Archibald Clavering Gunter

Baron Montez of Panama and Paris

A novel

Archibald Clavering Gunter

Baron Montez of Panama and Paris
A novel

ISBN/EAN: 9783337029135

Printed in Europe, USA, Canada, Australia, Japan

Cover: Foto ©Andreas Hilbeck / pixelio.de

More available books at **www.hansebooks.com**

BARON MONTEZ

OF PANAMA AND PARIS

A Novel

BY

ARCHIBALD CLAVERING GUNTER

AUTHOR OF

"MR. BARNES OF NEW YORK," "MR. POTTER OF TEXAS,"
"THAT FRENCHMAN!" "MISS NOBODY OF NO-
WHERE," "A FLORIDA ENCHANTMENT,"
"MISS DIVIDENDS," ETC., ETC.

NEW YORK
THE HOME PUBLISHING COMPANY
3 EAST FOURTEENTH STREET
. . . 1893 .

CONTENTS.

BOOK I.

A TRAGEDY OF THE EARLY ISTHMUS.

BOOK II.

THE FRANCO-AMERICAN.

BOOK III.

THE AMERICAN BROTHER.

BOOK IV.

THE STRUGGLE IN PANAMA.

BOOK V.

THE HURLY-BURLY IN PARIS.

BARON MONTEZ

OF PANAMA AND PARIS.

BOOK I.

A TRAGEDY OF THE EARLY ISTHMUS.

CHAPTER I.

THE RETURNING CALIFORNIANS.

" ANITA ! "

" Fernando, light of my heart ! Returned from the Pearl Islands ! " cries the beautiful Indian girl rushing to his arms and covering Mr. Fernando's olive face with the kisses of youth and love. Anita is but fifteen, and the heart grows fast under the sun of the Equator.

Fernando himself is scarce twenty, but he does not seem so ardent. He replies carelessly, " Yes, last night, by the *Columbus*," pointing to that little unseaworthy steamer as she lies languidly upon the blue waters of the Bay of Panama, about three miles from the town, and seven from the lovely Island of Toboga, from which these two are gazing at it.

" Last night, and you did not come to me ? you—away five days ! " answers the girl, tears coming into her eyes that flash through mists of passion like topaz stones.

" Last night I had business in Panama—great business." Then the young man says anxiously, " Is the *Americano* well ? "

" Yes."

" And *here ?* "

" Still here."

" He has not gone yet !   Blessings on God !   And his wife—the beautiful Señora Alicia, the lady with the white skin ?   She has recovered from her touch of the fever Panama ? "

"She is better.   They go to the mainland this after-noon."

" Ho–oh ! "

" To-morrow morning they take passage on the rail-way, to Aspinwall, and then go on the big vessel with the smoke to the great America beyond the sea."

"A–ah, she is well enough to travel ? "

" Yes, she is yellow no more ; her cheeks are red as the blossoms of the manzanilla."

" *Por Dios !*   She must be lovely as a mermaid of *Las Islas de las Perles !* " murmurs Fernando half to himself, but still not sufficiently low to miss the sharp ear of an Indian ; for at his words the dark eyes of Anita flash ominously, her full, round bosom pants under its white semi-transparent cotton drapery, and she mutters sav-agely to herself.

" What are you saying under your breath, Anita ? " cries the young man.

" Nothing !   I—I was only whispering a prayer to the Virgin for the young American lady's recovery, in the language of my tribe," answers the girl hesitatingly.

" *Diablo !*   No more of the language of your tribe !   I don't understand the language of your tribe ! " sneers Señor Fernando, giving the girl a little slap on her shapely brown shoulder and a nasty glance out of his bright eyes.   To this she does not reply, as she passes round the corner of the bamboo cottage, apparently overcome by some emotion she would sooner the gentle-man who has been speaking to her would not discern in her face.

" By all the saints of the cathedral, I believe the fool is jealous of my passion for the beautiful *Americana !* Anita jealous !   Did she but know there is an Anita at Cruces, another at the Island *del Rey*, and half a dozen more scattered between Aspinwall and Panama, little Anita of Toboga would have fine cause for jealousy," chuckles the young gentleman, smoothing his elaborate and spotlessly white shirt front, and settling the bright red sash around his hips, in the conceited way peculiar to South American dandies.

A moment after, he thinks: "What matters one Indian girl, more or less? Besides, to-day I have other things—they are going away to-day. How lucky I returned from the Pearl Islands in time! But now, *Por Dios!*—everything is arranged for the departure to-night of the American, his treasure, and his—beautiful—wife." He lisps this through his white teeth, as he looks lazily out over the Bay of Panama, and dreams a day-dream which seems to be a pleasant one.

It is shortly interrupted by a hearty American voice saying: "Back at last, Señor Montez. I hope you have brought the pearls. I was afraid we would not be able to wait for you. A gleaming necklace would be a very pretty present for my little girl in the United States."

With these words, a brown-faced, hardy and stalwart American, George Merritt Ripley, steps upon the bamboo portico and gives the man he addresses a hearty grasp of the hand. Ripley's manners are those of one who has been educated as a gentleman, but has to a limited extent thrown off the veneer of society among the rough and ready companions of Alta California.

This is apparent as he continues: "Light a cigar, my Spanish friend, and enjoy the view with me, this beautiful morning;" and, taking a camp chair, places his feet lazily upon the bamboo railing of the veranda, making a fine picture of a returning Californian of the fifties in his light woollen turn-away shirt, Panama hat, black trousers, high boots and belted revolver.

"*Gracias!*" The Spaniard accepts the offered weed and then suggests: "Your wife, I understand, is now sufficiently recovered, to continue her journey to the United States."

"Yes, thank God!" answers the American. Then his lip trembles a little, as he says: "Though our first day in Panama, I was afraid my Alice would leave me for ever;" and sighs: "That would have been the saddest parting on earth. My wife going to the embraces of our daughter she has not seen for four years—since we left her to journey to California."

"Why did you not take her with you to the land of gold?"

"What! take a child of twelve across the Isthmus in 1852? With its boat travel on the Chagres—its night at Gargona, amid the clicking of dice and the curses of the gamblers—its morning of miasma, going up the river to Cruces, and its mule ride through tropical forests infested by thieves and banditti? That would have been too great a risk; but now, with the railroad, our return is different and safe."

At the American's mention of gamblers at Gargona, and bandits on the Cruces road in 1852, a slight smile has rippled the olive features of the young man to whom he is talking.

As the returning Californian speaks of the railroad, the smile on the Spaniard's features changes to a scowl, but a moment after he assents laughingly: "Yes, it is different." Then a gleam of diabolical hope comes into his face, as he says: "I am glad the Señora is well enough to travel."

"Yes, we leave here this afternoon. That reminds me I must thank you for your kindness of the week. Had it not been for you, Alice would have remained in Panama, and perhaps have succumbed to the fever; but here on this beautiful island, the sea breezes and the perfume of the tamarind groves have been better for her than all the quinine in the universe, and all the doctors on earth. So I shall take her back to the East to meet our child, and a re-united family will settle down to a life of civilization, blessing God for the gold placers of the Sierras, for I have been very fortunate in California. My wife will be dressed very shortly, Señor Montez. Would you mind suggesting to the kind Anita that sea breezes bring appetite for breakfast?"

With this the gentleman returns into the little cottage of bamboo walls and palm-thatched roof, and Fernando Gomez Montez, looking after him, murmurs: "He has been *very fortunate!*" and thinks covetously of a strong iron-bound chest the returning Californian carries with him, whose weight indicates that it contains the gold of the Sierras.

Then his agile though sensuous mind wanders to the beauty that he knows the slight bamboo walls keep from his prying, inquisitive, hungering eyes—the beauty of the American lady—the white lady whose loveliness he has longed for since he has seen it—more than for the biggest pearl ever fished up from the blue waters of the Gulf of Panama.

So he chuckles, looking over his own personal charms which he thinks are great, for he has very nice regular white teeth and sparking dark eyes; his skin is a very mild chocolate color, and his slight, wiry, *petite* figure is clothed in immaculate white linen save where his bright red sash circles his dapper waist and falls down his right leg almost to his highly polished patent leather Wellington boots.

Then hearing a woman's soft voice within the bamboo walls, he mutters : " The Californian is bigger than I ; but she will forget him for me—the prettiest boy in Panama ! " and, gazing over the bay, sees in the distance, on the shore, the ramparts of the town, the white walls of its houses, and the glittering domes of its cathedrals.

Back of it are the savannas, green as emeralds, that glisten in the rising sun ; beyond, the Cordilleras droop to the lowest gap of that great ridge that divides the Atlantic and Pacific—so low here that twenty-five years after, they will draw all the gold from the stockings of the saving peasants of Brittany and Normandy, in the vain attempt to make the waters of the Pacific and Atlantic meet.

Behind the South American town rise two green hills —the nearest, called *Ancon;* the other, farther back, an advance peak of the Sierras, is the *Cerro de Filibusteres*— thus ominously named because Morgan, the buccaneer, first gazed upon the old Panama that he and his two thousand miscreants (gathered from all quarters of the earth) three days afterwards destroyed with lust and pillage and rapine and fire and blood.

Looking on this, Montez murmurs: "How peaceful ! how beautiful ! " Even his soul is struck by the lovely view before him, though he has seen it a hundred times, for to devils' eyes, heaven is sometimes lovely : and this looks like heaven—though it is not.

The sea breezes bring to him the scent of the tamarind, lime and orange groves. Around him is a mass of green —feathery green—of palms and bamboos, brightened

here and there by red and yellow blossoms, that are
strung, as if on florist's wreaths, from tree to tree, and
often dangle and droop into the limpid waters that lave
the shore of fair Toboga Island.

In front of him, and round to right and left, are waves
clear as blue diamonds, in which the fish are seen as in
some gigantic aquarium : the white shark, mixing with
shoals of baracuta, and now and then a shiver of pearly
water thrown into the air by flights of flying fish, that
glisten in the sun.

A little to his right, concealing a portion of the modern
town of Panama, are three or four islands—green to the
water's edge. Were he nearer to them, they would also
be brightened by the colors of innumerable tropical flowers, and made joyous by the songs of tropic birds. Beyond
these, on the mainland to the south, lie the ruins of the
old town of Panama—the one that Morgan made no more.
Farther towards the Equator, the mountain range, growing higher, disappears in the blue sky.

To the southeast, but beyond his eye, lie the beautiful
Islas de las Perles. Around him it is all green and golden
yellow and brilliant red—the foliage, fruits, and flowers of
the tropics ; about him blue ; at his feet the waters of the
Gulf ; above him the ether of a fairy atmosphere. Its
dreamy effect appeals to his sensuous soul. He gazes
entranced.

But as he looks his restless eyes catch, just on the right
of the new town of Panama, a little smoke that goes
peacefully into the air above it, and mingles with it. It
comes from one of the locomotives of the Panama Railway, completed but eighteen months before, and a gleaming smile, as bright and sunny as the day he looks on,
comes into the eyes of Fernando Gomez Montez, as he
thinks: "Our *mulateros* and the Chagres boatmen hate
this railroad that has taken from them the just dues
they filched from the stupid *Gringos* who travel across
our land. This iron track robs our honest *banditti* of
their chances of spoil and plunder on the Cruces mule
trail. To-night this helps me ! To-night I have both the
American's treasure and his wife ! "

Then he giggles and chuckles to himself, emotions
running over his mobile countenance, as fantastic,
bizarre, and changing as the many drops of the blood of

the various human races who in two centuries have passed across this highway of the world ; and Montez of Panama has a drop of nearly all the races of the earth within his despicable carcass, and each drop—the basest.

He has the drop that gives the cunning of the Spaniard ; the drop that holds the *bourgeois* greed of the Frenchman ; the drop that makes the watchful stealth of the Indian ; the drop that contains the savage cruelty of the Zulu warrior ; the drop that gives the *finesse* of the Italian ; the drop that comes from the Corsican and makes undying hate ; and, above all, one drop left by one of Morgan's buccaneers, that makes him more dangerous than all the other drops of wickedness in his blood, for it gives to him the determination and the bulldog pluck of the Anglo-Saxon.

Brute and bully as this buccaneer had been, he left his drop of blood to flow in the veins of this fantastic creature of all nations, to make him dangerous ; because it gave him that unflinching determination that has carried the Anglo-Saxon race to all quarters of the world, and made it dominant in every one of them.

But Montez awakes with a start. A merry voice is in his ear, a white, aristocratic hand is held toward him in friendly greeting. These belong to Alice Ripley, who with joy, hope, and happiness on her fair American face, is saying : " Señor Montez, our kind friend, you have been to the Pearl Islands for us—another favor for which to thank you ! "

" You are now quite well ? " he stammers, a little confused, though his eyes are bold enough to linger over the beautiful woman, as she stands before him, a white muslin dress floating about her graceful form, and some ribbons in her golden hair, giving color to a fair Saxon face, that is lighted up by radiant, happy violet eyes.

" Yes—quite well ! " she laughs. " So well, appetite has returned to me. I am impatient for breakfast, which kind Anita says is ready in the tamarind grove."

" You are—quite changed—you are more beautiful—"

" No," she laughs, " more happy. I am well once more —my husband is by my side. In ten days I shall kiss my daughter. Am I not a fortunate woman? But breakfast. *En avant*, George, and forward Montez ! " and Alice Ripley flits over the veranda towards the breakfast bower, made girlish by joy, and stands beside the green palms and red flowers, a picture that makes Señor Montez's eyes grow tender, and he would pity this lovely American lady he hopes this night to cut off from husband and friends, and home and child—but in all the polyhæma drops that run in his vile veins, there is no drop of pity.

But there are in his body, drops of blood that carry unbounded passion and intense desire, and gazing on this fair woman's blue eyes, and white skin, and graceful mobile figure, his eyes grow misty, as he mutters : " A rare flower for Fernando Gomez Montez of Panama to pluck —Ah ! This is a lucky day for the naughty boy of the Isthmus ! "

CHAPTER II.

" A TOBOGA BREAKFAST IN '56."

THEN this little disciple of Satan runs over what has brought him this great chance of good luck. He thinks of his earlier days.

He is scarce twenty now, but people develop rapidly under the hot sun of the Equator. He remembers the quiet little town of Cruces, in the mountains—at the head of navigation of the Chagres, where the good priest taught him his *Paternosters*, and where he chanted them each day in his class, mingling his Latin with howls produced by blows of a cutting rawhide in the hands of the *padre's* athletic and vigilant assistant.

This mixture of penance and prayer pleased the young Montez but little. His mother, who lived in a palm hut by the rapids of the Chagres, did the *padre's* washing ; his father was—Heaven knows where or who. There seemed no way of escape. They were about to make him an altar boy, and rebellious little Fernando cursed as he chanted and saw no prospect save of a life of prayer and penance, and candle carrying behind a decorated image of the Virgin, in its daily religious procession through the lanes of the little town. But just at this moment Cruces—buried from the world in the hills of the Cordilleras in the deadly slumber that had fallen upon the Isthmus when the route to Chili and Peru round Cape Horn succeeded the route via Panama, and the jingling bells of its mule trains were no longer heard crossing the mountain paths between Panama and Porta Bella—awoke and lived again.

The first rush of the gold seekers for California in '49 crossed the Isthmus.

Flying from church and prayer and penance, young Montez dodged fasting and discipline in the hurly-burly of that early Isthmus excitement.

At thirteen he peddled water, for ten cents a glass, to thirsty *Gringos.* A year after he did a thriving business in unripe bananas, oranges, and pineapples in the streets of Chagres. Next taking up with a *monté* shop, became " *muchacho diablo* " in a gambling establishment at Gargona, where he learned card sharping and thimble rigging. In the years 1851, 1852, and 1853 he was a handler of bad mules, which he leased out at exorbitant prices to the embryo pioneers and argonauts of California to cross worse roads from Gargona in the dry season, and from Cruces in the wet time, to Panama.

Perchance, he took a flyer or two, with one or two successful bandits, and some looted treasure came to him.

He had a knack of recovering lost children who disappeared together with their native carriers in this rush across the Isthmus, and restoring them to fond parents for large sums of money.

And during this time he learned one great principle that has been of much use to Napoleons of finance both in America and Europe—that is, not to steal *often*, but to steal *much.* The first invariably leads to disgrace and a prison—the second often to honor and a palace.

While doing all this, his facile mind became educated. He picked up French, from some Parisians crossing the Isthmus. Spanish was his native tongue. A smattering of Latin he had from the priest. English came to him from his vocation with the Californian adventurers ; and by devoting himself to one or two Portuguese, who travelled tremblingly across the Isthmus in those days, he stole from them a smattering of their language and any doubloons and Spanish dollars they might leave within reach of his grasping paws.

At length, the railroad completed in 1855 destroyed young Montez's means of livelihood ; but by this time he had sufficient to engage in other occupations, and turned his attention to dealing in pearls, precious stones, and other valuables he could pick up about the Isthmus, sometimes making trips to the Pearl Islands, and once or twice going as far as Ecuador and Peru, upon the English steamers that were now running down the coast of South America, and to Acapulco to the north, on the Pacific Mail boats, trading always with a rare facility and shrewdness that had come to him in a drop of Yankee blood left by a New Bedford whaler at Darien some hundred years before, and by a globule of the vital fluid of Israel, that had entered his poly-nation veins from an unfortunate Jewish pedler the Inquisition had burned, before the time of Morgan.

He was even now considered well to do, and his orders were good in the Hotel Franças in Panama, or in the restaurant of Monsieur Victor, the Isthmus Delmonico those days, but still as yet no grand *coup* had come to him.

Some ten days before the time he sits upon the veranda of the villa on the Island of Toboga, the steamer *John L. Stevens*, from San Francisco, brought its lot of passengers from California, to take route across the Isthmus by railway to Aspinwall, and so on to New York ; among them this American gentleman and his wife, who are occupying the pretty palm cottage this morning— Ripley ruddy in health, Alice beautiful as a pale lily, stricken with the fever picked up during a six hours' stay in Acapulco, and too ill to proceed on her journey. But for this, the American would have been the happiest of men, for he was a successful pioneer to California.

George Merritt Ripley had left a clerkship in Baltimore, and taken his wife with him, leaving his little daughter of twelve at school in the East, and had gone to California in 1852. He had made his first start in gold mining in Calaveras County, at Mokelumne Hill, and being sensible enough to see that placer digging was uncertain, and that trade in California at that time was a sure road to wealth, had taken his few thousand dollars, and entered into business in the thriving town of Stockton on the San Joaquin. In three years he had accumulated some sixty thousand dollars, which, in those days of cheap prices, large interest, and small capital, was the equivalent to half a million at the present.

Having enough to live upon in the East, his money properly invested in the growing towns of New York or Boston would in time make him even wealthy.

His wife, anxious to see her child (for four years is a long time to a mother's heart), had implored him to return to the Eastern States, which in those days all Californians called "home."

So, though his life on the plains of the San Joaquin had been a pleasant one, Ripley was delighted to turn his face from the crudities of the early California, to the more civilized existence of the Eastern world.

He had come on his way rejoicing, until the fever struck the woman he loved, so he had brought her to Panama to rest there—perchance to die there.

His trunks, checked through to the East, had gone on, all save one that contained their immediate necessities of apparel, and the *other* one ; the one that never left his eye —*the heavy one*—the one that took three natives to handle. These, together with his wife, were in Panama, when he chanced to meet Montez, who, having many arts and graces of a gentleman, had soon made George Ripley think him his friend.

Montez had recommended the change from the pestilent miasma of the mainland to the breezes that came fresh up the Gulf to the Island of Toboga, and in these zephyrs, health had come to George's wife, and despair had left the heart of the strong man who loved her.

During these days of his wife's convalescence, in one of his conversations with Montez, Ripley had mentioned a desire to invest a little of the gold he was bringing with him in the pearls of the Isthmus—which were cheap at Panama compared to New York. This treasure was all in his own care, for Wells Fargo's charges in these days, for the transmission of specie, were very high, and George Ripley thought himself strong enough to take care of his own money, having stood off bandits from his Mokelumne Hill mine and possessing that peculiar self-confidence that seemed to come with the air of the Sierras to all Californians in those early days. Therefore this foolish Ripley had evaded Wells, Fargo & Co.'s charges, and had everything he held valuable in this world with him in Toboga this sunny day—save his daughter in her Eastern school.

2

Musing over this, Fernando chuckles to himself :
" Brave *Americano*—fool *Americano!* "
Just here he is awakened from his reverie by the brave
Americano's voice in his ear, and the hearty grasp of the
fool *Americano's* hand upon his shoulder.   The voice
says : " Come along, Don Fernando Montez !   We are
hungry.   The odor of the breakfast is delicious—but my
wife insists upon our waiting for our kind host."   The
hand drags in friendly play the *petite* carcass of Fernando
Gomez Montez to see the prettiest sight his sparkling, all-
nation eyes have ever gazed upon—the blonde beauty of
the temperate zone contrasted with the dark loveliness
of the Equator, surrounded by a tropic breakfast *al fresco.*

It is under the shade of the tamarind trees, the perfume
from which is mingled with the odors of a feast for the
gods !

The aroma of Costa Rica coffee just burnt and ground
comes from a steaming urn that stands on the ground
near the fire of perfumed orange wood, upon which turtle
steaks are broiling, and luscious plantains and mealy yams
are cooking in its ashes.   A stew of rice and freshly
killed *Iguano* lizard, made hot with Chili Colorado, and
a slight suspicion of garlic—for Anita is an artist in the
cooking line—stands ready to their hands ; and fruits,
gorgeous as the sun that gave them their ripe beauty,
lie about them everywhere.

The American lady, lazily seated in a hammock, looks
coolly beautiful under the leaves that shade her—the
abandon of careless ease shows her still girlish figure in
graceful motion.   Her blue eyes would be very bright this
morning, were they not wistful at times when gazing
towards the East.   Anita posed like a bronze statue
stands near the fire, her orbs sparkling also, save when
looking at *la Americana* they glow with some unknown
passion like those of a Voodoo priestess !

So breakfast passes, Anita the presiding goddess of
the feast ; for to this Indian girl all the beauty of the
tropics has come in the fifteen years of her life.   She is
robed in white—some soft clinging Isthmus stuff, which
drapes her lithe figure, and displays the beauties of her
graceful limbs at every motion—and her little feet, bare
as when she was born, step so lightly they hardly rustle
the leaves under them.

The girl flits about, ministering to the appetites of Señor Montez and his guests, which seem to be very good, Montez apparently being happy, and a great joy beaming in the eyes of the American. His beautiful wife has roses on her fair cheeks, and in ten days they will be in their Eastern home; with them the one child of their love. Health and appetite are theirs, and their breakfast is almost like that of Arcady.

The coffee is of the sweetest aroma, the *Iguano* is done to a nicety, and the turtle steaks are juicy as those from a two-year-old buffalo cow. These being finished, they revel in the fruits of the tropics—oranges green as an olive, thin-skinned as a lady's glove, with one blood red shot upon each, to prove that it has ripened; melons, sweet limes, Avigado pears, and the mangoes for which Toboga is famous.

As appetite is appeased, conversation becomes easy.

" Why did you not ask Anita to tell me that I was keeping you from breakfast ? It is such a good one," laughs the every-nation gentleman.

" Anita did not seem to care for your coming," returns the American lady. " Perhaps she did not think her breakfast was as perfect as it is."

" Ah, Anita was sulky, eh ?" says Fernando, a little mocking snarl curling over his white teeth. " Anita has an Indian temper and Indian moods." He regards the girl with a sneer, and she returns him several flashes from her eyes, that would be reproachful, were they not almost vindictive.

" A little sullen, Anita—eh ?" jeers the host.

His tone would drive the girl to frenzy, did not the American lady suddenly say, " Please don't be cross with her. You do not know how kind she has been to me during your absence and my sickness ! " Then she turns to her husband and suggests : " We must not forget Anita's services when we leave her."

" No," cries the jovial Californian. " Anita shall have the biggest pearl that Montez has brought from the Islands."

At this mention of personal adornment, a smile runs over the volatile features of the Indian girl.

Fernando smiles also. What is Anita's is his. And everything is fish that comes to his net.

A second after, he gives a start. The American lady is remarking in grateful tones: "And what shall our offering be to you, Señor Montez, whose hospitality has given me health?"

"A present for me? *Mia madre!* you are too kind."

"Yes, mention what you like and you have it," interjects the Californian.

"Oh, if you wish me to say what I should regard with the greatest favor, it would be your—your beautiful revolver. There is none like it on the Isthmus,—none that shoots so truly, for I have seen your skill with it," answers Fernando, looking with longing eyes upon the fatal weapon of the American.

"My revolver," echoes the Californian with a start. Then he says, after a pause of consideration: "I will send it to you by express from New York. Until this journey is over, I cannot part with it. It has guarded my life and my property before. I feel safer with it by my side."

"Yes," returns Alice, "at his side by day, near his hand at night. George is superstitious, I think, with regard to it."

This conversation apparently does not please Señor Montez very greatly. The revolver has seemed to fascinate him. All through the meal his glances have sought the long Colt's pistol that carries six lives in its six loaded chambers as it hangs in the Californian's belt. A little spheroid of timid Cingales blood, poured into his veins from some East Indian ancestor, now brings a coward faltering into his bright eyes. He does not seem to enjoy the Avigado pear that he was eating with a good appetite a second before. Throwing it away with a "pish" of disgust, he cries: "Anita, quick, a cigar!" for nicotine soothes this gentleman's excitable nerves.

The Indian girl, at his command, draws out from a bundle of fragrant Toboga tobacco a fresh leaf, and rolling it in her deft and agile fingers, in half a minute it becomes a cigar. Thirty seconds more, a second leaf becomes another cigar. This she offers to the American, who follows his host's example. So lighting up, the two men puff away contentedly.

A moment after, Alice gives a start of amazement, for a third cigar has been tendered to her, and to her astonished refusal, Anita laughs : "You are not well enough yet to smoke. I had supposed now you are ill no longer you would enjoy it as I do." Then throwing herself into a hammock, this lazy bird of the tropic surrounds herself with wreaths of smoke, puffing them out between her white teeth, and playing with them as a juggler does with his baubles.

The sensuous scene appeals to even the energetic Californian's senses. He mutters : "This week at Toboga has seemed like a week of—of——"

"Of paradise ! " interjects his wife. "Since I have become well again, we have made a fairy land of it. Daytime in the hammock, sipping coccanut milk and *chicha* under the tamarind leaves ; dinners at Jacques' *petite* restaurant in the cocoanut trees, and moonlight in a canoe on the water. George said," here the lady blushes slightly, gazing at her husband with bride's eyes, "that it was more romantic than our wedding tour."

"A–ah, a—*new* honeymoon ! " sighs Montez. Looking at the beauty of this Northern violet, as she sits before him in the ease of this tropic Arcady—for Alice Ripley has imitated Señorita Anita in the hammock business, and sits lazily under the green leaves, one perfect foot and one delicate ankle carelessly swinging from under her white laces and muslin and ribbons— this gentleman's face suddenly flushes with a great delight, as he thinks : "A new honeymoon !—Yes— *for me !* " Then visions come to him, entrancing as the dreams of opium sleep, as he gazes at Alice Ripley through the clouds of his cigar smoke.

Mingled with the rustling breezes in the tamarind groves, as they sit there, the "silence—of—the—smoker " coming on them, is heard the voice of a rushing stream, which issues gurgling and foaming from the hill-side, and splashes into a little basin, a short hundred yards away, suggesting coolness.

The day is already burning, and the noise of this foaming stream apparently puts an idea into the fertile mind of little Montez, as he sits looking with sleepless eyes at the big Californian, through his wreaths of smoke.

He says : " How is a cool plunge this hot morning ? Why not a bath, Señor Georgio Ripley ? "

" A bath—delicious ! " ejaculates the American. Then

looking over the green water of the bay, he suggests,
" But the sharks ! "   •
" No sharks here," and Fernando points with a little
finger, adorned with some diamonds and a very delicately
trimmed almond-shaped nail, to the cool, limpid basin
worn in the rock by the unceasing flow of the living
stream for centuries. " That is nature's bathing place."
So the two go off together, through the thickets to the
shady pool, bearing with them handfuls of javoncilla
leaves, that will act as vegetable soap and make their
skins soft as those of children.

Looking on its limpid waters, dark under the palms and
only golden where the sun steals in upon it through little
breaks in the leaves, the American mutters : " This is
perfection."

Then Montez cries, " Quick, I'll beat you into the water.
You need not fear to undress here. Toboga has no
deadly lance-vipers or coral snakes like the mainland."

So undressing himself in the little thicket of broad-
leaved palms and feathery bamboos, George Merritt
Ripley, as he takes his plunge into nature's bath-tub, for
the first time in his journey really parts himself from his
revolver.

It is but for a short fifteen minutes, and Montez bathes
with him ten of them, but leaves the water *first*.

But in that five minutes, that one last plunge for Ripley,
something has happened to his weapon of trust that
had saved his life and his treasure from the bandits
of the Sierras and the highwaymen of the Californian
trails.

Not knowing this, George comes laughingly up the
bank, crying, " That last plunge was the most refreshing
of my life ! I hope you enjoyed your bath as well as I
did, Señor Montez."

" Perhaps better," returns his companion, who has as
yet hardly begun to dress. Fernando is apparently a lazy
man, and he has had something to occupy him, and a
little file that he has brought with him, during the five
minutes of Ripley's last plunge.

From now on, a confident air seems to come over this
every nation gentleman ; and when his eyes look at the
revolver which the American is strapping around him
again, they no longer shrink from it, but gaze at it in

confident triumph. So, walking up the path to the tamarind grove and bamboo cottage, Fernando chuckles to himself : "I am sure now—treasure and beauty."

₫ʿ:·

CHAPTER III.

THE RAILROAD STATION AT PANAMA.

ON the veranda once more, George Ripley suggests : "Would you mind showing us your pearls ? My wife is anxious to see your jewels, and we must be soon getting under way for the mainland."

"Yes, the *Illinois* arrived this morning at Aspinwall," returns Montez. "Her passengers will soon reach Panama. Soon there will be a Pacific Mail steamship in the bay. The *Golden Age* from San Francisco is one day overdue. When she comes in, her passengers will be moved eastward rapidly. If you are not at the railway station you may be left to spend ten days more with us. That would please me, *mi amigo;* but you—you are an American, and in a hurry. You do not enjoy life. You fly through it."

"And you dream through it, I imagine, Señor Montez," laughs Alice, coming on the veranda to meet the returning bathers. Then she says archly, "Dream no more ; show us your pearls, and become a man of business."

"That I will !" cries Montez, as he displays his jewels, and descants on the beauties of the large pink pearl he has, and the perfection of the white ones he holds caressingly in his hands, with the vehemence and volubility of an Armenian in the bazaar at Constantinople, and the shrewdness of a Hebrew pawn-broker in Seven Dials.

Fernando's trading powers, however, are thrown away ; for the American takes all the pearls at the seller's own prices, which though exorbitant for Panama, are cheap for New York.

"Come in and get our business over," says George ; and Montez following him and Alice into the bamboo cottage, the affair is completed. Opening a large buckskin bag, that is part of his belt, after the manner of early Californians, Ripley makes payment in gold-dust ;

for at that time gold was plenty, though coin was scarce, in the Western world.

Upon this yellow dross, Fernando's eyes linger lovingly, and from it roam gloatingly to the heavy iron-bound trunk of the Californian, and turning from this to the beautiful *Americana*, who was thrown her pearls in a string of white radiance around her fair white neck, his glance becomes more longing than ever.

Here George laughingly suggests : " Montez, you think jewels become her ?   Alice should have had these pearls when she stood in Edouart's gallery in Washington Street, San Francisco, and had this taken," producing from his pocket a tintype of his wife, a style of picture just come into fashion.

" Yes, I had two of them taken ; one for my husband, the other for my daughter ; Mary's was sent to her two months ago.   It will remind her of my coming," replies the lady ; then blushes a little, for Montez, in his native way, has cried out : "*Ah, Dios !*   It is celestial—but the sun has not done you justice, Señora Ripley ! "

The sun, however, has done very well, and the tintype has the blue eyes and fair hair of this charming American.

So charming, Montez fears to stay ; his passion may betray itself.   He mutters, " I will go and engage your boat, Señor Ripley."

" Yes !   Get a safe one, I don't care for speed.   Something there is no chance of capsizing," calls the Californian after him.

" I will be sure of that for my own sake, as well as yours," cries back the little gentleman, as he glides down the pathway, brushing with a bamboo switch the dust from his patent leather boots.

At the white glistening beach he selects carefully a boat, and is delighted to find among its crew a swarthy boatman, who is called Domingo.

Addressing him familiarly, and slapping him on the back, Montez says in his ear : " Old bravo, are you still up to *banditti* work as in '52, on the Cruces roads ? "

To this, Domingo, a gentleman with a pirate countenance adorned by two fearful scars, with a stalwart black frame, and a stout black heart beating in his black body, replies :   " *Si, Señor, mouches dinero, mouches sangui, mouches Domingo.*"

So Fernando knows he has at his hand, for this night's work, a man who will not be turned back for pity, nor blood, nor danger, from doing any wickedness that may come to his hand.

While this has been taking place on the beach, Ripley and his wife, during hurried preparations for their departure, are holding a conversation that makes the Californian open his honest eyes in astonishment.

His wife says to him, under her breath : " Now that Montez is away, I wish to tell you something : I am glad we are going ! "

" Of course ! To-morrow we will be one day nearer our daughter."

" It is not entirely that," whispers the lady, nervously, " but I fear to stay here."

" Why ? "

" Anita hates me."

" Impossible ! No one could have nursed you more faithfully during the fever, than the bright-eyed Indian girl."

" It is her bright eyes that make me fear her. Something new has come into them. Besides that, while you were taking your bath she told me that we had better go away as soon as possible. She told me——"

" Well, what ? " says the American impatiently.

" Only—that—if the fever returned to me here—I would not throw it off again. Toboga breezes are good for the first attack,—but after that,—like other medicines, —they lose their value."

While she says this in a hesitating, disjointed manner, a bright red flush has come over the features of the beautiful American lady, for Alice Ripley is telling her husband her first falsehood.

Anita's words had been to her : " Beware of Montez ! Montez loves you ! " and suspicion coming to her quick feminine mind at these words, Alice had noted some of the uncanny glances the polyhæma gentleman at times could not restrain himself from indulging in. But at the last moment, even when warning was on her lips, she has hesitated to tell her husband what she has heard and suspects—because the very thought of the thing brings blushing shame upon her.

So the modesty of this beautiful woman takes from her

husband one of his ropes of safety this day—his one chance of suspecting the man he thinks his friend, but who is even now bent upon his robbery and ruin.

"Well, let us give Anita her pearl—perhaps that will reconcile her to our going away," laughs the Californian.

This being done, they leave the palm-thatched bamboo villa, and come down the little rocky pathway to the beach at Toboga, to take departure for Panama.

Three stalwart natives carry the iron-bound trunk, and find it all they can handle ; another swings easily the lighter one that contains the wardrobe of George Ripley and his wife.

Looking around, Montez is happy ; for there is only a steamer of the English Steam Navigation Company in the harbor, one or two trading brigs and schooners, and the *Columbus* just returned from her voyage to the *Islas de las Perles,* and *no vessels of war of any nation.* No blue jackets can be landed to interfere with a plan that he has already set on foot among the desperate native classes of the town of Panama this fifteenth day of April, 1856.

Toboga is slumbering in the mid-day sun, as they stand upon the sandy beach. A lazy steward from the English steamer is buying fish and fruit from a big Indian *bongo* that has come from a neighboring island. There is a drowsy hum from a few bamboo huts, and pine board edifices that do duty as shops, and ship chandlers' stores, for this Island of Toboga is really the port of Panama, as the depth of water permits vessels to lie there at all times ; while off the mainland, the tremendous rise and fall of the ocean compels ships of burden to keep three or four miles out in the bay.

"I am glad you got a good, big, safe boat," remarks the Californian, "and I hope competent boatmen."

"Yes, that is all arranged. On board, *mi amigo*," cries Montez, offering a gallant hand to assist the pretty *Americana.*

But what the Indian girl has said to her makes this lady blind to his attentions, and she carelessly and lightly steps over the gunwale of the boat, and tripping to its stern, takes seat under its awning of many colors, ignoring the gentleman whose eyes follow her, an unknown suspicion in them.

A moment after, they are under way, black Domingo pulling a strong stroke oar, and three lithe natives keeping time with him, and dashing foam that looks like pearls and diamonds from the water, as they glide over this aquarium, in which Alice looking down sees countless fish.

As they move, she carelessly drops a dainty hand into the cool water, playing with its ripples. The next instant Montez quietly takes it in his and replaces it in the boat.

Perchance, unable to control himself, he has given its delicate fingers a tender pressure, for the lady's face grows angry.

"Would you like to leave your arm in that fellow's maw?" is Fernando's reply to her indignant glance, and he points to a huge white shark that is lazily patrolling the water a cable's length or so from the English steamer's stern.

Following his gesture with their eyes, the crew start and Domingo mutters : "*Diablo!* Toboga Bill!"

"Yes, that is the gentleman!" laughs Montez. "This desperado has just come up after the Peruvian steamer from a trip down the coast to Callao."

"So that is the terror of Panama Bay?" queries George, turning his eyes upon the great fish, who is as long as a ship's cutter, and whose dorsal fin makes a big swash of foam with every movement.

"Yes! There will be one or two less native boatmen, perhaps, before he leaves harbor!" returns Montez. Then he suddenly cries : "For your life, No!" and places a deterring hand upon the Californian's pistol, for Ripley is about to draw it.

"There is no danger in this big boat. Let me have a pop at the desperado," says George, still fingering his ready revolver.

"No, no! Your wife is here. He might charge the boat. He has upset canoes! Don't use your pistol!" murmurs the little every-nation rascal, his lips trembling and growing white.

"If he is so awful—don't shoot at him!" gasps Alice to her husband.

"If you tremble, of course not!" says the American, returning his revolver to his belt. "Though I had imagined Montez had better nerves."

This idea is that of the boatmen ; for one of them says
in Spanish to his fellow : " *Caramba !* I never saw the
muchacho diablo tremble before—at a shark, too ! "

But Domingo knows his old master better, and
chuckles to himself : " What was there about that
pistol of the *Americano* that Fernando did not wish him
to use it ? Ah ! It has been tampered with. This man
and this woman are to be our prey." And from now on,
the whites of his eyes grow blood-shot when they look
on the Californian and his fair-haired wife.

As they leave "Toboga Bill " behind them, fear seems
to depart from Montez ; he regains his spirits, but whenever a stray gull offers a tempting shot he looks nervous ;
perchance Ripley will test his pistol.

Three hours after, they make the landing at Panama,
having been assisted by the incoming tide, which has
just turned, and is here tremendous.

They come to the end of the long wharf of the railroad, finding there a little light-draft iron steamboat—
the *Toboga*—used in transferring passengers and mail
to the great Pacific steamers that cannot come nearer
than three miles of the town. Not six inches of water is
under the *Toboga's* keel. It must wait for the incoming
tide to free it, and make it float again, which will be
somewhere about ten or eleven o'clock this evening.

Clambering upon this wharf, which rises at this stage
of the tide quite high above the boat, Montez and Ripley
assist the American lady, who soon stands beside them.

" There will probably be no train for Aspinwall before
to-morrow morning. I think we had better go to one
of the hotels in the main town. It will be more comfortable," remarks Ripley.

" Very well," answers Montez, a shade of disappoint·
ment crossing his face, " the Hotel Français. But what
will you do with your trunk—the heavy fellow ? It seems
all that the three boatmen can manage."

" Of course, George, they can never carry it into the
town in this hot sun," remarks Alice, who, having hoisted
a dainty parasol over her head, stands watching the men.

" Let me suggest the Pacific House," returns Fernando,
pointing to a white board hotel just across the road from
the station. " It is but a step for your wife—and your
trunk."

To this proposition George assents, and they walk up
the wharf, followed by three of the boatmen, who struggle
under the heavy iron-bound chest, upon which the Californian, turning ever and anon, casts a wary glance. Behind them tramps old Domingo, slinging easily upon his
stalwart shoulder the light trunk containing the wardrobe
of the Californian, which does not seem to interest Ripley
at all.

Walking along the tracks of the Panama road, which
run upon this wharf, they soon come to dusty *terra firma*,
and find themselves in quite a crowd of passengers from
the *Illinois*, which has landed them at Aspinwall, on
the Atlantic side of the Isthmus, some few hours before.
These are making their preparations for departure, some
of them checking their baggage, and others having their
tickets examined ; a few, even now (fortunately for themselves), are taking their families on board the *Toboga*,
as the *Golden Age*, the incoming Pacific Mail steamer, has
been sighted.

Hearing this, Montez whispers to the Californian :
" The train for Aspinwall will be sure to leave early in
the morning. The Pacific House is the one for you,
it is so near the railroad depot."

So they pass in, and registering their names with
McFarlane, the proprietor, soon find themselves in a little
room on the eastern, and now shady, side of the house,
for the sun is already declining in the heavens.

This chamber is one flight up, retired and quiet as any
room can be in a house made of thin boards with parti-
tions of canvas and paper. To this the three natives
stagger with the heavy trunk, Domingo accompanying
them with the lighter one.

Here Montez says to the American, " *Au revoir !* " but
while doing this, suggests : " Won't you take a stroll with
me into the town ? You will find lots of the passengers
who are bound for California, seeing the sights. Why
not make an evening of it with me ? Dinner at the *Café*
Victor, and then, I believe, we have a circus in town
to-night."

" That would be delightful ! " cries Alice. A moment
after, she says thoughtfully, " but I am afraid I am too
fatigued for it."

" No thank you, Montez, old boy," answers George.

"I think I'll stay here with my baggage and my tired wife."

"Then *au revoir* again !" murmurs Fernando, and turns to go, but the Californian comes after him, and seizing his little fingers in his stalwart grip, says gratefully ; "This must not be the last we shall see of you ! Promise to come back here this evening. My wife and I must thank you again for your hospitality, and what you have done for us. I'll not forget to express the revolver to you from New York."

"Oh, do not fear—I'll return to you !" answers Montez, the Armenian drop in his blood coming to the fore, and giving his eyes a far-seeing, peculiar, subtle look. "Until this evening !" and whispering these words, he skips down the steps, giving one last longing parting glance at the fair American lady, who makes a pretty picture, her bright beauty being in strong contrast to the bareness of the room, as she carelessly sits upon the iron-bound trunk. Thus grouped these two treasures of the American look very beautiful to Señor Montez—they are now, he thinks, so nearly his.

As he reaches the doorway of the hotel he suddenly starts and says : "But I have much to do !" and so passes rapidly out of the Pacific House, where there is a good deal of drinking going on, and many glasses are being emptied to the first sight of the Pacific, by passengers eager to reach the land of gold.

Left together Ripley turns to Alice, saying : "It looks as if you would have a dull time, little woman, till to-morrow morning when we get upon the railroad for Aspinwall."

"Oh, I'll pass a little of it writing to Mary."

"Why, the child'll see us as soon as the letter ! "

"Not quite. We'll have to remain a day in New York probably. The letter will go right on. I'll tell her of our week in Toboga," returns the lady, taking from her trunk the articles for a hasty epistle. "Had you not better see about our tickets ? "

"They'll do in the morning," replies the gentleman who is looking out of the hotel window. "Besides, the crowd bound for California are giving the railroad officials all they want to attend to just now." And George amuses himself inspecting the movements of the throng outside as the sun goes down upon Panama.

After a little, his wife closes an epistle full of a mother's love to her absent dear one, telling her the day after she receives it she will be in her arms, and says, " George, just step down and put this in the mail at the railroad depot, before you forget as usual."

" Then the usual bribe," laughs her husband.

" Two, if you like," and the lady's lips receive his kisses, for these two are as much lovers as when they first became man and wife.

" Now hurry. For Mr. McFarlane's gong is going to sound for dinner soon," cries Alice.

So George Ripley goes down and posts the letter to Mary, his daughter, putting it in the strong grip of Wells, Fargo & Co., but does not come back to dinner with his wife—for this is the night of the fifteenth day of April, 1856—a night that at Panama severed husbands from wives and parted children from parents' love.

CHAPTER IV.

WHAT THE MOON SAW IN PANAMA.

MONTEZ, after gliding through the crowd about the railroad station, joins Domingo, who has been waiting for him, and the two stroll together along the dusty lane leading to the Cuinago, a quarter of the city composed of vermin, filth and native huts, in which the lower orders of this town of Panama make their habitat.

" You half understand my design, my worthy old desperado," murmurs Montez.

" *Si, Capitano mio*," returns the swarthier and more stalwart bandit.

" Then I will explain the rest to you. Listen ! " and Fernando hastily outlines a plan, which makes the other grind his teeth together in a wild kind of unholy chuckle. " *Diablo !* This will be a better night than any one of the wild days of my youth ! " and Domingo had once been a ship's boy with Lafitte, the last pirate of the Gulf of Mexico.

" Yes—it will be—*fine !* " laughs the other. " There are women and children among this crowd of passengers.

These people are not like the adventurers of '49. They
are going to be California farmers, not miners. Few of
them carry a revolver ; fewer still know how to use it."
"But your American friend bears a very large one."
"Yes, and is a dead shot ; but that is arranged," says
Montez.

"Ah, trust *el muchacho diablo !*" laughs Domingo, looking in admiration at his little mentor. Then he says
suddenly : "But the plan you have mentioned, will take
much time. The natives must be aroused."

"It is almost arranged now. You have but very little
to do. The keg of powder I have ordered is already in
those huts. You see our savage boatmen and muleteers
are prepared to use it," and Montez points to the crowd
of excited Indians, sambos, mulattos, negroes, Spanish
gypsies, and every other vile race of the Isthmus, who are
stimulating themselves in the streets of the native quarter
with *aguardiente* for some work they have on hand, and
are even now nearly all armed with old muskets, *machetes*,
or pistols.

Looking upon this, Domingo says : "That little
steamer," pointing to the *Toboga*, whose smoke-stack is
still visible at the end of the wharf, "has taken away
their livelihood from the honest *barqueros* here, by transferring the passengers that were their customers. Their
hatred will be an assistance to us. Besides, the railroad
has ruined our *mulateros*—they will not be backward."

"Not with American plunder in sight," laughs Montez.
"But they will need a leader—Domingo, you are the man
for that kind of thing : you like blood !"

"Ah, but, *demonios !* we have forgotten the police ! "

"We have not forgotten anything ! " replies the brighter
scoundrel. "The police are arranged for ; the governor, I think, is arranged for also. *A Dios* till six o'clock !
Do your work here ; I will do mine in the town ! Remember at six—the railroad station. There Montez will make
his start in life."

Leaving Domingo surrounded by a crowd of his old
cronies and chums, whom he will excite with strong *pulque* and bad *aguardiente*, Montez, turning away from the
native quarter, strolls through the Gargona gate, along
the *Calle de la Merced*, into the middle of the old town
of Panama.

Here he sees many of the passengers of the *Illinois*, who are buying jewelry of *Choco* gold and Panama pearls, *sombreros de Guayaquil*, and bright-hued stuffs, to take with them to California.

The sun is going down rapidly, flaming lanterns are beginning to appear in the shops; a few Spanish ladies, in short white petticoats and light chemises, scarcely concealed by graceful mantillas and *nelosos* floating from their dark hair, and draping their bare and gleaming necks and arms, are tripping with slippered feet hurriedly homeward.

The lights are twinkling in the Café Victor and the Hotel Français. The tingling of bells announces mules, ridden by dashing *caballeros* adorned with all the splendor of Spanish horse trappings. Still the streets seem curiously deserted; the lower classes have left them; few *mulateros*, boatmen, or *ladrones* are here; they are nearly all in the Cuinago, and those that are not yet there are hurrying towards the native quarter, as if going to a rendezvous.

Looking on this, Montez thinks: "This will be a glorious evening! But to make sure, I must see His Excellency."

He passes rapidly to the street San Juan de Dios, and stops before a low stone building, in front of which a negro sentry is parading, with dirty gun and bare feet. He says to him: "Colonel Garrido is here?"

"Yes, Señor, inside."

"I must see him."

And word being sent in, Garrido, Commander of Police, makes his appearance. He is half negro, quarter Spanish, quarter cur—all devil. Adorned with great tawdry epaulettes, and buttons and sashes, and a big sword, he wears long dark oily mustachios, which he strokes in an affected and military way.

"Ah, Señor Montez, *mio!*" he laughs, looking at the little man who has already placed his hand in his pocket and is chinking doubloons together. "You have come at last. I have been waiting for you!"

"Yes, I represent the law," says Montez. "There is going to be an outbreak. The *Americanos*, the passengers at the railway depot, will attack to-night our poor fruit pedlers."

3

"You told me of that yesterday."

"Yes! I am a prophet! Are the police prepared?"

"The police will do their duty. They are now ready," and Garrido chuckles and points into the *patio* where he has already mustered and armed the hundred vagabonds he calls the police of Panama.

"Then the *Americanos* will bully us no longer," rejoins Montez. "I thought that would be your decision. The *Americanos* have women and children with them, also considerable sums of money with which they are going to buy *ranchos* in California."

"But the men—those awful Yankee fighters," stammers the police colonel, growing nervous; "I remember them in '49 and '50. How they handled their revolvers!"

"Now—they do not carry many, besides—" Here Fernando's hand chinks a roll of doubloons into the outstretched palm of the officer of the law. "Besides—they are unprepared to fight—these rioters."

"A-ah, that settles *los Americanos*," laughs Garrido.

"But the governor—" suggests the other.

"Ah, the governor," mutters the colonel of police. "He is wavering."

"Wavering? *Diablo! Caramba!*" moans Montez. Then the drop of Morgan's buccaneer's blood coming to the front in this little man, he becomes tremendous. He cries out: "I'll see him at once! He shall waver no longer!"

So he directs his way to His Excellency's house, and begs that he may see the Governor of the town of Panama, but word is brought him that His Excellency is engaged.

At this Mr. Fra Diavolo grinds his teeth, writes four words on a slip of paper, and says: "Give that to His Excellency, curse him, and see if he dares to be engaged."

A moment after, the answer comes that he can see the potentate of Panama.

Young Fernando is received by this functionary, with a suggestive snarl. He says to this little every-nation gentleman: "What mean your threats, Señor Montez?"

"Nothing, only if the President at Bogota knows what I know, the Governor of Panama will occupy six feet of our quiet little cemetery within the month, though he will not die of yellow fever. Shall I tell him?"

"Certainly not!"

"Not if you do as you promised. There is no danger. The American Consul is a nothing! If it were Englishmen we were killing—*Santos!* that would be different."

"Very well, then! Garrido is arranged for?"

"Perfectly! Besides, these people are mostly unarmed; they have women and children with them. They will be easy. Likewise, the plunder will be great!"

"And my share?"

"Will be great also, as I promised."

"Ah! then I will know nothing about it! I shall go to sleep! I will not be awakened. *Buenas noches,* Señor Montez! Tell my people that I must be disturbed on no account—not for an earthquake—not even if a riot—nothing till to-morrow morning!"

"Very well, I will give your orders!" laughs Fernando. He is about to depart, when suddenly the governor queries: "How will the riot commence?"

"The *Americanos* shall do that!"

"The *Americanos*—how?"

"There are nine hundred and forty passengers; some one of them is sure to be drunk. Drunken men are quarrelsome!"

With these words Montez departs, whistling to himself a jaunty air from one of Verdi's first operas—the ones with melody divine in them—for this little gentleman has a drop or two of Italian blood, that make him a devotee to the Muses.

So passing along, he joins the stream of passengers bound for the railway depot.

Arriving there, the scene is much the same as when he left it, only there is a greater throng of passengers checking their baggage and seeing about their tickets. More ladies and children are going on board the *Toboga,* and the laughter coming from the saloons of McFarlane's hotel and the Ocean House (a rival hostelry) is louder. One or two drunken Americans are strolling about in front of the depot, and bantering in an alcoholic way some negro fruit hucksters, who are plying their trade with a defiant bloodthirsty vim, for they are waving the knives by which they cut up watermelons and pineapples, in a threatening and ferocious manner.

Just back of these stands Domingo and fifty or sixty

of his cronies, and perhaps a hundred more are scattered
from the depot, along the lane leading to the Cuinago.

Several American ladies, and their husbands and children, together with one or two Spanish señoras of the
better class, from the town, are looking at the scene,
which is made picturesque by torches, as darkness is
coming down.

It is a peculiar contrast of civilization and barbarism.

On one side, the long train of yellow railway passenger
cars ; the giant locomotive, that is powerless now because
it has lost its steam ; the railroad track ; the puffing
steamer at the end of the pier ; ladies and gentlemen
of Anglo-Saxon race, in the costumes of Paris and New
York, for some of the ladies wear little crinolines, that
are just now commencing to make their appearance on
the Boulevards and Broadway.

On the other side, the flaming torches of the negroes ;
their black, swarthy faces; the waving palms and bamboos and cocoanuts of the tropics ; the wild gesticulations
and jargons of the savage races who are half clothed, and
seem to excite themselves not only with *pulque* and *aguardiente*, but with some more subtle yet potent stimulant,
for their eyes blaze under the torch glow with some unholy
fire.

Between these aggregations—one white and civilized, one black and barbarous—stands one man—drunk
and disorderly—and he, alas ! of the Anglo-Saxon race.
He is bargaining with a negro huckster for a slice of
watermelon. He takes the watermelon, the watermelon
disappears ; the negro holds out his hand, demanding a
real.

" Go to the—the—d—devil ! " hiccups the drunken
American.

" A *real*, or your life's blood, *Gringo !* " screams the
negro savage, waving his *machete* in threatening gestures
about the American's head.

" Here's your ten-cent piece, Blackey ! Don't make a
muss," cries another Anglo-Saxon, stepping alongside his
compatriot, and tossing the negro the demanded coin.

" Curse it ! He—he was trying to b—b—bully me ! "
gulps the drunken American, trying to draw a revolver.

A second later, there is a sound of a pistol shot, and
riot and plunder, arson and murder, are let loose upon

the defenceless Americans, who. in a foreign land, burdened with their women and children, are almost helpless,
in the presence of a debased and armed mob.

The bell of the old church of Santa Anna, in the native
quarter, near the Gargona trail, is pealing an alarm.
Hundreds of blacks are running up the road from the
Cuinago, with wild cries and waving of muskets, *machetes*,
and pistols.

On this Montez looks and smiles, and as he does so, a
hand is laid upon his shoulder, and a voice cries in his
ear: " Stand the brutes off till the women and children
get on board the steamer ! " Then George Ripley, drawing his revolver from his belt, runs down the steps of the
hotel, and steps in front of the coming negroes.

A moment after, McLean of the Pacific Mail Company,
and Nelson of the railroad, stand beside him.

" Get the women on board the boat, quick ! If they
come another step, I shoot ! " cries the Californian.
" And I shoot to kill ! "

A moment more and he would try his pistol, and find
it useless, and thus perchance save his own life, did not
Montez hurriedly whisper to him : " Hold ! the police
are coming ! Hear their bugle ! "

At this moment its clear notes sound over the road
running from the town.

" Ah ! then all is well ! " mutters George, and puts up
his revolver.

Then a man named Willis, who has hastily rolled a six
pounder out of the railroad depot, and trained it loaded
to the muzzle down the lane running towards the Cuinago, which is crowded with coming blacks, turns it
away, crying : " Law and order ! we're all right now,"
and runs it back down the wharf, as headed, by Garrido,
the native police come marching with unsoldierly bare
feet, and carelessly carried muskets, to the front of the
hotel.

As they see the police, a cry of joy comes from the
American ladies and children, who have not as yet
escaped to the steamboat.

The bugle sounds again. A crashing volley from the
police.

" My God ! " cries George. " They have made a
mistake ! They are shooting at us ! They have killed

the child beside me ! There's its mother screaming over it."

Another crashing volley!

Mistake no more ! It is no riot. It is a MASSACRE !

Attacking negroes rush upon the railway station, butchering those they come upon, and plundering all. Trunks are broken open and looted ; and a little baby, torn from its mother, is tossed about by the savage men and more savage women of the mob, till it becomes a clot of gore.

Again the police fire !

More Anglo-Saxon blood !

A delicate American lady staggers to Ripley and gasps, " Tell my husband I—I was going to join—Harry Nesmith of Colusa— how I—died," then falls at his feet, a Minié bullet through her breast.

This sight brings recollection to the Californian.

With a muttered " My God ! my wife ! " George Ripley rushes back into the hotel to find and save, if possible, his wife and treasure. If not both, the woman he adores.

. Montez, Domingo and three blacks glide after him. The register of the hotel lies open in the deserted office. Tearing it to pieces, Fernando says : " There is now no record of the American on the Isthmus ! His fate will be unknown. To business ! "

A second later, amid crashing volleys, George Ripley, one arm around the slight waist of his wife, who is sobbing on his shoulder, one foot upon the trunk that contains the fortune he has risked his life to gain amid the Sierras of California, stands confronting the negroes ; foremost of whom, his eyes all blood-red now, is Domingo, a vermilion glow upon his black cheeks and white eyeballs, as if they were painted.

The ex-pirate cries : " Death to the *Americano !* Save the lady ! Her beauty gives her life ! "

To this Ripley's revolver makes reply ; the lock clicks, but no cartridge explodes. With a muttered curse he turns the cylinder.

They are springing towards him. Again the pistol, that has never failed him till now, when all depends upon it, gives no report to his clicking trigger.

" My heaven ! Someone has tampered with my

weapon!" he gasps ; and taking his wife's hand, turns to
fly, but at the door stands the man he thinks his friend,
and he cries : "Thank God ! In time, Montez ! "

And Alice joins his shout : "Dear Señor Montez, God
bless you for coming ! "

But tired of diplomacy, the savage drop coming upper-
most in him, this little every-nation fiend cannot for the
life of him keep down a smile of triumph and a mocking
laugh, as Domingo cries : " Fear not his pistol ! It will
not shoot. "

Then suddenly the American KNOWS !

He gasps : " My ruined weapon !—that bath at Toboga
—it was you ! *you !* YOU ! But, Judas, you go *first !* "

Reversing the revolver, with its butt end the Anglo-
Saxon strikes down two negroes who spring upon him,
and seizing Montez by the throat, is strangling him over
the trunk of his desires.

But at this moment there is a flash ; and, with a shriek,
such as comes only when hope has gone, Alice Ripley
sinks fainting on the dead body of her husband. For as
he has forced the every-nation traitor down, the back of
the Californian's head has come within two inches of the
pistol of Domingo, the ex-pirate ; and to the flash of its
explosion, George Ripley dies.

Looking on the scene, Fernando, rising, gasps—for the
breath has nearly left his body—to Domingo : " Quick !
the mules—before the massacre is over ! This treasure
is mine—all mine ! This beauty is mine—all mine !
Montez has made his first great start in life ! "

As he speaks, more volleys from the murderous police
outside tell of more bloodshed in the railway station,
and more cruel massacre of unarmed men and helpless
women and shrieking children, that, were they English,
would have been atoned for by the blood of the Governor
of Panama and his satellites and police ; but being
American, is left to the shallying procrastination of a
languid consul, and forgotten soon in the rush of the
great Republic towards what it loves best—gold.

Will the United States of America never learn to
protect its absent citizens, and make its banner, like the
Union Jack of England, a bulwark of defence to its
wanderers on the earth and on the sea ?

Some two hours afterwards, the moon rising high

above the Cordilleras of the Isthmus, lights up the Gargona trail leading into the mountains, where, on the back of a mule, is a defenceless woman insensible, in the arms of Montez, who rides hurriedly along, bearing her farther from any aid that civilized man can give, into the recesses of the upper valley of the Chagres. Domingo, ex-pirate, striding sturdily along in front of his master, mutters : " This has been a pleasant evening ! "

The glancing fireflies light up the lianas, parasites and creeping plants that hang from the great trees of the dense torrid forest. The silence is unbroken save by the tramp of the mule's hoofs as they scatter the decaying leaves, or the rustle of a serpent seeking his nightly prey—when, as he holds the fair victim to his heart, Montez starts.

Her lips are moving—sentiency is coming to her. She is shuddering, and murmuring: " My husband—killed at my side ! "

.   .   .   .

And under that same tropic moon, far out in the waters of the Bay of Panama, " Toboga Bill " and two other tiger-sharks, are munching over and playing with a something that was once George Ripley.

.   .   .   .

And, in a school dormitory, in far-away America, a child in the white dress of night is kneeling by her little bed, and praying, with happy eyes and expectant lips : " God bless papa and mamma, who are coming home to me again ! "

BOOK II.

The Franco-American.

CHAPTER V.

BLACK BLOOD CHANGES TO BLUE.

It had been a day of triumph for Panama and *le grand Français* Ferdinand de Lesseps, this first day of January, 1880—this day that inaugurated the opening work of the Canal Transatlantique; that was to make the commerce of all oceans one ; that was to wipe out from the sailor's log the tempestuous icy hurricanes of Cape Horn, and the more languid but equally retarding calms of the Cape of Good Hope.   By it France was to become richer, the world happier, and Ferdinand de Lesseps doubly immortal—this man of Suez and of Panama.

Five o'clock on the previous afternoon, welcomed by the braying of the one military band, and addresses from the Committee, and President of the State of Panama at the railway station, he had descended from the train bringing him from Aspinwall, soon to be rechristened Colon.

The bridge over the track of the Panama Railroad, from which the speeches were made, had been adorned with the flags of France and Colombia.

In carriages, the finest in the city, though not of the latest style, and the worse for twenty years' wear, Comte de Lesseps and his attendant party of engineers, politicians and fortune seekers, had been driven through streets, that for once in the history of Panama, and only once in its past, present, or to come, *were clean*.   They had been swept by municipal order, that their foul odors might not affront the delicate nostrils of the great Frenchman. Along the road from the railway station, leading up to the old Gargona road, and thence into the Plaza and the Grand Hotel, the huts and houses were especially white-washed for the occasion, to destroy germs of yellow fever, or *cholera Asiaticus* that had convenient resting place upon their palm-thatched roofs and mouldy beams.

This had been the suggestion of *Don* Fernando Gomez Montez, by this time one of the leading dignitaries of the city, banker, rich man, and general swell, who had impressed his views upon his *confrères*, by this pertinent remark: "*Caramba!* If all those delicate Europeans encounter Yellow Jack and *el vomito negro* before they commence operations, good-by to our canal which is to make us rich."

So the French party came with prancing of horses and shoutings from the crowd of creoles, negroes, and the general populace, between two battalions of native troops drawn up along the road, as ragged, as barefooted and as badly armed as in the days of '49 ; for this man and his nation were to bring wealth, commerce, and enter-prise to this city deserted since the days of the early Californian travel ; and Panama was to become even greater, richer, and more populous and important than the old town whose deserted tower stands in tropical jungle five miles to the south—the one that Morgan's buccaneers destroyed two hundred years before—the richest city of its size on earth.

Among the *élite* gathered to meet the great French-man had stood Fernando Gomez Montez, apparently not much older than when he had made his first great *coup* in life from the returning Californian, since which time he has devoted the plundered gold-dust of that night to commercial pursuits, and has built up for him-self a fortune, large for a Colombian city, but not great for Paris or New York.

His poverty he has learned by travel, for he has been both to France and America ; and his intellect, bright, wicked, and unscrupulous as ever, has been made subtle, cautious, and wary by experience. At twenty he *was* a great villain, at forty-four he *is* a great man, and therefore greater villain. To the audacity of the bandit he has added the *finesse* of the diplomat.

,,During the preceding day he has made his address at the railway station and at the banquet of the evening, and has been embraced by *le grand Français,* and petted with diplomatic tact, and called the hero local of the canal—for he had greatly assisted in obtaining from the Colombian Government the concession about to be sold to French stockholders for ten million francs.

On this day he has, with the inaugural party, sailed in the *Tobaguilla* around the bay, into *La Boca* of the Rio Grande, where young Mademoiselle Fernanda de Lesseps was to have inaugurated the work of the canal, by digging with childish shovel the first little sod of all the earth that separated the Atlantic and Pacific. But, as it had grown late, in this land where darkness comes on with sudden rush, they agreed to consider the entrance of the steamer into the river as the opening of the work of the canal—and omitted the shovelful of Isthmus swamp ; thus beginning the gigantic enterprise by a makeshift—one of the many that they made—till makeshifts were of use no more.

Returned from this excursion, to-night Fernando Montez is at one of the minor banquets that take place before the ball.

It is in one of the smaller rooms of the Grand Hotel. Several of the *attachés* of De Lesseps are at the table—a Paralta, a Diaz, and one or two others of the leading families of the Isthmus. It is a gentlemen's dinner party ; and though the great Frenchman is not there in person, all are enthusiastic about the canal which is to give every one a chance to grab a fortune.

Among them sits one Anglo-Saxon—a man of about twenty-eight years, who has a pleasant though weak face, surmounted by light hair, and adorned by a moustache and goatee, the cut of which are French. His costume is rather that of Paris than America, as far as a dress suit permits.

" The stock must be subscribed for at once ! " cries Montez. " The fever must not be let grow cold in France."

" Oh, trust De Lesseps for that ! " answers one of his satellites, Monsieur Dirks, Dutch engineer, who has dug canals in level Holland.

" Let me be the first to subscribe ! " says the Franco-

American.   Here he whispers to one of the French
attachés : " Please hand my name for the first one thousand shares to your chief, the Comte de Lesseps ! "

" The first one thousand shares subscribed for by an
American ! "   There is a buzz of excitement around the
table.   The champagne glasses clink.

" A health," cries Montez, " to the great Republic and
the American, Mr. Frank Leroy Larchmont ! "

" I beg your pardon ! " says the gentleman he toasts.
" Don't put me down as an American.   Register me as a
Franco-American—François Leroy Larchmont."

" But you live in the United States ? " says José Peralta
who sits next to him.

" I did *once.*   Now I consider myself a Parisian ! "
Which in truth he does.

" This gentleman who takes one thousand shares so
eagerly—I know his name—but what is he ? " whispers
Montez to the Frenchman sitting next to him.

" Oh, he is very rich, I believe !   That is all I know
about him.   He lives in Paris, has the good taste to like
France, and very seldom visits his native land."

.Then the banquet goes on, but during its conversation,
buzz and excitement, Montez' eye, sleepless and relentless,
never leaves the face of the Franco-American who has
taken the one thousand shares.

Fernando Gomez Montez has determined to make
himself one of the rich men of the world by this canal ; as
many more did about that time, some of whom succeeded.
He is shrewd enough to foresee, this cannot be by the
dividends it will pay to its investors, but in the immense
amount of money that must be handled, and rolled about,
and circulated from hand to hand and check book to
check book during its construction.

His subtle mind can easily grasp the idea that in this
great " grab game " some of it must come into his
clutches.   This gentleman, who rushes so eagerly into a
scheme just set on foot, whose face has a peculiar weakness not often seen in men of the United States, may
possibly be a very good chicken to pick in the great
pluckings and pickings that will take place during all the
financial evolutions of this great enterprise.

As soon as cigars pass about, and the formality of the
dinner becomes somewhat relaxed, he contrives to get

his chair beside that of Mr. Larchmont, and their conversation, from being that of first introduction, becomes freighted with some of the confidences of friends.

Mr. Larchmont, to Fernando's deft questioning, informs him that though educated partly in America, and his family entirely American, he has lived from his seventeenth year mainly in Europe and Paris. " Paris," he says, " I regard as my home. I have a young brother in the United States, who is only twenty now. I am afraid he is too American to ever become a Parisian like myself." But here their conversation is disturbed.

A dapper young man, with the quick address of one to whom time is money, and the manner of " no time like the present," enters the room, and says : " Pardon my stopping the champagne, Monsieur Dirks. I believe you are one of the engineers in control of the preliminary surveys of the canal ? "

" I have that honor," says the Hollander.

" Then, between drinks, permit me to ask you four questions. First, when do you expect to open the Panama Canal that has been inaugurated to-day ? "

" Certainly," replies the Dutch engineer, astonished at the abruptness of the address. " In five years at the latest. In 1885."

" You are sure ? "

" So confident that I would write it in letters twenty-four feet high ! "

" Then can you tell me how you are going to provide for the tremendous floods in the Chagres River that wash down, each rainy season, dirt enough to fill up the whole canal ? "

" That will be by means of a large dam and reservoir sufficient to hold the average rainfall of a week."

" But when the rainfall is more than the average, what will you do with it ? "

To this, the Hollander replies evasively : " Are you an engineer ? "

" No ! "

" Then why do you ask engineering questions ? " he replies sternly.

" It is because I am not an engineer that I ask engineering questions. If I were an engineer, I could determine things for myself."

"Ah, then I will tell you. The floods in the Chagres will be provided for—later."

"Then, the floods being provided for, what will you do with the higher rise of tide in the Pacific than the Atlantic?"

"That will be provided for later also!" returns the Dutch engineer savagely. And others of the Latin races at the banquet look with angry eyes upon this young man who stays their festival. Who is this creature that dares interrupt their night of triumph by impertinent queries that tend to throw doubt upon their grand scheme?

"Then, all this being settled, will you tell me how you are going to build the canal if you don't get the permission of the Panama Railroad, which by its concession from the Colombian government must give its consent before you can dig a barrelful of dirt out of your gigantic ditch?"

At this question, the guests rise with foreign indignation and South American swagger.

"That," shouts Dirks, wildly, "will be provided for by Monsieur le Comte de Lesseps. When he visits the United States, he will obtain from the Panama Railroad the requisite consent."

"Not unless he pays Trainor W. Park pretty well, if I know him," replies the young man. "I have just got time to telegraph your answer."

"Ah, you are an emissary!" cries a French *attaché*. "An emissary of the United States, that is now making such a shriek about the accursed Monroe doctrine!"

"I am no emissary!" the intruder gasps, dismayed, for two or three Latins have gathered about him threateningly, and one, a young *Chiliano*, is handling a carving knife as if it were a *cuchillo*. "I am merely a reporter for the New York——" He can say no more, for at this instant he is rushed from the room and hurled down stairs, which perchance saves his life, as the *Chiliano* does not reach him in time.

Looking on this, the Franco-American says disgustedly: "You see the crude manners of my countrymen. No wonder I fly from them! You will appreciate my embarrassment, Señor Montez, at this uncouth scene. I have been lately to New York, to try to induce my brother Henri to live with me in Paris, but he declines.

Over his actions I have no control ; but my ward, Made-moiselle Jessie Severn, as her guardian and trustee, I am taking with me to Paris. I made a short tour in America, and while in San Francisco, thought I would come to Panama, to see the opening of this great French enter-prise, and from here take passage in the *Transatlantique* line from Colon to France."

"The young lady, your ward, is with you ; " remarks Montez indifferently.

" Oh, yes ; she and her governess and nurse."

" Ah, she is not a young lady ? "

" Not yet. She is but ten. I am taking her to Europe, to educate her in the manner of my adopted country. I do not approve of the way in which girls are brought up in the United States. Heiresses in America become so bold and self-reliant. They even assert their independence to the extent of selecting their own husbands."

" Ah, an heiress ! " thinks Fernando, his eyes opening a little wider at the news, for here may be two fortunes to play with ; not only that of this rich gentleman, but also that of his ward.

So he proceeds to weave the first meshes in the web of the spider around this Franco-American fly. His con-versation grows jovial, and full of anecdote, repartee, and wit. Incidentally, by adroit questions that seem more suggestions than queries, he learns what he wishes to know of the other's character and life ; and, though it is conveyed to him with reluctance, discovers that Mr. Larchmont's father had been at one time a tailor in New York, and turning the money he had received for dress suits, overcoats, and trousers into city real estate, had become one of the magnates of Manhattan, though his elder son was almost ashamed to own him, notwithstand-ing the very handsome estates he had left behind him to his two sons and co-heirs.

" Ah ! " remarks Montez, to this revelation, " no one can avoid *bourgeois* ancestors in the United States ; it is land of trade and money." And he sneers at the tradesmen in his mind, as the robber always does at the merchant.

Then noting that the gentleman sitting opposite him seems somewhat ashamed of his commercial American ancestors, and drags into his conversation every one he

knows of title or rank in the Old World, Montez' occult
mind divines that to thoroughly and easily trap this man
who is ashamed of his commercial country and tailor
birth, he his captor must be of the nobility.

Then he mentions parenthetically : " Though you of
North America have no aristocracy, South America still
clings to hers. The Hidalgos of Spain never forget
that they are grandees. As such I remember my ancestors ! " and a drop of the blood of one of the Spanish
Conquistadores coming into his eyes, this gentleman
looks very haughty and exclusive to his Franco-American
acquaintance.

Shortly after, they stroll from the apartment in which
the little banquet has taken place, towards the ball-
room. As they pass through the corridor of the hotel,
which is brilliantly lighted, a charming figure trips toward
them. It is that of a beautiful little girl, who is dressed
like a sylph in gauze and fancy flowers and whitest
muslin.

She is attended by a French *bonne*, trying in vain to
restrain her charge, who comes eagerly towards the gentlemen, exclaiming, " Mr. Larchmont—Frank—Guardy !
Look what the count has given me."

She exhibits one of the beautiful decorations the charming gentleman had had made for distribution among the
ladies of Panama—a mass of colored enamel and solid
gold, and bearing the Colombian coat of arms, and an
inscription in Spanish announcing the inauguration of
Del Canal Interoceanic by Count Ferdinand de Lesseps.

These exquisite badges had been scattered broadcast
among the youth and beauty of Panama, little drops in
the ocean of expense that was to come, but bearing
promise of the lavish manner in which gold would be
thrown broadcast over promoters, jobbers, contractors
and employees—in short, on everyone engaged in this
gigantic enterprise—SAVE THE STOCKHOLDERS.

Delighted with her present, the child stands poised on
tiptoe, one hand held upwards towards her guardian, one
little foot advanced. With bare white arms and graceful
pose, the short skirts of childhood displaying fairy limbs,
she looks to Montez like a *ballerina* idealized. For she
has the blonde hair and blue eyes that dark nations love
so well ; and her figure, draped in the light dress of that

warm climate, gives promise of faultless development in an early future.

"This is my little ward," says Larchmont, examining the pretty bauble she holds up to him. "Miss Jessie Severn, permit me to present Señor Montez."

"*Baron* Montez."

"Ah!" is the little surprised exclamation from the American.

"Yes, we are old Castilians, we Montez, and like all Spanish Hidalgos, punctilio itself about our name and our titles. You will excuse my mentioning it to you," says Fernando, with a pleased smile at his own inspiration. "*Baron* Fernando Montez."

But here the little girl breaks in upon them, and says: "How curious, Mademoiselle Fernanda de Lesseps was to open the canal to-day, and you are called Fernando! Fernando Montez—that's a pretty name! I call little Fernanda, *Tototé*; must I call you *Tototo?*" Then she looks at the little figure of the ennobled gentleman, and gazes curiously at his jetty hair that is just beginning to show a little silver on the temples, and notes his mobile mouth play under his waxed moustachios, and his very white shirt, which has a decoration upon it—some old Spanish order he had picked up in some Peruvian cathedral. Next the blue eyes of happy childhood glance up fearlessly at the bright orbs of the new-made noble that have opal flashes in the gaslight; and, somehow, though this child had never felt fear before, her eyes droop before those of the all-nation gentleman, and she is happy when her guardian says: "Jessie, it is time for little girls to be in bed." So mademoiselle trips hurriedly off to her governess, followed by the sleepless eyes of Montez.

"You have made quite an impression on my little ward," whispers the guardian.

"Ah, you ravish me with delight!" cries Fernando.

And so he has; for the little girl is murmuring to herself: "Bluebeard, Bluebeard—naughty Bluebeard!" and trembles as she runs along.

The Hidalgo is pleased to see that his title has made an impression upon the Franco-American. He remarks, for the beauty of the child still lingers in his senses, "Miss Jessie will soon be ready to bless some happy man with her hand—this little beauty!"

4

" Pooh !   She is only ten.   That will be years from
now ! " says Larchmont easily.   Then he goes on : " But
I see in this tropic land the ladies develop early," and
casts his eyes over the bronze shouldered Inezes and
Doloreses, as they are trooping into the ballroom.

" Yes, we would marry her at fourteen here ! " laughs
Montez.   " But even in France, in a few years she will be
ready for her *trousseau*—about the time the canal will be
open.   You might celebrate both *fêtes* together, when
you have selected the husband."

Then the buzz of excitement coming in through windows that are always open, save during thunder storms,
in this torrid city, attracts the gentlemen.   They step out
to catch the night breeze that comes refreshingly to their
cheeks, and look down upon the great Plaza of Panama,
with its green plants and paved walks, in which the
crowd are promenading, the great cathedral standing at
their left.   For this is the old Grand Hotel—the one
that afterwards became the offices of the Panama Canal—
which is decked to-night for gayety.

Looking at the cathedral, a grim smile comes over the
face of Montez, and he sees in his vivid imagination a
bridal procession going up its great aisles to music of the
organ and chant of dusky altar-boys, and picturing the
bride with blue eyes and blonde tresses, thinks to himself : " Why not I for the bridegroom ?   I am not old !
She is rich.   The man beside me is weak.   Perhaps with
another fortune may come to me another beauty."

The noise of the moving crowds below breaks in upon
his reverie, and Larchmont suggests : " Suppose we see
the ball."

They go in to the dance where Spanish beauties, in
the ball-dresses of Europe, jostle French and Colombian
uniforms and black dress coats ; and the grand old man
dances quadrilles with lovely Inezes, Marias, and Manu-
elas, to have his agility telegraphed all over the world, so
that doubting French peasants may invest their stocking-
hoards in his newest and grandest enterprise, still thinking
him the man of Suez, when Ferdinand de Lesseps is in
reality beginning a dotage, awful in its consequences, to
his friends, his government and his country—because it
is unsuspected.

So the ball goes on to its climax, amid the strains of

the latest waltzes, and the clinking of champagne glasses in the supper room, and the laughing eyes of Spanish beauties, and the babbling tongues of sycophants and hangers-on.

And on this night of triumph, when De Lesseps inaugurates the work on the Panama Canal, this night Fernando Montez gives to himself nobility and a title that will give him weight in Europe and influence over weaklings like the one he has set his eyes upon this evening. So the black drops in his veins become blue, azure, and noble; even the little Congo negro he has in him changes to old Castilian, as he exclaims : " Fernando Gomez Montez, I ennoble thee ! Mule-boy of Cruces, I introduce you to Baron Montez ! "

Full of his project, this very night he obtains a printer, who, under great promise of secrecy, for which he is heavily paid, furnishes early the next morning the following striking *carte de visite.*

Baron Montez

*Panama
and Paris*

This looks so beautiful to him that he cannot refrain from trying its effect early next morning.

Old Domingo, who is older by twenty-four years since the night he assisted to make Montez rich, lives with him, not as servant, but as kind of half-way guest, for the old man is well-to-do. The old pirate knows the buccaneer maxim : " Every man his share ! " And he had had pirate enough in him to compel the moiety of the American's gold due him from Montez.

On this he has lived and prospered, and though well over seventy, is still as hale and hearty and old a sinner as can be found in South America—which furnishes as fine a sample of ruffians as Hades itself.

"How now, Señor? You seem happy!" is Domingo's greeting, as his mentor saunters on to his portico, having finished his alligator pear, sucked his orange, and drank his cup of coffee. "How now, Señor Montez?"

"*Baron* Montez!" corrects the gentleman addressed, severely.

"*Caramba!*"

"After this, *Baron* Montez! I have been ennobled," remarks Fernando, shoving his ornamental pasteboard beneath Domingo's rolling orbs.

"Ho oh! By the great fat Frenchman who is here?"

"Yes, the great Frenchman, who will make us all rich."

"Sant Jago! Another massacre! There are lots of them here now! Beauties, too! Would I were younger!" mutters the ex-pirate, his eyes glowing with pirate gleam.

"No, not this time. They have more to give us if we let them live!" returns Montez in grim significance.

· But the remembrance brought to his mind of that night in 1856, does not seem to please him. He looks curiously at Domingo, then gives a little sigh of relief; the appearance of his co-laborer indicates he will be forever close-mouthed. Time has made the rest safe. They are dead; even the beautiful Indian girl, Anita of Toboga, had become a hag at twenty-five, and died at thirty. Beauty that the sun nourishes most fondly, it soon scorches to death in these tropic climes.

So, with a contented smile, Fernando strolls off, to put his new nobility to use.

He sends up his card, with its coronet, to the Franco-American, and very shortly following it to that gentleman's parlor in the Grand Hotel, is greeted by a "Good morning, Baron!" and an effusive grasp of the hand.

For one second he starts, thinking some one else is addressed—it is not easy to get accustomed to nobility over night—then, with a smile, the "new creation" replies with affable *hauteur*.

Soon after, all others address him as Baron; none seeming to doubt his title, for these curious reasons: The French, knowing but little about him, think he is a true Spanish Hidalgo. His Colombian *confrères*, some of whom have known him even when he was an altar-boy in the Cruces chapel, think Fernando has received his patent of nobility in some peculiar manner from *le grand Français* De Lesseps. Besides this, they are very much occupied about a revolution that they have been intending to put in progress, but have postponed, fearing their political shooting and slaying might delay the opening of this canal. They will, however, go at this quite merrily, as soon as Monsieur de Lesseps leaves Panama. So it comes to pass that the ex-mule-boy of the Gargona trail, *el muchacho diablo*, becomes accepted by men as Ferando Gomez, Baron Montez, and prepares to air his title in the *salons* of Europe and the Parisian *Bourse*.

CHAPTER VI.

JESSIE'S LETTER.

AFTER this, the time passes pleasantly for the great Frenchman and his party at Panama in picnics, sight-seeing, and excursions around the beautiful bay. They run down to the Pearl Islands, and visit Montez' villa at Toboga. They view the ruins of the old city, and finally, the preliminary reports from the engineers being received, they one day put a little dynamite cartridge into the great mountain of Culebra, which will be the deepest cut on the whole line, and blow out an infinitesimal portion of its great side, little Mademoiselle Fernanda de Lesseps touching off the giant powder fuse, and announcing that work has really commenced on the great canal.

Then they depart, Monsieur de Lesseps taking steamer from Colon to the United States to obtain the proper concessions from the Panama Railroad Company necessary to his legally carrying out his project. Baron Montez and his Franco-American friend, however, leave the Isthmus direct for France, via Martinique and St. Lucia.

At Martinique they stop a day or two, and chance in a local museum to see one of the deadly snakes of that Island, the *fer-de-lance*, at which they all shudder, but Fernando turns very white and trembles ; so much so, that little Jessie, holding her governess' arm, says : "Mademoiselle, why is Baron Montez so afraid of a snake ?"

"*Mon Dieu !* my dear," replies the Frenchwoman, "everybody trembles at such hideous, crawling, deadly things. You did—so did I !"

"But I didn't nearly faint—and he is a man, and I am only a little girl !" And she looks with wondering, childish eyes after Montez, who has moved away from the sight.

But they soon leave this island. Two weeks later finds them at that centre of the French universe—the great city on the Seine—where Francis Leroy Larchmont settles down in a beautiful villa on the residential part of the *Boulevard Malesherbes* near the pretty little *Parc Monceau* with his little ward and attendants, and Baron Montez engages fine apartments just off the *Boulevard de Capucines*, where he can be near the Press Club and baccarat, an amusement in which he takes great delight.

He soon has hosts of friends, for he spends his money freely, hoping to get return from the same in the near future, with usurer's interest.

In this capital of France, De Lesseps, soon after returning from the United States, inaugurates his great scheme. The shares are taken by the peasants of France, every village has its subscriber, work is begun in reality upon the canal.

Then comes the time of harvest for Montez. He founds the firm of Montez, Aguilla et Cie.—Aguilla being practically a clerk, with a nominal interest—and for it obtains a contract for a portion of the work, at great figures. He circulates between Paris and Panama, dabbling in contracts, dabbling in shares, and making money in everything, for he knows what takes place on the Isthmus, as well as what goes on in Paris.

All the time he is doing this, investors' money is being squandered like water, and the shares of the Canal Company go lower and lower. But Montez loses not. He has become too near the Board of Directors to suffer; he knows too much of the inside politics of the scheme to permit its magnates to let him lose a single franc in this Canal Interoceanic.

Besides, he, by the diplomatic arts of entertaining and open pocket book, is now a boon companion with many a space-writer for the press—a class vigorously strong in shrieking their incorruptibility, and very pliable to the persuasive check book and bank bill, as impecunious classes generally are. Again, he has a few easy deputies of the *Corps Législatifs* under his thumb, owing to postponed debts at baccarat and many little suppers at *Des Ambassadeurs* and *le Madrid* and the Alcazar. In fact, he is a power at which the directors of the canal stand aghast, and would strike down were their enterprise upon a basis sufficiently solid for them not to fear what Fernando Baron Montez' ready tongue might hint to stockholders already becoming suspicious.

But stock and preferences in a losing concern, to make their owner rich must be converted into money of the realm and more substantial securities. To do this it was necessary to find purchasers ; and to beguile, allure and dazzle investors to transferring their gold to his pockets ; for shares in the Canal Interoceanic had been Montez' first, great and continuous effort ever since he had determined the enterprise must fall, even of its own weight.

His ready tongue, unscrupulous assertion, and, if necessary, direct and brilliant lies, had gained many listeners and some believers, notably among them one Bastien Lefort. This person, curiously enough, was a noted miser, who had lived to sixty, saving his accumulations, adding to them franc by franc the product of not only a life of toil, but a life of absolute deprivation. Beginning as a clerk in a small booth, he had saved and pinched till he had become a shopkeeper himself. Then he had squeezed and accumulated till he was worth nigh on to a million francs, each one of which meant not so much profit, but so much stint and discomfort and privation—even to lack of fire in winter and lack of food in summer. This hoarded treasure he did not dare invest in real estate—even city property sometimes depreciates. He did not dare deposit in a bank—banks fail—but kept his gold in safes of his own and the strong box of the miser.

All his life Bastien Lefort had said he was looking for an investment—one that would be sure as the Bank of France

but would return large usury—such an investment he
had been seeking for forty years. Within three months
after Baron Montez strolled into his little *magasin de
gants*, on the *Rue Rivoli*, to buy a pair of gloves, the
Panama philanthropist found it for him.

Among those gathered into these Panama ventures
is François Leroy Larchmont. From the year 1880 to
1887 Fernando has been gradually involving the wealth
of the Franco-American, who has become his bosom
friend ; and not content with this, has succeeded in drawing into the financial maelstrom that is now running over
Paris, the fortune of the orphan, the little girl, that her
weak guardian had in his charge, and which should have
been secured in consols and collaterals undoubted.

So one day, towards the close of the year 1887, Montez
thinks it time to speak, for all these years the loveliness of
this graceful girl—this American beauty—this fairy beauty, who is still in the schoolroom, but nearly a woman,
has appealed more and more to him. He has looked
upon it, and says it shall be his. He has whispered to
himself : "These people are in the toils. I am wealthy
as a New York nabob ! I will marry this beautiful creature. The loveliness of the Baroness Montez shall make
her a queen in the fashionable circles of this gay capital,
and I shall be one of its princes—I, Fernando Gomez
Montez, once mule-boy on the Cruces trail ! "

Thinking this, he one day calls upon his bosom friend,
François Leroy Larchmont, who is just admiring a newly
purchased picture, for this gentleman is a *dilettante* in
everything artificial, and dabbles in paintings, scores of
unproduced operas, and manuscript verses and novels ;
dealing with the prodigality of a connoisseur, and the lack
of knowledge of an amateur.

"I want to speak to you, Larchmont, *mi amigo*, on a
particular subject."

"Yes, but first admire the beauty of this picture,
Montez. The head is that of a newly discovered
Madonna ! "

"Ah, but not as beautiful as Mademoiselle Jessie, your
ward."

"Why, Montez, she is but a child ! "

"Nevertheless it is time she should marry. I wish to
speak to you of her ! "

Turning fiom his painting, in his nonchalant way, François Leroy Larchmont hears words that give him a fearful shock.

He remonstrates.

Then the easy tone of the friend changes to the voice of the master ; and before the interview is over, this weak and untrustworthy creature has given such hostage to his enslaver that makes him ashamed to look his lovely charge in the face ; for he knows in his feeble heart he has done the act of the dastard and the coward.

Now while this has been going on, several times in the years between 1880 and 1887, François Leroy Larchmont has received visits from his younger brother Harry Sturgis Larchmont, who has come over from the United States when his collegiate course has been finished, and has assumed, in his off-hand, American style, the *rôle* of a relative, and the good comradeship of a friend, to his brother's pretty ward.

This has been done in the easy manner of youth.

Once, on his visit after his college days at Yale, he had upheld her against guardian and governess in a way that had endeared him greatly to Miss Rebel.

It was one Fourth of July. Harry had come in the dusk of the day to dress for the banquet in honor of the United States at the American Minister's.

He is talking to his brother in the *salon* which looks out upon a little courtyard made pretty by flower beds, and a graceful *kiosk* in which the gentlemen sometimes take their breakfasts.

Harry has just remarked, " Frank, I'm sorry you sent a regret to Mr. Washburn's invitation. It looks as if you had forgotten George Washington and fire crackers."

" My dear Henri," lisps the elder brother, " I have promised to listen to a new manuscript comedy. Farandol, *le jeune*, its author, thinks I have influence with the management of the Palais Royal, and may get it produced. As for fire-crackers and such juvenile nuisances—" Here he gives a great start, and cries, "*Mon Dieu!* What is that ? Dynamite ? "

For a loud explosion has just come from the garden, and Parisians, in grateful memory of the Commune, always fear dynamite and Anarchists.

" I rather imagine that is a little piece of the Fourth of

July," laughs Harry, who has made Miss Severn a patriotic present of fireworks and fire-crackers this very morning.

A moment after, Jessie, with defiant face that is slightly grimed with gunpowder and burning punk, and a bunch of fire-crackers in her hand, is dragged into the room by her governess and an attendant maid.

" In spite of my protestations and commands she has exploded them in the bed of daisies, Monsieur Larchmont," says the duenna, looking with reproving eyes upon her charge who stands pouting but unrepentant.

"*Mon Dieu!*   My white daisies!" cries Mr. François ; then he remarks sternly : "This is most unseemly! Jessie, don't you know it is wrong to disobey your governess—wrong to make a noise, and disturb me with explosions?"

" Not on the Fourth of July!" mutters the child.   Then her eyes flash, and she cries, "I will fire them! I'm American! I ain't French, and I *will* fire them!" and emphasizes her declaration by defiant eyes and stamping feet.

"Oh, this is terrible!" murmurs Mr. Larchmont.

"If you would permit me," suggests the instructress, " I think Miss Jessie should be put to bed."

"What! for being a patriot?" cries Harry, intruding on the scene.   Then the young man goes on firmly, " Jessie shall celebrate the Fourth, and I'll help her."

" But, Henri," expostulates his brother, "the *gensd'armes* will arrest me.   It is violating a municipal ordinance."

" Then you pay the fine, or I'll do it for you," returns the younger man.   "You go off to your comedy reading, and Miss Jessie and I'll make a patriotic night of it."

"Will you?" cries the girl ; then she comes to him and puts her arms about him, after the manner of trusting childhood, and whispers, "I knew you would. You're a Yankee, so am I."

"You bet!" says Harry, giving way to slang in this moment of patriotic enthusiasm.   "You and I, Jessie, are the only Americans in this house."

"Well, have your will!" replies the older brother.   "I'll go off to the reading and get away from the noise.—Jessie, come and kiss me good-night."

"I won't," returns Miss Jessie.   "You would have let

Mademoiselle put me to bed if it hadn't been for Harry
—Harry's my *chevalier*."

"You won't kiss me," mutters the child's guardian.
Then he astonishes his brother, for he goes to his pout-
ing charge, and says: "I beg your pardon, little one.
Won't that get a kiss?"

"Yes, two!" answers Jessie, and gives him three very
sweet ones, for her guardian is very kind to her, and generally lets her do her will except when it disturbs his
ease or puts him to trouble.

So Harry and Jessie go off to their fireworks, where,
amid revolving pin-wheels and colored lights, the little
lady in her dainty Parisian dress looks like a miniature
Goddess of Liberty, though Mademoiselle, her governess,
shakes her head ; and the maid, whose white apron has
been soiled and her cap put awry, and her skin somewhat bruised by the struggles of Miss Rebel when she
had been dragged in, mutters : "If I had my way with
Miss Vixen, I'd smack her good."

After this Miss Jessie looks upon Harry Larchmont as
her Court of Appeals from all decisions against her childish
whims. And when, some time after, a pretty trinket of
gold and jewels, commemorative of this event, comes to
her from New York, it does not tend to make her forget
her Fourth of July champion.

This very year, when he is making a little tour of Europe, Miss Severn has renewed her trust in him, and they
have grown greater friends. The exquisite beauty and
grace of the girl have appealed to him, as they would to
any man, though she has seen but few, being still kept
at her studies much closer than Mr. Harry Larchmont
thinks is necessary. For, on leaving for his German trip
he has remarked to his brother ; "Why not bring Jessie
over to America, put her in society, and marry her to an
American?"

"She is too young for society."

"She is not too young to have a good time. Give her
a chance at a beau anyway. Whether she marries or
does not, just at present is of no particular moment ; but
her enjoyment is!"

"I will consider your suggestion, Henri," says the
brother, a wistful expression coming over his face, but
his answer is cut short.

"Confound it ! Don't call me Henri. Do you sup-
pose I would ever call you François?" bursts in the
younger brother. Then he goes on quite dictatorially,
" Frank, be an American, and a man. Leave this foreign
place where you are dawdling away your existence ! "
"And what are you doing in America ? "
" Nothing ! "
" Am I not doing the same in Paris?" says the other,
with an attempt at a laugh, which changes into a sigh as
he continues, " I wish I could leave Paris ! "
" What keeps you ? "
" My interests."
" Pooh ! your fortune is well invested, and you can
sell this pretty little villa at a profit, even now, notwith-
standing Panama shares have gone down ! " answers the
younger brother. So, departing upon his journey, he
thinks he will have an hour in Dresden, a week in
Vienna, three days in Berlin, and get home for the first
Patriarchs' ball of the season in New York.

Curiously enough, this young gentleman, though a
man of fashion, has a good deal of action in him ; though
nominally he does nothing, he is energy itself, killing
time by athletics, hunting, pigeon shooting. He is very
good at some of these sports, which, if they do not
exactly elevate a man, at least keep his muscles in condition, and his mind active. He has been a great foot-
ball player, and is still remembered in his college as a
wonderful half back. He leads the German at Delmonico balls, with a vigor that startles the languid
youths who perform in the cotillon ; and young ladies
are very happy to have his strong arm as a guide, and his
potent elbow as a guard from collisions in the dance, for
he has not yet forgotten an old football trick.

His innocent looking elbow has many times caused
young Johnnie Ballet, who dances so recklessly, and
Von Duzen Van Bobbins, who prances about so carelessly,
to wonder why they so suddenly get extremely faint and
out of breath, when they come in contact with his deft
elbow. But they have not played on college *campi*, and
do not know how effective this elbow has been in putting many a Princeton rusher out of play, and many a
Harvard slugger on the ground, in the desperate scrim-
mages of the football field.

It is late in 1887 when Harry Larchmont goes away for his German tour, in the careless, easy frame of mind that he has been wont so far to run through life. Three days afterwards, at Cologne, he receives an agitated letter from Miss Jessie Severn, praying him to come to her for heaven's sake, before he leaves for America. Its end gives this easy-going young athlete a start, for it closes :

"*Dear good Harry, as you love the memory of your mother, don't let your brother know I wrote this.*
Your frightened to death
JESSIE.*"

CHAPTER VII.

"NO ! BY ETERNAL JUSTICE ! "

THE words are blotted with tears, and the whole appearance of the epistle is such as to give the young man a shock. He throws this off, however, remarking to himself," Pshaw ! she's only a child in short dresses yet ! I presume she must have been naughty. Even if she has been disobedient she needn't fear Frank, he is gentleness itself to her." But this evasive kind of reasoning does not suit him. After communing with himself fifteen minutes the action of the man comes into play. He was dawdling by the Rhine. He dawdles no more. And in one hour afterwards he is *en route* to Paris, as fast as an express train can take him.

Arriving there next day, he goes over from the *Gare du Nord*, as fast as a *fiacre* can take him, to the pretty little villa on the *Boulevard Malesherbes*.

"Ah, Monsieur Henri, you have come back from Germany," says the footman, opening the door, a grin of welcome upon his Briton face, for this young gentleman has endeared himself to the servitor by many fees.

"Yes, you need not mention the matter to my brother, if he's at home," says Mr. Larchmont, "but I presume he is out ?"

"I think he is at the *Bourse*."

"At the *Bourse ?* That is rather astonishing."

"Oh, he goes there every day, now," answers the man.

"The dickens!" ejaculates Mr. Harry, and this information would set him wondering, did not another idea fill
his mind. He says : "Step upstairs, please, Robert, and
tell Miss Jessie that I am here, and would like to see
her."

"Mademoiselle Jessie is at her lessons," replies the
footman, "and I don't think the governess cares to have
her disturbed."

"Never mind about the studies, Robert, I have only a
few hours to stay in Paris. Just show me up to the schoolroom, and I will break in upon the lessons, and help her
with them," returns Mr. Harry, and walks up to find Miss
Jessie and get a surprise.

As he opens the schoolroom door and looks in upon
her she is prettier than ever, but not wearing out her blue
eyes over books, though there is a troubled look in them.
She springs up with a cry of joy, and, as he gazes at
her, he notes that during his few days' absence an occult
change seems to have come over the girl. Her short
skirts had seemed to him her proper costume ; now as
she glides toward him they appear too juvenile.

She utters a warning "Sh-h-h !" and puts a taper
finger to her lips, then whispers : "My governess is in
the next room. She thinks I am studying, but I was
thinking—thinking ;" next gasps, "Harry ! Dear good
Harry ! God bless you for coming to me !" and the
pathos in her manner, and look in her eye, tell him that
a great trouble has come into this child's life.

"I am here," he says, astonished at the girl's manner,
"to do anything you wish, Jessie ; but it seems to me you
should have applied to my brother, who is your guardian,
before coming to me."

"It is he who makes me come to you !"

"My brother?"

"Yes ! Your awful brother is using his authority as
my guardian. After the horrid manner of the French, he
has betrothed me."

"Be—betrothed you?" stammers the young man shortly
in intense surprise.

"Yes, to that odious Baron Montez !"

"What, that old stock-jobber? He's twice your age !
You are but a child."

"I am seventeen, and, in spite of training, an American

seventeen ; and that is old enough to know that I never will marry Baron Montez ! " cries Miss Jessie, angry at the suggestion of youth, more angry at the thought of Montez.

" Oh, ho, you love another ! " laughs the young man, who tries to take this matter quite easily before the ward, though great indignation has come to him against the guardian.

" No, I love no one ! I hate everyone. Rather than marry Fernando Montez," falters the girl, her lips growing pouting and trembling, " I'd sooner go into a convent."

Whereupon the gentleman says, in offhand manner : " Pooh ! Pooh ! No convent for such a beauty as yours."

" And you will save me, even though your brother uses his authority as my guardian ? "

" Certainly ! " says the young man.

" Swear it ! "

" Very well, you have my promise," returns Harry who is loath to take the affair seriously ; " but I don't think you need have troubled me. Had you spoken to my brother, he would have most assuredly not tried to coerce your inclination in such a matter."

But here Jessie's words bring astonishment, disgust, and displeasure against the man he calls brother, to the gentleman facing the excited girl. She whispers: " I have told your brother ! I have told him that I loathed, I detested, I hated the man he wished me to marry ! "

" And he did not listen to you ? "

" No ! He said it was absurd for me to rebel against his lawful authority. That I must, and I should, do what he told me."

" He did, did he ? Then hang him ! I swear you shall not ! " cries the young man, for something in Jessie's manner tells him she is speaking from her heart. " You shall only marry the man you want to ! "

So he leaves the young lady reassured, and strolls over into the *Parc Monceau* (his brother not having returned from the *Bourse*), and communes with himself in the exquisite little pleasure ground, looking at the beautiful *naumachie* and rock grotto, and would reflectively toss stones into the lake, did not a *gend'arme* restrain him.

And all the time his eyes grow more determined, and the indignation in his heart against his brother increases.

Then he strolls back to the house, and Mr. François Larchmont being at home, walks into that gentleman's library, with a very nasty look upon his countenance.

"You here?" says Frank, starting up with unnerved face. "This is a surprise!"

"Yes," says the other nonchalantly. "In Cologne I received a letter from Miss Severn—I suppose we must call her Miss Severn, since you consider her old enough to marry. By the by, I think you had better have her governess put her in long skirts; she's been growing lately."

While he has said this, notwithstanding Harry's manner, Frank's face has become white. He suddenly asks: "Did that stop your journey?"

"Certainly! An appeal from a woman would stop any man's journey. I have seen your ward. She tells me what I find it very hard to believe—that you wish to exercise your authority as her guardian, to coerce her into marrying this South-American stock-jobber, and gambler—Baron Fernando Montez. Is it true?"

"It is," falters the other. "I wish her to marry him!" Then he goes on suddenly, noting the look of disgust upon his brother's face, "Don't misunderstand me, Henri, it is necessary. She has now arrived at the age when it is best for her—for any young woman—to enter the world ; and to do that in France, it is necessary for her to take a husband."

"But not such a husband."

"He will give her title."

"Pooh! titles are common here."

"He will accept her—and this is the important part of the matter—without a *dot*."

"*Without* a *dot?* Why, she is worth a million dollars in her own right."

"Nevertheless she will have no *dot!*"

"What do you mean? gasps the other.

Then Frank bursts out hurriedly : "Don't look at me so. I have lost Jessie's money in speculation."

"Then you must make it up out of your own fortune. You are a very rich man!"

"I *was*."

" Good heavens ! have you lost that also ? "

" Yes, it is involved. At present I could not, if called upon, hand over Miss Severn's fortune, which was entrusted to me by her father's will, when I gave her to her husband. In France it would be demanded at once, if any one else except Baron Montez married her."

" And you have lost all this money—in what ? "

" In the shares of the Panama Canal, I think."

" In the Panama Canal, you *think?*" sneers Harry. Then he scoffs : " You—you are the only American who has not made money out of that giant fraud ? You are so afraid of being thought a man of business, that you have let that swindling South American make you bankrupt ? "

" I—I do not know—my affairs are involved. I have entered into so many speculations with Baron Montez."

" Ah, he has your money ! " cries the New Yorker. " He has Miss Severn's money. He has got the *dot* before. Now he will take the bride, generous man, without it, but she shall not marry him ! I have sworn it ! "

" Great heavens ! You would ruin me ! "

" I would ruin everyone to save this girl's happiness ! "

" You—you love Jessie ? " gasps Frank with twitching lips.

" As a brother ! That is all. But it is well enough to see she is not wronged by you ! "

" You forget I am her guardian ! "

" And I am her protector ! She shall not marry Baron Montez ! I'll prevent it with my fortune—with my life ! Do you suppose I will stand by and see a lovely, beautiful, young American girl sacrificed on the altar of your speculations ? No ! By eternal justice ! "

" You will save her ? " asks François Leroy Larchmont, a curious wistful look coming into his uncertain eyes.

" Yes ! "

" God bless you ! " cries the man, and sinks down into a chair, sobs in his voice, but no tears in his eyes.

" Why do you thank me for saving her from your friend ? "

" He is not my friend ! I hate him ! I fear him ! I loathe him now, but I am in his power ! But thank God !

5

Henri," and the weak man has seized his brother's hand and wrung it, and is muttering to him : "Thank God ! you will save her—save her from marrying him—save her for me—for me—I love her ! "

"Not for you ! " cries the other, breaking away from his brother's grasp, and an awful contempt coming into his soul. "You are not worthy of her. You love no one but yourself, and that not well enough to fight for your own hopes, desires or loves ! When you renounced your country, you gave up manhood ! But I'll save her for some good American ! "

With that he leaves his brother, who has sunk down, and is cowering away from Harry Larchmont's indignant eyes, and goes up to again see the lovely girl her guardian's weakness would have sacrificed, and tells her to be of good cheer, that he will save her. "Only one thing—procrastinate this matter," he adds. Then he queries wistfully, "Can you be woman enough to procrastinate ? Are you still a child ? "

"Why not defy him ? With you by my side I'll snap my fingers in Montez' face."

"That," says the young man, wincing a little, "will require a sacrifice from me." For he knows, if matters come to a climax now, to give this girl her fortune and keep his brother's name in honor before the world, will sadly cripple his means and make him comparatively poor.

Looking in his face the girl says suddenly : "No, I see it is important. I am not child enough to ask too much. I will do as you say."

"In every way ? "

"In every way."

"Then procrastinate. Get my brother to bring you over to New York for this winter ; put off the wedding till the spring—till the autumn. If Frank demurs, tell him you will write to me, and that will settle the affair, I think."

"You—you are going away ?" falters the child, growing pale at the thought of his desertion.

"Yes, I am going away."

"Why ?"

"To save you."

"How ?"

" To find out more about this man, who has my brother in his power—this Baron Montez of Panama and Paris. Here he is surrounded by all the Panama clique ; there is no rent in his armor that I, an American, unaccustomed to the ways of Paris, can pierce. If he has a flaw in his cuirass, it is at the other end of the route. I am going to Panama. Please God, I'll nail him there! I leave this evening for England. Then to New York, to arrange several matters of business, for if the worst comes to the worst——"

" You will permit me to be sacrificed ? "

" Never ! It is for that I go to New York."

" But if the worst comes to the worst, you——"

" It is for that reason that I go to New York. Don't ask me questions. Only know that I am forever your protector. What my brother has forgotten, I will do ; his dishonor shall be effaced by me."

" His dishonor ! " cries the girl. " What do you mean ? "

" Nothing that I can tell you ; but good-by, Jessie. Be sure of one thing—that you need never marry Baron Montez of Panama ! "

" God bless you ! " cries the girl, and gives him the first kiss she has ever given him in her life. But it is the kiss of the child, not of the woman. The kiss of grati-tude—the kiss that beauty gives to the knight that risks his life to save her from the giant Despair.

.   .   .   .

Twenty-four hours after, Harry Larchmont sailed for New York on the *Etruria,* and a month later his brother brought his ward to America upon the *Gallia;* but Baron Montez said to him, " Remember, *mon ami,* you must bring her back by Easter. Spring-time in France will suit Mademoiselle Jessie's beauty."

Four weeks after the Larchmonts arrive in New York a letter comes to Fernando, from a co-laborer of his in the Panama scheme, one Herr Alsatius Wernig, who is in America on some joint business, and will shortly pro-ceed to the Isthmus.

This epistle contains some curious news about the Larchmonts.

After reading it the Baron's face grows grave for a moment, then it suddenly lights up. Montez, with a

jeering smile, exclaims : "What ?   That idiot who plays
football and takes the chance of being killed *for fun !*"
A moment later he remarks meditatively: " There is
always danger in a lunatic ! " and an hour afterwards
sends a carefully prepared cablegram to Herr Alsatius
Wernig in New York.

BOOK III.

The American Brother.

CHAPTER VIII.

THE STENOGRAPHER'S DAY-DREAM.

*[Extracts from the diary of
Miss Louise Ripley Minturn.]*

" A TYPEWRITER, I believe ? "

" A stenographer," I reply as sternly and indignantly as an Italian tenor accused of being in the chorus, " *stenographer !* "

" Oh, excuse me, mademoiselle ! Certainly, a stenographer—that is what we require. What salary will you ask to go to Panama, to act as stenographer ? "

" To Pan-a-*ma ?* " There is an excited tremolo in my voice as I say the words, for the proposition is unexpected, and the distance from New York perhaps awes me a little. " Panama, where they are constructing the great canal ? "

" Certainly, mademoiselle. It is because they are building the great canal that I ask you the question."

" What will be the cost of living there ? "

" That I hardly know. It will not be small, I am certain, judging by the bills of expense I have seen from there."

" Very well," I reply, American business tact coming to me, " if I go, we will say thirty dollars a week, and expenses."

" You are able to take stenographic dictation in English ? "

"Certainly."

"And in French?"

"Yes; but that will be ten dollars a week more."

"And in Spanish?"

"Perfectly. Ten dollars extra."

"Ah," remarks the little clerk, who is half American and half French, "your charges are high; but every one gets their own price—on the Isthmus."

Prompted by this ingenuous remark, and actuated by American business greed, I ejaculate hurriedly: "I also take dictation in German, which will be another ten dollars a week."

"Let me try you," says the little man; and in six minutes he has given me English, French, Spanish and German dictations, to my astonishment, and I have taken them down, and read them correctly, much more to his amazement.

"Your work is perfectly satisfactory in every language," he replies. "You will come on the terms you mentioned?"

"That is, sixty dollars a week, and expenses there and back," I say, "if I go."

"Ah, you are not certain you would like to leave New York? You have ties here?"

"None," I reply, a tremble getting into my voice, as I think of my loneliness, and of my mother, who passed away from me but a year before.

"You would like time to consider the proposition?" suggests my interviewer.

Looking around upon the dingy copying establishment of Miss Work in Nassau Street, the girls slaving over interminable legal documents on their type-writing machines, and thinking of the drudgery that has been, and still promises to be my lot, I say desperately: "Yes, I will go!"

"Very well. Remember, you must sign a contract for a year from to-morrow. That is till the twentieth of March, 1889."

"Yes."

"You must be ready to start the day after to-morrow."

"Certainly. Only, of course, as I said before, my contract includes a first-cabin passage to and from Panama."

" It shall be as I have promised. Call at the office of Flandreau & Co., No. 33½ South Street, to-morrow at eleven, for your instructions and contract. Good afternoon—Miss Minturn, I believe your name is?"

" Yes; make out the contract for Louise Ripley Minturn. But you have not told me the name of the person by whom I am to be employed."

" Montez, Aguilla et Cie., Contractors Construction, Panama. You can ask about them at the agents of the canal, Seligman & Co., bankers, or the French Consul —are these references satisfactory?"

" Perfectly," I gasp, overcome by the solidity of their sponsors as I sink back, before my Remington, overwhelmed with what I have so hurriedly, and perhaps rashly done, as the dapper little clerk, bowing with French empressement to Miss Work, and with a wave of his hand to the other typewriting ladies, leaves the apartment.

Montez, Aguilla et Cie. Where have I heard the name before, and Panama—the place my mother used to talk to me about when I was a child. My mother—all thought leaves me save that I have lost her forever, and tears get in my eyes.

A few minutes after, time having brought me composure, I step over to Miss Work, a sharp Yankee business woman of about thirty-five, and tell her my story.

" I supposed you would go, Louise," she says kindly, " when I recommended you for the position. I am very glad that you have got a situation that will enable you to save money. There is, I understand, plenty of it on the Isthmus. I presume you are anxious to go home and make your preparations."

Then she settles with me for the work I have done, at the same time telling my companions of my good fortune, which makes a buzz in the room even greater than at lunch-hour, as they come clustering about, to congratulate, and wish me a pleasant journey and good luck, and all the kind wishes that come into the hearts of generous American girls, which even toil and drudgery cannot harden.

Just as I am going, Miss Work, after kissing me good-by, remarks : " Be sure and make every inquiry about your employers, and under whose protection you are to go out to Panama, as the journey is a long one ; though I know you are as well able to take care of yourself as any young lady who has been in my employ, and I have had some giants, both physical and intellectual."

"Thank you.   I'll remember what you say," I reply, and turn away.

As I reach the head of the stairs, there is a patter of light feet after me, and my chum and roommate, Sally Broughton, puts her arm around my waist, and says : "I shall be at home early, too, Louise dear, to help you pack, and do anything I can for you.   But," here she whispers to me rather roguishly, "what will Mr. Alfred Tompkins say to this ? "

"Say ! " reply I.   "What business is it of Mr. Alfred Tompkins, what Miss Louise Ripley Minturn does ? "

" Notwithstanding this, I'll bet you dare not tell him."

" Dare not tell him ?   Wait until this evening, and see me," I answer firmly, as I step down the stairs on my way home to East Seventeenth Street, just off Irving Place, where Sally and I have two rooms—one a parlor and the other a bedroom, for joint use, that we call home.

Notwithstanding my defiant reply, as I am being con-veyed by the Fourth Avenue cars to my destination, Sally's remark has not only set me to thinking about Mr. Tompkins, one of the floorwalkers and rising young employees of Jonold, Dunstable & Co., but also of— *some one else.*

Mr. Tompkins' blond face fades from my imagination. His yellow hair becomes chestnut ; his English side whiskers transform themselves into a long, drooping, military mustache ; his pinkish eyes become hazel, flash-ing, and brilliant.   His slightly Roman nose takes a Grecian cast.   His wavering chin changes into a firm, strong, and dominating one.   His five feet eight, grows into six feet in his stockings.   In short, Mr. Alfred Tompkins of Jonold, Dunstable & Co.'s dry-goods estab-lishment, expands into Harry Sturgis Larchmont of the United and Kollybocker Clubs, the leader of cotillons at Newport, Lenox, and Delmonico's, the ex-lawn-tennis champion and football athlete.   I go into a day-dream of stupid unreality, and call myself—IDIOT !   What have I, one of the female workers of this earth, to do with this masculine butterfly of fashion, frivolity, luxury, and athletics?

Still—I am a Minturn!

He dances with my first cousins at Patriarch balls. He takes my aunts down to dinners in Fifth Avenue residences, and plays cards with my uncles at the United and Kollybocker Clubs; a second cousin of mine is one of his chums; though they all apparently have forgotten they have a relative named Louise Ripley Minturn, one of Miss Work's stenographic and typewriting band at No. 135½ Nassau Street, New York, in this year of our Lord, one thousand eight hundred and eighty-eight.

My drifting away from my fashionable relatives had been easy: the drifting was done by my father, when he married my mother. He had no money. Neither had my mother, and so they drifted.

The thought of my mother brings Panama into my mind, and I give a start, for it calls back the sad tale she had told me so often, in my early girlhood, though before her death it had become even an old story to her: the statement of the unrecorded fate that befell her parents upon the Isthmus, no detail of which was known to her, she being a girl of sixteen at that time, at a school near Baltimore.

Her father, George Merritt Ripley, and her mother, Alice Louise Ripley, were returning from California. Enthusiastic letters said they came laden with the gold of the Sierras, to bring all the blessings of wealth and love to the one daughter of their heart. They had arrived in Panama in September, 1856. Since that time, no word had ever come of their own fate, or that of the treasure they brought with them.

Their daughter had tried to discover—the lady principal of the school at which she was, had made repeated efforts to learn of George Merritt Ripley and his wife from the American Consul and the agent of the railroad company—but could never discover anything save that my mother's parents arrived at Panama by the steamer *George L. Stevens* from San Francisco and then disappeared.

The lady principal, however, was kind; and my mother, having no near relatives who would assume the care of the orphan, had remained at her school—partly as pupil, partly as music teacher—until Martin Minturn had met her, after he was in his middle age, and had already, during the War of the Rebellion, lost his fortune, which he had invested in Southern securities.

Turning from the world, perhaps embittered by his losses, he had become one of that class least fitted to battle with its storms and currents—a scientist and philosopher. He was professor of chemistry in a Baltimore university, and came three times a week to lecture at the young ladies' seminary in which my mother lived a tame and passionless existence as instructor on the piano.

Mutual sympathy for the misfortunes that had come upon them brought them together. They loved and married.

Inspired by his love for her, my father had determined to again take up the battle with the world. He had brought his wife with him to New York, and after eight years of heart-breaking disappointment as an inventor and the maker of other men's fortunes, had died, leaving my mother with very little of this world's goods, and burdened by myself, a child of six.

My father before his death had drifted entirely away from his rich and fashionable relatives in New York, who once or twice, in a half-hearted manner, had tried to aid him, and then had finally shut their doors against the man of ill fortune who only came to them to borrow.

Too proud to ask assistance from those who had turned their backs on her husband, my mother again devoted herself to teaching, this time in a New York school. Here she had lived out her life for me, giving me all she could obtain for me by parsimony and self-denial—a first-rate education, for which God bless her! my dear mother, who has gone from me!

At last she died, and I, left alone in this world at eighteen, was compelled to put my talents into bread and butter. A fair musician, I was not artist enough to become celebrated. A poor music teacher is the veriest drudge upon this earth. I had studied stenography, and was an accomplished linguist. That seemed a better field. To the moment of writing this, it had been a hard one, though the previous year had been to me generally a pleasant one, and I had made a friend—not a fair-weather friend, but an all-weather friend—Sally Brough-

ton, who sat at the next typewriter to me, at Miss Work's.
Mr. Alfred Tompkins of Jonold, Dunstable's establishment, and Mr. Horace Jenkins of the rival dry-goods
house of Pacy & Co., had also become known to me.
These gentlemen are chums, though the haughty
Tompkins, whose business place is on Broadway, rather
looks down upon his Sixth Avenue factotum.

Mr. Jenkins greatly admires Miss Sally Broughton.
Mr. Alfred Tompkins—but why should I mention a
matter that hardly interests me? My life is so lonely, I
must talk to some one at times—though Mr. Tompkins
says, I am told, that I have a great and haughty coolness
in my manner.

I have also seen, met, and spoken to the athlete, who
fills my mind, at the house of his uncle, Larchmont Delafield, the great banker.

Here the conductor of the Fourth Avenue car disturbs my meditations by calling out in stentorian tones:
" TWENTY-THIRD STREET ! "

With a start, I remember Seventeenth is my destination, and jump off the car, reflecting that my musings
have cost me an unnecessary promenade of six Fourth
Avenue blocks.

While making this return trip, my mind goes wandering again. It seems, now that I am about to leave New
York, to take me to the object that has most interested
me in it—the frank hazel eyes, that have appeared to be
always laughing, when I have seen them, and the graceful athletic figure of Harry Sturgis Larchmont.

So getting to the little bedroom and parlor *en suite*
that Miss Broughton and I call home, I take out my
diary, and in its pages go back to the time I first met
him.

His uncle, Mr. Larchmont Delafield, had had a good
deal of stenographic and typewriting work done at Miss
Work's office. Mr. Delafield, being anxious to complete
some very important correspondence, was confined to his
house by an attack of gout. I was sent to his house on
Madison Avenue, one evening, to take a dictation from
him.

Arriving at his mansion about half-past seven o'clock
in the evening, I found evidences of an incipient dinner
party. A magnificent woman and very charming girl,

both in full evening dress, preceded me up the grand staircase. The footman was about to show me after them into the ladies' reception room, when I told him my call was simply one of business with his master.

A moment after, I found myself in the study of the banker, who was apparently in one of those extraordinary bad tempers, peculiar to gout.

"Shut the door, John!" he thunders at the domestic, "and keep the odors of that infernal dinner out of my nostrils. I long for it, but can't have it!"

"Yes, sir," replies the footman, about to retire.

"Stop!" cries the banker. "Tell my nephew, Harry Larchmont, to come up and see me at once. Has he arrived yet?"

"Yes, sir, with Mrs. Dewitt and Miss Severn."

"Of course—of course—with Miss Jessie Severn! the girl with the plump shoulders that she shows so nicely," says the old gentleman, with a savage chuckle. "Tell him to come up—that I want to see him instantly, though I won't keep him long."

A moment after, Mr. Harry Sturgis Larchmont stalks lazily into the apartment, in faultless evening dress, decorated with a big bunch of lilies of the valley, and looking the embodiment of neat fashion.

"Harry, my boy," says the banker, "I want to see you for a moment."

"So I was just told. I'm awful sorry the doctors won't permit you to join us," returns the young man, giving the elder a hearty grip of the hand.

"Don't speak of the dinner," mutters old Delafield. "My mouth waters at the thought of the canvas-back ducks now. But it is of this I wish to speak to you. You must occupy my place, as host, with Mrs. Delafield. I know I can leave my reputation for hospitality in your hands."

"I'll do my best, sir," replies young Larchmont. Then he gives a sudden start of horror, and ejaculates: "Great goodness! My taking your place as host entails my taking that fat dowager, Mrs. John Robinson Norton, in to dinner."

"I'm afraid it does, my poor boy," grins his uncle, "but I spoke to my wife, and pretty little Miss Jessie Severn sits on the other side of you. You have only to

turn your head to see her blue eyes and plump shoulders.
She has also exquisite ankles ; you should have kept her
in the short dresses she came over in from Paris a month
ago.   You're kind of half guardian to her, ain't you ? "
runs on the old man.

"It is necessary to drape a young lady's ankles to
bring her out in society," returns Mr. Larchmont.
"Miss Severn is now *out*.   Mrs. Dewitt is chaperoning
her.   Besides," the young man goes on, playfully,
"you're too old for ankles.   At your time of life the
ballet ! "

"If you didn't know, Harry, that you were my favorite nephew, you wouldn't dare such wit," chuckles the
uncle.   Then he goes on : "I suppose you feel so financially comfortable already, that you never think of my
will ? "

"'Thank God, I never do, dear old uncle !" says the
young man, earnestly.

"Besides, if you marry Miss Severn, she'll have a
pretty plum," goes on old Delafield.

At this the nephew suddenly looks serious, and I
think I detect a slight sigh.

Somehow or other, as I look at Harry Sturgis Larchmont, I begin to dislike the pretty little Miss Jessie
Severn.   I had seen this gorgeous masculine creature,
when I was sixteen and enthusiastic, at a football game,
and had gloried in his triumphs on that brutal arena.

Interest begets interest, and as the young gentleman
turns to go, he casts inquiring gaze upon me.   This is
answered by his uncle, in the politeness of the old school,
as he says : "Miss Minturn, let me present my nephew,
Mr. Harry Larchmont."

"Miss Minturn has kindly consented to act as my
stenographer this evening, on some important business,
that cannot be delayed ; " interjects the elder man, as
the younger one bows to me, which I, anxious to maintain
my dignity, return in a careless and nonchalant manner.

A moment after, Mr. Larchmont has left the room.
While his uncle chuckles after him *sotto voce :* "A fine
young man !   I wish that French brother of his, Frank,
the Parisian la-de-da, was more like him—more of an
American ! "   Then he snaps his lips together, and says :
"To business ! "

"But your dinner!" I suggest hurriedly, for I have somehow grown to sympathize with the old gentleman's appetite.

"My dinner? My dinner consisted of oatmeal gruel, which was digested two hours ago, thank Heaven! To business!" cries the old man.

With this, he commences to dictate to me a number of letters on some very important and confidential transactions. As we go on, these letters approach a climax. I have been at work nearly two hours, when an epistle to the president of a railroad, who, he thinks, is attempting some underhand game with its preferred stockholders, makes the old gentleman intensely angry. His face gets red ; as he continues, his letter, from being that of a business man, becomes one of vindictive and bitter animosity. His asides are, I am sorry to say, strong almost to the verge of profanity. His hands tremble, his voice becomes husky, and as he closes the letter with "Yours *most* respectfully," Larchmont Delafield utters a savage oath, and rising from his chair, after two or three attempts at articulation that end in gasps and gurgles, falls back into it. I am alone with a man apparently stricken with an attack of apoplexy, brought on by his own passions.

I hastily open the door. The noise of laughter and gayety downstairs, comes to me, up the great staircase. The perfume of flowers, and the faint music of the orchestra, tell of revelry below.

. I hesitate to make this scene of gayety one of consternation and sorrow. I hurriedly press the button of an electric bell.

A moment after, a footman coming to me, I say : "Please quietly ask Mr. Harry Larchmont to come up to his uncle. Mr. Delafield wishes to see him immediately."

"I can do that easily, now," replies the man. "The ladies are in the parlor, and the gentlemen are by themmen in the dining-room."

I wait at the head of the stairs. Mr. Larchmont coming up, says : "My uncle wishes to see me, I believe."

"No!" I reply.

"No?—he sent for me."

"*He* did not send for you—*I* did."

" You ? " The young man gazes at me in astonishment.

" Yes ; I did not wish to disturb the gayety of the
party below. Your uncle has had a seizure of some
kind—a fit ! "

" Thank you for your consideration," he answers, and
in another second is by the side of the invalid, and I
looking at him, admire him more than ever.

•ʄThis gentleman of pleasure has become a man of action.

" Some cold water on his head—quick ! " he says
sharply. I obey, and he lifts his uncle up, and proceeds
to resuscitate the old gentleman by means that are
known to athletes. While he is doing this, he says
rapidly to me : " Ring the bell, and give the footman
the notes I will dictate to you."

As I do his bidding, and sit down ; never relaxing his
efforts to bring consciousness back to his uncle, the
young man dictates hurriedly :

"*Dear Sir:* Come to Mr. Larchmont Delafield's, No. 124½ Madison
Avenue, at once. He has had an attack of epilepsy or apoplexy—I
think the latter. Simply ask for Mr. Delafield. There is a dinner
party below.

Yours in haste,

HARRY STURGIS LARCHMONT."

" Triplicate that letter," he says. " Send one to Dr.
George Howland, another to Dr. Ralph Abercrombie, and
the third to Dr. Thomas Robertson ; you'll find their addresses in that directory."

As I finish these the footman comes in.

" Not a word of this, John," Mr. Larchmont says, " to
anybody ! Take these three letters, go downstairs, and
give them to three of the servants. There are half a
dozen in the kitchen. Tell them they must be delivered,
each of them, within ten minutes—and a five-dollar bill
for you."

A quarter of an hour later, the young man has partially
revived his uncle.

A moment after, one of the doctors summoned stands
beside him, and says that the attack is not a serious
one, and that the old gentleman will be all right with
rest and care.

" Very well," replies Mr. Harry ; " if that is the case, I

will go down to the dinner party. No one has been
alarmed—not even Mrs. Delafield—and all owing to the
thoughtfulness of this young lady, to whom I tender my
thanks." He bows to me and goes down to the festival
below, while I gather up my papers and dictation book,
and make my preparations for departure.

A few minutes afterwards, I come down the great stair-
way also, and stand putting on my cloak in the hall.

As I do so, through tapestry curtains, that are partially
open, I see, for the first time in my life, one of the great
reception rooms of a New York mansion. Lighted by
rare and peculiar lamps, each one of them a work of art,
adorned by numerous pictures, statues, and costly *bric-a-
brac* from the four corners of the earth ; embellished and
perfumed by hothouse plants and flowers ; and made
bright by lovely women in exquisite toilettes, and men
in faultless evening dress, the scene is a revelation to me.

But I linger only on one portion of it.

In front of a large mantel-piece stands Harry Larchmont, talking to a young lady who is a dream of fairylike loveliness in the lace, tulle, and gauze that float
about her graceful figure. She is scarcely more than a
child yet, but her eyes are blue as sapphires, her chin
piquant, her laugh vivacious, her smile enchanting. I
am compelled to admit this, though for some occult
reason I do not care to do so.

For one short second I compare the face and figure in
the parlor with the one I see reflected in the great hall
mirror beside me. A flash of joy ! It seems to me
I am as pretty as Miss Jessie Severn. Perchance, if I
wore the same exquisite toilette, my lithe figure and bru-
nette charms would be as lovely as her blonde graces.
Perhaps even he——

Here fool's blushes come upon me. His voice sounds
in my ear.

It says : " I have excused myself for a moment from
my guests, to again thank you, Miss Minturn, for your
presence of mind and thoughtful action this evening.
The night is stormy—you have been kept here late."
Then he turns and directs the man at the door : " John,
call up the carriage for Miss Minturn."

He holds out a hand, which I take, as I stammer out
my thanks, and looking in his eyes, I know he means

what he says. Perhaps more—for there is something in his glance that makes me, as I go out of the massive oaken doors and down the great stairs, and pass through the little throng of waiting footmen, and take the equipage his care has provided for me, grow bitter, for the first time in my life, at my fate.

As I ride to my modest rooms in quiet Seventeenth Street, I clinch my hands, and mutter : " Had my mother's parents not disappeared upon that Isthmus of Panama, their gold might have made me the guest, instead of the stenographer. At dinner he might have gazed upon my pretty shoulders—not Miss Jessie Severn's."

Fool that I am, I think these things ! For I have admired this young gentleman's victories on the football field, and his presence of mind and action more this evening. " He seems to me a man who might make a woman—" But I stop myself here, and gasp : " You are crazy ! Typewriter ! you are crazy ! "

Reaching home, I take out my clicking Remington, and over the correspondence of Mr. Delafield the banker, Miss Minturn the stenographer tries to forget Mr. Harry Larchmont the man of fashion.

CHAPTER IX.

THE ANGEL OF THE BLIZZARD.

Two days after, I received a brief note from Mr. Larchmont, which simply stated he was taking care of his uncle's minor matters of business, during that gentleman's recovery, and enclosed to me a check for my services as stenographer, the amount of which, though liberal, was not sufficient to make me think it anything more than a simple business transaction.

Then one week afterwards came the blizzard, that crushed New York with snow-flakes, that stopped the elevated railways, and blocked all transportation by surface cars ; that confined people in their houses on the great thoroughfares, as completely as if they had been a hundred miles away from other habitations. That dear delightful, fearful blizzard, in which I nearly died.

6

On Monday morning, March 12th, I am awakened by Miss Broughton, who is peeping out through the casements. She crys: "Louise, wake up! This is the greatest storm I have ever seen."

"Nonsense! It's spring now," I answer sleepily.

"Yes, March spring!—cold spring! Jump out of bed and see if it's a spring atmosphere," returns Sally, with a castanet accompaniment from her white teeth.

I obey her, and the spring atmosphere arouses me to immediate and vigorous action. In a rush I start the gas stove, and, throwing on a wrap, walk to Sally's side, and take a look at what is going on in the street.

"Isn't it a storm!" suggests Miss Broughton enthusiastically. "A beautiful storm! A storm that will stop work. A storm that will give me a lazy day at home!"

"You are not going down to the office?" I say.

"Through those snow banks?" she replies, pointing to six feet of white drift on the opposite side of the street, in which a newsboy has buried himself three times, in an unsuccessful attempt to deliver newspapers at the basement door.

"Certainly," I reply.

"Impossible!" she says. "You will make a nice, lazy day of it, at home with me. We will do plain sewing. You shall help me make my new dress." Sally always claims me on lazy days. In my idle moments, I think I have constructed four or five costumes for her. This time I rebel.

"If you are not going to work, I am!" I say decidedly.

"Through those drifts?"

"Certainly!" I reflect that I have some documents Miss Work has promised this day. They are legal ones, and admit of no postponement.

"Well, you may be able to get to the office," says Sally, "if you are a Norwegian on snowshoes, or an angel on wings."

This angel idea is a suggestion to me. "The elevated is running!" I answer, and point to the Third Avenue, down which a train is slowly forcing its way. The station is only a short distance from me. I will take the elevated. Surface cars may be blocked, but the elevated goes through the air.

Miss Broughton does not reply to this, though I presume she has her doubts about the feasibility of my plan, for the storm is coming thicker and heavier.

But breakfast over, she steps to the window, looks out, and says disappointedly : " Yes, the Third Avenue trains are still running. I presume you can go, but how about getting back again this evening ? "

" Pshaw ! " I reply, " it will be all finished in an hour."

A few minutes afterwards, well equipped for Arctic travelling, I, with a desperate effort, get out of the door, and for a moment am blown away by the wind. I had no idea the storm was so severe. But I struggle on, and finally reach the Third Avenue station, to climb up its icy stairs and be nearly blown from them in my ascent to the platform. From this, I finally struggle on board a down-town train, which contains very few people. The guards have lost their usual peremptory tones. They do not cry out in their bullying manner, " All aboard ! Step on lively ! " as they are prone to do on finer days, but are trying to get warm over the steam-pipes in the car. The blizzard has even crushed them !

We roll off on our journey, amid gusts of wind that nearly blow us off the track, and flurries of snow that make it impossible to see out of the windows. In about quadruple the usual time, however, we creep alongside the City Hall station platform.

It is now half-past nine. I alight, and am practically blown down the stairs, though a snowdrift at the bottom receives me, and makes my fall a soft one. Then I fight my way along Park Place and into Nassau Street. The storm seems to get stronger and fiercer, as I grow more and more feeble. Midway I would turn back, but back is now as great a distance as forward ; and one end of the journey means the comfortless railway station, where perchance no trains are leaving now. The other terminus is Miss Work's office, where there will certainly be a fire, company, and occupation. By the time I shall be ready to go home, the storm must be over.

So I struggle on, and fight my way through snowdrifts, to finally arrive, in an almost exhausted condition, at 135½ Nassau Street.

A long climb up the stairs, for the building is not pro-vided with an elevator, and I find myself on the top floor, which is occupied by Miss Work's establishment. Here, to my astonishment, the door is still locked. Having a pass key, I a moment after enter, to my consternation, an empty room, and a cold one. Miss Work, who is punctuality itself, is not here. I reflect, she will undoubtedly arrive in a few minutes. She must come.

While thinking this, for the atmosphere does not permit of delay, I am hurriedly making a fire in the grate, which has not been attended to over night, the man in charge of the building apparently not having visited it this morning. Fortunately there is plenty of fuel, and I soon have a roaring fire and comfort.

Then I move my typewriter where I get the full benefit of the cheery blaze, and sit down to my work.

Time flies. No one comes. Having nothing to eat, I pass what should be my lunch hour over the keyboard of my Remington, thinking I will have my task finished and go home the earlier. But the papers are long ones, and being legal, require considerable care and accuracy, and as I finish the last of them I look up.

It is nearly dark. My watch says it is only three o'clock, but the storm, which seems to be even heavier than in the morning, causes early gloom. I look out on the wild prospect. As well as I can determine, in the uncertain light, glancing through flurries of snow, not one person passes along sidewalks that are usually crowded with humanity.

What am I to do? I am hungry! I am alone! Even in this great building I am the only one, for no sound comes to me from the offices down stairs, that at this time in the day are usually filled by movement, hurry, and activity.

Sally will be anxious for me. Though, did not my appetite drive me forth, I believe I should attempt to make a night of it in the great deserted building. I should probably be frightened, though I should barricade myself in. I should probably see ghosts of lawyers and legal luminaries who have long since departed, from these their old offices, to plead their own cases before the Court of Highest Appeal. But hunger! I am more afraid of hunger than of ghosts. Besides, it is so lonely.

I decide to force my path to Broadway. On that great thoroughfare there must be some one! I lock the door, come down the stairs, step out on the street, and give a shiver. During the day it has grown much colder, though in the warm room I had not noticed it.

My first step is into an immense snowdrift. Through this I struggle, and reaching the corner of the street am literally blown off my feet, fortunately towards Broadway. Thank Heaven! it is a very short block, though it seems to me an eternity before I reach the thoroughfare that yesterday was the great artery of traffic in New York, but now, as I gaze up and down it, seeking some human face, seems as deserted as a Siberian steppe.

The shops are all closed, even the drug stores. There are no passing vehicles, no struggling pedestrians. The traffic of the great city has been annihilated by this prodigious storm. Telegraph wires, that last night were overhead, have many of them fallen. There is nothing for me but to struggle onward.

I turn my face to the north—up town—where three miles away Sally is waiting for me, with a warm fire, and I hope a comfortable meal. Towards this I force my way —for a few minutes.

Then I trip over a broken telegraph wire that lies in the snow. As I stagger up again, for a moment I am not certain which way I am going. Good Heavens! if I should turn back on my tracks?

The wild snowstorm about me dazes me, confuses me, benumbs me, and makes me stupid. The strength of the wind forces me to hold my head down; I try to see which way I have come by my tracks in the snow— but there are none! The gusts are so violent, my footsteps have been obliterated almost as I made them.

Desperate, I look around me, and see, through snow flurries, the light in the great tower of the Western Union Telegraph Building. It seems awfully far away, but gives me my direction; and I struggle northward once more, staggering through drifts—sometimes falling into them, no voice coming to me—alone in a living city that is now dead—killed by the snow. Darkness has fallen upon the streets, and enshrouds me. Still I fight on. There are hotels farther up the street. If I could get to one—if I could get *anywhere* to be warm!

I have passed the Western Union Building, I think— I am not sure—my faculties are too benumbed for cer-

tainty. All I know is, that I am cold—that I am benumbed—that I am hungry—that I am weak—that the
snowdrifts grow larger—the snow flurries stronger—the
piercing cutting wind more fierce and merciless—and,
above all this, that I am unutterably sleepy. I dream
even as I struggle, and then I cease to struggle, and only
dream—beautiful dreams—dreams of what I long for—
dreams of warmth and comfort, of bounteous meals and
generous wine.

And even as this last comes to me, something is poured
down my throat—something that burns, but vivifies—
something that brings my senses to me with sudden shock.
I hear, still in a half dreamy way, a voice that seems
familiar, say :   •

" Pat, that is the worst whiskey I have ever tasted ; but
I think it has done me good, as well as saved this young
lady's life."

" By me soul, it has saved mine several times to-day ! "
is the answer.

Then the other voice, the familiar one, goes on : " Do
you think you can get us up town ? "

" Faith, I've been half an hour coming from the Western
Union Building. You may bless God if I make the
Astor House alive."

" Then somewhere, quick ! This will keep her warm."

I feel the burning stuff pour down my throat once more,
and give me renewed life and sentiency. Strong arms
lift me into a cab, a rug is wrapped around me. I open
my eyes. Beside me sits a man, to whom I falter, my
teeth still chattering, " I—I was lost in the snow."

Even as I say this, the familiar voice cries : " Your
tones are familiar. Who are you ? "

I answer : " Miss Minturn."

And the voice cries : " Good heavens ! Thank God
I saw you from my *coupé* in time ! "

And I, still dazed, gasp :. " It is Mr. Larchmont, is it
not ? "

" Yes : don't exert yourself, you are weak. In a few
minutes we will have you at the Astor House, warm and
comfortable. Have no fear."

And somehow or other, his voice revives me more
than the whiskey. I am contented—even happy.

But the storm is still upon us ; and though there are

two strong horses attached to the *coupé*, fighting for their own lives through the deepening drifts, it is nearly an hour before lights flash on the sidewalk, and I am assisted into warmth and comfort and life once more, in the Astor House parlor.

There I thaw for a few minutes, during which he sits looking at me, though I am dimly conscious he has given some orders. Having entirely regained my senses, I falter : " I must go home ! Sally will be anxious about me ! "

" Where do you live ? " he inquires shortly.

" Seventeenth Street."

" Then you could not live to walk home to-night, and no carriage could take you there. There is but one thing for you to do. The housekeeper will be here in a moment. She will take you to a room. Go to bed, and take what I have ordered for you."

" What is that ? "

" More whiskey—but it is exactly what you want. In two hours they will have dried your clothes, and you can come down to dinner with—with me." His " with me " is rather embarrassed and diffident.

I do not reply, and Mr. Larchmont almost immediately continues : " Or, if you prefer it, the dinner can be sent up to your room."

I shall feel quite lonely—it will appear ungrateful. " I will be happy to meet you in the dining-room," I answer.

A moment after, everything he has arranged is done. I go with the housekeeper, a kindly woman of large build and comfortable manner, and find myself excellently taken care of.

Two hours afterwards, feeling like a new being, I enter the dining-room. It is only half-past seven, and Mr. Harry Larchmont is apparently waiting for me. It is a pleasant, though, perhaps, to me, embarrassing meal. The room is crowded with people that the storm has forced to take refuge in the hotel—Brooklyn men, who cannot get across the East River ; Jersey men, who are cut off from home ; and down-town brokers, who are unable to reach their up-town residences. The place, in contrast to the dreadful dearth of animal movement in the streets outside, is full of life, bustle, and activity.

" I think I have arranged very well as regards dinner,"

remarks Mr. Larchmont. "We'll have to be contented with condensed milk, but we shall have some Florida strawberries, and Bermuda potatoes and asparagus." As we sit down, he says suddenly : "Who is Sally ? "

"Sally ? Ah, you mean Miss Broughton ?"

"Yes, the young lady you said would be anxious about you."

"Oh," I answer, " Miss Broughton is my chum ! " Then we get to chatting together, and I give him a few Sally anecdotes that make him laugh. As the meal goes on I grow more at my ease, and become confidential, and tell him a good deal of my life, my work, and my battle with the world. This seems to interest him, and once, when I am busy with my knife and fork, I catch his eyes resting upon me, and they seem to say : "So young ! "

But I won't have his sympathy ; so I make merry over my business struggles, and tell him what a comfortable little home Sally and I have.

Altogether, it is a delightful meal for me, and I am not sorry that Mr. Larchmont lingers over it. He grows slightly confidential himself, over his coffee, explaining to me that he has had some very important telegrams to receive from Paris ; that the up-town wires were all down, and he had been so anxious about his cables, that he had contrived to get as far as the main office of the Western Union Company ; that he thanks God he succeeded in doing so, though no cablegrams had come to him. "Because," he concludes, looking at me, "if it had not been for the cables, you might have been still outside in the snow ! "

A few minutes after, he startles me by saying, it seems to me with a little sigh, "I must be going ! "

"Where—into the storm ?" I gasp, amazed.

"Only as far as French's Hotel, just across in Park Place."

I know "just across in Park Place" means three long squares—an awful distance, which might kill a strong man in this driving storm.

"You must not go ! " I cry.

"Under the circumstances, I must," he replies, and rises, to cut short remonstrance. Then I go out with him from the dining-room into the hall, a blush on my cheeks, but a grateful look in my eyes, for I know it is to save me any embarrassment this night that he will make his desperate journey through snowdrifts and pitiless wind.

We have got to the ladies' parlor now. He turns and says earnestly, " I have made every arrangement for you, I think, Miss Minturn, not only for this evening, but for to-morrow, in case you should be compelled to remain here. I am more than happy, and bless God that I met you in time."

And I whisper: "You have been to me the—the angel of the blizzard ! "

At which he smiles a little, and his grasp upon my hand tightens as he bids me good-night.

Then he is gone into the storm.

I go to my room ; a fire is burning brightly there. Sleep comes upon me, and happy dreams—dreams in which I make a fool of myself about "the angel of the blizzard."

The next morning everything has been arranged for me. After a comfortable breakfast, I discover that the storm has ceased, but the streets of New York are still impassable. Then I get a newspaper, and learn that the indefatigable reporters have somehow got information of nearly everything. Glancing over its columns, I give a sigh of relief. In the long list of accidents, escapes, and deaths on that twelfth day of March, 1888, I note that my adventure has not been reported, though I read that French's Hotel had been so crowded that people had slept upon the billiard-tables and floors of that hostelry, and one up-town swell had been obliged to content himself with the bar-counter. I guess who the up-town swell was who did this to save me any embarrassment or anxiety, and I bless him !

I bless him again, when, in the afternoon, I find that the streets can with difficulty be navigated, and the porter coming up, informs me that a carriage has been ordered to take me, as soon as possible, to my address in Seventeenth Street.

At home, I am welcomed by Sally, with happy but anxious eyes. She cries : " Oh, Louise ! I thought you were dead ! "

" Oh, no," I reply nonchalantly, " I did a day's work."

" And then ? "

"Then I went to the Astor House."

"Did you have money enough with you for that? I hear they charged ten dollars a room."

"That bill is liquidated," I return in easy prevarication.

"But you had a carriage ! I noticed a carriage drive up with you. How will you ever pay the hackman? They charge twenty-five dollars a trip."

"Never mind my finances. I am home safe once more. And you ?" I answer, turning the conversation.

"Oh, I nearly starved ! · I would have starved entirely, had I not forced my way to the grocery store. I have been living on crackers and cheese, bologna sausage, and tea without milk."

"I have been enjoying the 'fat of the land.' You had better have gone down with me, Sally. You would have had a delightful day," I continue airily to my pretty chum, who looks at me in partial unbelief.

Then the next morning comes a joy—a rapture—a surprise ! It is a bunch of violets tied with violet ribbon, with the name of a fashionable florist emblazoned on it, and with it this card :

Compliments of

Mr. Harry Sturgis Larchmont,
who hopes Miss Minturn has
thoroughly recovered from the
storm.

United Club.

Fortunately, Sally is out when this arrives, so I avoid explanation. When she comes in, the flowers soon catch her bright eyes. She ejaculates, "Violets ! Where did you get violets, Miss Millionnaire ?" and smells them to be sure they are genuine—not artificial.

"Why do you call me Miss Millionnaire?"

"Well, no one but a Miss Millionnaire can live at the Astor House during blizzards, and perambulate in carriages at twenty-five dollars a trip, and have great big bunches of violets at a dollar a blossom! Gracious! They must have cost thirty dollars! Every flower on Long Island was destroyed by snow." Then Sally's eyes open very wide with inquiry, and she says coaxingly: "Who sent them?"

"Oh," I reply in easy nonchalance, "I gathered them!"

"Gathered them? Where?" These are screams of unbelief.

"Off the snowdrifts on Sixth Avenue, over which they have placed a sign 'Keep off the grass!'"

"That means you will not tell me," says Sally, with a pout.

"Precisely!"

"What makes you fib so much lately?" she mutters disappointedly.

"It is not a fib—that I will not tell you."

"Very well! I shall inform Mr. Tompkins!" replies Sally spitefully, which threat causes me to burst into hysterical merriment, I am in such good spirits.

I write to _him_ at his address: "I am quite well. I thank you for the violets, but for the rest—thanks are too feeble. I only hope some day the mouse may aid the lion. L. R. M."

I initial this note.

Somehow I don't know how to end it. I have grown strangely bashful and diffident lately.

That was only a week ago. Once since then I have seen him at the theatre, in attendance upon ladies, one of the party being Miss Jessie Severn.

As I have looked at him I have noticed that a good deal of the lightness has left his face, and a portion of the laughter has departed from his eyes. Has some cloud come over his life?

As I look over my diary and recall these things, a sudden thought strikes me. I am going away without bidding him good-by. That will be hardly grateful. It is half-past four: he may be walking on Fifth Avenue. It would hardly be wrong to say "farewell" on a crowded street.

Five minutes, and I have flown over to that fashionable promenade, and am strolling up its thronged sidewalk. I am in luck. Near Thirty-first Street I see him stepping out of a fashionable club. But there is another gentleman with him, almost his counterpart save that he is ten years older, and has a foreign and un-American air and style about him. This must be Harry Larchmont's French brother—the one Mr. Delafield had sneered at.

Of course I cannot speak to him now. To my passing bow Mr. Larchmont responds with more than politeness. As I pass, I catch four words from the gentleman who is with him. "She is deuced pretty!"

Fortunately I am beyond them; they cannot see my blushes through the back of my head. What would I not give to have heard Harry Larchmont's reply!

As it is, I shall not even bid him good-by. I return curiously disappointed to our rooms on Seventeenth Street.

CHAPTER X.

A CHANCE MEETING AT DELMONICO'S.

As I enter from my unsuccessful promenade, Sally's sweet lips give me a kiss, and Sally's laughing voice says: " Well, Miss Lazy, I beat you home after all! "

Then, as if sudden suspicion has come to her, she cries: " Did you meet him? "

" Him—who? " I gasp, as a startled blush comes upon me.

"Why, Mr. Tompkins, of course! "

" Mr. Tompkins? " I reply icily, " Do you suppose I would go out walking with Mr. Tompkins? "

"Oh, you didn't think I meant Alfred! Who did you suppose I meant? Is—is there some one else? Those violets! Are you keeping a secret from me? " and Sally's bright eyes are gazing into mine with sudden and embarrassing inquiry.

Whatever have been my wild thoughts about this gentleman of clubs and cotillons and fashion, I have made no confidant of my chum, nor any one else—nor ever shall !

To turn the conversation from this dangerous ground, I suggest: "Come ! Help me pack my trunk, as you promised to."

" Not till to-morrow," answers my volatile companion. " You must keep your best dress out for to-night."

" To-night—why ?"

" To-night Mr. Tompkins and Mr. Jenkins have requested the pleasure of escorting us to the theatre."

" The theatre ! I have too much to do."

" Nonsense ! Your trunk isn't such a very large one. I'll help you to-morrow. Besides, you'll spoil our party. I can't go out with *two* gentlemen. This will be your last chance to do me a great favor."

As she says this, Sally's blue eyes are fixed in entreaty upon mine. The thought of parting from her makes me pliable to cajoling. "Very well !" I assent.

" Ah ! I thought I could persuade you, and have already arranged the party," says Miss Broughton, who is even now in her best bib and tucker, and looks very well in it—her bib being a handsome fur-trimmed jacket ; and her tucker, a pretty and modest fawn-colored cloth dress, that drapes her rather under-sized, but plump figure, with graceful folds.

" This will make him happy," she continues thoughtfully. " He comes to take us to dinner——"

" He—who ?"

" Mr. Tompkins, of course ! It is to be at the Dairy Kitchen, where they have music. We will have a jolly time ! But goodness, hurry ! I hear his step upon the stairs, and you are not yet in festive array !"

Thus adjured, I retire to our bedroom, and in fifteen minutes come out to meet Mr. Tompkins, who is talking to Sally, as she puts on her hat. As I enter, their conversation floats to me.

" She is so deuced haughty !" says the gentleman.

" Haughty ? How absurd ! She's affability itself," returns the young lady.

" Yes, to girls !" answers Mr. Tompkins snappishly. Then he turns and sees me. My efforts at personal adornment seem to be pleasing to him, for I catch a stifled "By Jove !" as he regards me, and Sally gives

a little cry, partly of surprise, partly—I am vain enough
to think—of admiration ; for before my glass, a sudden
thought had flown into my mind. " Perhaps at the
theatre I may meet *him !* " And I had drawn upon the
utmost limits of my wardrobe, to make myself as alluring
as possible, with, I think, very good effect.

Perchance this accounts for Mr. Tompkins' more than
usually effusive manner, as he greets me with, " How are
yer ?" and then murmurs : " This is exquisite, Miss
Louise. I take it as a personal compliment ! "

" I never compliment anybody ! " I reply icily.

Then I grow red a little, for it has suddenly struck me I
have been complimenting Mr. Harry Larchmont. My
blushes seem to please Mr. Tompkins. He shows a
rapture in his face which embarrasses me. A moment
after, he suggests : " You have something on your mind ? "
For I have got to thinking of Panama, and have placed
my latch-key on the table, instead of putting it in my
pocket.

" Yes," I reply, " there is something on my mind. I
am going——"

A biting pinch from Sally's quick fingers makes me
pause—half in astonishment, half in pain.

A second after, getting opportunity as we put the
finishing touches to our toilettes in the little bedroom,
she whispers : " Don't tell him now."

" Why not ? " I ejaculate.

" Because you'll spoil our theatre party. I can't explain now ; but don't tell either of the gentlemen till we
get home. Promise ! "

" Certainly. It is a matter of indifference to me whether
Mr. Tompkins or Mr. Jenkins ever know of my departure ! " I answer.

So we rejoin our escort, who is a florid little fellow,
not much over five feet seven, with a quick, dapper walk.
He wears the conventional evening dress of the day, embellished by a heavy gold chain across his vest, that does
not seem to me to be exactly the mode. At all events,
Mr. Larchmont never wears one.

A moment after, we are under way for the Dairy
Kitchen, a gorgeous restaurant on Fourteenth Street,
that accommodates the well-to-do hundred thousand, and
furnishes them with a very fair dinner at a reasonable

price, accompanied by the music of an indifferent orchestra, and the discordant sounds of half a hundred
waiters, who clash their dishes together with vivacious
activity.

Under its brilliant arc-lights we meet Mr. Jenkins,
one of the floorwalkers of Pacy & Company, who says in
a loud voice, that is suggestive to me of "Cash!": "I
.have kept this table for you for twenty minutes, and am
hungry."

"Then you must wear your dress coat in the store. I
don't think you ever get away till at least a quarter *after*
six, at Pacy's," sneers the haughty Alfred Tompkins.

Mr. Jenkins, crushed by this business sarcasm, regards
us in gloomy and hungry silence, as we take seats at
his table, and Mr. Tompkins suggests: "Have you
ordered the *menu*, Horace?"

"No! What's that?" asks Jenkins suddenly, at which
I stifle incipient laughter, and Miss Broughton suggests
with playful sarcasm: "Perhaps he thought it was the
oysters!"

At Sally's badinage Mr. Jenkins grows so savage, that
I turn the conversation, by hastily asking: "To what
theatre are you going to take us?"

After giving the necessary orders for our entertainment,
Mr. Tompkins condescends to furnish me the informa-
tion I ask. "I have procured tickets," he says, "for the
Paragon."

"The Paragon!" Sally screams in horror. "Why do
you always take us to the Paragon? Now if it had been
Fauntleroy, that I have been dying to see for six months,
that would have been something like. Couldn't you do
it now? It is getting near the end of its run."

Here Mr. Jenkins candidly remarks: "Fauntleroy
tickets are not on the bargain counter yet."

At this soft insinuation Mr. Tompkins hems and blushes.

The theatres that Mr. Tompkins patronizes, are always
those that have on their boards either unsuccessful pieces,
or plays that have been performed so long that, their first
flush of glory being over, the management are liberal
with complimentary tickets. His position as floorwalker
in a leading dry-goods establishment gives him rather a
command of these tributes of managerial favor, for he
has been quite successful, in his day, in making full houses

for them ; and several times the employees of his house,
have attended some of our leading theatres almost in a
body, giving them the appearance of great prosperity and
crowded houses.   To " first nights " Mr. Tompkins seldom invites any one.   In fact, he says he does not like
them.   He prefers a play to grow mellow and old, and to
receive the polish of one hundred and fifty performances,
before he visits it.   At the Paragon, however, he sometimes invites people to " first nights," though at the box
office it is always said :   " We are sold up to Q."

Consequently it is the Paragon to which Mr. Tompkins
is going to take us this evening.

At his announcement, my heart sinks ; for I am very
certain Harry Sturgis Larchmont will not be in its orchestra chairs or boxes : and a half hysterical regret, for
which I anathematize myself, comes into my mind.
" Perhaps I will not see him before I go."

Noting my pre-occupied manner, Mr. Tompkins in his
most dulcet tones suggests : " Is the something on your
mind, that Miss Sally spoke of, destroying your appetite ? "   Then he whispers, a Romeo timbre in his voice:
" Is it about *me*—Alfredo ? "

At this I give a start.   The romantic tone of the gentleman—Sally's hint not to tell him of my departure.   A
sudden suspicion comes into my mind, that makes me
very icy and haughty to Mr. Tompkins.

A few minutes after, we all stroll over to Broadway
to take car to visit the Paragon, a little theatre where
they sometimes have very good plays, but rarely full
houses.

The performance this evening is a pleasant one, and
the party leave the theatre in very good spirits, except
me.

We walk over to Fifth Avenue, and turn down this
great thoroughfare, crowded with rushing cabs and
carriages coming from the theatres.   During our walk
Mr. Tompkins announces to us that he has had a
great stroke of business luck ; that he has been promoted
to a higher department, with a better salary.   He has
apparently kept this piece of news to impress either Mr.
Jenkins, Sally or myself.

As we approach Twenty-sixth Street, this gentleman's
good fortune seems to have made him financially reck-

less. He suddenly says : " What do you say, young ladies, to supper at Del's ? "

" Supper at Del's ! " ejaculates Sally in unbelief.

" Certainly."

" Catch me ! " gasps Miss Broughton and pretends to be overcome. But Tompkins repeats sternly : " I mean it ! A supper at Del's ! "

" This is too good a chance for Jenkins to refuse. He answers, " Right you are ! " and promptly leads the way.

For a moment I am about to draw back. An awning is up on Twenty-sixth Street; a cotillon, or dinner dance, or Patriarchs' ball, or something of that kind is going on in the ballroom up-stairs. It is quite probable that Harry Sturgis Larchmont may be there. I may meet him in the restaurant or the hall, and I shrink from this fashionable gentleman encountering me under the escort of the florid Tompkins.

But Sally pulls at my arm, whispering : " A supper at Delmonico's ! It is the chance of your life ! "

Hesitation would be absurd. I know she will try and drag me in if I do not go, and I follow them.

Looking on our party as we pass in, I am content with Miss Broughton and myself, though the gentlemen do not impress me " as to the manner born " to the glories of this fashionable restaurant. Sally's dress is certainly very nice. My own I *know* is all right. Besides, the hall boy, as he takes and checks our wraps, is politeness and humility itself. The haughty head waiter, however, impresses me more strongly, as he precedes us, remarking : " *Table pour quatre !* "

Our escorts' clothes, however, do not impose upon me. True, they both wear swallow-tail coats, but their fashion is not of·the latest mode ; and their vests are not of the white duck I see some of the gentlemen at the neighboring tables wearing. Besides that, both of them have three horribly big exaggerated studs in their shirt fronts.

I am delighted when they sit down and hide their watchguards from view ; for this atmosphere is one to disclose slight defects in the dress of either man or woman.

The room is a blaze of electric light. The toilettes of the ladies, some of whom are in graceful and beautiful evening gowns, having just come in from the opera,

are nearly all magnificent; the dress suits of the gentlemen, perfect in detail.

"This time we have a *menu*," remarks Mr. Tompkins
proudly, and shows it to Mr. Jenkins, as the waiter places
it in front of him.

A moment after, he surreptitiously passes the *carte
du jour* to me, muttering: "Confound it! It is printed
in French. Won't you assist me, Miss Louise?" my
knowledge of that language being known to him.

"I'll save you the trouble," laughs Sally. "The other
side of the card is in English."

Then Mr. Tompkins, his face covered with embarrassment, orders oysters, some cold partridges, ice-cream, and
a bottle of champagne ; and thoughtlessly being lured
into unknown fields of extravagance by the waiter's suggestion, adds terrapin to his bill of fare, and we have a
very pleasant meal of it.

My ears, however, are devoted to the conversation at
the table next us. The people there are giving me information that interests me. One of the ladies remarks
carelessly : "Mrs. Dewitt, I hear, goes to Europe on
Saturday. I believe she chaperons Miss Severn."

"Of course Mr. Larchmont goes with his ward," is the
reply of a gentleman.

"Oh, certainly ; they leave on the *Aurania*. They
say Mr. Larchmont is interested in pretty Miss Jessie
much more personally, than as trustee of her estate, and
guardian of her person."

I catch no more of this conversation, as the party giving it to my ears now rise and leave the restaurant.

Soon we are going also, Mr. Tompkins looking sorrow-
fully at his bill. As we reach the hall, the incident comes
to me that I have dreaded, yet hoped for. I again see
Harry Larchmont's pleasant face.

He is talking to a gentleman standing near the office.

His friend says : "You lead the cotillon with Miss
Severn, I understand, to-night?"

"Yes, for the last time—perhaps." This with a little
sigh.

"Why the last time?"

"I am going away."

This confirms the news I have just heard of him from
the party in the restaurant.

A moment later, his glance catches mine. The hall-
boy is about to hand me my wrap.

In a second he stands beside me, with outstretched
hand, which I do not refuse, and says : " How do you
do, Miss Minturn ? No after effects from the blizzard ? "

" No," I reply, " only gratitude."

But the blizzard has left an after effect on me. I turn
mý head away, my cheeks are burning.

" Nonsense ! " he replies lightly. " Don't think of the
affair in that serious way. I regard it now—only with
pleasure."

" What ! When you slept on a counter that night," I
return.

As this is going on, he is cloaking me with that deft
ease which indicates the squire of dames, while Mr.
Tompkins, who has hurried to my side to proffer a
similar attention, stands glaring at this unknown swell
who is acting as my cavalier for the moment.

A second later, Mr. Larchmont whispers : " I am most
happy to have seen you before I go away.

" Oh, I am going away also ! " I reply.

" Indeed ! Where ? "

" On the *Colon*——"

He interrupts this with a little start, saying : " On
the *Colon?* Then I shall only say *au revoir*," bows,
rejoins his friend, and the two go up-stairs, from which
the sound of music tells us of the coming dance ; while
I look on his departing figure, wondering what he means.

During this, Sally has been gazing at me with very
large eyes ; and as we pass out, is questioning eagerly :
" Isn't he very handsome ? Who is he ? "

I reply, attempting nonchalance : " Mr. Harry Sturgis
Larchmont."

This announcement is received by unbelieving sneers
from both Mr. Jenkins and Mr. Tompkins, who have read
many times of Mr. Larchmont in the society columns of
their morning newspapers.

" What ! " screams Sally, careless of overhearing cab-
men, " the leader of cotillons ? the howling swell ? "

" I don't know about the howling swell," I reply, " but
I believe he leads the cotillon this evening."

" Good heavens ! Why did you not introduce me ? "
This is a sigh of unutterable reproach at lost opportu-

nity ; then Sally goes on impetuously : " I would so like
to know a *real* swell before I die ! "

At this uncomplimentary speech, Jenkins grinds his
teeth, as he walks by her side, and Mr. Tompkins grows
pale, for he fears I have told the truth.

So we go home, they all questioning me, " How did I
know him ? "

This Sally answers for me.   She says proudly : " He
is a relic of her former life.   You know that Louise is
Miss Minturn—one of the real Minturns.   You can read
of her cousins, aunts, and uncles every day, in the society
columns of the papers.   They are dancing now, perhaps,
with Mr. Harry Sturgis Larchmont."

At this suggestion comes the thought that he is dancing
now with Miss Jessie Severn, and the idea which has been
in my mind so often, comes up with renewed force.   Had
not misfortune befallen my mother's parents on the Isthmus, I might have been dancing the German with him,
in her place, and this makes me severe—severe with poor
Tompkins, from whose remarks I turn with disdain.

By this time we are at our home in Seventeenth Street.
Mr. Jenkins leaves us at the door, apparently not having
forgiven Miss Sally for her remark about a *real* swell.

A moment after, Mr. Tompkins bids us adieu, and
turns to follow him.

I am about to bid him good-by as well as good-night
and tell him of my intended departure ; but Sally whispers to me : " He will know to-morrow."   Then as the
young man disappears she archly says : " Yes, he is sure
to turn up to-morrow.   He turns up every day.   Perhaps Mr. Tompkins will sleep better to-night if he does
not hear the news until to-morrow."

" Don't talk nonsense ! " I return, as we run up together to our rooms.   In the parlor, Miss Broughton,
who has been in high spirits all the evening, suddenly
changes her mood.

She looks at me wistfully, and says : " Louie, only one
night more together after this ! "

Then we two lonely ones in this world gaze at each
other, and our eyes grow dim ; and after we have gone
to bed I hear dear little Sally sobbing, until sleep comes
to us both and gives us rest.

The next morning Miss Broughton has apparently regained her spirits. She whispers : " You will write to me often, and if you don't like it there, come back."

" I have a contract."

" Come back, contract or no contract. They can't chain you there. With sixty dollars a week you can save money to pay your own passage."

" And you ! " I say anxiously. " What are you going to do ? "

" Oh, I'm all right ! " she runs on. " I have got Laura Dutton to come and take your place. She won't be such pleasant company, but is of a motherly disposition, and I think will keep me in good order."

So, breakfast being over, I am compelled to go to the office of Flandreau & Co., to sign the contract, and complete my arrangements for departure.

There I meet the dapper little clerk again, who is very polite to me, and has the contract drawn up, to be signed in duplicate, by which I bind myself for one year to furnish my stenographic services to the firm of Montez Aguilla et Cie., contractors construction, Panama, for the sum of sixty dollars per week and the various other emoluments that had been agreed to between us.

These documents are in printed forms in Spanish, apparently being in general use by the Panama firm to cover their agreements for labor.

Somehow or other, the name of the firm—Montez Aguilla et Cie., seems to me familiar.

These contracts I take to Miss Work, who has advised to this effect, and she gets a young lawyer in a neighboring office to see if they are what I wish. I translate them to him, and this gentleman pronounces them, in his judgment, satisfactory. I put my name to them, and returning to the office in South Street, they are signed by Flandreau & Co. as agents for the firm with which I contract.

My ticket for Panama, for a first-class passage, is given me, and I am informed that the captain of the steamer *Colon* will take charge of me as far as the Atlantic side of the Isthmus. There Mr. Stuart, the agent of the Pacific Steamship Company at Colon, will see about my railroad ticket, and transfer me across the Isthmus. I am given letters of introduction to both these gentlemen, and sufficient money in hand for any reasonable expenses that may come to me upon the voyage.

All this has been done by one o'clock in the day, and I depart for our rooms up town, I purchasing on the way a little *souvenir de remembrance* for Sally.

Miss Broughton is waiting for me, for she has given up her day's work to pack my trunk and see the last of me. This packing does not take long. My wardrobe, though good, is not extensive ; but I have purchased a few light and I think pretty gowns, suitable for a warm climate. So together we soon make quick work of the trunk. But this very packing brings the past back to me.

Among the mementos left me by my dead mother are a few things she had received from her own. One is a picture of a beautiful lady in the dress of thirty years ago. It is a tintype, bearing on the back : "*Edouart's Gallery, Ambrotypes and Daguerreotypes, 634 Washington Street, San Francisco.*" There is also a package of letters my mother had received as a schoolgirl, from her parents in California. These I have looked over before. Some time on the Isthmus I will read them again.

Perhaps I may learn the fate of the writers at Panama. Perhaps I may regain the treasure that was lost with them. Perhaps I may be— Pshaw ! Nonsense ! Their fate came on them thirty years ago.

We have had our dinner, and eight o'clock comes, and with it Mr. Tompkins. The trunk is now out in the parlor, strapped and labelled.

This trunk seems to give Mr. Tompkins a sensation. Almost as he wishes me good-evening, it catches his eye. He says hurriedly : " You are going away ? "

" Yes, to-morrow."

" And where do you think she is going ? " interjects Sally.

" To Long Island," suggests Mr. Tompkins uncertainly.

" To Panama for a year—under contract at sixty dollars a week—and first-class passage there and back ! " cries Miss Broughton.

" To Panama ! " gasps the gentleman. " Impossible ! "

" Look at that trunk ! Read its label ! " returns Sally.

" Miss Louise Ripley Minturn, Panama, via steamship *Colon.*"

Reading this, Mr. Tompkins believes, and sinks down,

overcome, upon our little sofa. But only for a moment. Then conviction has such an awful effect upon him, that Sally and I stare at his emotion.

He rises, an inch added to his height, a desperate determination in his face, and cries : " Put that trunk away ! Unpack it at once ! I forbid you to go ! "

His manner is so extraordinary, and there is such a wild light in his eyes, that Miss Broughton, having raised the Romeo in him, runs away from it into the other room, with a stifled giggle.

This is perhaps fortunate, as Mr. Tompkins' emotions have suddenly become of a most embarrassingly ardent nature to me. At last I realize why Sally has prevented any knowledge of my departure reaching the romantic Tompkins before. He is given to the emotions in their most violent and dramatic form.

Looking at me he mutters in reproachful tones : " And you kept it from me ? " then again cries out in a desperate way : " But I will not let you leave ! "

However, I steady myself and say determinedly : " That is impossible ! I have signed a contract."

" I want you to sign a contract with me ! " he returns, an awful romantic significance in his voice, " a contract to be my wife."

He is coming towards me. In another moment his arm will be about my waist. With a gasp of consternation, I place the trunk between us.

From the other side of it he still addresses me. " Yesterday I was made very happy. My salary was raised. It is sufficient to support a wife. Tell me, Miss Minturn —Louise, that you will enjoy that salary with me ! " He reaches to seize my hand, but three feet of trunk prevent him.

" I am glad to hear of your business success, Mr. Tompkins," I reply, trying to stifle any emotion that may be in me.

" Your Alfred's success ! " he cries. " Call me Alfred ! " and steps to my side of the trunk, but I, with a deft spring, keep it between us.

" Will you marry me ? " he asks in eager tone.

" No ! " I answer desperately, for his hand has caught my arm, and there are kisses in his eyes, " No ! Never ! "

Then comes an awful scene. He reproaches me for

having made him love me—me, who had hardly given him a thought—who had not even cared enough about him to guess what Sally's insinuations had meant.

Finally he exclaims : "I know it now ; you love another !" and grinds his teeth.

"Another ?" gasp I. "I forbid you to continue ! "

"Why not ?" he cries. "Why not ? Didn't your eyes tell me your hideous secret last night at Delmonico's when you looked at the swell? Harry Sturgis Larchmont, that's his name ! What chance have we workingmen against these gentlemen of fashion ? But, frivolous girl, I warn you of him ! With my last word, I, Alfred Tompkins, warn you ! "

With this invective he departs.

I pray God he will be happy. True hearts are scarce in this world, and though Alfred Tompkins' love for me is perhaps not of the most exalted type, still he has given me the whole of it.

Then Sally comes out to me and whispers : "You have sent him away ? "

"Of course ! "

"I knew you would, ever since you looked, last evening, at the swell in Delmonico's. Why, what awful blushes ! but they're very becoming, Louise."

"Nonsense !" I cry. "Don't dare to speak such ineffable idiocy. No more of Mr. Tompkins ! "

"No more of Mr. Harry Sturgis Larchmont?"

"No more of anyone !" and I turn from the subject, though Sally brings it back to me several times upon this last evening we spend together. The last night of our friendship ! If I come back, I will be changed, and she— Any way it will be different !

But at present we are all in all to each other, and mingle our farewells with tears and caresses, and promises to never forget each other.

So the morning comes to us, and my trunk is taken away by the expressman, and Sally and I go down to the great steamship, at its dock in the North River. I present my letter of introduction to the captain, and find that I have a very pleasant stateroom, all to myself. Here Sally and I bid each other farewell. A moment after, I give a start.

Alfred Tompkins is standing before me. He says,

heedless of Sally's presence: "Whether you change your mind or not, I have come down to bid you good-by!"

And I whisper to him: "I can't change my mind! You will forget me in time."

Then the cry comes up of "All ashore!"—the cry that is separating me from the land of my birth. And Sally and Mr. Tompkins have gone across the gang-plank to wave adieu to me as the steamer leaves its dock.

Other farewells are being said. Husbands are parting from wives, and sisters from brothers, and a lot of fashionables are waving farewell to some gentleman comrade. Carelessly I turn to look at him.

I give a gasp of astonishment. What does it mean to my life? The man waving an adieu to his friends, and standing carelessly on the bulwarks of the ship—the man sailing away with me to Panama—is Harry Sturgis Larchmont

Sally and Tompkins have seen and recognized him too. I see it by the look of amazed alarm upon their faces. Good heavens, if they think it an elopement! I give a start of horror, and fly to my stateroom dismayed and overcome at emotions that give me curious joy and bashful fear.

CHAPTER XI.

AN EXILE FROM THE FOUR HUNDRED.

FOR two days, on the plea of seasickness, a vague bashfulness keeps this young lady in retirement, in spite of kind messages from the captain, brought by the stewardess, suggesting it will be well for her to get her "sea legs" in working condition, and that his table looks lonely at dinner-time; for the skipper, being an admirer of lovely women, has given her this post of honor, somewhat to the young lady's astonishment.

Not being seasick—for the weather is by no means tempestuous—she has devoted herself to writing up her diary, which has fallen behindhand in the two or three days previous to her departure from New York.

On the morning of the third day, the stewardess, opening Louise's stateroom door, with that young lady's coffee in her hands, says, in her good-hearted darky way : "Miss Minturn, Cap'en's compliments, an' hopes to see yo' at breakfus'."

Then getting no answer to this but a piquant yawn, for the young lady is sleepy, she runs on in her *patois :* "'Deed it 'ud be a pow'ful shame if yo' don' go, honey. De vessel ain't rockin' mo' dan a baby's cradle. Dis am reg'lar Bahama wedder."

"Can I wear a light dress?" the girl asks suddenly and rather anxiously, reflecting, in a sleepy way, that her new summer gowns are her strongest points in wardrobe ; and desirous, like other Eves, to make a good appearance on her first entry into the dining *salon.*

"Laws ! Yo' could wear angel's wings, yo' could, to-day, an' be comfo'table ! " returns the stewardess.

"Oh ! " cries Louise, laughing. " I have no wish for a celestial toilette. Nun's veiling will make me near enough to the angels at present."

Soon after, stepping upon the deck, a vision of summer loveliness, she feels sorry that she has confined herself to her stateroom so long. The vessel is ploughing her way through a sea that is strangely blue, and quiet as the waters of an inland lake, save for its long ocean swell. The sky above her is also azure, and the glorious sun makes the bracing sea breezes a little languid, as they toss the girl's hair about, and give undulation to skirts and draperies that outline as pretty a figure as ever stood upon a ship's deck. She draws in the salt air, which is just strong enough to give buoyancy to her step and roses to her cheeks, and is happy that she has left New York with its March winds behind her, and sailed into a sunny sea.

Everything is tropical.

She looks about, an indefinite bashfulness in her radiant eyes, as if she hoped, yet almost feared, to see someone, and notices the passengers are nearly all in the toilettes of midsummer: the gentlemen mostly sporting white linen suits or flannels ; the ladies in light yachting costumes, with dainty sailor hats, or other delicate dresses suggestive of the tropics.

The gong is sounding for breakfast. Miss Louise,

with a little disappointed pout upon her lips, for somehow she has not seen what she has been looking for, is
about to go a little diffidently into the dining *salon*. But
at the companion-way a cheery voice greets her. The
captain is at her side, saying pleasantly—for this old sea-
dog has a quick eye for pretty girls—" I hope you have
got a salt-water appetite, Miss Minturn. Delighted to
see you on deck. I was afraid you might make the
voyage 'between blankets.' "

" In such beautiful weather that would have been
horrible," replies the young lady.

" If you had not come out to-day, I was going to send
our saw-bones to see what was the matter with you,"
returns the captain.

"Oh!" says the young lady, withdrawing her hand
from his vigorous and hearty grasp, for the skipper has
been giving its taper fingers a cordial squeeze, " I never
take doctor's prescriptions."

" Neither do I!" laughs the seaman; "so come down
and take some of our cook's."

A moment after, they are at the breakfast table, the
waiter placing a chair for Miss Louise at the left hand of
the captain, as the latter introduces his pretty charge to
the people immediately about him. During these pre-
sentations, the young lady discovers that the chair at the
captain's right is occupied by the wife of a French
engineer connected with the Panama Canal Company.
She is going to join her husband on the Isthmus, and is
very *petite*, rather timid in her manner, and delighted
when she learns that her new acquaintance speaks
French.

Immediately beyond this lady is an American, Colonel
Clengham Cleggett by name. He is in some way connected with the American Commission for the Panama
Canal, and is at present enthusiastically praising the
French management of that gigantic enterprise, probably
because he receives therefrom a handsome salary. A little farther down the table is a very pretty American girl
going by way of the Isthmus to meet her *fiancé*, who is
an orange farmer in Los Angeles, California, where she
is to be married to him. Her name at present is Miss
Madeline Stockwell.

These things come to Miss Minturn in a dreamy man-

ner.   With change of latitude, the atmosphere seems to
have changed also.   Though the flag of the United States
floats over her, she is apparently no longer in America.
Everything about her is so foreign !

The conversation at the next table, coming from
several young Central Americans returning to their coffee
plantations, is Spanish.   The balance is almost entirely
French.   There is but one subject of remark—the
Panama Canal.   For nearly all of the passengers are
connected with it, and get their bread and butter out
of it, being employees of the Canal Company, of the
various contracting firms engaged in constructing it,
returning from leave of absence to their duties on the
Isthmus.

The only exceptions to this, besides those mentioned,
are a couple of English Chilians bound for Valparaiso,
and a representative of Grace & Company, going to
Lima.   Therefore the name of *le grand Français*, Ferdinand de Lesseps, and his colossal enterprise, is on
everybody's lips.

But even as these things come to her, the young lady's
pretty hazel eyes are looking diffidently, yet anxiously,
about her.   She is wondering where Mr. Larchmont sits
in the dining *salon.*   She rather hopes it is far from her;
next suddenly wishes the reverse.   Even as this thought
is in her mind, a great blush comes over her beautiful
face, she turns her head away for a moment, confused,
for Harry Larchmont, coming down in summer flannels,
take's the vacant seat next to her.   Looking at the
beauty beside him, he gives a start of surprised pleasure,
and ejaculates : " I was afraid you were overboard! "

The captain says : " Harry" (for this young man's easy-
going way has made him familiar with nearly everybody
on shipboard), " let me introduce you to Miss Minturn.
She is the derelict of the ship.   You should know her.
She is one of your set in New York."

To this peculiar information, Mr. Larchmont says with
the instinctive good breeding of a man of the world :
" Yes, I know Miss Minturn very well, I am happy to
say."

"Of course you do ! " laughs the captain.   " She
danced at the Patriarchs' ball with you the other
evening."

" No, you are referring to my first cousin, Miss Fanny Minturn," ejaculates Miss Louise, suddenly finding her tongue, and not wishing to sail under false colors.

" Miss Fanny Minturn is your cousin ?" says Mr. Larchmont, a look of surprise passing over his face, for which the young lady does not bless him, for into her quick mind has flown this thought : " Why should this gentleman be astonished at Miss Minturn of Fifth Avenue being the cousin of Miss Minturn the stenographer ?" As she thinks this, chagrin makes her its prey. She imagines the captain's politeness and seat at his table came because he had supposed her one of the elect of New York. Fortunately for her peace of mind, she soon discovers that she does this jovial, good-hearted seadog injustice, as he don't care anything for Fifth Avenue. All he cares for is pretty girls ; and Miss Minturn's face and figure having pleased him, he has given her a seat at his table, and will favor her with personal attentions during the voyage, that he would hardly give to an ugly countess.

As the look of annoyance leaves her face, the conversation becomes more general, though ever and anon, during its commonplaces, the pretty young lady seated at Harry Larchmont's side, catches his eyes upon her, and she interprets their glances to say : " What the dickens brings you here ? "

Perhaps her piquant face asks the same question, for after a little he suggests : " This meeting is unexpected to you, Miss Minturn ; you now discover what I meant by *au revoir* at Delmonico's."

" Why—I—I had supposed you were bound for Paris," says Louise.

" No. My brother goes to France with Miss Severn and Mrs. Dewitt," answers Larchmont, looking serious.

"'Then you are *en route* California, I imagine ?" asks the girl a little anxiously.

" Only as far as the Isthmus." The young gentleman does not look very happy as he says this, and astonished meditation comes over the young lady. This bird of fashion might run away from winter in New York to the orange groves of California, or to gay St. Augustine, or the Riviera, or even Egypt ; but why should Harry Larchmont make a pilgrimage to Colon and Panama, with their

swamps, miasmas, and yellow fever? She is sure of one
thing—that it is not for pleasure. She recollects that he
sighed when he said, at Delmonico's, it might be the last
time he would lead the cotillon.

He affords no solution to the problem, though he
gives the young lady several pretty commonplaces, and
the conversation at the table runs along in a desultory
way; but it is a conversation that delights the girl who
is listening to it. She perceives the narrow limits of Miss
Work's typewriting room have opened, and let her pass
out into the world of finance, of politics, of diplomacy—
the little world that dominates the greater one. As she
thinks this, the girl's eyes grow bright with excitement
at the new life that is coming to her.

Across the table from her a discussion is taking place
as to whether the United States will interfere in case the
rights of the few remaining American stockholders of
the Panama Railroad are ignored by the Panama Canal
Company that has purchased it. Colonel Clenghorn
Cleggett is apparently the most bitter Gaul in the discussion, and is verbally trampling on his own countrymen
with savage vehemence.

"Rather an un-American chap," remarks Mr. Larchmont *sotto voce* to Miss Minturn. "According to his own
stories, Cleggett was a Congressman, and yelled Monroe
doctrine until he received a French appointment."

"Then he is a mercenary traitor," says the young lady,
with the quick decision of youth and womanhood, in a
whisper that brings her pretty lips very close to Mr.
Harry's ear, for their seats at table permit easy confidence.

A moment after, she suddenly goes on, "How much
you know about the Canal!"

"I've been making a quiet study of it lately," answers
the young man, and rather gloomily attacks his breakfast.

Then silence comes over Mr. Larchmont. Having
come in late to breakfast he is apparently making up for
lost time, so the young lady could keep her ears open
and her mouth shut, did not the captain's occasional
attentions compel reply.

He insists on her tasting the various dishes he recom-
mends; and knowing the strong points of his cook, she
discovers she has fared very well by the time the skipper
rises to leave the table. The young man beside her is

just finishing the last of his coffee hurriedly, and is apparently about to address her, when the captain, offering a gallant arm, says : " Let me show you my ship, Miss Minturn ; " and with that seizes upon Miss Beauty, and takes her up the companionway, to instruct her in various nautical matters.

After a few minutes, the captain's attention is demanded by his first officer, and Harry chancing to saunter out from the smoking-room, the seaman turns his charge over to him, saying : " My boy, complete my instructions. Miss Louise now knows the difference between a topmast and the smokestack."

Then going away to his duty, he leaves the two facing each other.

The gentleman looks pleased and eager. The lady's eyes turn to the water, as it flows past, a slight blush on her fair cheeks, a little confusion in her eyes. She is thinking of the blizzard and—the violets.

Mr. Larchmont says laughingly : " Miss Minturn, since you have been under the captain's instructions, will you please educate me ? "

So they shortly find themselves seated in two steamer chairs which the young gentleman, for some occult reason, has placed very close to each other.

" What a languid sea breeze! " murmurs the girl, making an alluring picture of laziness as she dallies with her white parasol.

" Not as languid as the blizzard," laughs Harry.

Whereupon the young lady turns on him grateful eyes, and whispers : " You were very kind to me ! " then looks over the water.

" Ah ! you like me in the *rôle* of rescuer ? " returns the gentleman, suggestion in his voice.

"On shore, perhaps ; but here your remark indicates collision, hurricane, shipwreck, and 'Man the life-boats! ' " replies Louise, growing a little pale at her own imagery. Then she suddenly ejaculates, " What a pretty little ship ! "

" By Jove ! " cries Larchmont, hastily producing his field-glasses, and inspecting the pennants of an exquisite schooner that is just abreast of them, with every white sail set to the southern breeze.

" Why, she looks like a toy compared to our steamer !"

remarks the young lady ; and noting the gentleman inspecting her signals, continues : " You appear to know
the boat."

" Yes, that is the *Independent*, Lloyd Pollock's schooner
yacht," answers Harry. " Pollock is bound for the West
Indies, for a winter cruise. He is one of the most charming 'do-nothings' in the world. He spends his life seeking summer." Then he sighs, " Two months ago I was
a ' do-nothing ' also." This last remark is perhaps produced by the sight of the steward serving cocktails on
the yacht's deck.

" Well, why not join him ?" suggests Louise. " Mr.
Pollock is a friend of yours ?"

" Yes, an intimate."

" Then hail him. He is hardly too distant, even now.
Ask him to take you on board," continues the girl, who
is a little piqued at her companion's sigh. " Your trip
to the Isthmus does not please you."

" I am better pleased to be here than on board any
yacht in the world," answers young Larchmont stoutly;
and looking upon his companion concludes that he has
spoken the truth. Then a new idea seems to come into
his mind, for he goes on suddenly : " You are journeying to California, Miss Minturn ?"

" No," says the girl, " what makes you think that ?"
and turns wondering eyes on him.

" Why," he answers, a little hesitation in his manner,
" I had heard a young lady on board was *en route* to California to be married. When I saw you at the captain's
table alone, and in his charge, I presumed you were the
fiancée."

" I am *not* going to California, and I am *not* going to be
married !" utters Louise decidedly. " That young lady "
—she indicates by her parasol Miss Madeline Stockwell,
who is seated by the side of a young Costa Rican—" is
the coming bride." Smiles are upon her fair face, for
she is glad to find Harry Larchmont has been speculating upon her. She laughs, " Could you not tell it ? I
thought brides could always be guessed."

To this the young man replies : " If brides could be
guessed by tremendous flirtations, I should have selected
Miss Madeline Stockwell. How do you think her *fiancé*
would enjoy looking on that ?" and he points to the

Costa Rican, who is stroking his moustaches with one white hand, and with the other devotedly fanning the pretty Madeline, as she sits languidly on her campstool, a picture of contented ease, apparently having forgotten the orange grower.

Then the two become merry, for somehow Mr. Larchmont's face, when Miss Louise had announced to him ··she is not the coming bride, has given that young lady good spirits. So they go to joking with each other, and have quite a merry time of it, until Harry brings catastrophe upon their *tête-a-tête*.

He says incidentally : " By the by, Miss Minturn, you remember that gentleman who was with you at Delmonico's the other evening ? "

" Oh, yes ! " she replies carelessly. " Mr. Alfred Tompkins ; he came down to bid me good-by."

" Then it was he ! " ejaculates Harry, a peculiar look coming into his face. " He is a very curious man."

" Indeed ! Why ? "

" Why, he ran to the end of the dock just as we cast loose, and shook his fist at the ship, and called out, ' You infernal scoundrel ! ' For a moment I wondered if he was not anathematizing me ; but a French gentleman standing beside me took it to himself, and crushed your friend with a volley of Gallic invective. Consequently, I know he did not refer to me."

There is meditation, yet questioning, in his voice ; perhaps there is a little roguery in his glance ; for the young lady has turned suddenly away, and a big blush has come upon her. She knows the reason of Mr. Tompkins' violence, and in her heart of hearts is gasping : " Good heavens ! he thought I was eloping with—if Harry Larchmont should ever guess ! "

A moment later, the gentleman startles Miss Louise again. He says : " You are not a good sailor, I am sorry to see."

" Why ? "

" Because every little lurch of the vessel seems to make you wish to look over the taffrail. Besides, you were sea·sick in your cabin for three days."

" No, I was not ! " replies the girl indignantly. " I— I had some writing to do."

" Ah, then you are a good sailor. You like yachting,

8

of course ? "   This is said as if everybody yachted ; and
Louise bites her lip, and hates him for making her con-
fess ignorance of that fashionable amusement.   Then
great joy comes to her.   She remembers the catboat
Tompkins hired in summer, and called a yacht.   She
had been on it *once* at Sheepshead Bay, with Sally Broughton, and putting her soul in her words, she answers
sweetly : " I *adore* yachting ! "

Then she grows very angry again, for he has glanced
at her surprised.

A moment after, he goes on, unheeding indignant
looks : "If you adore yachting, and I love yachting,
suppose we imagine this ship a yacht : we have yachting
weather."

"What difference," says Miss Minturn petulantly,
" does it make whether we consider we are on a steamer
or a yacht ? "

" Only that on yachts people get better acquainted with
each other.   There is something in the very deck of a
yacht that makes people feel *épris.*"

" We will consider this a *steamer,*" mutters the girl
piquantly yet sternly.

Her glance disconcerts the young man ; but ·he says :
" You play, I know."

" Passably."

" On the piano ? "

" Yes, on the piano, the guitar, banjo, and harp.   My
mother was a music teacher."

" The guitar—you have one with you ? "

" It is in my stateroom."

" Then we will have musical nights on deck ; dancing
waves—romantic moonlight—the——"

Harry's eyes are speaking as well as his lips, when Miss
Minturn cuts him short with, " My evenings are devoted
to writing."

" Oh, letters for home ? "

" No, my diary."   As this slips between the young
lady's pretty lips, she clinches her teeth together, as if
trying to cut it off, and grows very red, for he is whispering : " A diary ! a young lady's diary ! I am devoted to
such literature.   Give me a peep at yours ? "

" Oh, gracious ! " ejaculates the girl, for sudden
thought has come to her : " If he should see it with his

name on every other page !" Very red, but desperately calm, she goes on : "That diary is under lock and key, and shall remain there. No one will ever see it."

"Not even your husband—when you marry ?" suggests the gentleman.

" He less than anyone ! "

" Of course not ! The diary would be very sad read-.ing for the future husband," answers Harry, putting pathos in his voice. Then he says consideringly : "I am glad, however, it is a diary. Diaries can be left till to-morrow. I was afraid it was some of that awful stenographic work ; that I might hear the click of the typewriter in your stateroom."

" 'Typewriters," cries Louise, "are for the Isthmus."

" For the Isthmus ? "

" Yes. Don't you suppose there is any business done on the Isthmus ?" answers Miss Minturn, with savage voice ; thoughts of typewriters do not charm her soul this pleasant morning. " Is the Panama Canal all talk and *no* work ? "

Now this latter announcement seems to have a very potent effect on the gentleman with her. He mutters : " I am afraid so." Then continues : " I am going to the Isthmus myself, on business—business on which——"

Here Louise eagerly interjects, delight in her voice : " So am I ! I am going out to be the stenographic cor-respondent of Montez, Aguilla et Cie."

At these words Harry Larchmont starts, looks at his companion with sudden scrutiny, perhaps even suspicion. A moment after, apparently changing the tone of his speech, he says, with an attempt at a laugh : " So am I."

" What ! Stenographer for Montez, Aguilla et Cie.?"

" No, not exactly that, but I am going to be a clerk also."

" You a clerk ? You, who have led cotillons ? You, who are one of the lazy birds of the world ?" gasps the girl, astounded.

" That is a thing of the past, now," he says contempla-tively. " You see," here a sudden idea flies into this gentleman's mind, and he becomes apparently confidential, " when a man in the class I have been running with dis-covers, to put it pointedly, that he is 'dead broke——'"

" Dead broke ? "

"That's what I said. He finds very few avenues of employment open to him that are sufficiently lazy to suit his disposition."

He makes the last pictorial, by reclining very languidly on his steamer chair, and murmurs, "You look happy at my news."

"Happy?—I—" stammers the girl. "Of course not!" But her eyes belie her words, for there has flown into her soul a rapturous thought : "This man and I are now equal in this world's goods." After a moment she goes on suggestively :

"Why, you might go on the stage, with your voice and figure."

"Thanks for your compliment !" he laughs. Then, growing serious, says : "On the stage ! Every dramatic jackal of the press would have run me down in their columns as coyotes do a buffalo that has left his herd. Besides, do you think a man becomes an actor without study ? And I have never studied anything."

"Why, you must have studied something—football for instance !" laughs Louise. Then she says, her eyes growing large with admiration : "I saw your wonderful game four years ago."

"Yes," he replies, "I am an athlete, but not a prize fighter ; prize fighting leads to the stage, not general athletics. Consequently," he goes on, as if anxious to stop discussion on this point, "I applied to my uncle, Mr. Delafield, who has some influence in business circles, and he has obtained for me a clerkship in the Pacific Mail Steamship Company's office at Panama. I think it will suit me. They only have three steamers a month ; between times I can lie in a hammock, smoke cigarettes, eat oranges, and suck mangoes."

"Yes, I think it would suit you," says the girl mockingly ; and looking at him, acquiesces with him, but does not believe him. His speech seems to her not genuine. Up to the time she had told him she was the correspondent for Montez, Aguilla et Cie., his conversation had been frank and ingenuous ; from that time on, it has appeared to be forced.

A moment later the captain breaks in on her meditation, saying : "Harry, I think we'll have to change watch now. It's my turn below."

And Mr. Larchmont, to whom this conversation has grown embarrassing, for he is not a young man to use ambiguities easily, and tell white lies with the straightest of faces, but who feels it necessary to disguise the reason of his visit to the Isthmus to any one connected with Baron Fernando Montez, yields up his seat, and strolls off to meditate over a cigar.

Then the captain attempts to make play with the beauty of the ship, but finding her unresponsive to his nautical wit and humor, suggests lunch ; for she is thinking, " If it is true ? If he is a clerk—there is no gulf— Harry Sturgis Larchmont and I are equal before the world ! " And it is joy to her, for this girl loves the man, not his reputed wealth or social position.

So the day runs on, and Louise gets to watching this young man who has been so much in her thoughts, and what she notices makes her wonder still more

There is a certain Carl Wernig, a gentleman who the captain tells her is of prodigious wealth and great influence in the Panama Canal Company. This person seems to be interested in the movements of Mr. Larchmont. The two having picked up a hurricane deck acquaintance, Miss Minturn hears him mention to Mr. Larchmont that he knows his brother François in Paris.

" I call him Frank," says the New Yorker rather curtly. " An American name is good enough for me, though I believe my brother has Frenchified his since he has been promenading the *boulevards*."

But nothing seems to check this German in his interest in Mr. Larchmont. He joins him, at every opportunity, on deck, laughingly questions him as to his trip on the Isthmus, as if anxious to know what he intends doing there. To these Herr Wernig receives the short answer that Harry is "busted," and is going out as a clerk to Panama.

The next morning, Miss Louise, who has spent some part of her night meditating upon the gentleman of her thoughts, gets a surprise when she comes on deck and stands by the captain's side, looking at the Island of Salvador, with its white light-house.

The skipper says suddenly : " By Jove ! "

" Why do you make such extraordinary remarks ? "

asks the young lady, a little startled at the bluntness of
the seaman's exclamation.

"Why, look at that young springall, Harry Larchmont, sauntering along the deck as unconcernedly as if it
were an every-day occurrence ; and yet I understand
Mr. Cockatoo lost one thousand dollars at poker last
night ! Those young bloods think the skipper does not
know what is going on in this ship, but the skipper
does."

To this Louise does not reply. A curious problem is
in her mind. She is wondering how a man, who yesterday told her he was "dead broke," seems not even to
give a passing thought to the loss at cards of one thousand dollars that will be "hard-earned dollars" to him
very soon.

As she goes down to breakfast she thinks : "Can it
be the carelessness of financial despair, or is it from force
of habit ?"

She had known Larchmont was regarded as rich, even
in New York, where a million dollars goes not over far.
Is this exile from the Four Hundred, though he has not
gone on the stage, acting some part ? Does he wish the
real object of his journey to the Isthmus to be unsuspected and unknown ?

CHAPTER XII.

A WILD-GOOSE CHASE.

THIS latter idea, circumstances that occur later in the
day tend to confirm.

Mr. Larchmont, after having eaten a hearty and comfortable breakfast, is apparently not overburdened in
mind by last night's losses. Leaving the companionship
of his social equals in the *salon*, he for some curious
reason devotes himself to the second-cabin passengers.

The privilege given him by his ticket permits his
wandering all over the boat, and he avails himself of it
by taking a long promenade in that portion of the ship
where those who are compelled by financial considera-
tions to take inferior accommodations make their exercise.

His absence rather astonishes Miss Louise, who is dawdling out a tropical forenoon, seated on a steamer chair, under stern awnings, and surrounded by the light conversation of people talking to kill a nautical day, that is made up of three supreme events—breakfast, lunch, and dinner, with minor intervals between. Not greatly amused by the conversation of some of the young gentlemen of the boat, with whom she appears to be a general favorite, she meditates, and reproach comes to her. She has shut herself up in the cabin on the evening before, and has not enjoyed the moonlight, as Mr. Larchmont had suggested. Perchance, had she given him her society, he would not have turned to poker ! This last thought is a spasm of delight too charming to be analyzed.

As she languishes amid fan and parasol and sofa cushions and surrounding gallants, her bright eyes suddenly become animated ; to her astonishment she notes that Mr. Larchmont is interesting himself with the second-cabin passengers. He is taking his exercise in their company, and has become friendly with several of them.

Apparently he does not love them well enough to eat with them, for he returns to first cabin at meal-times.

This is in Miss Minturn's mind, as the young gentleman takes seat beside her at the lunch table, for she remarks caustically : " Mr. Larchmont, you do not seem to enjoy second-cabin table as much as you do second-cabin society."

" Oh," he replies, stifling a grin : " there are some curious characters amidships ;" then, after a little reflection, continues : " Besides, I am training myself for associations that may come ultimately to a poverty-stricken individual." This assertion is made with a laugh which does not seem to be genuine, from one prognosticating a fall in his social environment.

But lunch over, this young gentleman is again at his business in the second cabin. He seems to have taken a particular fancy for a short, dried-up-looking little man, whose dress and appearance proclaim the French shopkeeper.

In the afternoon, a refreshing breeze having sprung up, most of the passengers take a leisurely promenade on deck ; and Miss Minturn follows the fashion. She has some of the gentlemen of the ship at her side, among

them Herr Wernig. A few scraps of conversation, that
are carried by the breeze to them, from Mr. Larchmont
and his second-cabin chum, appear to be in French;
Harry apparently making very hard work of the Gallic
vernacular.

As the young lady only has ears for what floats to
her from the forward part of the ship, her inattention is
not complimentary to the gentlemen about her, and one
by one they drop away from her, until she finds herself
tête-à-tête with the German financier.

This gentleman's large bright eyes—one of which has
a cast—have been often rolled towards her since she has
made her appearance the day before ; for he has a quick
optic for feminine beauty, and the young lady's exquisite figure, graceful movements, and vivacious countenance, have affected Herr Wernig in a manner that he
would consider complimentary, but Miss Minturn would
by no means approve. Therefore he has contented himself with admiring the bright face by his side, which is
somewhat dreamy this afternoon, though the young
lady's inattention has not been flattering to a self-pride
with which he is well provided.

Finding himself alone with her, he breaks in upon her
brown study with dominant manner, and slightly foreign
accent, remarking : "Miss Minturn, your friend, young
Mr. Larchmont, seems to be attempting to improve his
French. If he learns French from Bastien Lefort, he
will acquire the language of the *bourgeois*, not the aristo-
crat."

"Ah, you know the person Mr. Larchmont is talking
to?" says the girl, suddenly growing interested.

"Oh, yes, everyone on the Parisian *Bourse* knows him.
He is a large investor in canal stock."

" And yet he takes passage in the second cabin," returns
Louise, astonished.

" Yes, he is going to examine the works for himself,"
replies Wernig, smiling sarcastically. " He is a man
who saves his *sous*. My only surprise is, that he did
not go in the steerage." Then he shrugs his shoulders,
and his large eyes roll themselves about in a manner he
considers expressive of admiration, as this foreign gentleman suggests : " Why discuss others, Miss Minturn,
when there are more charming people on board—much

more charming—much more beautiful—and so—so delightful ?" His eyes indicate quite pointedly to whom he refers.

At this, the young lady gives a little start, and, a *soupçon* of scorn coming into her voice, replies : "Then you will be compelled to make your charming conversation——"

"A what ?" cries Herr Wernig enthusiastically.

"A soliloquy !" suggests the girl sharply, and turning on her heel, gives him a very piquant but formal courtesy of adieu.

Perhaps Mr. Larchmont has observed her conversation with Herr Wernig, for he shortly afterwards leaves his second-cabin chum, and coming aft, takes place beside her, as she is lazily looking over the taffrail. At all events he mentions it ; for he asks, a trace of annoyance in his voice : " What do you find interesting, Miss Minturn, in that old foreign duffer ? "

"Ah, it is you, is it, Mr. Larchmont ? " answers the young lady, turning a pair of beautiful but uncompromising eyes upon him ; for she has been somewhat chagrined at the desertion of her companion of yesterday. Then she goes on quickly, " What old foreign duffer ? "

" The one you were walking with a few minutes ago—the man with big eyes, and a cast in the largest one."

" Oh, your friend," murmurs Louise.

" My friend ? "

" Yes, the one who knows your brother in Paris, so well."

At this, a shade comes over Mr. Larchmont's face, as he murmurs : " Yes, he told me he was acquainted with Frank."

" Perhaps your chum of the second cabin is also a friend of your brother's," replies the piqued young lady, affecting an archness which does not seem to raise Mr. Larchmont's spirits, for he replies with gloomy and morose tone and sneering voice, " You evidently don't know my brother in Paris ; he does not associate with second-cabin passengers."

Then, to turn the conversation, he attempts a cheerful and playful : " Where's your guitar ? This will be a night for guitars. This evening we will pass Cuba where guitars, mandolins, and dulcimers make music for the

gay fandango.   We should keep in the atmosphere.   The
guitar this evening, eh, Miss Minturn ?"

"No," determinedly replies Louise, who likes not his
bantering tone.   "I shall write this evening."

Perhaps some subtle beauty in the girl—perhaps the
natural buoyancy of youth—has caused Mr. Larchmont's
bad spirits to entirely disappear, as he returns lightly :
"Ah, the diary !   We have not seen that yet.   I must enjoy that wonderful diary, even if I have to steal it !"

"Never !" says the girl hoarsely, looking out over
the horizon, the redness of confusion upon her cheeks,
for she cannot meet his eyes whenever the diary is mentioned.

"Why not ?"

Then Louise grows desperate, for he is smiling an
awful smile.   She mutters : "You shall never read that
diary—never !   I will throw it overboard first."

Here he surprises her ; he whispers impulsively : "How
anger becomes you !"   As in truth, it does, for Louise
Minturn is a girl whose spirit is even more beautiful than
her face, and in excited moments her soul shining out
through radiant eyes becomes wonderfully dominant over
her delicate and mobile face.

A moment after, Harry continues : "Yes, throw the
diary overboard—do anything with it, but don't write
in it this lovely night."

"Why not ?"

"Because—" he hesitates slightly, then goes on with
the audacity that is beloved by women ; "because I
want your company.   You will take pity on me, and
drive away the blues—wont you ?   Promise me."

And the girl answers slowly : "Y-e-s."   For there is
an appeal in Harry Larchmont's dark eyes, and it is the
first time he has ever asked a personal favor, though he
has given her many.

She turns away, murmuring : "Good-by !"

"You are going ?"

"To be sure—to put my guitar in order."

"Then *au revoir* until dinner."

"Oh, I had forgotten dinner !"

"What !   Forgotten dinner ?" laughs the gentleman.
"Oh, guitars and mandolins !   Here is a romantic soul !"

Whereupon, covered by some sudden confusion, she

hurries to her stateroom ; and though she tunes her
guitar, doubtless some of its chords are a little false, notwithstanding this young lady has a very correct musical
ear.

For some occult reason, she does not make her appearance at dinner, until the second course.   Perhaps it is
because she has lingered, arraying herself in a new gown
of softest folds and most radiant whiteness.

As she steps into the cabin, young Larchmont stops
hastily in his fish, and mutters to himself : " Undine ! "

She does not hear this, for the skipper at the head of
the table suddenly breaks out with a chuckle, continuing
a conversation that Louise has broken in upon : " I had
supposed, Harry, you were in charge of Miss Minturn
here, while everybody tells me you have been making
love to the second-cabin passengers."

" Miss Minturn, I believe, has discharged me, in favor
of Herr Wernig, the Franco-German capitalist," remarks
Mr. Larchmont, as if disposed to put the brunt of the
fight upon the young lady just taking her seat beside
him.

This suggestion of Herr Wernig makes the girl angry,
and the captain's remark does not add to her self-control.
He returns : " Well, it seemed very natural that you and
Miss Louise should become comrades.   You dance the
cotillon with her cousin in New York, and ' birds of a
feather flock together ' ! "

Here the young lady interjects : " Yes, he dances with
my cousin, Miss Minturn of Fifth Avenue, but she is
very different from Miss Minturn the stenographer, of
Seventeenth Street."   Then she says, unfalteringly :
" Captain, you seem to be laboring under a misapprehen-
sion.   I am not an exotic of fashionable New York.   I
am simply a young woman who makes her own living.
This is not a pleasure trip to me.   It is a matter of business.   I am going out to be the stenographic correspondent of Montez, Aguilla et Cie."

At this a little hush comes about the table.   The ladies
glance at her, some with astonishment, some with careless
indifference—one or two with surprised admiration, most
of the gentlemen joining apparently in the latter.

The captain suddenly says : " My dear young lady, I
would rather have you sitting at my table than any Fifth

Avenue girl I ever met.   Harry "—here he looks at Mr.
Larchmont—"seems to be of the same opinion.   And I,
as skipper of this vessel, would much sooner have him
sitting by you on moonlight nights" (this last is a little
whisper for her own particular ear) "than the German
capitalist over there."   He nods towards the table where
Herr Wernig is discussing his champagne with his third
course.

But this announcement, that the girl has perhaps carelessly but very candidly made, seems to produce a difference in several people, in their bearing towards her.
Among the ladies, some who had been quite effusive to
the supposed belle of fashionable Fifth Avenue grow
distant, perhaps supercilious ; a few, those of undoubted
social position, are, if anything, kinder to her than before ;
one or two of them, in leaving the cabin, making it their
business to stop and speak to Miss Minturn.   The gentlemen seem about the same ; to Mr. Larchmont, this
announcement of course makes no difference, he has
known it all along.

As Louise rises from the table, he whispers: " Remember your promise.   Cuban breezes, moonlight and
music ! "

But this news about the beautiful American girl, which
after a little time drifts to his ear, seems to make one
gentleman unusually joyous, and to affect his spirits even
more than the champagne, of which he is unusually
lavish this evening.

This is Herr Wernig, the Franco-German capitalist ;
and very shortly after, getting on deck, he strolls to
Miss Minturn's side, his manner effusive, and his tone
even more affable than it had been in the afternoon, and
whispers, " My dear Miss Louise, I am delighted to hear
you are a stenographer—the stenographer of my grand
friend, the Baron Montez of Panama and Paris.   It will
be a very fine position for you.   I have great influence
with the firm.   I shall try to advance you."

" Please do not trouble yourself on my behalf, in any
way ! " replies Louise ; then laughs : " It would do no
good.   I am under contract.   They will not raise my
salary for a year."

" But I insist—I must—I will apply for you ! I cannot
help it, my dear young lady.   I have much business with

your firm—in fact, confidential relations—I'll ask them, when on the Isthmus, to appoint you my stenographer."

Here Mr. Larchmont suddenly puts his camp-stool between Miss Louise and the German gentleman, to whom he whispers: "Herr Wernig, when you have any letter-writing to do, you come to me.   I am corresponding clerk, also, of the Pacific Mail Steamship Company. I am not as good a stenographer as Miss Minturn, but still I think I can do all the correspondence you wish—perhaps *more*."   The "more" is emphasized, as he happens to get the leg of his steamer-chair over the German's toe, and seating himself on it, his one hundred and seventy-five pounds of athletic material makes Herr Wernig writhe.

He snarls: "Sir, do you know to whom you are talking?   You clerk !   I will have you discharged from the Pacific Mail."

"You'll have me discharged?" laughs Harry.   Then a bantering tone coming into his voice, he says: "Oh, please don't !   For God's sake, think of a young man left to starve on the Isthmus!"   Next bursts into a sudden shriek of laughter, which indicates, if the worst comes to the worst, he has a stout heart, and will make out to subsist upon plantains, oranges, and bananas, that can be had for the plucking, in that land of tropical plenty.

But his laugh is lost upon the German gentleman, who has gone sullenly and silently away.

As he turns to Miss Minturn, Larchmont's laugh ceases, for he sees something in the girl, that he has never seen before—her soul !   And as it shines from her radiant eyes, it is more beautiful to him than all else he has seen of her, which up to this time has seemed to him the fairest of womanhood.

Besides there is something in her glance that makes him extraordinarily but unaccountably happy.

All through this evening, the young man seems to be in the highest spirits, as well he should be, having the beauty of the ship by his side.

They are a little apart from the rest of the passengers —just enough to make them *tête-à-tête*—but hardly sufficient to excite remark.   The moonlight, shining over silver waves, streams on the deck, and makes it bright,

but leaves them in shadow.   One red ray, like a gigantic
calcium, mingling with the moonlight on the water, comes
from the lighthouse on the eastern point of Cuba ; a
shore that looks olive beneath the moonlight, but under
the sun would be green as an emerald, and beautiful
with flowers, could they but see them, but the soft
breeze wafts over the water, odors that are magic as
those of fairy-land.

Looking on this, Harry Larchmont whispers to the
young lady at his side : " Now give to this scene, music !
Complete it, and let us forget all else in this wide world
—except you and me."

There is a suggestion of romance in his tone, but beneath all there seems a sorrow, which arouses the sympathy
of this girl, who, until these last few days, had supposed
that Harry Larchmont's life was as bright as that of any
mortal upon this earth.   While she sings a little romantic, plaintive, piquant Spanish love song, just fitted for
this moonlight night, she wonders what cloud has come
over him.   Then, at his request, she sings another, and
being made enthusiastic by the scene and its surroundings, gives her heart to the melody, and her beautiful
contralto voice very shortly draws others of the loiterers
on deck about her.

Apparently this throng does not please Mr. Larchmont ;
he rises, and says : " Thank you for a perfect evening,
Miss Louise," and so passes away from the girl, though
she notes that he does not go to the card-room, but rather
seeks his own cabin.

Then the loungers around her beg for another ballad ;
and she sings it, but her heart is not in it.

A moment after, she leaves them, notwithstanding their
entreaties for more Spanish melodies, and passing to her
own stateroom, sits and looks out over the moonlit
water, breathes in the perfumed air, and dreams a dream
that is so happy she would continue it, did not the
stewardess come and put her light out, and destroy
romance with common every-day shipboard rules and
regulations.

In her berth she gets to thinking, and murmurs to herself : " Poor fellow !   What can have come into his life
to make it sad ? "   Then awful distress comes upon her ;
she suddenly gasps, " He is parted from Miss Severn !

That is the reason of his unhappiness ! " and feels that her heart is drifting away from her, to a man whose love is given to another.

As for this object of her sympathy, he is not dreaming— he is *swearing*. He is saying to himself : " Dolt ! Idiot ! Why did you make an enemy of that fellow Wernig ? He might have helped you in your investigations about Baron Montez." Then he suddenly mutters : " I am glad I did it, anyway ! Did he suppose a beautiful American girl would look with anything but disgust at such a creature ? What did he mean, anyway? " Here he suddenly grinds out between his teeth : " If I were quite sure, I'd knock his foreign head off ! "

A moment after, he meditates gloomily : " But I have other fish to fry than fighting Wernig. I am fighting Montez, not for Jessie's sake, but for my own. I don't want to give up two-thirds of my fortune to save my weak brother's name and give his ward her *dot*. What can I find out on the Isthmus anyway ? It is the last straw ! I fear I am on a wild-goose chase. But the game is never lost till time is called, and I have got a few months yet ! "

Whereupon he lights a cigar, strolls out of his cabin, and would shatter a fond idea of Miss Minturn's, did she see him ; for he goes to the card-room, and plays poker most of the night, to drive away thought ; this time with better success than the night before.

The fickle goddess smiles upon him, and he wins considerable money ; some of it from Herr Wernig, who has apparently forgotten this young gentleman's impertinence of the early evening, though once or twice there is an ominous look in his eccentric eye as he rolls it towards his fortunate opponent.

CHAPTER XIII.

THE BUNDLE OF LETTERS.

THE next day Herr Wernig has become again effusively affectionate and thrusts his society upon Mr. Larchmont, though that young gentleman gives him but little chance, as he is again devoting himself to the second-cabin passengers.

This time, he has dropped the society of the man Bastien Lefort for that of one of the second-cabin ladies. This lady has a little child of about five. With paternal devotion Harry takes this tot up and carries it about, as he talks to the mother. This attention seems to win the lady's heart. And he spends a good deal of the morning promenading by her side. By the time he returns to lunch in the first cabin, "his flirtation," as they express it, has been pretty well discussed by the various ladies and gentlemen of the after part of the ship. Of course it comes to Miss Minturn's pretty ears, and sets her wondering.

After an afternoon siesta—for the boat is now well in the tropics, and everybody is drifting with it into the languid manners of the torrid zone—Louise strolls on the deck for a little sea breeze, and chancing to meet the gentleman of her thoughts, puts her reflections into words.

This subject is easily led up to, as Mr. Larchmont even now has in his arms the little girl from the second cabin.

"Miss Louise," he says, "this is a new friend of mine. This is pretty little Miss Minnie Winterburn, the daughter of a machinist on one of the Chagres dredgers. Her father has been out there almost since the opening of the railroad. He is by this time used to yellow fever."

"And her mother?" suggests the young lady rather pointedly, for Harry's speech has been made in a rambling, semi-embarrassed manner.

"Oh, her mother," returns Mr. Larchmont, "is on board in the second cabin. She is much younger than her husband—third or fourth wife—that sort of thing, you understand. I have brought the little lady aft to get some oranges from the steward." Which fact is apparent, as the child is playing with two of the bright yellow fruits. "If you will excuse me, I'll return my little friend to maternal arms, and be with you in a minute. Let me make you comfortable on this camp-stool."

Arranging the seat for her, Harry strolls off with the little girl. As he walks away the young lady's eyes carelessly follow him; suddenly they grow tender. She notices the careful way he carries the little tot, and it reminds her of how he had borne her through the snow and ice of that awful New York blizzard.

Apparently the emotion has not left her eyes when Larchmont returns to her; for he says, his eyes growing tender also: "To-night we will have another musical evening?"

"Oh, I'm not going to sing for you this evening," ejaculates the young lady lightly, for seats beside each other three times a day at the dining-table, and the easy intercourse of shipboard life have made her feel quite *en camarade* with this young gentleman, save when thoughts of her diary bring confusion upon her.

"Why not?"

"Oh! second-cabin society in the daytime, second-cabin romance at night."

"Was there a *first*-cabin romance last night?" asks the gentleman, turning embarrassing eyes upon her.

"No—of course not—I—I didn't mean anything of the kind!" stammers Louise.

"Indeed! What did you mean?"

"I meant," says the girl, steadying herself, "that you seem to prefer second-cabin society during the daytime —why not enjoy it also in the evening?"

Whereupon he startles her by saying suddenly: "How a false position makes everything appear false! I presume, Miss Minturn, you imagine I enjoy the *patois* of Monsieur Bastien Lefort, and the good-hearted but homely remarks of the wife of the machinist—but I don't!"

"Then why associate with them?"

"That for the present must be my secret! Miss Louise, we have been very good friends on shipboard. Don't go to imagining—don't go to putting two and two together—simply believe that I am just the same kind of an individual as I was five days ago." Then he brings curious joy upon her, for he whispers impulsively, a peculiar light coming into his eyes: "No, *not* the same individual!" and gives the young lady's tempting hand, that has been carelessly lying upon the arm of her steamer-chair, a sudden though deferential squeeze; and with this, leaves her to astonished meditation.

9

She does not see him till dinner, which he eats with
great attention to detail and dishes. But, though he
says very little, every now and then he turns a glance
upon her that destroys her appetite.

At dessert, this is noted by the captain, who in his
affable sailor way, with loud voice suggests : " What's the
matter with your appetite, Miss Louise ? Has the guitar
playing of last night taken it away ? Not a decent meal
since yesterday."

"Oh," replies the young lady, "the weather is too hot
for appetite ! "

"But not for flirtations ! " says the awful sea-dog.
Then he turns a winking eye upon Larchmont, and
chuckles : " Remember, Harry, kisses stop at the gang-
plank ! "

" Not with me ! " says the young man, determination
in his face and significance in his tone : " If I made
love to a girl on shipboard, I should make love to her—
always! I'm no sailor-lover ! " With this parting shot
at the skipper he strolls from the table, and goes away to
after-dinner cigar.

" By Venus, we've a Romeo on board ! " cries the
captain. " Where's the Juliet ? " and turns remorseless
eyes upon Miss Minturn.

Fortunately this little episode has not been noticed by
any of her fellow passengers, nearly all of them having
left the table before Mr. Larchmont.

A moment after, Louise follows the rest on deck, blushes
on her cheeks, brightness in her eyes, elasticity in her
step. She is thinking : " If he loved me, he would love
—*always*. Did he mean that for—" Here wild hope
stops sober thought ; but after this there is a curious dif-
fidence in her manner to Mr. Larchmont, though she does
not avoid his companionship—in fact, from now on, he can
have her society whenever he will, which is very often.

This evening he asks for more songs, and gets them,
perhaps even more soulfully given than the evening
before. So the night passes.

And the next day is another pleasant tropic one, that
the two dream out together under the awnings, with
bright sunshine overhead, and rippling waves, that each
hour grow more blue, running beside them as the great
ship draws near the Equator.

And there is a new something in both their eyes, for the girl has thrown away any defences that her short year's struggle with the world of business may have put about her, and is simply a woman whom love is making more lovely ; and the gentleman has forgotten the conservatism of his conservative class, and is becoming ardent as the sun that puts bronze upon their blushing faces.

So the second evening comes upon them, and the two are again together on the deck, and the strings of the girl's guitar seem softer and her voice is lower.

Then the crowd on deck having melted away, their moonlight *tête à tête*, as the soft blue ripples of the Caribbean roll past them, grows confidential. Drawn out by the young man, Miss Minturn, gives him her past history, which interests him greatly, especially that portion referring to the disappearance of her mother's parents on the Isthmus.

He suggests, " In Panama, perhaps you may learn their fate."

" But that was so long ago," says Louise.

" Nevertheless—supposing you look through your old letters. It won't do any harm. Let me help you. It will give us a pleasant morning's occupation," goes on Harry, quite eagerly.

" Don't you think you could be happy without the letters ? " laughs Louise. Then she suddenly whispers : " Oh, they are putting out the lights ! " and rises to go.

" Blow the lights ! " answers Larchmont, who is out of his steamer-chair, and somehow has got hold of Miss Louise's pretty hand. " Promise the morning to me."

" The whole morning ? "

" Why are you so evasive ? Promise—will you ? "

" Yes, if you will stop squeezing my hand. You—you forget you have football fingers ! " gasps Louise ; for his fervid clasp upon her tender digits is making her writhe.

" Forgive me ! "

" O-o-oh ! "

He has suddenly kissed the hand, and the girl has flown away from him.

At the companion-way she turns, hesitates, then waves adieu, making a picture that would cause any man's heart

to beat.   The moonlight is full upon her, haloing her exquisite figure that is draped in a soft white fluttering
robe that clings about it, and would make it ethereal,
were not its round contours and charming curves of
beauty, those of the very birth of graceful, glorious
womanhood.   One white hand is upraised, motioning
to him ; one little slippered foot is placed upon the
combing of the hatchway.   Her eyes in the moonlight
seem like stars.   Her lips appear to move as she glides
down the companion-way.   Then the stars disappear, and
Harry Larchmont thinks the moon has gone out also.

He sits there meditating, and after a little, his lips
frame the words : "If I did, what would they say ? "
Then rising, he shakes himself like a Newfoundland dog
that is throwing the water from him, tosses his head about,
puts his hand through his curly hair, laughs softly, and
says to himself : " Hanged if I care what anyone says ! "

Curiously enough, he does not go to the card-room
this evening, for he paces the deck for some two hours
more, meditating over three or four cigars that he
smokes in a nervous, excitable, fidgety manner.

The next morning, however, as Miss Louise, a picture
of dainty freshness, steps on the deck, he is apparently
waiting for her.   His looks are eager.   There is perchance
a tone of proprietorship in his voice as, after bidding her
good morning, he says : " A turn or two for exercise
first, then breakfast, and then the letters ! "

" Oh, you are beginning business early to-day," laughs
the young lady, whose eyes seem very bright and happy.

" Yes.   You see I want all your morning."

" Then you will have to read very slowly," suggests
Miss Louise, " or the letters will not occupy you till
lunch time."

" After the letters are finished, there will doubtless be
something else," remarks the young man confidently ; and
in this prediction he is right, though he would stand
aghast if he knew what he prophesied.

So the two go down to breakfast together, and make
a merry meal of it, as the captain, occupied by some ship's
duty, is not there to embarrass them by sea-dog asides
and jovial nautical jokes that bring indignant glances
from the young man, and appealing blushes from the
young lady.

They have finished their oranges when Mr. Larchmont says eagerly : " The letters ! "

" They are too numerous for my pocket ! " answers the girl.

" You have not read them ? "

" Not for years. In fact, I've forgotten all there is in them, except their general tone ; but I fished them out of my trunk last night."

" Very well ! Run to your cabin, and I'll have steamer chairs in the coolest place on deck, where the skipper will be least likely to find us," replies Harry ; and the young lady, doing his bidding, shortly returns to find a cosy seat in the shadiest spot under the awnings, and Mr. Larchmont awaiting her.

" Ah, those are they ! " he says, assisting her, with rather more attention than is absolutely necessary, to the steamer chair beside him, and gazing at a little packet of envelopes grown yellow by time, and tied together with a faded blue ribbon. " These look as if they might contain a good deal."

" Yes," replies the girl, " they contain a mother's heart ! "

Looking over these letters that cover a period of four years, they find that Louise is right. They have been carefully arranged in order. Most of them are simply descriptions of early life in California, and of Alice Ripley's husband's efforts for fortune and final success ; but every line of them is freighted with a mother's love.

The last four bear much more pointedly upon the subject that interests the young man and the young lady. The first of these is a letter describing Alice Ripley and her husband's arrival at San Francisco *en route* for New York, and mentioning that she encloses to her daughter a tintype taken of her by Mr. Edouart, the Californian daguerreotypist.

" You have the picture ? " asks Mr. Larchmont.

" Yes," says the girl. " I brought it with me, thinking you might like to look at it," and shows him the same beautiful face, the same blue eyes and golden hair that had delighted the gaze of Señor Montez in far-away Toboga in 1856.

" It is rather like you," suggests Harry, turning his eyes upon the pretty creature beside him.

"Only a family likeness, I think," remarks the young lady.

"Of course not as beautiful!" asserts the gentleman.

"I wish I agreed with you," laughs Louise. Then she suddenly changes her tone and says: "But we came here to discuss letters, not faces," and devotes herself to the other epistles.

The second is a letter written by Alice Ripley from Acapulco, telling her child that sickness has come upon her; that she is hardly able to write; still, God willing, that she will live through the voyage to again kiss her daughter.

The third, in contradistinction to the others, is in masculine hand-writing, dated April 10th, 1856, and signed "George Merritt Ripley."

"That is from my grandfather," says Louise.

Looking over this letter, Larchmont remarks: "A bold hand and a noble spirit!" for it is a record of a father's love for his only daughter, and it tells of the mother's illness and how he had brought his wife to Panama, fearing death was upon her, but that a kind friend, he has made on the Isthmus, has suggested that he take the invalid to Toboga. That on that island, thank God, the sea breezes are bringing health again to her mother's cheeks.

There is but one letter more, a long one, but hastily written upon a couple of sheets of note paper. This is inside one of Wells, Fargo & Company's envelopes, for in 1856 the express company carried from California to the East, nearly as much mail matter as the United States Government.

It reads as follows:

"PANAMA, *April* 15th, 1856.

"MY DARLING MARY:

"I write this because you will get it one day before your mother's kisses and embraces. Can you understand it? When you receive this, I shall be but *one* day behind it—for it will come with me on the same steamer to New York; but there, though I would fly before it, circumstances are such that it will meet you one day before your mother.

"Tears of joy are in my eyes as I write; for by the blessing of God, once more I am well and happy, and so is your dear father.

" How happy we both are to think that our darling will be in our arms so soon ! We are *en route* to New York. Think of it, Mary— to you ! We left Toboga this morning.

" I am writing this in the Pacific House where we stay to-night, to take the train for Aspinwall to-morrow morning.

" The gentleman who has been so kind to your father and me, has come with us from Toboga, to see the last of us. He has just now gone into the main town of Panama, which gives me time to write this, for your father and I have remained here. It is so much more convenient for us to rest near the station, the trunk is so heavy—the trunk your father is bringing filled with California gold-dust for his little daughter. I have a string of pearls around my neck, which shall be yours also. Papa bought them to-day from Señor Montez."

At this Harry, who has been reading, stops with a gasp, and Louise cries : "Montez ! That's what made Montez, Aguilla et Cie. so familiar ! Montez ! It was the name in this old letter ! " Then she whispers : "How curious ! Can my employer be the man of this letter ? "

" He is ! " answers Harry, for while the girl has been whispering, he has been glancing over the last of the manuscript. He now astounds her by muttering : " See, here's his accursed name ! "

" What do you mean ? " stammers Miss Minturn.

" That afterwards," goes on Mr. Larchmont ; then he hastily reads :

" This gentleman has been inexpressibly kind to us. George says that he saved me from death by the fever, because he took us to the breezes of Toboga.

" On parting, my husband offered him any present that he might select, but Señor Fernando Gomez Montez (what a high-sounding name !) said he would only request something my husband had worn —his revolver, for instance—as a souvenir of our visit.

" I am hastily finishing this, because I am at the end of my paper. There is quite a noise and excitement outside. Papa is going down to see what it is, and will put this letter into Wells, Fargo & Company's mail sack, so that my little daughter may know that her father and mother are just one day behind it—coming to see her grow up to happy womanhood, and blessing God who has been kind to them and given them fortune, so that they may do so much for their idol.

"With a hundred kisses, from both father and mother, my darling, I remain, as I ever shall be,

"Your loving mother,

"ALICE LOUISE RIPLEY.

"P. S.   Next time I shall give the kisses in person ! Think of it ! Lips to lips !"

"Does not this bear a mother's heart ?" whispers Miss Louise, who has tears in her eyes.

"Yes, and the record of a villain !" adds Harry impulsively.

"What do you mean ?"

"I mean this," says the gentleman.   "Last evening you told me that your mother's parents and treasure disappeared during a negro riot upon the Isthmus on April 15th, 1856, the day this letter was written.   Their gold was with them.   That was their doom !   Had they not carried their California dust under their own eyes, they would have lived to embrace their daughter !"

"What makes you guess this ?" asks the girl, her face becoming agitated and surprised.

"I not only guess it—I know it !—and that he had something to do with it !"

."He—who ?"

"Señor Fernando Gomez Montez !"

"Why, this letter speaks of him as a friend who had saved her life !"

"That was to gain the confidence of her husband, so he could betray him.   Why did he ask for George Ripley's revolver, so as to leave him unarmed ?   His nature is the same to-day !   He has also betrayed another bosom friend !" says Harry excitedly.

"Tell me what you know about him !" whispers the girl eagerly.

To this, after a momentary pause of thought, Larchmont replies : "I will—I must !"   And now astounds her, for he mutters : "I need your aid !"

"My aid !   How ?"

"Listen, and I will tell you all in confidence," answers

the young man. Then he looks upon her and mutters :
" You have no interest to betray me ? "

" Betray *you ?* " she cries, " you who saved my life ?
No, no, no ! " and answers his glance.

" Then," says the young man, " listen to the story of a
Franco American fool ! "

" Oh, don't speak of yourself so ! "

"*'" No," he laughs bitterly, chewing the end of his mustache ; " I am referring to my brother ! "

" Oh, your French brother ! " cries the young lady,
" the one your uncle sneered about."

" The one I shall sneer about also, and you will by
the time you know him ! " This explosion over, Mr.
Larchmont goes on contemplatively : " My brother is
not a bad fellow at heart. Had he been brought up
differently, he might have had more force of character,
though I don't think it would have ever been a strong
one."

Then his voice grows bitter as he continues : " There
is a school in New Hampshire, or Vermont, called Saint
Regis, the head-master of which, had he lived in ancient
Greece, would have been promptly and justly condemned,
by an Athenian jury, to drink the juice of hemlock, and
die—*for corrupting the youth of the country ;* because he
makes them unpatriotic and un-American. This gentleman is a foreigner—a man of good breeding, but though
he educates the youth of this country—some five or six
hundred of them—he still despises everything American.
He calls his classes ' Forms,' after the manner of the
English public schools. He frowns upon base-ball because it is American, and encourages cricket because it is
an English game. He tries to make his pupils foreigners,
not Americans. Not that I do not think an English-
man is better for England, or a Frenchman better for
France, but I know that an American is better for
America ! Therefore he injures the youth of the United
States. However, it has become the fashion among certain of our better families in New York to send their
boys to his school, to be taught to despise, practically,
their own country.

" Frank was sent to Saint Regis, and swallowed the unpatriotic microbes his tutor stuffed him with. After he
left there, Yale, Harvard, or Princeton was not good

enough for him.   He must go to a foreign university.
Which, it did not matter—Oxford, Cambridge, Heidel-
berg—anything but an American university.   His guardians foolishly let him have his way.   He took himself
to Europe, ultimately settled in Paris, and practically
forgot his own country, and became, as he calls himself :
François Leroy Larchmont, a Franco-American.

" This would not probably have weakened his character
altogether, for there are strong men in every country,
though when a man becomes unpatriotic, he loses his
manhood ; but with Frank's loss of Americanism, came
the growth of a pride that is now, I am sorry to say,
sometimes seen in our country—the pride of the ' do-
nothing ' ; the feeling that business degrades.   With that
comes worship of title and an hereditary aristocracy,
armorial bearings, and such Old World rubbish."

" Why !   I—I thought you were one of that class ! "
ejaculates Miss Minturn, her eyes big with astonishment.

" Oh !   You think this is a curious diatribe from a man
who has been called one of the Four Hundred, a good
many of whom are devotees of this order," Mr. Larchmont mutters, a grim smile coming over his features.

" Yes, I—I thought you were a butterfly of fashion ! "
stammers the girl.

" So I was—but of *American* fashion !   Now I am a
man who is trying to save his brother ! "

" From what ? " asks Louise.   " From being a Frenchman ? "

" No, from losing his fortune and his honor ! " remarks
Harry so gloomily that the young lady looks at him in
silence.

Then he goes on :   " My brother's worship of title, his
petty pride to be thought great in a foreign capital, got
him into the Panama Canal, and the clutches of Baron
Montez—God knows where he picked up the title.   This
man became my brother's bosom friend, as he became,
twenty odd years before, the bosom friend of the man
whose letter I hold in my hand ! "

He taps the epistle of George Merritt Ripley, and continues :   " This man was a strong man.   He had to be
killed perchance, to secure his treasure.   My brother,
being a weak one, needed only flattery and persuasion."
Then looking at the girl, Harry's tones become persua-

sive ; he says : " I am going to the Isthmus to try and save my brother's fortune, and that of his ward, Miss Jessie Severn, out of which they have been swindled by this man, who probably ruined your chances in life, and made you struggle for livelihood in the workroom when you should have aired your beauty and graces in a ball-room. Will you aid me to force him to do justice to my brother? Your very position, thank God ! will help you to do it ! "

But here surprise and shock come to him. His reference to Miss Severn has been unfortunate.

Miss Minturn says slowly : " My position ?—what do you mean ? "

" You will be the confidential correspondent of his firm. You will perhaps discover the traps by which Montez has purloined my brother's fortune."

" Do you think," cries the girl, " that I will use my confidential position against my employer ? "

" Why not, if he is a scoundrel ? "

" That is not my code. When I became a stenographer I was taught that the confidential nature of my position in honor forced upon me secrecy and silence ! " And growing warm with her subject, Miss Minturn goes on, haughtiness in her voice, and disdain in her eye : " And you made my acquaintance—you tried to gain my friendship, Mr. Larchmont—to ask me to do this ? "

" Good heavens ! I never thought of it before these letters brought home this man's villany to you, as well as to me ! " gasps Harry. " I was simply coming to the Isthmus to fight my brother's battle, to win back for him, if possible, his fortune ! To win back for Miss Severn, her fortune ! "

" And for that," interjects the young lady, " you would make me do a dishonorable—yes, a series of dishonorable acts. You would lure me to act the part of Judas, day by day, to my employer, to bring to you each evening a record of each day's confidences ! How could you think I was base enough for this ? How could you ? "

Then seizing the letters that have brought this quarrel upon them, and wiping indignant tears from her eyes, she whispers with pale lips : " Good-by, Mr. Larchmont ! "

" Good-by ? "

"Yes, good-by! I do not care to know a gentleman who thinks I could do what you have asked me!"

She sweeps away from him to her own stateroom, where she bursts into tears; for, curiously enough, it is not entirely his hurried, perhaps thoughtless proposition, that makes her miserable, and has produced her paroxysm of wrath—it is the idea that he is fighting for Miss Severn's fortune. "He loves her," sobs the girl to herself, "and for that reason he would have made me his tool to give her wealth."

After she has left him, Mr. Larchmont utters a prolonged but melancholy whistle. Then he suddenly says: "Who can divine a woman? A man, thinking he had lost a fortune through this villain Montez, would have seized my hand, and become my comrade, to compel the scoundrel to do justice to us both! But she—" Then he meditates again, and says slowly: "I wonder—was there any woman's reason for this? Her eyes—her beautiful eyes—had some subtle emotion in them that was not wholly indignation. They looked wounded—by something more than a business proposition!"

Then a sudden pallor and fright come upon this young Ajax, as he falters to himself: "Great heavens! if she *never* forgives me!"

CHAPTER XIV.

LITTLE PARIS.

NEITHER Harry Larchmont nor Miss Louise Minturn make their appearance at lunch this afternoon upon the *Colon.*

At dinner, only monosyllables pass between them, which the captain noticing whispers into Miss Louise's pink ear to make it red: "Didn't I tell you kisses stop at the gang-plank?"

Just here the sea-dog's attention is fortunately attracted by what is happening to another young lady under his charge.

Miss Madeline Stockwell, the pretty girl who is going to California to be married to the Los Angeles orange-grower, oblivious of the vows she is journeying to take, has been indulging in a flirtation with the young Costa Rican, which has gradually grown from mild to tempestuous ; from tepid to boiling hot !

This young gentleman, not understanding English very well, has failed to catch what has been generally known about the ship, of this young lady's engagement. But now, the voyage drawing to a close, some one has been kind enough to inform him, in good Spanish, that Miss Madeline, who has entangled him in the silken meshes of love, and whose bright eyes have grown to be very beautiful to him, and whom he has had wild dreams of transporting, after Church ceremony of course, to his coffee plantation near San José, is already promised to another !

So all the afternoon Don Diego Alvarez has been going about with a Tibault glare in his eyes, and is now eating his dinner in a gloomy, vindictive manner, cutting into his salad as he would into the orange farmer's throat, were he within knife reach.

Soon after, all go on deck.

Here is his opportunity. He steps towards the pretty Madeline, who has been hiding from him in her stateroom most of the day, and whispers something in her ear, at which she turns deathly pale, for she is now mortally frightened at this demon of Spanish love that she has conjured up, and that will not down.

Noting this, the skipper, laying his hand on Larchmont's shoulder, whispers to him : "Harry, will you do me a favor ? "

" Certainly, if possible."

" Well, here is a matter in which I cannot interfere unless I go to extreme methods. Young Alvarez is frightening that foolish girl. She has been silly enough to encourage him, and Spanish blood, when encouraged and then jilted, is sometimes obstreperous. Now you kindly take care of the young lady this evening. To-morrow morning we will be at Colon, and after I have landed her, pretty Miss Madeline Stockwell can handle a Spanish flirtation as she pleases. Don't leave her alone with him—that's a good fellow ! "

Now Mr. Harry is exactly in the mood for something desperate himself. He has just had another short but exciting *tête-à-tête* with Miss Minturn, in a little dark spot of the deck that the rising moon has not yet intruded on.

"You have not changed your mind about me, I see?"
he has whispered, noting that Louise's eyes are still
uncompromising in expression.

"Certainly not ; about your proposition!"

"And you accuse me of attempting to gain your
friendship with the idea of making it?" the young man
has asked hotly.

"It would seem so.   Why else?"

"Why else?   You are too modest.   Don't you think,"
he has gone on warmly, "that you have other attractions
than being the stenographer of Baron Montez?   Didn't
I treat you with consideration before that?   Did I ask
your aid until those accursed letters showed me that you
were probably his victim as well as my brother and
Jessie?"

"Oh, it is for Miss Severn's sake that you ask me to
do a thing I consider dishonorable?   Learn that I consider a stenographer's conscience as valuable as an heiress's money!" the girl has muttered very haughtily, for
her position makes her over-sensitive.   "Please do not
speak to me again until you remember it also!"

So turning away, she has left Larchmont in a very bad
humor, for he feels he is badly treated.   He has muttered to himself sarcastically : "I wonder if she thinks I
saved her from the snow that night, because I *divined*
she was going to be the stenographer of Montez, Aguilla
et Cie.?   She's as unjust as she is beautiful."

Consequently at present Harry is about the worst person the captain could have chosen to pour oil upon the
troubled waters of Miss Madeline Stockwell's flirtation,
although he accepts the office with alacrity.   He whispers
to the skipper : "See me cut the Costa Rican out!" then
proceeds to join a *tête-à-tête* that is becoming exciting ;
for young Alvarez has just placed his hand upon his
heart, and said with a rolling of the eyes : "Señorita,
remember it is his life or my own!   Tell that to your
orange rancher!"

"Good evening, Miss Madeline!" interjects Harry ;
and is very effusively received by the girl, who would be
pleased at any time to receive attentions from this *élève*
of New York society, but at this moment would be
happy to have Old Nick himself intrude upon her interview with Don Diego.

It is a little trembling hand that the American takes in his as Miss Stockwell whispers nervously : " I—I am delighted to see you, Mr. Larchmont. Permit me to present Señor Alvarez. I—I cannot always understand his Spanish. He speaks so fast and ex—excitedly."

"Can't understand him, eh?" says Harry ; "then permit me to be your interpreter ;" and coolly places a steamer-chair between the young Costa Rican and his *inamorata.*

Next turning upon the astonished Don, he mutters rather surlily : "Supposing you say to me what you were going to say to her."

"Say to you, *Americano,*" gasps the astounded Alvarez, "what I was going to say to the light of my soul, the Señorita Madeline?" Then looking at the American contemptuously, he says : "Bah! you do not interest me !"

"Don't I?" replies Harry courteously. "Then perhaps Miss Maddy will be kinder to me. Don't you think a promenade this pleasant night would suit you?" and he offers his arm to flirtatious Miss Stockwell, and takes her away, leaving the Costa Rican grinding his teeth at him, for Mr. Larchmont has a very tender manner with pretty girls, and Alvarez, noting his devotion to the young lady in the moonlight, includes him in his vendetta with the orange farmer, as rival number two.

Harry's attentions to Miss Stockwell are not unobserved by Miss Minturn, who thinks to herself : "He has not succeeded in gaining me over to his plans. Therefore I am of no more interest to him. See how he *proves* the truth of what I accuse him !" This feminine logic makes Louise's heart grow very hard to Harry Larchmont, as he paces the deck of the *Colon,* whispering idle nothings to Miss Madeline Stockwell ; for this young lady has a habit of thinking all men in love with her, and rolls her eyes most affectionately at the big fashionable creature, who she thinks has fallen before her charms.

So Louise, growing desperate, mutters to herself : "If he shows indifference, why not I?" And Herr Alsatius Wernig chancing to come along, she receives his effusive attentions with a great deal more kindness than she has hitherto shown to him, and puts him in the seventh heaven of expectant delight, though ever and anon Mr.

Larchmont turns an evil eye upon her, as he passes her on the deck.

Consequently Miss Louise Minturn and Mr. Harry Larchmont, who had greeted each other this morning so warmly, go to bed this evening with bitter feelings in their hearts towards each other. Not the bitterness of hate, but the bitterness of love, which is sometimes equally potent, and ofttimes produces as unpleasant results.

As for Miss Stockwell, she is radiantly happy. She imagines she has got rid of one flirtation that bothered her, and taken up another that she thinks will not bother her.

Later in the evening, Mr. Larchmont, after packing his baggage, and getting in general order for going ashore next day at Colon, sits down and writes a letter, giving to it one or two sighs, and one or two imprecations ; and just before going to bed, remarks : "So far, I don't think my trip to Panama has been a success ! " for this very evening he has added another enemy to his list—Don Diego Alvarez, the Costa Rican.

The next morning, bright and early, every one is up, for land has been sighted !

From the deck, they see the distant Andes of South America.

Then, after a time, from out its mists, they can distinguish the *Tierras Calientes*, that rise, a mass of tropical verdure, before them : from which, wafted by breezes over sparkling waves, are the odors of myriad plants and flowers. For what has been blustering, chilly spring in New York, is now early summer under the Equator.

Then churning the blue waters, the great ship enters Navy Bay, and before them lies Manzinillo Island, on which stands the town of Colon—a mass of low red brick structures, brightened here and there by palm trees ; embellished on its sea side by a number of parallel wharves that go straight into the bay, lined with the shipping of all nations.

To their left are the pretty residences of the officers of the canal, on the Island of Christophe Colon, to which a causeway has been filled in, at great expense, by the ever-lavish Canal Interoceanic.

Then the steamer running into her dock, ranges alongside the wharf, and ties up to it.

All of this would have been noted with a good deal of interest by Miss Minturn, did not a more personal matter take up her attention.

In the last moments of a voyage, just before landing, some of the niceties of ship etiquette are forgotten ; and taking advantage of this, a pleasant-looking round-faced woman, very neatly dressed, and leading by the hand a pretty child, leaves the second cabin, and coming to Miss Louise, presents a letter saying : " Mr. Larchmont asked me to give you this."

Looking over it, the girl is astonished by the following :

Steamer Colon, March 30th, 1888.

"DEAR MISS MINTURN :

" Though you may consider it an impertinence, I take the liberty of making this suggestion to you. I have been thinking over the position in which you will be placed—a young lady, unknown, and alone in a foreign city—Panama.

" Of course the firm by whom you are engaged, and Mr. Stuart, will do everything they can for your comfort ; but still perhaps the matter of domicile may be a difficult one to you. You should have a home with some company and some protection.

" Under the circumstances I venture to suggest to your favorable consideration, Mrs. Silas Winterburn. She has rooms and board in the Spanish family of an old notary named Martinez, in Panama— that is, when she is not with her husband, who is stationed with his dredger at this end of the Canal.

" The Martinez family, she informs me, will be able to accommodate you, at a reasonable figure. Consequently I presume to mention this to you.

" Yours most respectfully,

" HARRY STURGIS LARCHMONT."

Looking at these words, the girl sees the handwriting that came on the card with the violets, and her heart grows softer to the gentleman whose hand has penned this note.

She says to the woman : " I am happy to meet you, Mrs. Winterburn. Mr. Larchmont has been kind enough to mention that you could assist me in obtaining a domicile in Panama ; " and holds out a welcoming hand.

This is cordially gripped by the woman, who replies :

"Thank you very kindly! I hope you will come with me. It will be so nice to have some one to talk to in English. The other time I was there, I did not understand Spanish, or French, and it was so lonely!"

As she says this, the steamer is at the wharf, and Louise finds herself face to face with a kindly-looking florid gentleman, whom the captain introduces as Mr. Stuart of the Pacific Mail, and to whom Miss Minturn presents her letter of introduction.

As he is reading it, Mrs. Silas Winterburn and her pretty child have been hugged, kissed, and hugged again, by a peculiar-looking man, who was once tall, but has apparently been shrivelled by the sun from six feet one to five feet ten.

"Miss Minturn, this is my husband!" says the woman very proudly.

And the man adds: "By Plymouth Rock and Sanctus Dominus! I'm almighty glad to grip such a pretty girl by the hand."

"Oh, how do you do, Winterburn?" remarks Stuart cordially, looking at the mechanic.

"Quite spryish, governor," is the answer.

Here Miss Minturn takes opportunity of explaining what Mr. Larchmont had suggested in the letter.

After a moment's consideration, Mr. Stuart says: " I really think that would be the best plan for you in Panama. Of course I shall see you safely on board the cars, and that all preparations are made for your pleasant transport across the Isthmus. But though I can engage rooms for you in Panama, by telegraph, I do not think for a young lady situated as you are, they will be as pleasant as those in the family of old Martinez, the notary, where you will have at least American society and the protection of honest Silas Winterburn and his wife."

"Oh, everybody knows me," remarks Silas, "from Colon to Panama, and from the Atrato to Chìriqui! I am the American pioneer of the Isthmus!"

"The pioneer of the Isthmus?" echoes Louise, astonished.

"Yes! *Caramba!* I beg your pardon!—I beg *your* pardon! I sometimes swear in Spanish from force of habit. I was a fireman on the first through train on the railway in '55."

" And have you been here ever since ? "

" I've buried three families here, of yellow fever," says the man, wiping a tear from his eye. Then he goes on in a happier voice : " But I've got started with number four ! " And looking with loving eyes upon his wife, he whispers : " I think she'll last me through. The other three were timid things from factories in Mass'chusotts, and most died of fright at the thought of Yellow Jack ! "

This is said in a manner that astonishes Miss Minturn, for Silas seems to suffer agony at the remembrance of his three lost families, but to be equally happy in the contemplation of the present one.

By this time they have all got ashore, Louise noting that Mr. Larchmont is well ahead of her, and already in conversation with one or two officers of the Panama Railroad, who chance to be Americans he has seen in New York. This young man's chief object now seems to be to make acquaintance with everybody on the Isthmus, and apparently he is succeeding.

Then genial Mr. Stuart shows his pretty charge over the town, which consists chiefly of two rows of houses and stores running the length of the island, with the Panama Railroad shops on the south end of it, and the attachment called Christophe Colon at the north, and the canal, which is the Chagres River turned from its course, running past it : all this with a few palm and cocoanut trees thrown in, a mangrove swamp behind it, and a series of wharves in front of it that run out into the blue waves and soft surf which ripples upon a beach of coral sand.

Half an hour of this is sufficient ; then Mr. Stuart puts Louise on the train beside Mrs. Winterburn, the happy Silas and his little daughter occupying the opposite seat. The cars are crowded by a heterogeneous mass of foreigners. The bulk of the conversation however is French, for this canal with its thousand officers and myriad laborers in 1888, had made the Isthmus from Colon to Panama practically a French colony.

Mr. Larchmont is not on the car in which Miss Minturn is seated. Therefore she does not speak to him, though she would have liked to ; for she is beginning to repent of her hasty expressions towards him, which had been caused not only by his proposition, but by Miss Severn's connection with it.

She is even now thinking, "His letter this morning brought me protection, when I had treated him harshly. He has done me *many* kindnesses; and I have refused to do him *one !* I don't think I could ever bring myself to his proposition, still I forgive him for making it. Yesterday, jealousy made me cruel!"

Then she mutters to herself: "Jealousy! Pshaw! I am not jealous! Whom am I jealous of?" And glares around as if to find out the person on the train, but only catches the eye of Mr. Winterburn.

This eccentric says: "What's the matter, sissy? Are you looking for a beau? There's plenty here. *Por Dios !* I beg your pardon for the swear. Most every one's unmarried about here. By all the saints in the Cathedral! bachelors and widowers predominate."

"You—you seem to be very well acquainted with the Isthmus, Mr. Winterburn," stammers the girl, throwing off meditation. "You say you are a pioneer?"

"Yes, had the fever in 1856 and got acclimated. Since then I have found it as healthy as the Penobscot—for me! Other people sicken and die, but I thrive. I reckon, when we were building this railroad, we planted a man for every tie. Now I think the Canal is even beatin' our average."

This eulogium upon the climate of the Isthmus gives Louise a shiver; she turns the conversation by suggesting: "You must have seen many curious things here?"

"Yes, everything from revolution and riot, to balls and fandangos."

"Revolution and riot!" says the girl, and is about to ask him something eagerly, when glancing out of the car window she suddenly ejaculates: "How beautiful! How fairylike!"

For the train has run out of Colon, and leaving the island, is dashing through the swamps of the Mindee that are fairylike in beauty, but awful in miasma and death.

So they come to the mainland with its rank vegetation, in which are trees of a myriad species, flowers of a thousand hues, vines and creeping plants, each different from the other, making a thicket that is a garden.

So passing Monkey Hill, they reach Gatun, getting here a first glimpse of the main Chagres ; and turning up its valley, the cars run under great lignum vitæ trees covered with parasites, and palms of every species, from the giant *grandé* to those of smaller stem and more feathery leaves.

Every now and then, they pass a little native *rancho* with its thatched roof, and inevitable banana plantation. These are varied by occasional orange groves, and now and then a glimpse of the Chagres River, quiet and limpid in this the dry season, and rippling peaceably between banks of living green to the Caribbean. It is now disturbed, here and there, by the huge dredgers of the American Company—great masses of machinery that scrape the mud of the river from its bottom, to build up side walls to protect its banks.

" It is one of them fellows that I work on as engineer, Miss Minturn," says Winterburn, looking up from his little daughter, who has grown tired, and is sleeping contentedly in his lap.

Now and again they get glimpses of trading stations for canal laborers, some of them kept by Chinamen, till finally they arrive at Bohio Soldado.

"That's my place of residence ! " ejaculates Silas, who has now become communicative. " But I've three days leave, and so I'll see you and the old lady through to Panama. Do you note that p'int ? " he says, after twenty minutes more travel, " that's the head of the dredging, and from there on, the Canal Company tackles not mud, but rocks. And rocks," here he whispers to the girl, a curious twinkle in his eye, " is what'll down 'em ! "

And then passing the great bridge over the river at Barbacoas they run up the other bank to Gargona, and from that on, by gradually increasing grades, come to Culebra, where the Canal people have their deepest cut to make.

" Oh, goodness ! " cries the girl, " what an enormous excavation ! "

" It's the biggest in the world," answers Silas. Then he whispers confidentially, " But there is five times as much more to dig."

" Why," cries Louise, " they'll never do it ! "

" Not this trip ! *Por la Madre !* assents Winterburn solemnly.

But other views drive Culebra from the girl's mind. They are descending the mountain ; before them the great savanna that leads to Panama, and the white waters of the Pacific. Running down through hills that gradually become smaller, they come to the Rio Grande station, and first see the river that is to be the western waters of the canal.

From there on, dashing over savannas ever green, they note at their right hand, some gray buildings on a hill.

" That's the Canal yellow-fever hospitals, where the poor critters will get a little breeze," says Silas, eager to do the honors of the Isthmus.

But leaving these, three miles away they run into a little station where carriages with native drivers are waiting for them, to drag them through dirty lanes into the town of Panama itself.

This is now a little Paris. French people jabber about them at the station, and the language of Normandy and Brittany dominates the Spanish tongue ; for *la belle France* has come over the Isthmus to capture Panama.

Twice before this has been attempted. Twice with success ! Once Morgan and his daring band of every-nation freebooters came up the Chagres, and conquering, bore away with them the treasures of the western ocean. Then American enterprise fought its way with iron rail through the swamps of the Mindee, and up the valley of the Chagres, and through the gate of the mountains, and reached this town, to take its tribute from the commerce of the world, and pay to stockholders the dividends of Dives.

And now comes France—not to cross the Isthmus, but to drive through it, and thus levy toll upon the navies of the sea !

The Isthmus, subdued twice, will it be conquered again ? Nature—the awful giant nature of the tropics—will it triumph ? Will this land go back to nature, and become silent as when the Spanish *Conquestadores* first landed on its shores to make the Indians curse the white sails which bore to them a Christianity that came with blood and bigotry, to make them slaves ?

BOOK IV.

THE STRUGGLE IN PANAMA.

CHAPTER XV.

WINTERBURN'S MUSEUM.

STRIKING a bargain with a mulatto charioteer, half in the English tongue, half in Spanish, Winterburn procures a carriage, and the party take route up the lane leading from the railway station ; and passing into the old town of Panama, between houses whose balconies come very close together, they reach the *Calle del Catedral* or Main Street.

A moment after, Miss Minturn gives an exclamation of pleasure, for they have come out on the great plaza of the town, and the sunshine is upon it, making it look very bright and pleasant compared to the dark streets through which they have passed.

They drive along this, past a little *café*, with seats and tables on the sidewalk, after the manner of Paris, and then in front of the old Grand Hotel—the one in which Montez had made the acquaintance of the Franco-American. This is now devoted to the offices of the Panama Canal Company—the upper floors being used for business purposes, and the lower one being turned into a general club full of billiard-tables for the use of its employees ; all lavishly paid for by the money of the stock-holders.

Then they come to another *café* or restaurant, more elaborate than the first, whose tables and chairs are upon the sidewalk like those of the grand Boulevard *cafés* in far-off Paris. Turning the corner, across the Plaza with

its walks and tropic plants, the girl sees the great Cathedral of Panama, old with the dust of centuries.   But this
is distant and ancient; and the Grand Central Hotel and
a lot of offices are near her and modern.

At the old Club International, they turn away from the
Plaza and go towards the sea wall and the 'Battery;'
and after passing through more narrow streets with overhanging verandas, they come to the house of the notary,
Martinez.

Here Mrs. Winterburn is received in voluble Spanish,
by the wife of the official, a Creole lady of about thirty-
five, but looking much older, and her numerous progeny ; all of them daughters, ranging from twenty-two
to fourteen, and all of them, in this rapid sunny part of
the world, of marriageable age.

Louise's Spanish soon makes them her friends, and she
finds herself settled very comfortably in a room that
looks out over a wide veranda on a little *patio*, or enclosed
courtyard, around which the house is built.   This courtyard has a few plants and flowers, in contradistinction
to most of the Panama *patios*, whose inhabitants are too
lazy to put into the earth anything that merely beautifies,
though the land only requires planting to blossom like
Sharon's Vale.   Her apartment is up one flight of stairs,
for there are stores underneath, and the family, as in
most of the Spanish portions of Panama, live over
them.

. Inspection discloses to Miss Minturn that she has a
clean room, with whitewashed walls and matting upon
the floor ; a white-sheeted bed, and a few other articles
of furniture that are comfortable, though not luxurious.
At one end of her room swings a hammock.

"Hammock, or bed!   You can take your choice, señorita!" laughs the old Spanish lady.   "But if you take my
advice, you will choose the hammock—it's cooler!" and
leaves her alone.

Then Louise looking around, finds there is a veranda
overhanging the street, to which a door leads directly
from her room.   With this open there is a very good
draught, which is pleasant, as it is now the sultry portion
of the afternoon.

Soon her trunk, which has been attended to by kindly
old Winterburn, arrives, and the girl unpacking it, makes

her preparations for permanent stay, and looking out on the prospect, thinks : " How different this is to Seventeenth Street in New York ! " Then she murmurs : " How quiet ! and this for a whole year ! " and sadness would come upon her ; but she remembers there are Anglo-Saxon friends in the house with her. She thinks, " Were it not for his thoughtfulness I should be alone and home-sick. And I was unkind to him—not because of his proposition, but because "—then cries—" I hate her anyway ! "

After this spurt of emotion, being tired with the railroad trip, and worried over Mr. Larchmont, Louise thinks she will take, after the manner of the Spanish, a *siesta* and forget everything ; and climbs into her hammock.

Being unused to this swinging bedstead, she gives a sudden shriek, for she finds herself grovelling on the floor ; the management of this comfort of the tropics not being an accomplishment that is acquired in one *siesta*.

But the heat will not let her sleep, so she goes into a day-dream, from which she is aroused by one of the young ladies of the household coming in, and crying : " Señorita Luisa, I have brought you some cigarettes ! "

" For me ? I never smoke ! " laughs the American girl, partly in dismay, partly in astonishment.

" Not smoke ?—and you speak Spanish ! " says the Isthmus maiden in supreme surprise. " Let me teach you ! "

She lights up, and lolls upon the bedstead, telling the young American lady, to whom she seems to have taken a great fancy, that her name is Isabel, but all who love her call her Belita, giving out incidentally the *petite* gossip of Panama, between deft puffs of smoke that rise in graceful rings about her.

Louise sits looking at her dreamily, thinking that Panama is a very quaint and quiet place, as it is to her, this afternoon.

Mr. Larchmont's experiences, however, are different. He drives into the town over much the same road as the Winterburns have taken, but stops at the Grand Hotel, and would engage a suite of apartments of most extraordinary extent and price for a man depending upon the salary of a clerk in the Pacific Mail Steamship Company, or any other clerk for that matter, except, perhaps, some of the Canal Company, who are paid most extravagant prices ; but suddenly Harry remembers he is supposed only to have one hundred and fifty dollars a month for his stipend, grows economical, and chooses quarters that do not please him and make him swear—this luxurious young man.

Then having made himself as comfortable as the heat will permit, attired in the whitest linen, and a wide-brimmed *sombrero de Guayaquil,* which he has purchased in the French bazaar as he drove into town, Harry Larchmont steps out to see the sights of this arena upon which he has come two thousand miles, like a knight of old, to do battle for a young maiden, against the giant who has her in his toils.

Like Amadis de Gaul and Saint George of Merry England, on his journeying he has found another Queen of Beauty to look upon the combat ; and though her place is not on the imperial daïs, and under its velvet canopy, still one smile from her would make his arm more potent, his sword more trenchant, his charge more irresistible, and nerve him to greater deeds of "daring do," than those of the maiden for whom he battles, or those of any other maid in Christendom.

So with chivalry in his heart, and a great wish to strike down Baron Montez, the evil champion opposed to him, though scarcely knowing where to find rent in his armor of proof, Sir Harry of Manhattan steps out upon the *Plaza de Panama,* to see a pretty but curious sight.

A Spanish town turned into a French one !

Not some quaint old village of Brittany, or Normandy, but a bright, dashing, happy-go-lucky, "*Mon Dieu!*" Can-can, French town ! In fact, a little part of gay Paris transferred to the shores of the Pacific. A modern French picture in an old Spanish frame.

As he leaves the hotel, the *Café Bethancourt,* just across the street, is filling up with young Frenchmen arrayed very much as they would be on the *Champs Élysées* or *Boulevard des Italiens.* They have come in, as they would in *la belle Paris,* to drink their afternoon absinthe.

Open carriages, barouches, landaus, are carrying the magnates of the Canal management, with their wives and their children—or perhaps some one else—about the Plaza preparatory to their drive to the Savanna ; which, unheed-

ing the mists of the evening, they will take as they would
in the *Bois du Boulogne*, though the miasma of one breeds
death, and the breezes of the other bring life.

All this looks very pretty to the gentleman as he strolls
through the Plaza, between green plants and over smooth
walks, and notes that about this great square none of
the surrounding buildings, save the great Cathedral and
the Bishop's Palace, have now the air of old Spain. The
rest have become modern Parisian *cafés*, offices, hotels,
bazaars, or *magazins*.

After a few moments' contemplation of this, the young
man says to himself : "But I came here for work !
To discover the weak spots in this villain's armor, it is
necessary for me to know those who are acquainted with
him, those who have business with him ; in fact, the world
of Panama ! And to become acquainted with these novel
surroundings, first my letters of introduction."

So he starts off, and after a few inquiries, finds the office of the American Consul General, which is just opposite the Bishop's Palace, in the *Calle de Comercio*.

Fortunately this dignitary is at home, and Harry, pre-
senting his credentials, is most affably received, for his
letters bear very strong names both socially and politically, in the United States.

"I'll put you up at the Club International immediately," says the official. "There you will meet everybody ! Supposing you drop in there with me this
evening ? "

"Delighted ! " returns Harry, "provided you will dine
with me first—where do they give the best dinners ? "

"Oh, Bethancourt's as good as any."

"Well, dine with me there, will you ? Half-past seven,
I suppose 'll be about the hour."

"With pleasure," answers the representative of America. And Mr. Larchmont, noting the official has business
on his hands, leaves him and saunters off to kill time till
the dinner hour, curiously enough asking the way to the
house of Martinez the notary, but contenting himself
with walking past and giving a searching glance at its
windows, though he does not go in.

Then he strolls back to the hotel to dress, and being
joined by the consul the two go to the swell *café* of Panama, where Mr. Larchmont gives the representative of

Uncle Sam a dinner that makes him open his eyes and
sets him to thinking, " What wondrous clerk has the
Pacific Mail Company got, who spends half a month's salary upon a *tête-à-tête* and that to a gentleman ? Egad, I'd
like to see this young Lucullus entertain ladies ! " a wish
this gentleman has granted within the next few days, in a
manner that makes him and the whole town of Panama
open their eyes ; for Harry suddenly goes to playing
a game at which he cannot be economical.

This comes about in this manner. Larchmont and his
new friend are enjoying their coffee, seated at one of the
tables outside ; scraps of conversation coming to them
from surrounding tables.

The one next to them is occupied by two excitable
and high-voiced Frenchmen, one an *habitué* of the Isthmus ; the other a later arrival.

" I wish," says the new-comer, " that I could get some
definite word out of Aguilla about their contract with
me.   But he puts me off, saying that Montez when he
arrives will attend to it.   Now Baron Fernando likes the
great Paris better than the little one.   He has not been
here for a year.   I am waiting two months, and I'm
rather fatigued ! "

" You won't have to wait much longer," laughs his
companion, the Panama *habitué*.   " Baron Fernando will
shortly arrive."

" Ah, has his partner told you ? "

. " No, Aguilla never says anything."

" Then how do you know ? "

" How ? " says the old resident, with a wisely wicked.
smile.   " By that ! " and he points to a placard hanging
on a wall near by.   Following his glance Harry Larchmont sees that it announces that Mademoiselle Bébé de
Champs Élysées of the Palais Royal, Paris, will shortly
make her appearance at the Panama Theatre.

" When Mademoiselle Bébé is announced, Baron Montez very shortly afterwards steps on the stage," continues the gentleman at the table.

" Ah, she is a friend of his ? " queries the other.

" *Sans doute !*   So much of a friend that she never
comes here without her *cher ami*, Baron Montez, arriving
very shortly after her."

" You seem interested in the conversation next us,

Larchmont," whispers the consul. "Do you know the famed Baron Montez?"

"A little!" answers Harry abstractedly, for he has just thought what he thinks a great thought, and is pleased with himself.

It is something after this style : "Perhaps here is a flaw in my enemy's armor of proof. Perchance Mademoiselle Bébé de Champs Élysées has the confidences of her *cher ami* my adversary. Mayhap from her I can gain some knowledge that may give me vantage over him!" Then he laughs to himself quite merrily. "By Jove! what great friends Mademoiselle Bébé and I shall be!"

With this rather unknightly idea in his mind, the young gentleman proceeds to pump the consul and everyone else he meets this evening, about the coming dramatic star at the Panama Theatre, and very shortly discovers that De Champs Élysées is a young lady, who, though she is by no means prominent on the Parisian boards, is considered a great card in Panama.

This has been chiefly owing to the push that has been given to her artistic celebrity by the devotion of Baron Fernando, who has lavished a good deal of money and a good deal of time upon this fair *élève* of the *cafés chantants* and the Palais Royal.

After a little, anxious to learn more about her, Harry proposes to his guest that they drop into the theatre. So they saunter to the temple of Thespis where a Spanish opera company that has come up from Peru is giving "High Life in Madrid," which is so much like high life in Paris embellished by the chachucha and fandango instead of the can-can, that it greatly pleases the mixed French and Spanish audience.

Though every one else is interested in the performance, Mr. Larchmont is not. He is devoting himself to discovering all about the attraction that is to follow it. Getting acquainted with one of the *attachés* of the theatre, he learns that Mademoiselle Bébé de Champs Élysées will arrive within a day or two, and appear probably the next Monday. That she is not a very great singer ; that she is not a very great actress ; that she is not a very great dancer ; but that she is "a very *diable*," as the old doorkeeper expresses it.

"However, Monsieur is young, handsome, and I hope rich. So he can soon see for himself," suggests the old man with a French shrug of the shoulders.

The opera over, Harry and the American official go to the Club International, which has been moved from its former quarters on the Grand Plaza, to a house called "The Washington," somewhat nearer the railroad, and in the old Spanish quarter. Here they find some billiard-playing, some chess, and lots of Frenchmen, Spaniards, and in fact a good deal of the male high life of Panama.

Mr. Larchmont is introduced right and left, and being anxious to make *friends*, soon has lots of *acquaintances*, for his off-hand manner wins everybody. All that he learns here, using both tongue and ears with all their might, satisfies him on one point, and that is, that Mademoiselle Bébé de Champs Élysées will know the secret thoughts of Baron Fernando Montez, if any one does.

So he chuckles to himself : "I'll nail this scoundrel Samson of Panama by this naughty Delilah of Paris!" and considers himself a very great diplomat, and a wonderful card-player in the game of life, as he goes to bed about three o'clock in the morning, which is a rather bad time for an industrious clerk to retire to rest, if he wishes to be at his duties in the Pacific Mail Steamship Company's offices early the next morning.

But even as Harry turns into bed, he mutters : "If she had been kinder, I should not have done this thing!"

Still, notwithstanding his buoyant nature that considers half the battle won, this young gentleman, as he closes his eyes, gives half a sigh, and wonders what has been lacking in his life this day ; then suddenly becomes wide awake, as he mutters : "By Jove! I have not seen her face—I have not looked into her eyes—or heard her voice for twenty-four hours!"

Next grows angry and indignant and cries out : "Hang it! I *will* go to sleep. No woman shall keep me awake!"

But notwithstanding this determination, he tosses about on a sleepless bed for an hour or two, and wonders if it is the mosquitoes of Little Paris.

As for the object of his thoughts, she has passed a quiet evening with the Winterburns, and the family of old Martinez, who has lived a long time upon the Isthmus, and tells her anecdotes of the earlier days of Panama, before it became, as he calls it, " a French colony."

Some of his daughters are musical, and Louise and they sing snatches of the old operas together, in duos, trios, and quartettes, to the accompaniment of mandolin and guitar ; music which seems in keeping with the tropic evening and quiet of this Spanish portion of ,,Panama, which is half deserted after nightfall.

Winterburn breaks in after each selection with a quaint mixture of American applause and Spanish bravos, some-times saying with a sigh : " To-morrow I'll have to be going off to work on my Chagres dredger again at Bohio Soldado."

" You have lived on the Isthmus a long time," remarks Miss Louise. " I suppose now you're used to it."

" Well, yes, pretty well. I've been on it so long that I know everything about it."

Then he astonishes the girl, by ejaculating suddenly : " Would you like to see my museum ? "

" Your what ? " asks Louise.

" My collection of curiosities. I've got most enough to run a dime show, in the U. S. Just let me add a couple of San Blas Indians, a live crocodile, an anaconda, and throw in a Spanish dancing girl, and the pen with which De Lesseps signs Panama bonds, and *diablo !* I will do a fine business on the Bowery ! "

" The Bowery ! " says his wife. " Why, Silas, have you ever seen the Bowery ? "

"Yes, I saw it on my third wedding tour, ten years ago," he remarks contemplatively. " Sally—she was the one before you—was very much taken with it also. I'll give you a show at it, too, Susie, some day."

On this cheering remark Miss Minturn breaks in, say-ing : " The museum, quick ! "

" Then I'll accommodate ! " replies Silas genially. " I always like to accommodate pretty girls, even when they're thick as candles in a cathedral, as they are about here," and he looks around at the various señoritas of the Martinez family, with a jovial chuckle, and a horrible *soto voce* remark : " Perhaps some day, if I live long enough, I'll be marryin' one of ye."

So they all troop into a big room at the end of the house, which had once been occupied by domestic *impedimenta* of the Martinez family that are now crowded out by the collection of this pioneer of the Isthmus.

It is a conglomeration of odds and ends picked up in nearly forty years of the Tropics. This he proceeds to walk around, giving a lecture very much after the manner of exhibitors of similar collections in the United States.

"Here," he says, "ladies and gentlemen, is the first spike that was ever driven in the Panama Railroad. I know it's genuine, for I pried it out and stole it myself.

"This," he shouts, pointing to a hideous saurian of tremendous size, "is an alligator I killed myself down on the Mindee in '55. There were lots of them there in those days—big fellers ! This chap is reported to have eaten a native child, but I don't guarantee that !

"Here," and he points to some curious images, "are some of the old statues taken from Chiriqui temples. Dug 'em up myself, and can swear to their bein' the *real* genuine. Archæologists declare that they take us back as far as the times of most ancient record, equivalent to days of Pharo's Egypt.

"Lot number four is a bottle of snakes of my own killin' also. The one with the big head is what the natives call the Mapana down on the Atrato, whose bite is certain death. Here is a Coral, likewise deadly. Killed it in the ruins of old Panama. And that reminds me—by-the-by, Miss Louise, I want to give you a little advice about snakes in this country. Most people will tell you there ain't none about here. So there ain't, in town here, and along the works of the Panama Canal and Railroad. But I remember in the days in old Gargona, when the passengers went down from the board hotel to take boat for Cruces early in the morning, and a negro boy always went ahead, swinging a lantern, to scare the crepeers away. When you go into the country, you wear high boots, and don't skip around old trees in open-work stockings !

"Here is a counacouchi," and he points to a stuffed snake some thirteen feet long. "The natives here call it a name I can't pronounce, but it is the same as frightens people in Guiana under the high title of ' Bushmaster.' It is the deadliest and fiercest viper on earth. He don't wait for you to come at him—he comes at you. Look at them inch and a half fangs! There's hyperdermics for ye!" And he shows the two fangs of that deadly snake, some of which inhabit the more inaccessible parts of this Isthmus of Panama, together with the no less dreaded lance-headed viper—the Isthmus prototype of the hideous *Fer de lance* of Martinique, and Labarri of Guiana, scale for scale, the only difference being that climatic changes have given different coloring to the snake.

"Oh, no more of this," shudders Louise. "I shall dream of snakes!" and turns away to examine a hideous idol.

While doing this, she cries suddenly: "What is this?" and points to the branch of a large tree, in whose solid wood is imbedded a powder canister, which bears the stamp "Dupont Rifle Powder, 1852," though age has rendered it scarcely legible.

"The first," says Silas, "is an idol that the Indians used to worship before the Spaniards taught 'em better. The second is a proof of the wonderful growth of all vegetable substances in this rapid land. I was working my dredger on the main Chagres last rainy season. It was just after a flood, and there was a pile of brushwood coming down the river, when 1 seed somethin' glisten in the floatin' rubbish, as it went past me, and fished this out, and brought it over here. That tree must have been growin' around that old Dupont powder canister that probably some California miner flung away, for perhaps thirty odd years, and has now become part of it.

"Well! you have not much curiosity, though you are a Yankee!" laughs Louise.

"Why?"

"Because you have never removed the lead stopper from it. There might be something inside."

"Oh, open it, Silas!" cries his wife. "Perhaps there's money in it!"

"Oh, leave that for a rainy day. Ye can spend an afternoon investigating it, when I'm on the dredger. At present I am goin' on with the museum: Lot number six. Bow and poisoned arrows. Have been used by the San Blas Injuns in fighting off surveyors and explorers. The high mountainous nature of the country prevents their bein' conquered, and at present they are the only politically free people in the State of Panama!"

"Hush!" cries the old notary, laughing. "Don't touch on politics, my friend Winterburn."

"Oh, ho! Is there another revolution on foot?" inquires the Yankee, and goes on with the description of his collection.

Some of his curiosities are very peculiar, notably an idol with revolving eyes.   ·

After a time, Miss Louise grows tired of idols, bows and arrows, snakes, lizards, and jaguars, and suggests that they leave the balance of the curiosities for another day, as she is anxious to be at her post early in the morning.

Alone in her room, Silas' warning about snakes impresses her so much that she climbs into her hammock, thinking with a shudder that it is safer than the bed. But she can't sleep in the hammock and crawls timidly to the bed, and there forgets about snakes, for her pretty lips murmur—"Harry" as unconsciousness comes over her and closes her bright eyes.

CHAPTER XVI.

THE DUPLICATE TINTYPE.

THE next morning Miss Minturn, having American business methods in her mind, makes her appearance, after an early breakfast, at the office of Montez, Aguilla et Cie., on the *Calle de Paez*, but finds that it is not open, and is told by a negro boy who is in charge of it, that if she will call at eleven o'clock, they will be ready for business.

Consequently, though somewhat astonished, the young lady takes a walk about town, and going towards the bay, finds herself in the market of Panama, where a number of negro women and mulattoes are doing a thriving business in yuccas, frijolis, beef cut in long strips (*tassajo*), fruits, and fish.

Tempted by some of the beautiful fruit of the Isthmus, Louise buys an orange, and walks nonchalantly, eating it, towards the end of the railroad track which runs out on the wharf into the bay. Nearing this, she sees a building that is now almost in ruins, carelessly deciphers on it the words "Pacific House," and suddenly gives a start. This is the place from which the last letter of Alice Ripley had been written to her daughter in the far-away United States.

It brings the epistle home to her ; Montez comes into her mind, and she wonders : "Can it be true—the wild accusations that the American has made against him ? If he has ruined one friend in Paris, may he not have destroyed another frank, trusting soul upon the Isthmus ? "

Filled with these thoughts, the girl strolls slowly down the wharf, to see a figure that appears familiar to her. It is that of the second-cabin passenger on board the *Colon*, Bastien Lefort.

The old man is sitting looking over the beautiful waters of the bay, which, as the tide is in, are now rippling at his feet. His eyes have a dreamy, far-off expression, and he is muttering as if broken-hearted, words that come to Miss Minturn something like this :

" Five hundred thousand francs ! *Sapriste!*—for the residence of the Director General ! Seven hundred and fifty thousand francs ! *Mon Dieu !*—for his country palace ! Millions for luxury, the pigs—the swine—but little for work ! "

Then to her astonishment, the man suddenly becomes very animated, for he utters a snarling, shrieking " *Sacré!* What shall I do ? The savings of a life ! " and goes dancing and muttering up the wharf in a semi-demented, semi-paralyzed manner.

But the beauties of the scene bring back her thoughts to it. It is fairy-land !—and a fairy-land she had never seen before, for no stage picture was ever so beautiful. The dainty islands of Flamenco, Perico, Tobaguilla, and in the distance far-away Toboga, rise before her from blue water, green—eternal green !

To the south, blue water ;—though this seems to her west, for the points of the compass are wondrously changed here, to those not knowing them.

To the east, the coast running away to the far-off tower of deserted old Panama, and back of it green savannas and mountains that rise from it, islands in an emerald sea. To the north, the old gray ramparts of the city.

But the sun is coming up upon this scene of beauty, and warned by its heat, the girl leaves the wharf and returns to the town of Panama, to make her appearance at the office of Montez, Aguilla et Cie.

Here she is received by the junior partner Aguilla, who is an old, pleasant, round-faced, honest-mannered Frenchman, one of the *bourgeois* class, who had been taught in his youth to save pennies, but now, in this era of extravagance, runs his business quite liberally.

· "Ah," he says, "Miss Minturn!" speaking to her in French, to which she replies in the same language. " I had received advices of your leaving New York from our correspondents, Flandreau & Company, who have forwarded to me your contract. Your duties here will not be difficult, nor unpleasant, I hope. You will chiefly take my dictation, and forward my letters, doing any other correspondence that may be entrusted to you. An American stenographer was engaged, at the suggestion of my partner, the Baron Fernando Montez." The old gentleman speaks with great reverence of his titled associate. "He thought an American would have less interest in discovering any of our confidential transactions, and would be more difficult of approach than any one we could employ here. Your engagement, Miss Minturn, is a tribute to the respect my partner and I feel for the business honor of the United States."

Then the old gentleman chuckles in a theatrical way : " *Voilà* Remington !" and shows her, in an adjoining office, a newly imported type-writer.

." It came with you, on the same steamer," he laughs.

"Oh, I brought mine with me also ! " says the girl.

"Ah, that will be convenient, if one gets out of order. Besides," here a sudden idea strikes this gentleman, " I occupy a villa belonging to Baron Montez, on the Island of Toboga. We will have this sent there. I have often correspondence that requires attention on Sundays. Sometimes I will ask you to make a picnic to Toboga, on a bright day, where you will be pleasantly received by my wife who lives there. Thus we can save a delay of twenty-four hours in our correspondence."

A few minutes afterwards, Miss Minturn's own machine, which has been sent from his house by the notary, arrives, and the young lady finds herself at her old occupation again, and playing upon the well-remembered but perhaps not well-beloved keys.

She is delighted to find she has a room to herself. It is immediately behind the private office of Monsieur Aguilla. The large general offices, three or four of them, are occupied by numerous clerks who go about business in a French way, with a good deal of excited jabber and volubility.

Miss Minturn's first day's correspondence is chiefly with the Panama Canal Co. Everything with that institution is done by letter. However, there are some outside epistles, one to the agent of the railroad at Colon, and another addressed to Domingo Florez, Porto Bello, State of Panama, enclosing a draft upon the Railroad Company at Colon, for the sum of fifty dollars.

" You can keep that form of letter," remarks Aguilla, after dictating it, " as you will have to send a similar one every month to the old man, as it contains his remittance —his dividend on his Panama stock."

Then the old gentleman looks with quick, eager eyes at the deft hands of the young lady, as they fly over the keyboard.

He laughs as he goes away, and says :

" You are like an artist on the piano. I feel quite proud of our firm ! We have the only stenographer and typewriter on the Isthmus ! "

This sets the girl to thinking. She the only stenographer in Panama—what could have put it into their heads? But the remark of Aguilla satisfies her on this point. They fear that their affairs would not be as private in the hands of some one who knew more about the state of business on the Isthmus—some one who perhaps might find it to his interest to disclose some of their contracts with the Panama Canal Company—one or two of the letters to that concern having made Miss Minturn open her bright American eyes, and wonder with her bright American mind, if there is not jobbery and rascality contained between their rather ambiguous lines.

But this is none of her business, and getting through with her work, Louise soon becomes interested in the movements of her fellow-clerks, a few of whom are now introduced to her by the head of the house.

Most of these are young Frenchmen ; although there

are a few Spaniards and Chilians, there are no Americans among them. But, curiously enough, there is a Chinaman ! He has charge of the accounts of the various laborers hired upon certain excavation contracts that the firm is engaged upon, and also carries accounts with several Chinese stores and booths scattered along the works of the Canal, between here and Colon.

Two of the clerks, however, interest her. They are both great dandies, one of them a young Parisian named Massol, and the other a Marseillais named D'Albert. These two young gentlemen are apparently well up in the office and have good salaries, as they stroll off to the Bethancourt for lunch, while the bulk of the employees are perfectly content with the more democratic and less expensive *La Cascada*, which is more convenient to the *Calle de Paez*.

Noting the employees going away, the young lady steps into Monsieur Aguilla's private room, and says : "What must I do now ?"

"Why, do what the rest of them have done. Run away to your breakfast ! "

"Will I have time ?" asks the girl, astonished, recollections of the rush of Nassau Street coming to her.

"Oh, certainly ! There will be nothing for you to do till half-past two—say three o'clock. I will be here at three. Perhaps I may have a few letters."

So the girl trips away quite lightly, though the sun is warm, wondering to herself : "Sixty dollars a week for *this !* At this rate I would have earned six hundred dollars a week at Miss Work's."

But she soon discovers that the heat is such that one cannot labor as vigorously in Panama as in New York.

When she gets home and has a *déjeuner à la fourchette*, she is very glad to escape from the sun, and under the cool veranda lounge out a couple of hours in a hammock *siesta*. It does not take long for old Sol to destroy even Anglo-Saxon activity in this land of the Equator.

So the week runs along, and grows heavy to her, for by this time she has become very anxious to see the bright face of Harry Larchmont. She has, however, heard about him several times from the loquacious clerks, D'Albert and Massol, the former of whom questions her regarding the young American.

He remarks one day : "Mademoiselle, you came by the same steamer with Monsieur Larchmont, the new clerk of the Pacific Mail Company?"

"Yes," replies the girl, "why do you ask?"

"Why? Because he is the most wonderful clerk in the world. His salary, I have inquired and discovered, is one hundred and fifty dollars a month. He spends one hundred and fifty dollars in a night. Now, if he were rich, he might be a clerk in other lands, but nobody who is rich would ever come down here to slave."

Then he suddenly strikes his head, and says : "*Mon Dieu!* perhaps he is an embezzler! Perhaps he has fled from the United States!" for there are several of these gentry upon the Isthmus.

The girl answers, with indignant eyes : "Embezzler! What do you mean? Mr. Larchmont is a member of one of the richest families of the United States!"

"Oh, indeed! And mademoiselle is angry!" replies the young man. Then he bows to her mockingly, and remarks suggestively : "Monsieur Larchmont is also one of the handsomest men in the United States!"

Watching them as they go to breakfast, Louise notes with flaming eyes and indignant face D'Albert and Massol emit sly giggles, and indulge in shrugs of shoulders, and slight pokes in each other's Gallic ribs.

Going off to her own afternoon intermission she smites her pretty hands together nervously, once or twice, and murmurs : "Yes, handsome! God help me! *Too* handsome for my happiness!" Then she says suddenly : "What a fool he is! Could he not have seen it was Miss Severn made me angry?"

So the time is heavy on her fair hands. Silas Winterburn has already gone back to his dredger on the Chagres, and Mrs. Winterburn devotes herself chiefly to her child and rummaging in her husband's museum in the daytime, and listening to the music of the young ladies at night ; for this is almost the only recreation that Louise has found.

According to Spanish custom, young ladies cannot go out by themselves, and old Martinez does not seem to ever think of taking his daughters to evening amusements.

"If they would only go to the theatre," thinks Miss Minturn, "I could perhaps invite myself to go with

them. There I might see him! What shall I do to
pass the coming nights that are even now so long?"

And she has thoughts of writing a novel, or poetry,
or some other wild literary thing that young ladies
when driven by *ennui*, resort to, to bring despair upon
publishers.

So Saturday arrives, and Louise imagines she will
have a Sunday holiday, and thinks of doing the Cathedral.

But before leaving the office for the afternoon, a large
mail comes in, and Aguilla taking it in his hands says:
"Behold our Sunday work! Make up a little picnic.
Ask one of your young lady friends, the Martinez, I
believe you live with, or some one else, to come
with you to Toboga. Run down to-morrow. I have
had the new typewriter sent there. You will have a
little office all to yourself in my villa. Come and pass
the day with us, and take a two hours' dictation from
me. The *Ancon* goes down every morning, and you
will enjoy the trip, I think. The expense, of course,
will be mine."

"Thank you," replies the young lady, "I shall be
delighted to come," as in truth she is; for she knows it
will be a pleasant excursion, having heard of the beauties
of Toboga Island from other people besides her employer.

So she asks Mrs. Winterburn if she will not go with
her, thinking she will be more protection, and perchance
needs more recreation than the voluble Spanish girls,
who seem to find their life in Panama a pleasant one, notwithstanding there is a dearth of suitors, as old Martinez
has no great *dot* to bestow upon his numerous progeny.

Thus it comes to pass that Miss Minturn and the
wife of the engineer, one bright Sunday morning, run
down through the limpid waters of the bay, upon the
steamboat which lands them amid the palms, plantains,
and cocoanuts of Toboga Island, which is very fair—fair
as when George Ripley looked upon it in 1856, though
now slightly more modern.

They tramp up the little hill, and over the same walk
that Fernando had skipped down that 15th day of April,
and come to the villa of Baron Montez of Panama,
which has been greatly enlarged from the bamboo and
palm-thatched cottage of its early days.

Seated on a veranda overlooking the bay, Louise finds the genial Frenchman and his family, and they make her at home, and treat her very kindly ; and after a pleasant lunch, she takes half an hour's dictation from the business man.

"Now," he says, " I think you can write all these letters and have time to return to Panama this afternoon ! "

He leads her into quite a large room which had once been used as a bedchamber, but which has been made into a temporary office, for there is a bureau, chest of drawers, and washstand in it. In this has been set up the typewriter.

Working rapidly, Louise finishes the letters in less time than she had expected.

As she hands them to Aguilla, he remarks : " Have this paper put away in the bureau. Make everything permanent for yourself. This dictation has been a great success ! I am a day ahead in my week's work. We will have more of these Sunday dictations."

"Very well," answers the young lady, " I will put the paper and envelopes in the drawers of the bureau."

"Yes, I believe it is empty," he replies. " I don't think the room has been occupied for a long time, though my partner slept in it years ago, before even the Canal."

So he leaves Mrs. Winterburn and Miss Minturn together, for the girl is putting on her wraps.

Susie says suddenly : " I will put away the paper for you, so we will have more time to catch the boat."

"Thank you, I think the top drawer will be all I want," answers Louise, by this time engaged with her hat-strings.

"What a pretty picture ! " suddenly exclaims the matron, from the depths of the bureau.

"Indeed ? " says the young lady nonchalantly.

"Yes, I reckon she must have been some sweetheart of the Baron's," laughs the lady. " It's quite your facial expression. Look ! " and she thrusts the picture under the girl's vision.

And suddenly Louise's eyes grow great with startled surprise, and stare at a portrait ! For it is the counter-part of the one she showed Harry Larchmont that day upon the *Colon*—the one even now she is carrying in her pocketbook.

She gasps—she almost staggers !

"Why, what's the matter, dearie ?" cries Mrs. Winter-burn.

"Nothing, but a great surprise! Something that I may want," says the girl suddenly, a kind of horror com-ing into her eyes,—"want you to bear witness to. See !" She has opened the pocketbook. "Compare these two —the one found in this deserted room—in the unused bureau—it is the duplicate ! It is the picture of Alice Ripley, who disappeared on the Isthmus over thirty years ago !"

And she holding them before the astonished woman's face, Mrs. Winterburn says, also growing pale : "Oh, goodness gracious ! They are just the same ! She was a relative of yours ?"

"Yes, she was my mother's mother," whispers Louise. "She and her husband were robbed here of a fortune which should have been mine—at all events, it disap-peared. This picture I am justified in keeping ! But say nothing of it—not even to your husband."

"Why, Silas can help you in the matter ! He knows everything about the old Isthmus in those days !" gasps Mrs. Winterburn.

"Until I tell you—not a word to him ! I must con-sider."

The girl's hand is laid warningly upon the woman's arm, as Aguilla coming in, says : " Hurry, my dear young lady, or you will miss the boat !"

"Yes," answers Louise. "Thank you for your hospital-ity !" and goes down the path falteringly, leaning upon Mrs. Winterburn's arm.

So falteringly that Aguilla remarks to his wife : "Is sickness coming upon that poor child so soon? See, even now she looks pale—her limbs tremble. Can the yellow fever have found even her youth and beauty ?" and sighs, turning away his face, for he has seen many a young face go down before Yellow Jack in this town of Panama.

But as they approach the landing, Louise starts and gives a jeering laugh, for Mrs. Winterburn has whispered to her : "Do you think he is the murderer ?"

"He ? Who ?"

"Why, Aguilla, the man in the house."

"No!" cries the girl. "He is as kind-hearted a Frenchman as the sun ever shone on! He has an honest heart! Though I think there is another who is not so scrupulous! But for God's sake, keep silent! My future depends upon your promise!"

"Very well!" says the lady, "though I'd like to have told my husband!"

"I'll tell him if necessary," answers Louise.

Then they board the steamer, which ploughs its way back over the blue water to Panama, making the trip in about an hour; and all this time Miss Minturn is in a brown study, no flight of flying fish attracts her, no big shark draws her gaze—her eyes look out on the blue water but see it not.

She is thinking: "He divined! He knew! I'll tell Harry Larchmont! I'll beg his pardon! I'll tell him what a fool I was! I'll ask his aid, and if Montez is guilty, I'll help him throw the villain down!"

Now she becomes desperately anxious to see this man she has turned her back upon. She throws away mock modesty. Excitement gives force to her character.

Soon after they reach her home in Panama, Martinez says: "You are not tired; your eyes are very bright; your face has plenty of color, Señorita Luisa; why not take a walk with me and my daughters, on the Battery? Everybody goes there on Sunday afternoons, to hear the band play. It costs nothing."

"Willingly!" cries the girl, for sudden thought has come to her: "If everybody goes to hear the band play, Harry Larchmont will be there!" She can speak to him. She can apologize and ask his advice and aid.

So they all stroll off to the Battery, which is but a step for them, and climbing up on the old ramparts, that have the city prison beneath them, they see the town in its glory—the white dresses of the ladies, the gay colors of the negroes, the fashions of Paris displayed in ancient setting of rare beauty; blue water on one side, the old town on the other; underneath, prisoners wearing out their lives in sepulchral heat; and overhead, gay Panama.

The crowd is brilliant as a butterfly and light and airy as the blowing breeze. The military band is playing, and the scene is radiant with French color and French vivacity, but it has tender Spanish music, for the band is South

American, and Spanish music always brings love to young girls' hearts.

So there are tears in Louise's brown eyes, and she is looking anxiously for Harry Larchmont, when suddenly there is even more than the usual French buzz about her, and she sees a beautiful woman in the latest mode of Paris, sweeping with bold eyes and flaunting step, and brazen look through the assemblage. The eyes of all are turned upon her, and she is laughing and flirting her parasol about her, and crying: *"Bichon! Viens ici! Bichon! Vite!"* to a French poodle that has been shaved in artistic manner, and is led by a maid beside her. She is talking to a gentleman whose form the girl recognizes and starts as she sees his face, for it is Harry Larchmont, and he has shut off all admirers from this lady's side, and is talking to her, making play with his eyes, as if he loved her.

Then there is a whisper in the girl's ears. It is that of old Martinez the notary, who knows everybody and says: "Turn away your heads, girls! It is that awful French actress—that fearful Mademoiselle Bébé de Champs Élysées, the heroine of a hundred loves, the *chère amie* of Baron Montez, the financier."

But Miss Minturn does not turn away her head! She looks straight at the gentleman, who on seeing her is about to speak, but as her eyes gaze at him, his eyes droop, abashed, a flush of shame runs over his cheeks, that for one moment have become pale, and his lips tremble a little, though they force themselves to try to speak, as Louise Ripley Minturn, the stenographer of Seventeenth Street, New York, cuts Harry Sturgis Larchmont, of fashion and Fifth Avenue, dead—dead as the yellow fever!

CHAPTER XVII.

VADALIA CARDINALIS.

THEN Mademoiselle de Champs Élysées and Harry Larchmont pass on, the crowd gathering about them with hum and chatter and merry voices, and screening them from her view; and the girl, who has thoroughbred pluck, and whose eyes have looked the gentleman very straight in the face, suddenly feels faint, and thinks the sun has gone out of the heavens, for love, trust, and faith in humanity have gone out of her heart also.

She notes, in an abstracted way, that Martinez is making some little joke upon the appearance of the Frenchwoman : for though he has told his daughters not to look, the old notary's eyes have devoured the beautiful yet too highly colored picture La Champs Élysées has made.

After a little the young Martinez ladies suggest going home, and Louise is very glad, and departs with them to her lodgings, carrying her head quite high and haughtily, though she has a heart of lead and iron within her wildly panting bosom.

But she has left a picture in the eyes of Harry Larchmont that he will never forget ! That of a girl with a light straw hat, the ribbons floating in the breeze above her lovely head—a graceful figure posed like a statue of surprise, one little foot advanced from under white floating draperies, the other turned almost as if to fly. A sash of blue shining silk or satin, knotted by a graceful bow about a fairy waist ; above it, a bosom that pants wildly for one moment, and then seems to stop its beating, as her hand is wildly pressed upon its agony. But the face ! The noble forehead ; the true, honest, hazel eyes, which flash a shock of unutterable surprise and scorn for debased mankind, and nostrils panting but defiant ; pink cheeks that grow pale even as he looks upon them ; rosy lips that become slowly pallid, the lower trembling, the upper curled in exquisite disdain ; the mouth half open, as if about to speak—then closed to him for ever ; and over all this the infinite sadness of a woman's heart for destroyed belief in what she had considered a noble manhood.

And his heart stops beating, too, for even as he looks at her comes a sudden rapture, then a chill of horror—rapture, for at this moment he guesses that she loves him; horror, because he knows she will love him no more.

Turning from this picture of pure womanhood, he sees beside him the woman for whom he has lost all hope of gaining what he now knows has been his hope in life. For the shock of her disdain has told him something a false pride had made him fight against believing : that he,

Harry Larchmont of the world of fashion, loves Louise
Minturn of the world of work with all his heart and all
his soul.

Though Bébé de Champs Élysées utters her latest
piquant drolleries imported from Paris, and tries her best
to amuse and allure this handsome young American who
strolls by her side, and whom she supposes rich, for he
has squandered money on her, she finds him but poor
company.   He contrives to reply to her, but her flaunting affectations seem more meretricious to him than
ever.

After a little time he excuses himself to Mademoiselle
Bébé, and leaves this fascinating siren surrounded by a
crowd of gentlemen admirers, for her notoriety, as well
as beauty, have given her quite a following of high-life
worshippers in this town of Panama.

As he goes away the band is playing one of the Spanish love songs Louise had sung to him in the moonlight
on the *Colon's* deck, and he mutters to himself, crushing
his hands together, " My dear little sweetheart of the
voyage !   Fool that I was !   I have lost her for a fan-
tasy ! "   Which is true, for no love of Bébé de Champs
Élysées had ever entered Harry Larchmont's heart.

He had gone into this affair rather recklessly, simply
seeking information that he thought she could give, and
for which he was willing to pay.   As to its moral sense, he
had given it very little consideration.   It had simply
occurred to him that by it he might destroy his adversary.
In New York he would doubtless have hesitated before
embarking in a matter that might bring scandal upon his
name ; but here, in this far-off little place, which has the
vices of Paris, without even its slight restraints, he had
dismissed this aspect of the affair from his mind, with
the trite remark : " When you are in Rome, do as the
Romans do ! "

So Baron Montez not being on hand, Harry Larchmont has obtained a passing introduction to this siren of
the *Boulevards* upon her arrival.   He has made his
approaches to her quite cautiously, and with all the secrecy
possible, not wishing to form part of the *petite* gossip
of Panama.   Having spent quietly considerable money
and considerable time in trying to insinuate himself into
her good graces, he has succeeded in gaining perhaps

more of Mademoiselle Bébé's regard than he himself would wish.

Her confidences, for he has been compelled to approach the matter very deftly, have been so far only confidences as to what kinds of jewelry she likes most. In fact, a great deal of her conversation has been in regard to the wondrous string of pearls that a merchant has brought from the *Isle del Rey*, that are, as she expresses it, "dirt cheap!" For this young lady has an eye to business, and knows that the traders of Panama have not as fine diamonds as those of Paris, yet in pearls they sometimes equal, sometimes excel them.

Her promptings and petitionings have been so persistent, that Harry knows that the gift will probably win from her the information that he wishes, and that when the pearls of Panama adorn Mademoiselle Bébé's fair neck, she will perchance in a gush of rapture open her pretty lips, and tell him what she knows, if he pumps her deftly.

So this very Sunday he has this string of pearls in his pocket, having purchased them the evening before, and was about to present them to her.

But even while he is arranging a little *coup de théâtre* that may unloose the siren's tongue, she has insisted upon his visiting the Battery in her company; for this lady likes to make public display of her conquests, and Larchmont is a very handsome one. Some sense of shame being on him, even in this free-and-easy, out-of-the-way place, Harry has declined her invitation.

But Bébé's temperament will not brook denial even in little things; she has turned upon him and said: "*Mon ami*, are you ashamed to be seen by the side of the woman to whom you express devotion? If I thought that, my handsome Puritan, I should hate you—you have never seen Bébé's hate."

Under these suggestions he has yielded, and been led very much like Bichon, her poodle, in triumph to the Battery of Panama, there to meet what fate had prepared for him.

But now shame changes this man's ideas. He mutters to himself: "The cost is too great! I will not win success at the degradation of my manhood! though, Heaven help me! I fear I have already paid the bitter price!"

From this time on he visits Mademoiselle de Champs
Élysées no more.

But his desertion produces a curious complication, and
brings the siren's undying hate.

Among the gentlemen who pay their devotions on the
Battery this afternoon to Mademoiselle de Champs
Élysées, immediately after Harry's departure, is young
Don Diego Alvarez, who has lingered in Panama, waiting
for the steamer to carry him to Costa Rica. This fiery
young cavalier still hates, with all his Spanish heart, Mr.
Harry Sturgis Larchmont. His regard for him has not
been increased by his apparent success with the coming
celebrity at the theatre. He has learned that Larchmont is a clerk in the Pacific Mail, and sneers at him as
such, and laughs to himself: "What will be the effect of
my news on the mercenary *diva?*"

So he strolls up to her, and enters into conversation,
remarking : "I am delighted, Mademoiselle Bébé, to see
at least one woman who admires a handsome man, even
if he has no *other* attractions."

"You don't mean me?" laughs the lady in gay unbelief.

"Certainly, you !"

"And who is the gentleman? Of course I've never
seen him *yet.*"

"Why, that American, Señor Larchmont."

"Oh, Henri," says the young lady in playful, easy
familiarity. "Henri has plenty of *other* attractions.
Besides good looks, he has money !"

"Money?" sneers the Costa Rican.

"Yes, *money !*"

"But not *much* money."

"He has enough to promise me the great string of
pearls that have just come from the islands !"

"What? This clerk in the Pacific Mail Company, at
a beggarly salary, buy the great string of pearls?" scoffs
the Costa Rican.

"This clerk in the Pacific Mail Steamship Company !
Whom do you mean?" gasps the fair Bébé, growing pale.

"The Señor Harry·Larchmont."

"Impossible ! "

"You can convince yourself of the truth of what I
have said, easily enough to-morrow, or this evening, if
you are in a hurry," laughs Don Diego.

'And he promised me that string of pearls, the *misé-rable!* He played with my heart!" gasps the lady, plac-ing her hand where that organ should be, but is not. "A clerk in the Pacific Mail—an accountant—a beggarly scribbler! But I will investigate! Woe to him if it is true!"

Being a woman of her word, not only in affairs of the heart but in matters of business, this lady makes inquiry and finds that what she feared is true; and would have vented her rage upon Mr. Larchmont had he appeared before her. But Harry keeping aloof, she changes her tune in reference to this gentleman, for she is an incon-stant creature, longing most for what she has not. She mutters: "The poor fellow! I frightened him away by my extravagance. I would have forgiven his being a clerk, he is so handsome!"

But the pearls being still in her head, she thinks she would like to take a look at them; that, perhaps, as Baron Montez is coming, he may be induced to purchase them; and she goes to the shop of Marcus Asch the jeweller near the Cabildo, and asks for the baubles that she will gloat over and admire. But they inform her that the pearls are gone.

"Gone? Absurd! They were here last Saturday!"

"Yes, but Señor Larchmont bought them."

"*Mon Dieu!* Impossible!" she screams; and then going away, mutters: "Malediction! if he has given them to another!" but sends the gentleman who has bought the pearls a most affectionate note.

And perchance if Harry could have seen her then, he would have bought from her with his pearls any revela-tions of chance words Montez had let fall in the con-fidences of the champagne glass or *petite* supper; for Bébé, like Judas, will betray her master for the ten pieces of silver as often as they are laid at her feet.

But Larchmont does not receive her note. He has gone away, along the line of the Canal, towards Aspin-wall.

So she grows very angry and thinks to herself: "What other one has received what were bought for me? I will punish this traitor!"

That afternoon Baron Montez arrives in Panama.

This gentleman is apparently quite happy and contented as he drives up from the railroad station in company with his partner and Herr Wernig, and enters his office, hardly noting that there is a bright-eyed girl who looks up from her work in the room behind the private office with curious interest at him. His years have been successful ones, and though there are two gray locks upon his temples, his eyes are as bright as of yore, and his intellect as vivacious, though tempered by contact with other brilliant minds.

He gets through his business rather quickly in his office, saying to Aguilla, who would be effusive, "To-morrow, *mon ami*. To-night my comrade Herr Wernig and I will talk over old times."

So the two go away together to the Grand Hotel, where Montez has the finest apartments and is received by Schuber the proprietor with much deference and many bows; for though the Baron has been careful never to have his name upon the directory of the Panama Canal, still he is known to be in very close touch to its management and control.

After dinner the two stroll up to the theatre where Mademoiselle Bébé is waiting for her *cher ami*, with many evidences of petulant affection, one of them being a revelation of "*l'affair Larchmont.*"

First greetings being over, this little *poseuse* affects a jealousy she does not feel. She pouts and mutters, "You came not to Panama, Fernando *mio*, as soon as you promised." Then her eyes flash from absinthe or some other French passion, and she cries, "Ah! It is that little minx of the *Boulevard Malesherbes!* But I'll teach her when I go back!"

"I pray you not to mention that young lady's name!" says the Baron, looking at her rather curiously.

"Tut! Tut! What do I care for those savage eyes of yours, *Monsieur le Baron?*" laughs the lady. "I can have other admirers!" As she easily can; for even now she makes a most alluring appearance, her *costume de theatre* being such as to display beauties of the figure as well as the face; of which Bébé de Champs Élysées has many, though most of them are of the "Robert le Diable" enchantress order.

But Montez not answering her, she babbles on, "You don't believe me! You have not yet heard of the hand-

some young American whose eyes are as bright and big
as your friend Herr Wernig's, though *mon* Henri's are
straight, not crooked."

"*Mon* Henri's," mutters the Baron, giving her an under
glance.

"Yes, *mon* Henri, who is wild with love for me. So
wild, he offered me a great string of pearls worth a fortune. But for your sake, ingrate, I repulsed him!"

"Ha, ah! *ma chère!* That means, you want a string of
pearls!" laughs Fernando, who knows this lady's tricks
and manners very well.

"I do!" answers Bébé, "but not from him! Had I
wished them from him, they would have been mine! I
think, from certain hints of his, he wanted some revelation from me. A revealing of some of your careless
remarks over supper table and champagne glass, of your
connection in business with his brother, Monsieur François Larchmont."

"Larchmont!" cries Montez. "Oh, it is that younger
brother who has come here to the Isthmus?"

"*Certainement!*"

This suggestion makes Fernando very serious. Though
Montez is a great man, like most great men he has a
weakness. A drop of blood from a Gascon adventurer
in his polyhæma veins, makes his tongue over a champagne glass sometimes throw away careless hints of
things it were wiser not to speak of. This is especially
his nature when he has been triumphant; and he has
been triumphant so many times over the careless trust of
François Leroy Larchmont, that he fears he may have
dropped some suggestion that the lady beside him might
under duress, or lured by gold, betray. And did she but
know it, poor laughing *méchante* Bébé's tongue has been
doing some industrious work on her sepulchre just
now.

Baron Montez looks at her curiously, then as she
stands babbling to him, waiting for her cue at the side
scene, puts off this short-skirted, white-shouldered siren
with a few careless words; and shortly after, leading his
Fidus Achates, Herr Wernig, from the theatre, plies him
with some very pertinent questions about the young
American, as they stroll towards the Plaza.

After getting his answers, Fernando gives a chuckle

and ejaculates : "*Parbleu!* This young bantam has come to fight me on my own dunghill!"

Then he listens in an abstracted way as Herr Wernig goes on in further explanation : "You wrote me about him. I watched him carefully. He is supposed to be a clerk in the Pacific Mail Steamship Company's office, but he does as he pleases. He also had quite a flirtation on the *Colon* coming out, with that pretty stenographer in your office."

"Oh, yes," remarks Montez, "the girl I saw this afternoon. I remember I told our agents in New York to engage one. I thought an American would be less dangerous than a French one to our confidential communications. Personally, I always write my own letters of importance, but poor Aguilla is not good with his pen, and requires a correspondent."

"*Poor* Aguilla? *Rich* Aguilla! He's your partner," laughs the German.

Here from out Montez' white teeth issues a contemptuous "Bah!" and Herr Wernig, after a pause of thought, gives a little giggle.

"As to the young lady stenographer, I will ask her some questions in the morning. You say she was *épris* with this Larchmont?" murmers Fernando, puffing his cigarette very slowly.

"Oh, very much, but there has been some trouble. She has not spoken to him since they left the steamer. I saw her cut him very directly on the Battery last Sunday, when he was walking with Mademoiselle Bébé, for whom I understand he bought the big pearls, but did not deliver them."

Into this Montez suddenly cuts : "You leave to-morrow morning?"

"Yes, by a quick steamer to St. Thomas, and then to Paris."

"Of course! to add your weight, Wernig, to the Lottery Bill that is to permit the Canal here to make one last big gasp before it "—here Fernando lowers his voice —"dies."

"Certainly!"

"You need have no fear. The bill will go through the *Corps Législatif*. Then a spark of life, but after a little time there will be an end of the ditch. However,

it is very important that this Lottery Bill pass, for you
and for me. By it we will get the moneys due us from
the Panama Canal Company, which are at present delinquent. After that no more contracts for me ! ”

“ For me also ! ” laughs the German. “ Don't you
think I have seen this as well as you ? ”

“ Ah, you have come here to clean up—so you need
not return ? ”

“ Yes, I have done so pretty effectually.”

“ I am here to clean up also, and very thoroughly. If
the Lottery Bill did not go through, work would stop
here at once, and there are some in this dirty little town
who would call themselves my dupes, and perhaps wish
my blood—the blood of poor, scapegoat Montez—the
innocent blood ! But in two months I shall be safely
out of all this, so *vive la loterie !* ”

“ I wonder you did not remain in Paris till the bill
passed ! ” says Wernig inquisitively.

“ That was impossible ! ” returns Fernando. “ Besides ”
—here he whispers to the German who bursts into a
guffaw and cries, “ What ! The Franco-American ! ”

“ Yes ! He is doing the buying ; he is at my suggestion making himself amenable to French law. But you
leave to-morrow morning for Colon,” continues the
Baron. “ I must bid you *adieu* to-night. I am not an
early riser.”

Then the two go into some more private confidences,
but as Montez bids Wernig good-night, he whispers these
curious words : “ In a month you will see me in Paris.
In a week or two I shall be away from here, and leave
nothing behind me—*nothing !* ”

Then looking around, he waves his hand with foreign
gesticulation, and laughs : “ I will have eaten them all
up—I have such a big appetite ! ”

And the German seizes his hand and chuckles : “And
so have I, my brother ! ”

So after a farewell glass of wine at the *Café* Bethancourt, these two part, with many expressions of mutual
esteem, and many foreign embraces, and even kisses,
they so adore each other ; though Wernig has made up
his mind to eat Montez, and Montez has made up his
mind to devour Wernig.

Far away Australia, among other wondrous birds,

beasts, fishes, and reptiles, has given birth to a most
marvellous insect—the *Vadalia Cardinalis!* Its appetite
is phenomenal, its voracity beyond description. Though
not destructive to vegetable life, were it large enough,
it would eat the entire animal world.

There is also a lazy lower order of insect that lives
dreamily upon the leaves of the orange-trees of California, known by the name of the Cottony Scale. Its form
of life is so low that it seems more a white incrustation
on the beautiful plants than an insect who lives upon
their leaves and life.

Into the orange orchard, dying from myriads of Cottony Scale, the planter lets loose a few *Vadalia Cardinali.*
These prey upon and eat up the lazy white Cottony Scale
with incredible rapidity, and the beautiful plants, bereft
of what is drawing their life away, survive and flourish.
But after the *Vadalia Cardinali* have eaten up all the
Cottony Scale insects in the orange plantation, with incredible voracity they fall upon and devour each other,
and the survivors again devour. Each hour they become
fewer and fewer, until there are but two *Vadalia Cardinali* left. And these two battle and fight with each
other till one is victorious and destroys and devours his
opponent. And from that orchard that once was white
with myriads of Cottony Scale glistening in the tropical
sun, and here and there a red spot of *Vadalia Cardinali*,
but one insect crawls away, seeking for further prey for
his all-devouring jaws—one *Vadalia Cardinalis!*

Such an insect is Baron Montez of Panama. He has
already eaten up and destroyed outside stockholders
and investors in Panama securities—the weaklings, the
Cottony Scales—such as François Leroy Larchmont and
Bastien Lefort. Having devoured the Cottony Scales,
he is now about to eat his own breed—his partner Aguilla,
his old chum Wernig, his early companion Domingo the
ex-pirate, who has invested his savings under Montez'
advice, and half a hundred other cronies of his, who
have assisted in his work of despoiling the lower order
of animal life. He will be the only *Vadalia Cardinalis*,
who will leave his own particular plantation on the orange
farm called the Canal Interoceanic.

Perchance he would be wiser, perchance he would have
less care, perchance he would be more successful, if he

let a few others save himself have a little of the pickings of his schemes ; for even Cottony Scale bugs writhe in anguish sometimes, and some of the men he is about to devour are *Vadalia Cardinali*, ferocious, implacable, and cunning. For instance, Domingo the ex-pirate, and Aguilla, who has swindled many in his time in his honest *bourgeois* way. But to eat all is Montez' nature ; he is a *Vadalia Cardinalis.*

CHAPTER XVIII.

BÉBÉ'S LITTLE PRESENT.

SOME instances of this come under Miss Minturn's bright eyes the next morning, in the office. Old Aguilla is still smiling, happy and contented, but after a short but excited private conversation with the Baron, who has come in languidly about eleven o'clock, the junior partner appears anxious, *distrait*, nervous, and uncomfortable.

"Never mind, my old man," laughs Montez, looking on Aguilla's gloomy face. "The *Corps Législatif* will surely pass the Lottery Bill, and then all will be well."

Reassured by this, Aguilla goes about his business. But a few minutes after, there is a terrible commotion in the office. Bastien Lefort has been admitted to the private office of Baron Montez.

He is screaming at him so everybody hears : "*Mon Dieu !* You have come at last ! I have been waiting for you ! You ! You !! who lured me to invest my all in this bubble of extravagance ! One hundred thousand francs for this ! A million for that ! All thrown away ! Rascality and fraud ! *Sacré nom de Dieu !* the savings of a lifetime ! "

He shrieks this out so wildly that the clerks run into the private office, thinking him a madman who will perchance attack the Baron.

Montez, cool and calm, says : "Restrain yourself ! *Mon cher* Lefort, this is nonsense ! Are not your dividends paid you regularly ? "

"Yes, my dividends," groans the man. "But the principal ! The Canal will never be built ! "

"Oh, nonsense! The Lottery Bill will pass next month —and then, my boy, then!"

"But my shares have gone down so much!

"Oh, but then, the Lottery Bill, then—wait!"

"I do not understand," murmurs Lefort. "I cannot understand!"

"Of course not. You are not a financier, you are a glove-merchant. Leave it to me! Place yourself in my hands—the Lottery Bill—go back to Paris—remain quiet —the Lottery! All will be well!"

"Oh, but the extravagance—the throwing away of precious gold!" murmurs Lefort undecidedly.

"You speak to me as if I were one of the directors," remarks Montez, "when I am but a stockholder like yourself. We are both stockholders! Still, when we are in Paris, we will go to the directors and explain to them things that they do not know ; or perhaps you had better remain here, and keep me posted when I go to head-quarters in Paris. I will see you again."

And he puts off the broken-down miser with fairy prom-ises, until the old man smiles and says : "Yes! Yes! my dividends—I still receive them! I will still believe!" and so goes away.

Then Montez devotes himself to his private correspond-ence, taking great care over one long letter, during the writing of which he sometimes refers to a large black pocketbook that he produces from an inner pocket of his vest, not his coat. This appears to be filled with papers and memoranda. When he has finished with it, he returns it very carefully to his safe vest pocket again.

All this comes under Louise's bright eyes, as she is seated at her typewriter in the room behind the private office. The day is hot, and the door has been left open for draught. Miss Minturn has set herself to watch this man she suspects, and now that he is near her, though the keys of her Remington click unceasingly, every sense is alert as to what passes at Montez' desk.

A few moments after, she comes face to face with him, and his easy, affable manner interests her as well as as-tonishes her.

After finishing his private correspondence, Fernando calls in Miss Minturn, and dictates a few unimportant letters to her ; most of them being in response to invitations to dinners and *fêtes* from the resident managers of the Canal as well as a few other local magnates of finance and trade in this town of Panama.

The last of these finished, as Louise is about to go, he asks her a few questions : how she likes Panama—is she pleasantly located in the house of Martinez, the notary—she boards there, he understands—and hopes she will enjoy herself upon the Isthmus, and that her labors will not be too severe.

He would, in his quiet off-hand way, get a good deal of information from her, were the young lady not *en garde ;* but she simply thanks him for his interest in her comfort, and turns to go.

Just here a sudden idea seems to enter his head. He calls out after her : " By the by, Miss Minturn, do you known the address of Monsieur Henri Larchmont ? "

" No," replies the girl, suddenly returning.

" Ah, I'm sorry. I would have sent him a letter I have for him from his brother François in Paris. He intrusted it to me."

" Why did you think I knew Mr. Larchmont's address ? " asks Louise, hurriedly, her cheeks growing a little red.

" Oh ! ha ! ha ! My friend Herr Wernig said you and the gentleman were quite companions on the steamer."

" Since the steamer, I have not seen him," says Louise ; an intonation in her voice, Fernando does not quite understand.

" So your comradeship ceased at the gang-plank. It often does ! " laughs the Baron languidly. Then he continues : " Doubtless it is just as well. Monsieur Henri is rather a gay youth. Besides, I think there is a pretty Miss Jessie Severn in Paris. Eh, mademoiselle ! " And would go on, a little banter in his tone, but the girl's face astonishes him.

She mutters : " I beg you leave my private affairs alone ! " Then for one second there comes over her fair face an awful look—one he has seen before somewhere—a look that opens the pages of his memory.

" Have you any other letters ? "

" No, not to-day," he stammers as she leaves him.

He thinks : " What was that in her eyes—so like the eyes of the American señora of thirty years ago ? But

this girl's eyes are brown, not the blue eyes that I love!
Besides, Alicia had blonde hair that I adore! Pooh!
Let the past be the past!"

And he thinks of other blue eyes—those of the present
—that he hopes to go back to, and the lovely rebellious
face of pretty pouting Jessie Severn, whom he has left in
far-away Paris, with a weak guardian even more in his
power than ever, who has said, when Montez returns the
reluctant beauty shall be his bride.

He mutters: "When I come back, she is mine, and
that must be very soon. I have here a letter!" He
looks at the one he has been writing, "but mails are slow.
I will send a telegram."

Which he does, addressed to François Leroy Larchmont, 238½ *Boulevard Malesherbes*, Paris.

Then calling a clerk he says: "Cable that on the
instant!" and goes to musing again: "I wonder what
the woman did with the string of pearls that I never
could find? Did Domingo steal them? Ah—but what
matters it?"

Then a smile passes over his face, and he laughs.
"This American stenographer is jealous of Jessie Severn!
Why? Because this young dandy—this brother of
François Leroy Larchmont—loves my *fiancée*. For what
reason does he come to the Isthmus? To destroy me so
that he can wed her?"

Then suddenly the undying hate of Corsican blood
comes into Montez' face, mixed with the drop of in-
flexible determination descended to him from Morgan's
buccaneer, as he mutters: "I have it! He stays on the
Isthmus! Like the man who bought pearls thirty years
ago, the man who buys pearls now, remains! I will fix
him! *Caramba!* But I will fix *him!*"

He muses a little while over this; then sends for the
Chinaman who attends to the real-estate affairs of the
firm, and makes some inquiries about certain properties
belonging to them in Panama. After hearing the report
of the Celestial clerk, a grim smile passes over his face,
and he thinks laughingly: "It is not always you can kill
two birds with one stone!"

Mademoiselle Bébé de Champs Élysées has been rather
exigeant in the last few months. She has reproached
her dear Baron several times, with not being as liberal

as he used to be.   She has complained that his devotion
to Mademoiselle Jessie Severn, the ward of his friend
François Leroy Larchmont, has made him more provident
of his pocketbook than was his wont.

Her hint the evening before, at the theatre, makes him
fear that he may have some time, in careless confidence,
dropped into her ear secrets that may be dangerous to
him in Paris ; for he knows the time is approaching when
there will be such an explosion about Panama Canal
affairs that will make any scandal fatal.

Mademoiselle Bébé de Champs Élysées is returning to
Paris.   If his coming marriage enrages her—if she can
find a higher bidder for any secrets of his that may be of
advantage to his enemies, he knows very well she will
sell them.

Meditating on this, he takes Mademoiselle Bébé out
for a drive this afternoon, over the savanna, on his return
passing near the outskirts of the town a very pretty little
villa.

While they have been approaching this place, the
Baron and his fair companion have been engaged in a
somewhat acrimonious discussion.

Mademoiselle has been pouting and chiding : "You
come to see me no more !   You only remained at the
theatre a few minutes last evening !   You brought me
no jewels from Paris ! "   Then she has suddenly cried
out : "Ah, it is because of that designing young American—the one it is rumored in Paris you are to marry.
Do you think your Bébé will let you desert her so easily
—*mon cher* ? "

"*Diable ! ma petite !* " says the Baron grimly, "not
while I have any money left."

Next he smiles and says : "But you can have many
more admirers—this Monsieur Larchmont—he adored
you ? "

"Adored me ! " cries Bébé ; "he adores me still—he
worships me ! "

"You have but to speak the word—he will come back
to you ? "

"Would not he—if I would let him !   But then, Fernando *mio*, it would break your heart ! " babbles Bébé,
her vanity destroying the truth.   She would go on and
lie a little more, did not she suddenly stop and cry :

"What are you laughing at?" for the Baron can't keep in a diabolical chuckle.

"Only my little joke!" murmurs Fernando. But had she known what Fernando's little joke meant, poor little Bébé would have plucked out her pretty red tongue from between her rows of pearly teeth, rather than have told vainglorious lies, each one of which is a nail in her coffin.

"You reproach me for not being generous," grins the Baron, "when I have a present all ready for you."

"What, in your pocket?" cries Bébé enthusiastically, about to make sudden investigation for hidden jewels.

"Oh, no! It is not in my pockets."

"Then where is it?"

"On the mound there!"

"What do you mean?"

"Why, that pretty little villa. It is yours, if you wish," and Fernando points.

"You will give it to *me*?"

"Yes, it will be more pleasant for you than your apartments at the hotel, and more private. You shall have a pony-carriage to drive out there."

"Oh, you darling!" cries Bébé, clapping her little Parisian gloves together with joy. "Let me look at your new present! Is it furnished?"

"I think so."

There is a little pathway running from the road, and the negro coachman stops his horses at some distance one side of the door.

Fernando scowls at the lackey but says nothing, and assists Mademoiselle Bébé out. It is but a step.

The Baron has the keys in his pocket. Entering, they examine a very pretty *bijou* of a tropic residence, quite handsomely furnished in modern French style, which had been occupied by Monsieur Raymond, one of the engineers of the Panama Canal; but he and all his family have died some weeks before, of yellow fever.

Montez has no hesitation in entering it. He knows the pathology of the disease too well; that any one who has once had this scourge and lived, is safe from it forever afterwards. And Fernando, in his early Isthmus days, had passed a few weary weeks recovering from the touch of Yellow Jack.

"How beautiful!" cries the lady, clapping her hands. He says : "*Ma chérie*, you like this?"

"It is delightful!"

"Here you can have your own little parties—here you can invite Monsieur Larchmont to call on you."

Then noting reluctance on the lady's face, the Baron goes on laughingly : "Do not hesitate—I do not mind it! In fact, it will be a favor to me. I would like to meet this gentleman. There are certain facts about his brother, of which I shall ask you to pump him. Your Fernando is not jealous. Is it a little compact between us?"

"Oh, certainly!" laughs Bébé. "I would do anything for this villa! Monsieur Larchmont shall reveal to me everything you wish to know! Now, *mon cher*, our little dinner."

So he and the lady leave the house, and drive through the streets of Panama to the Plaza, and from there on the road out to La Boca, where, at the Garden of Paradise, with its palms and tropic foliage growing in its miniature glen, Mademoiselle Bébé and Baron Montez have one of Monsieur Clemont's charming *petite* repasts with sparkling wine that makes Bébé very brilliant. Then Fernando murmurs : "It is time for the theatre, *ma petite*." And the two return to town, Montez appearing in a very good humor, and Bébé being a mass of smiles of delighted avarice, and of newly acquired wealth.

The next day Fernando Montez, having made all the arrangements, Mademoiselle de Champs Élysées is installed in the Villa Raymond. There is little or no trouble about servants, the Chinese clerk who attends to the real-estate affairs of the firm has hired them with Celestial astuteness, engaging only those who have passed through the yellow fever, and therefore do not fear it.

Mademoiselle Bébé enjoys her triumphs at the theatre each evening, and drives out therefrom to the pretty cottage that has as many germs of Yellow Jack and *el vomito negro* in its cedar walls, as it has crevices to hold them.

Each day La Champs Élysées expects to see among her admirers at the theatre, Harry Larchmont, for she has written him another pressing letter, begging him to come to see her at the Villa Raymond, and hinting that even without the pearls, he will be very welcome at her side.

But Harry Larchmont is upon the works of the Canal, poor fellow, on another wild-goose chase. For here, though he discovers that there is lots of rascality and swindling in the various contracts of the Canal Inter-oceanic, still there is nothing that will bring anything definite home to Baron Montez, or to his firm. Nothing by which he, by any peradventure, can wring back from Fernando the fortunes of his brother or Miss Severn.

He has gone into this affair seriously, and has spent some time making his investigation a thorough one. He has passed twenty-four hours with Winterburn on his Chagres dredger, learning all the machinist can tell him of the workings of the Canal. The dredgers, he notes, are doing their work thoroughly. The American Company is keeping its contract.

Then he has passed along to the more difficult work, the big mountain cuts. He has pumped the foremen of the various gangs of laborers, drawing information from them, by his pleasant address, and his generous use of cigars, and noting with astonishment that they are doing their work pretty much after antique methods; that if they have any steam drills or modern appliances very few if any are used ; that like the Pharaohs of Egypt and Louis Fourteenth of France, the contractors of this nineteenth-century achivement depend upon the myriad hands of men.

One night during his investigation, one long night, cut off by a rain-storm, he has been compelled to pass in a cabin near the great cut of Culebra, with a foreman of one of the gangs.

This has been with particularly bad physical results as regards himself, for in the same cabin had been care-lessly left an open can of nitro-glycerine, the fumes of which give headaches such as mortal man cannot endure, but mortal man remembers forever. They are of a peculiar kind—once felt, never forgotten.

From this journey, Harry has returned to Panama with a downcast heart, knowing that there is lots of rascality in the atmosphere, but feeling that he is grasping at air.

He is sure of one thing, and that is, that any dollars his brother may have put into the Canal Interoceanic are as much lost, from an industrial investment standpoint, as if he had thrown his money into the Atlantic Ocean itself.

So as Larchmont enters the Grand Hotel, immediately on his return, he has about made up his mind, in a half broken-hearted way, to give up the affair entirely—to devote the great part of his fortune to giving Miss Jessie her inheritance, saving his brother's name, and—but he will not think of this.

He meditates wildly: "I must see her! I must try and explain! I cannot go with Louise thinking me what she does!" Then he jeers himself: "She'll never believe me! No woman would!—and I doubt if any man!" and so goes to the office of the hotel.

Here he is very affably received by the clerk, who hands him two letters addressed in a French feminine hand he does not know.

He opens them wonderingly. They are both in the same bold yet dainty chirography, and from Mademoiselle Bébé. The first begs him to come and see her and bring the pearls. The second sings the same tune, but tells him she lives at the Villa Raymond, and she will forgive and love him without the pearls.

To these he mutters, "Never!" As he turns away from this, for there is a commotion outside. He looks out.

It is a funeral procession, large and impressive, wending its way to the great Cathedral, for the ceremonials of the Catholic Church, in these South American countries, are ofttimes grand and imposing. Otherwise, this one would create no commotion, for there are a great many funerals about this time, in the town of Panama.

Turning to the clerk, Harry asks: "Who of importance has died lately? Whose death march is that?"

"Oh, that!" says the clerk, "have you not seen the mortuary placards and heard the news? That is the funeral procession of Mademoiselle Bébé de Champs Élysées, of the Theatre. The careless, thoughtless creature went to live in the infected Villa Raymond. She took the yellow fever four days ago, and died this morning."

Then the clerk wonders whether Mr. Larchmont has not the yellow fever also, for he has grown deathly pale, and almost staggers, and is muttering to himself: "Good heavens ! if the scorn of that pure American girl had not come between me and her—I should have visited the Villa Raymond—and perchance been in my coffin also."

Looking on this procession—the lighted candles and solemn black, the Baron Montez, who acts as chief mourner, smiles to himself, and murmurs : " Bébé's little present disagreed with her ! But that Larchmont—he escaped me ! "

This seems to affect Fernando's spirits, for he is superstitious, as he says to himself : " Is it a premonition ? Will he conquer in the end ? "

So returning from his solemn duties, he seems to be very sad. His spirits have left him.

So much so that old Aguilla, who has a tender heart, pats him on the shoulder with his fat *bourgeois* hand, saying : " My poor boy—cheer up ! Cheer up ! We know how you loved her—but courage, *mon brave !* "

Soon after Montez does cheer up, for this very afternoon he hears incidentally that Harry Larchmont is sick, and has been taken to the rooms of one of the clerks in the Pacific Mail, a young American, George Bovee, who had conceived a great affection for him. Though he is not sick of the yellow fever, his exposure in the open cuts of the Canal, full of the miasma from decaying vegetation, has brought to him the malarial fever of Panama, which is sometimes as deadly even as the other.

At this, the *Vadalia Cardinalis'* step grows light, and his smile more baleful, as he says to himself : " I triumph ! See how my enemies fall before me ! "

CHAPTER XIX.

WHISPERS OF THE DYING.

MISS MINTURN does not hear of Larchmont's mishap so soon as Montez. Her labors at the office are not great ; but outside of it, sensation has come to her.

On the very day of the Baron's interview with her, she returns to the house of Martinez for her afternoon *siesta,* but instead of rest receives excitement.

She is met almost at the door by Mrs. Winterburn.

That lady, as is her wont, has been killing the long hot day by rummaging through the articles in her husband's museum. She now says affrightedly : " I've been waiting for you ! Come in with me—there is something in that powder canister ! "

" What powder canister ? "

" The one imbedded in the growing branch my husband took from the Chagres River. You remember what he told us about it that evening ? "

" Yes," answers Louise carelessly, " but I am tired. Why not tell your story to the Señoritas Martinez, and keep it for me in the evening ? "

" The Martinez are all asleep. Come in with me—I want you to see what there is in it. I think they are valuable. Besides that, there is a writing that I have not read. I fear it is a will—that the pearls will not be mine honestly," says the woman.

" After that you will let me take myself to my darling hammock ? " pouts Louise, anxious for beauty-sleep.

" Yes."

A minute after, they are in the old lumber-room, and coming to the branch with its powder canister, Susie Winterburn unscrews the lead stopper that has made it watertight, opens it, and reveals something that for a moment makes Louise give a cry of delighted astonishment ; then afterwards a gasp of horror.

She takes out therefrom a long string of beautiful white pearls that glisten even in the subdued light of the room. These are wrapped in a woman's cuff.

The pearls are fresh and glistening as when first plucked from ocean's bed ; the cuff is a little soiled and yellow by age, but has on it some hasty writing in red, that has been scribbled with a piece of pointed wood, or something of the kind. It reads, though disjointedly, with horrible intelligence, as follows :

" Come to my aid—these pearls will pay you. The place is called Caperiha—I am in a hut imprisoned by the little river.

" My husband was killed in the Pacific Hotel, Panama, by Montez and Domingo.

" Domingo watches me, and is my jailer.

" Come quick ! To-night he comes to me—to-night the snake will kill me !

" ALICE RIPLEY."

13

These letters appear to be in red ink, but as the girl examines them, she shudders, for she guesses they are in the blood of the woman who wrote them.

She has read this aloud in her agitation, and it has produced a great effect upon Mrs. Winterburn. That lady says: "When do you think it was written? We must alarm the authorities!"

"What? To rescue a woman who wrote this thirty years ago?"

"How do you know it was so long?"

"Because the time she speaks of is the massacre of 1856—April 15th—I have read accounts of it in the Panama *Star*. I know all about it."

"How did you come to know that?"

"How? Because the handwriting of this woman is the handwriting of my murdered relative, Alice Ripley, the beautiful woman whose picture you saw at the villa of Fernando Montez—the duplicate of which I brought with me from New York."

"Oh, sakes of mercy! What are you going to do?"

"Avenge her!" answers Louise in strident voice. Then she mutters dejectedly: "But first I must find out more about the matter."

"Then why not ask my husband? He knows most everything about the Isthmus in them days."

"Yes, I'll telegraph him at once! His address is Bohio Soldado!" cries Louise, and turns to go about her errand, but pausing, whispers: "Not a word of this to anybody! It may bring danger upon me!"

"Danger upon *you*?"

"Yes. Do you suppose a man who would murder in 1856, would hesitate to murder *now*, though he is a Baron, and rich?" mutters the girl, and would fly from the room.

But Mrs. Winterburn says suddenly, running after her: "Take these—these are yours!" and presses the pearls into her hands.

And Louise says: "We can settle that afterwards. But not a word to anyone—and remember where these came from. You may have to make oath to the same!"

So leaving Mrs. Winterburn in a half-comatose state from surprise and agitation, Louise Minturn hastily goes to the telegraph-office, and sends such a despatch to

Silas Winterburn, that he makes his appearance in Panama the next morning.

Meantime Miss Minturn contrives somehow to get through her work this afternoon.

Before she is out of her hammock the next morning, she is gratified by a rap upon the door, and Silas' jovial voice saying : " What do you mean by scaring a man to death with telegrams ? I thought my wife or baby was dead ! "

" Why," cries Louise through the door, " I said nothing about them."

" That's what's the matter. You merely telegraphed me to come for God's sake ! Ain't that kind of a telegram enough to scare a man who has lost three families ? "

" Very well ! Now that your mind is relieved, I would like to speak to you for a few minutes : I will be out in five."

As tropical toilets do not take long, Miss Louise trips out within the time specified, an agitated but beautiful picture. Together they go to the museum. There turning to him, she says : " Your wife has told you ? "

" No, she hinted at somethin' about this 'ere canister," replies Silas, laying his hand on the object ; " but Susie was too agitated to be quite intelligible."

"Very well then, I will tell you the story," answers Louise.

And she does, giving him the full details of everything, showing him Alice Ripley's letters, the duplicate tintypes, then puts before him the contents of the powder-canister, the glistening string of pearls, and the letter on the cuff, which she reads to him, though her voice trembles. His voice trembles also, as he answers her : for she is questioning him rapidly : " You know the place this was written from ? "

" What, Caperija ? I should think I did—though she's spelled it wrong, just as it is pronounced, poor critter ! It's about four hours by canoe, when there is water enough to get there, from Cruces, up the Piqueni, one of the headwaters of the Chagres. It's a miserable hole, on the old deserted road to Porto Bello. She threw that powder canister into the Piqueni, and it floated down into the Chagres, washed up against some tree growing on the banks, and lingered there till the tree grew round it. Then it was washed away by some flood, and so it came into my hands, thirty years afterwards!"

"You believe, then?"

"Certainly! People don't throw away pearls like these for fun. This was a woman's last despairin' effort."

"You believe that Montez and Domingo killed her husband, George Ripley, in 1856?"

"Why, Holy Virgin! I was there!" cries Silas.

"You were there?" gasps the girl.

"Yes! That night was impressed upon me, for I had to git for my life on to the steamer. I remember like yesterday, before the muss commenced, seein' a big Californian stand off the crowd, till the police came and shot down the women and children. Just as I fled, I saw that black Domingo run into the Pacific House, followin' the big Californian; and, durn me, if Montez wasn't with him!"

"You think I can prove their crime?"

"It will be pretty difficult against Montez! Thirty years has passed. He is rich and powerful, and a Baron —though that don't count here—but riches do, everywhere!"

"Then, how to get evidence?"

"You are in Baron Montez' office. You have seen that worthy gentleman—young lady, do you think you will obtain it from *him!*"

"No," mutters the girl, "never from him personally."

"Then, as to Domingo, the black nigger; he's probably dead! I ain't seen him round here, or on the railroad, for years. He must be nearly eighty."

"I know him! I have written to him! He is alive!" cries the girl, remembering the letter to Porto Bello.

"Great Scott! *Por Dios! Muchos diablos!* Beg pardon!" ejaculates Silas, astounded. "Alive! Well," he goes on, reflectively, "I don't think you will be able to get anything from him, if Domingo's got his senses left. I'll make some inquiries around town, and see what I can pick up; but I reckon you won't be able to put any salt on either of those two old gray birds' tails."

So he goes away, while Miss Minturn proceeds to Montez, Aguilla et Cie., to get another sensation. About twelve o'clock in the day she sees a tall black man, dressed in Spanish style, with long sash and wide *sombrero*, with two terrible scars upon his face, and wool white as the driven snow, come into the office. Though his eyes are bright, and his step seems elastic, there is the gray of old age upon his face that makes his scars seem red.

This creature steps in, and walking up to the great Baron Montez, who is writing at his desk, slaps him upon the back, and cries : " Ah, ha! *diablo muchacho !* "

To this Montez, springing up, falters : " *Parbleu*, Domingo, my—my old comrade ! " and tries to greet him quite effusively, though he does not look overpleased to see him.

Domingo's eyes are still sharp, and he jeers : " What ! not happy to see your old friend and *compañero*, Domingo of Porto Bello ? " Then he snarls : " You need not be frightened ! I have not come for my dividends on the stock of this big ditch they are digging and digging, and will dig forever. Those are paid regularly by old man Aguilla, your partner."

"Of course, the dividends come regularly," murmurs Montez.

" I should think so. If they did not, you would hear from Domingo of Porto Bello! "

Then he goes on : " But how do they make money digging the ditch? Do they get paid for digging it ? "

Miss Minturn is trying to hide her agitation by playing on the keys of the Remington, for she has heard this conversation through the door, that is always left open on account of draught, and knows that she is sitting almost in the presence of the two murderers of Alice Ripley.

Domingo of Porto Bello cries : " What's that ? "

" What ? "

" The noise like the clicking of a thousand pistol locks ! "

" A typewriter."

" What's that ? "

" A little thing," remarks Montez, " that takes down what is said to it. Would you like to see it ? "

So he brings in Domingo to look upon this wonder of the nineteenth century. And the girl can hardly keep her hands upon the keys, though she gazes eagerly and

takes in the face of Domingo to her memory, never to
forget it.

The ex-pirate says: "She takes what you say, *down?*"

"Yes."

"And puts it on paper? Ah, ho! This is wonderful!
She must be a smart girl. Why does she sit there forever? Is she a slave? Of course she's a slave. No one
but a slave would work like that!"

Then he suddenly cries, for at his words, Louise has
looked up again with blazing eyes:

"*Maldito!* The same eye as the white lady—the
blonde lady! You remember her, Montez? you remember the good old days! You remember——"

But Montez suddenly interrupts. "Nonsense! I remember too many!"

"Ah, but no white ladies with snakes, eh?"

"Sh—sh! what is the matter with you?" cries Fernando. "Come to lunch. You ramble, old man, you
ramble!"

After Domingo has gone out, Montez comes in to Louise
and says: "This is an old dependent, who is now in his
dotage. I presume he was a wicked boy in his day. I
think, between you and me, he must have been a
pirate."

"Oh," cries the young lady, "did they ever have pirates
here?"

"Yes, but long before you were born. You should go
down and see the old town that Morgan destroyed!"
suggests Montez, going out.

Pondering on this, Louise thinks her employer curiously
evasive, and guesses quite shrewdly that it is to cover
up some agitation produced by the remarks of his old
dependent Domingo of Porto Bello.

As soon as possible she flies off with this story to Silas
Winterburn, who remarks: "Well, they're both here,
and I guess that's about all the good it will do you! I
reckon you'd better take the pearls and be contented to
let the matter rest, my dear young lady!"

"Never!" cries the girl. "I'll have the truth from one
of them in some way!"

"Well, seems to me you're takin' about as long a
job as buildin' a cathedral!" mutters Winterburn, "but
I don't think I'll be able to do you any good further

than to give my evidence about the powder canister, if you ever should get them into court."

Suddenly his voice becomes solemn, and he whispers : "For the love of heaven and Santa Maria, my dear young lady, don't let either of these gentlemen know what you're drivin' at, or that you're a relative of the robbed and murdered Californians. They didn't stop at murder then, and I don't think either of them have improved by age. Promise me to be very careful ! "

"I will," replies Louise, " very careful, for that is the only way to succeed."

She would go on devoting her mind to this business, but Winterburn, as he goes away, gives her a little further information.

"By the by," he says, " I was in Kophcke's drug store half an hour ago, getting some liniment to take with me for bruises on the dredger, when that young Californian, Bovee, came in to get some medicine, and told me about poor Larchmont."

"*Poor* Larchmont ! "

"Yes, the nice young fellow that gave my wife the letter of introduction to you. He spent a day on my Chagres dredger—the day before I got your telegram."

"Well, what of him? *Poor* Larchmont?" gasps the girl, growing white.

"Oh, it ain't as bad as that," cries Silas. "He ain't dead yet ! "

"Not yet? O heavens ! What do you mean ? "

"Why, he's got the fever."

" The fever ! The *yellow* fever ? "

"Not the yellow fever ! "

"Thank God ! "

"But the Panama fever—the malarial fever, though sometimes it's most as deadly, but they get over it quicker."

"Where is he ? "

"In the rooms of George Bovee, one of the clerks of the Pacific Mail."

"Do you know where the house is ? "

"Yes ! "

"Then take me to him, quick ! And I will bless you for this kindness ! "

"What are you going to do ? "

"Nurse him !" whispers Louise.   "Nurse him till he lives, or——"

"What?"

"Till I die !"

And led by the kind-hearted engineer, she goes to the quarters of the young American, which are three open rooms, with plenty of sea-breeze.

They are received at the door by a gentleman who looks in astonishment at the beautiful young lady, as she says: "You are Mr. Bovee? You are a friend of Mr. Larchmont's?"

"I hope so. And you?"

"I am Miss Minturn of New York. Mr. Larchmont saved my life in the New York blizzard. I have come to nurse him ! "

And the young American, taking off his hat, says: "Thank God ! We have got a nurse—a woman nurse—a tender-hearted nurse ! God bless you, Miss Minturn, for coming ! We need one ! He is very low ! " Then noting how pale Louise is, he thinks it is from fear, and whispers : " Do not be alarmed. His disease is neither contagious, infectious, nor epidemic."

"Were it all three," answers the girl very solemnly, " I'd nurse him ! "

Then Bovee leads the way into a room, where on a little cot-bed, his face sometimes as white as the sheets, with awful chills, and red with the fever at others, lies Harry Larchmont, and she whispers to him : " Do you know me ? "

The eyes, opening, smile at her, and the teeth chattering with malarial chill, gasp: " Louise ! " and a hand, hot as the sands of the desert, clasps hers, as he mutters : " God bless you ! "

But suddenly he utters an awful cry : " Angels have come ! " Then moans, " My God ! too late ! too late ! " and the delirium is on him.

In it he mutters things that almost break his nurse's heart, for he babbles of the girl in Paris, and shrieks : " She shall not marry Montez."

But Louise sits in martyrdom by his bedside, and they nurse him day and night, and they fight death for him, and she fights strongest of them all—stronger than his friend—stronger than the doctor—catching words of delirium that sometimes wound her heart, for she mis-construes them.

Once during his delirium, he gives her unutterable joy, for he shrieks : " No more ! No more attempts to lure the secrets of Montez from the lips of the horrible French-woman ! " Next he sobs the tears of delirium, and cries out : " But it was to save my brother's name without destroying myself. To save that poor girl from that villain Montez ! "

And his nurse goes out from the room, and clasps her hands together, and looks over the hot sunny water of the Bay of Panama, from the veranda, and murmurs : " Thank God ! The man I love is worthy ! but his heart is given to another ! The whispers of the dying are al-ways true ! It was not to gain the smiles of the French-woman, but to win Montez' secret, that my Harry seemed what he was not—a villain ! "

And the tears come into her eyes and run down her pale hopeless face, as she smites her hands together and links them in despair, muttering : " I can call him my Harry now, because—because he is *dying !* "

For the doctor this morning has given her no hope that the patient may live.

CHAPTER XX.

DOMINGO OF PORTO BELLO.

Now, this absence of the young lady from her office duties she has explained in person to Aguilla, who has said in his kindly way : " That's right, my dear. If you can save a victim from the fever, do so. There are so many who are not saved," and gives indefinite leave of absence.

This being reported to Montez, he meditates : " Ah ha ! The pretty Louise loves him yet—this Harry Larchmont—though he loves my *fiancée* in Paris ! " In-cidentally meeting, that day, the doctor who attends Larchmont, the Baron makes careful inquiries on the plea of being the intimate of Harry's Parisian brother, and is informed that there is no hope of his recovery.

So he laughs to himself :

"Again I triumph ! See how my enemies fall before me ! I leave this place clear ! To-morrow I go away from Panama forever ! To my wedding day—to enjoy the beauty of Jessie Severn—to be rich as a prince—to be one of the great ones of the earth. I have eaten up everyone ; though they do not know it, they are in my jaws now ! "

And they are ; for he has made such arrangements that none of them will ever see any of the gold of Panama. Domingo's stock will be lost to him ; he will receive his dividends no more. Aguilla, his partner, is ruined, or will be soon after Montez gets to Paris. Wernig, his chum, will have hardly a fighting chance, and François Leroy Larchmont no chance at all. Everyone has been eaten up by this *Vadalia Cardinalis.*

Montez, with his astute mind, has looked over the field. He knows the Canal Company, lottery or no lottery bill, will not last out the year, and with this failure must come such an explosion from French investors, that will upheave even France itself.

Investigation must show jobbery and fraud almost unequalled in the history of the world.

So he has withdrawn himself from the storm, as far as possible. He has made large investments in American securities. These are in the hands of a New York banking house, solid as a rock—one that has little to do with France—one that has never in any way been interested in French securities, or the Canal Interoceanic.

"I can live on that, a Fifth Avenue nabob, in America, if the worst comes to the worst," he thinks, as he consults the black pocketbook he always carries with him, and which day by day, and night by night, is his own particular care.

So he makes his preparations for departure in very happy mood.

As he is bidding Aguilla good-by, that gentleman says to him nervously : " You are sure the Canal Lottery Bill will pass ? "

" Certain as that I stand here ! " cries Montez.

So Fernando goes away from Panama, receiving merry *adieux*, and passing over the railroad to Colon. At Matachim he looks up the Chagres River towards Cruces, and his eye says : " Adieu forever ! "

Taking steamer on the Atlantic side, Baron Fernando Montez goes to New York, where he will spend a fortnight, looking after his American investments, and seeing that they are as certain as securities can be.

Within a week after he has gone away from Panama, there comes a commotion in the office. He has left certain letters written in his own hand, to be delivered. Bastien Lefort brings in one of these, and mutters in a broken voice : " Where is the Baron Montez ? *Sacré Dieu !* I am a ruined man ! "

Being informed that the senior partner has gone away, he wrings his hands and interviews the junior.

After reading his letter, Aguilla himself turns pale, and his fat face becomes thinner, and he also gasps : " *Mon Dieu !* " Then he shuts himself up in his private office, and tears run down his fat face—the *bourgeois* tears for loss of money—for he moans to himself : " If what this letter tells me is true, Montez has destroyed me also. My God ! my children ! How can I stop him ? What hope is there ? "

But into this scene comes a happier face. Louise Minturn, radiant as the sun, though her young face bears lines of care, from ceaseless watching and careful nursing, comes in half crying, half laughing : " Thank God ! he is saved ! The doctor says he will live ! You understand me ? I am back for work, Monsieur Aguilla ! The doctor says Harry—Mr. Larchmont will live."

But before Aguilla can answer, there is a harsh voice outside, and a terrible thump on the door, and in strides the black man with the two great red scars and the white wool.

He cries hoarsely : " Where is this *ladron*—this Montez ? I have had his letter read to me. It says my gold is gone. I, Domingo of Porto Bello, will wring his slippery neck ! "

" Montez has gone—to—to France ! " stammers Aguilla, for the appearance of the ex-pirate frightens him.

" To France !—Thousands of miles from me !—But you his partner are here—in my grasp ! " howls Domingo, and seizes poor Aguilla by the throat, growling : " Tell me, liar ! Tell me, dog ! Tell me, where are my dividends, or I will strangle you ! "

Old as Domingo is, Aguilla cannot get away from his grasp, though he contrives to gasp out : " You want —your month's dividends ? "

" Yes !   This letter says I shall have none ! "

" You shall have them ! "

" Now or your life ! "

" Certainly !   The — the   fifty   dollars ! "   stutters Aguilla, and pays it agitatedly out of his pocket ; forgetting even receipt for same, though this is not natural to his *bourgeois* nature.

" *Ah, Diablo !* " cries Domingo, chinking the silver and gold.   " Now for the pirate's delight—the rumshop ! " and goes off, leaving Louise and Aguilla gazing at each other astonished and dismayed.

Then Aguilla says suddenly : " Thank Heaven none of the clerks heard ! " and looks into the outer office, which is quiet—the employees are all at their lunch.   At this Louise, turning to the Frenchman, queries : " What does this mean ? "

" I cannot tell you at present," he answers.   " Come to-morrow ! "   Then looking at her he says consideringly : " I may have a curious mission for you.   It will be very important.   Come to-morrow for instructions."

" You do not want me to-day ? "

" No, go back and nurse your sick friend.   My little daughter is sick also.   I must go to Toboga ! "

So Louise, happy to get to the bedside where she has fought death and won, goes back to her vigil beside the couch of Harry Larchmont the American, and beside his bed is a telegram ; but the doctor says, " Not yet ; he is not strong enough."

The next day she blesses God again, for he is better, and his brain is clear, but he is weak—so weak ; though there is a look in his eyes that indicates he is happy, as she ministers to him with the tender hand of loving woman : the tender hand that comes to men in sickness : the tender hand that men should remember, but which they ofttimes forget when health makes them strong.

And the doctor coming, she whispers to him : " It is a cable—shall I ?—dare I ? "

" Not yet," says the man of science.   " But to-morrow, perhaps, if all goes well.   He is improving fast—thanks to his good nurse ! "

"Thanks to his good doctor," answers Louise with happy blushes, and goes back to her labors at Montez, Aguilla et Cie., very happy, to find on her desk plenty of work.

It is mostly routine labor that she can answer without dictation, for a note has been made on every letter. She goes to work at these, for Aguilla, who comes in once, says : "I am cabling to Paris. I shall have nothing to say to you of what I spoke of last night, until I receive answer," and keeps away from the office, apparently very anxious as to his return despatches.

So the girl, stealing one hour from her work, to spend at the bedside of Harry Larchmont, comes back late in the afternoon, to finish up her letters, and sits writing at the typewriter, till all the other clerks have gone away and left her, and the rapid night of the Isthmus is growing near.

There is no one in the building.

She has finished her last letter, and is rising to go home, when the door opens with a bang, and a hoarse voice speaks to her. The voice of a man half drunk with *aquardiente*—half wild with rage. She gives a gasp, and her heart beats wildly, for she, Louise Minturn, is standing alone, face to face with Domingo, the murderer of Alice Ripley and her husband.

His eyes have a pirate gleam in them, and his black heart is throbbing with deep pants beneath his black bosom, that is partly bare, for he has torn away the shirt in rage, or drunkenness.

She would fly to the door, but he closes it and locks it. The key goes into his pocket as he cries : " Lefort, the miser who is weeping for his gold, says mine is gone also ! The miser sobs ! The pirate kills ! "

Next a cunning gleam comes into his eyes that are red, and he whispers : " You are the one who writes in the magic box. You take down the words in the air ? "

And the girl gasps, " Yes ! "

" Then put it down, that I, Domingo of Porto Bello, may swear to it, and hang this villain Montez—who has robbed me of my gold, and hang myself, Domingo ! "

And the girl, with pale face and trembling hands, stands looking at him, and he with half-drunken voice, cries : " Put it down ! Put it down, or I will kill you ! Put down the story of the white lady with the pearls ! ''

Then Louise, sinking into her chair, with trembling hands, does as she is bidden, and takes down the story of the ex-pirate, crazed with drink and rage, told with the florid gestures of the tropics ; delivered with the intensity of the savage.

" You know me, Domingo of Porto Bello ? ''

" Y—e—s," falters Louise.

" Put it down ! You know Fernando Gomez Montez, mule-boy of Cruces, who calls himself Baron ? ''

" Yes ! ''

" Put it down ! You know the night in '56, when we killed 'em here—women and children—we killed 'em ? ''

" My Heaven ! ''

" *Put it down !* You know the Californian—you know the Señor Georgio Ripley—the white lady— the lady with the pearls ? ''

" Yes ! ''

" 'Tell how we killed the man, and stole the gold and the woman ! That Montez gave me little gold, and kept much ! Put it down, how that night we tossed the dead man to the sharks ! ''

" My God ! '' cries the girl.

" PUT IT DOWN! Put it down how we bore the beautiful woman into the mountains, along the Gargona trail, up through the hills into the Cordilleras, over the old Porto Bello trail, grown up with weeds over which the mule stumbled, but I strode on. How the monkeys howled and the jaguar screamed as we passed through the tree vistas in the dark night ; how the moonlight shone on us through the boughs and hanging vines and palm leaves. How the day came on—above us the birds and sunshine, around us things that love darkness—the crawling snake, the timid tapir, the crouching tiger. And the lady—the white lady—regaining her senses, cried to us, and we took her to the hut by the river, where she struggled, and cried to God for her husband. *Mia madre !* how she cried ! Cried as the women cried on pirate ships, when their husbands were cut down by cutlasses, or pistolled before their eyes. I, Domingo, tell you so. *Put it down !*

" Put it down how Montez told her he loved her.

How the beautiful eyes shone with hate upon him ! Tell of the lovely form drawn up erect ! How she turned upon him in the hut, and swore to kill herself, by the God of Gods, rather than love him ! How he, to see if we were pursued, left her imprisoned in the hut, giving her one day to decide whether she would love him willingly or unwillingly. How I, Domingo, watched her, that I might steal the pearls from her. I could have torn them from her, but she might have told Montez, and I feared Montez. And I fear Montez yet, for he is stronger—cunning little Montez ! Montez *el diablo muchacho !*

"Put it down how she looked out of the little hut—out of the window, and saw the Indian snake charmer—the snake catcher. Tell how she watched across the river-bank ! How the birds fluttered frightened—how that awful snake—the one I have seen kill a comrade in Saint Lucia, when I was a boy on Lafitte's ship—the one they call the yellow snake—the lance-head—the Labarri of Guiana, and Macagua of the Caribs. How the Macagua, eight feet of living death, with black forked tongue that moves unceasingly, and lurid eyes that never quail, crawled over the bank of the river, in pursuit of the bird ; how the snake charmer, with long branch, pinned his head to the ground, and seized him, and laughed in his very fangs, as I watched—I, Domingo, watched ! Tell how the woman, crazy with despair, beckoned to the snake charmer, for she knew not his lingo, while he held it—the death spirit—the great long serpent with the bands of black upon his back, that tapered down and left all scales of yellow on his belly—the living coil with death at its head, and long, sharp fangs, from which the venom dropped—how he put it in a water gourd, and bound over it deerskin, and held imprisoned the living death, that would affright even a man like me—PUT IT DOWN !

"And the lady—the white lady—looking with desperate eyes—with eyes that were growing crazy—beckoned the Carib, and he plunged into the rapids, and waded across, for she held up one white pearl of the string to allure him to her—one glistening pearl, worth money anywhere. Put it down ! And the man coming to her with his vase of living death, she seized from him the gourd that held the Macagua snake, and dropped into

his hand the pearl. And the snake charmer laughed,
and I, Domingo, knew a desperate woman meant death
to one or both of us, if we entered into her hut, or death
unto herself. How I chuckled : ' Here is an unknown
joy for Montez who will be coming soon, for Montez
loves this woman with the sunny hair and the blue eyes,
and skin white as the Santo Espiritu flower !'

"Then, as night comes on, Montez is back and says :
' There is no pursuit !'

"And I said : ' Ha, ha ! there may be ?' That was to
myself, for I had seen her write something, but I knew
not what she did with it.

" And Montez said to me : ''Is she there ?'

"And I said : ' She is—go in !'

"I laughed—I, Domingo, laughed. And as he entered,
I saw this woman rise up as a spirit of the sea ! Her
white limbs and bare bosom, the garments torn from them
by the brambles of the forest, gleaming in the last sun
rays ; her eyes—blue as the waves and flashing like those
of women who walk the plank.

"Upon this loveliness Montez one moment gloated,
then he cried to her : ' I love you ! I will be your
husband ! I will take the place of him who is lost
to you !"

"And she cried : ' Never !'

"And as she cried out, Montez sprang towards her, and
then, between them both, I saw her hold the living snake,
and laugh : ' Come now ! I love this better than I love
you !'

"And the Macagua snake, not knowing which to bite,
waved his head, and hissed a sharp hiss, with his fangs
uplifted, as she chased Montez with the living death
around the hut, and then again around ! And he with
awful screams sprang through the door.

" And the snake bit her, and the woman cried : 'I love
him best !'

" And so she died ! *Put it down !* Behold the story
that will hang this Baron Montez, who robs me of my
dividends of gold ! PUT IT DOWN ! PUT IT DOWN !
that I may swear to it—I, Domingo of Porto Bello—
the last living pirate."

But there is a swooning woman, who can put down no
more, as Domingo, ex-villain, ex-murderer, and last of the

pirates of the Gulf, staggers out, and says to the Frenchman, Bastien Lefort, who is walking moodily outside :

"I have put it down—what will hang the villain
Montez, who has robbed both you and me, my Frenchman of the heavy heart ! I have put it down !"

CHAPTER XXI.

AFTER HER !

SOME little time after this, the girl lying half swooning
over her typewriter, by an effort, forces her mind to its
work ónce more, and taking the awful dictation with her,
goes tremblingly out of the building, and is happy to find
herself in the streets, with people moving about.

This terrible tale has affected her nerves, and she
shudders, turning corners, even on the open streets
of Panama, for she sees the Macagua snake in her
imagination, and a woman crazy with despair holding
it on high, pursuing the shrieking Montez in the hut,
careless as to which one it gives death. But the very
horror of the tragedy ultimately gives her strength.
She thinks of the cruel fate of Alice Ripley, and deter-
mines to avenge it, and this nerves her to do things
Louise Minturn could hardly have brought herself to do,
until Domingo the ex-pirate had told his awful story to
her shuddering ears.

She is so excited, that she fears her agitation may
communicate itself to the invalid. She knows this
night she is no fit nurse for anyone.

So she sends a message to the young American, Bovee,
in whose room Harry Larchmont still lies ; and, receiving word that the invalid is doing very well, remains at
home and goes to bed herself.

The next morning she awakes her usual self ; for
youth and hope give brightness to the eyes and elasticity
to the step of this fair young maiden—even in this
sickly town of Panama—now that Harry Larchmont is
getting well.

She comes into the sick-room quite cheerily this morning, and is very happy, for the patient is much better.

14

A moment after, the doctor, who is present also, says to her inquiring glance : " Yes, you can give him the cablegram now."

This she does, and is sorry for it.

Glancing at it, the sick man utters a faint cry, and tries to struggle up in his bed.

" What's the matter ?" whispers the doctor, seizing him.

" My brother! " shouts Larchmont, agitation giving him for a moment strength. " My heaven ! He is wax in Montez' hands ! I must go to Paris at once, or he will marry her to that villain before I get there ! It's—it's a cable from Jessie."

These words put a knife in Louise Minturn's heart.

After a little, when the doctor has quieted the patient, telling him he will soon be able to travel, she mutters : " I must go! " And despite Harry's pleadings for more of her society, falters from the room to her office labors at Montez, Aguilla et Cie., murmuring to herself in broken voice : " How anxious he is to get back to the side of his love—the girl in Paris ! All he fears is that he will lose her ! "

At the office she contrives to get through her work, which is very little just now, though Aguilla says : " In a few minutes I will have something to say to you ! "

She is at her typewriter. Suddenly she shudders ; Domingo stands before her.

The wine has left him now, and he says insinuatingly, a cunning gleam in his eyes : " What did I do last night ? Did you see me ? Did the old drunkard swear to any wild tale, eh, *muchacha bonita ?* "

The girl, steadying herself, replies : " No, though you might have—you had a letter to write, old Domingo —only you were a little overcome with wine—too much to speak it to the air. If you will tell it to me now, I will put it down for you."

" Oh, I told you nothing—that was well ! Never be- lieve the stories of the drunkard ! " he chuckles. " But I have a letter to write to *mi amigo*, Baron Montez—one he will not bless you for sending."

And he dictates one to her, of a threatening kind, in case he shall lose his gold that he has saved during his many years, and be left in his old age without money to buy for him the pleasures of life. This finished, he snarls: "Send that to Montez with the compliments of Domingo of Porto Bello!" and goes off to the wine-shop, for there is still some money in his pockets.

Thinking over the matter, Louise is glad she has given him no hint of his revelation. Domingo drunk, and Domingo sober, are two different creatures. Domingo drunk will babble his awful tale into her pretty ears: Domingo sober will cut her white throat for telling it.

A moment after, she hears something from Aguilla that expels for the moment all thought of the ex-pirate from her mind.

He leads her cautiously into his private office, and says: "This that I tell you is a secret. I have been kind to you, while you have been here, have I not?" and pats her hand as if to beg a favor.

"Yes," answers Louise, "very kind and considerate, and I thank you for it."

"Then in my extremity, remember it! You are the only one I can trust to do this thing. My clerks here are either those who might betray me, or have not that certainty of character that is necessary in this delicate mission."

"What do you wish?" asks the girl, nervously; for his manner is impressive.

"This! and remember—I am placing my fortune in your hands—the fortune of my family that I have worked all these years to gain! I want you to prevent my partner, Baron Montez"—here his voice grows very low—"from *ruining me!*"

"Ruining you?"

"Sh—sh! Not so loud! Yes. What he has done here, to those about him, makes me know I am not safe in his hands. I fear he will destroy the ledgers of our firm in Paris, because those ledgers show that I am rich—not as he is—but still enough. There is but one chance for me. You must go to Paris!"

"To Paris!" gasps Louise, then thinking of the invalid still pale and weak and needing her nursing, she mutters, "Impossible!"

"Imperative!" answers Aguilla. "You must leave to-night!"

"But my patient?"

"Leave him here. He is out of danger, I am not.
My salvation depends on your acting for me—*in time!*
I shall give you tickets for the fast steamer leaving Colon
to-morrow morning, to connect at St. Thomas with the
English line for Southampton. The British ship calls at
Cherbourg. From there go to Paris, immediately! At
the office of Montez, Aguilla et Cie., deliver to the gentleman in charge, Monsieur Gascoigne, my written order for
you to examine the ledgers of the firm, and take off certain reports therefrom."

"But," stammers Louise, " Montez is there. If he
means to do what you fear, he will refuse!"

"Montez is *not* in Paris! He did not go there direct.
He will stop two weeks in New York—*that is our chance!*
You will get there, probably, a week before him! In that
time you must take a record of the ledgers for the first
four months of 1881. That was the time when we sold
out most of our stock and got clear of Canal Interoceanic.
Have your excerpts attested by Monsieur Gascoigne before a notary. Then if Montez destroys the books or
loses the books—or they fly away into the air, I am safe
—I have the records!—he cannot rob me!"

"But why not go yourself?"

"At this moment it is impossible! My wife and child
are sick—perhaps dying—I cannot leave them! There
is no time but now! I must trust to you! Will you do
it?"

"Yes, if possible!" cries Louise, a sudden wild thought
in her brain. "I will tell you in an hour!"

"Very well! If you will not go, I must try and get
some one else, though I know of none who would do as
well!" murmurs Aguilla.

Then the girl flies off to the bedside of Harry Larchmont.

"What does the doctor say about your going to
Paris?" she asks hurriedly.

"Not for a week yet—at best!"

"Then I will go to Paris for you!"

"You? How will you prevent Baron Montez marrying Jessie Severn?" and the invalid stabs his nurse again.

"Do you suppose you could control my brother?" he
goes on reflectively, "who is now either fool or imbecile,
in Paris?"

"No, but I can do something else for you!" murmurs the girl, whose lips tremble at the mention of Miss Severn's name. "You told me once, you wanted the secrets of Baron Montez. What secret do you want most?"

"The most important to me," murmurs Larchmont, "would be the real or true record of his transactions ··with my brother. The statements he has furnished Frank, I have looked over; they are incomprehensible, involved, vague. I do not believe them true!"

"I will betray them to you!"

"Impossible!"

"I will betray Baron Montez to you! I will use my confidential position to destroy him!" cries Louise, her face excited.

"Oh, no!" answers the man. "You told me your business honor would prevent your doing that!" Then he falters: "Not even to save me a fortune or my brother his honor, will I permit you to do what you may one day blush for!"

"My business honor is to business men—not monsters, murderers, and bandits!" answers the girl, the light of passion coming into her eyes. "I will destroy this man as he has destroyed those of my blood—remorselessly as he did them!" and she tells him the story of Domingo, the ex-pirate, and the mission that Aguilla would give her in Paris.

But he whispers: "No! no! Montez would kill you, if you brought danger upon him! For my sake, do not go!" and kisses his nurse's hand, murmuring "Promise!"

"I must go!"

"Not till I go with you. Promise!"

But she does not understand, and breaks away from him; but lingers at the door and kisses her hand to him, though her face says farewell.

From Harry's side she flies back to Aguilla and says: "I accept. I will do what you wish, faithfully and truly!"

"Then I have hope!" answers the Frenchman, and chuckles in his *bourgeois* way. "I knew you would! You are a true girl! I have had everything prepared! Here are your tickets to Paris, complete in every particular. Here is money for your expenses!" And he gives her more gold than she has ever had in one lump in her life before. "Spare no expense. This letter to the firm will give you the opportunities you want, if you get to Paris before Montez—that is the vital point!"

Then she suddenly says: "Where shall I stay in Paris? A young lady alone, I am told, is very unpleasantly situated."

"I will give you a letter to a friend of mine, a man of family," answers Aguilla. Writing this last and handing it to her, he gives her another thrill—for he says: "You must leave this afternoon!"

"This afternoon?" ejaculates Louise.

"In two hours! The steamer leaves Colon to-morrow morning, and time is vital!"

"Then get a carriage for me," answers Miss Minturn, who having once made decision carries it to the end. This being done she flies to the house of Martinez the notary, and astonishes them all. She says she is going away.

"Next month?"

"No, now!"

"Now? *Sanctus Dominus!*" And the Spanish family, not accustomed to haste, jabber excitedly about her as she packs her trunk. Feeling she has not strength to say good-by to the man for whose sake she is *really* going, Louise scribbles a hasty note of farewell to Harry Larchmont; and even while writing it, Aguilla has come for her with a carriage—he is in such a hurry.

The two drive down to the railroad, the Frenchman repeating his instructions as he puts her on the train.

Then Louise Minturn, as the cars run out of Panama, the excitement of departure leaving her, falters: "Who would have thought it this morning? I am going to Paris to fight Harry's battle—to win his love for him—to win her fortune back!"

Her lovely eyes cannot see for the tears, and she murmurs: "God help me! The happier I make him, the more unhappy I make myself! I wonder if he will ever know?" Then determination coming to her, she cries: "I pray God not!"

That evening a little note is brought to Harry Larchmont, as he lies in his cot, in the town of Panama, and he mutters: "Louise has broken her promise! She has left me ! She has gone where danger and death may come upon her ! "

" Calm yourself, Harry ! " says his friend Bovee ; " she has only gone to Paris, and Paris is not fatal to *all* pretty women."

" But you don't know—he may kill her ! "

" He—who ? "

" Baron Montez ! "

At this his friend looks curiously at him, and thinks he is raving again ; so curiously that Harry says : " You need not fear. My head is as sane as yours, only— God help me ! She has left me ! "

" Oh, you're convalescent now—you can get along without your nurse ! " laughs Bovee.

" *Not when I love her !* " answers Larchmont. " Love her with my heart and my soul ! "

" Then," says Bovee, after a pause of astonishment : " I can give you better medicine than the doctor—the best medicine in the world ! "

" What's that ? "

" She loves you ! "

" My God ! What makes you think——? "

" She's awfully jealous of that little girl in Paris—and between ourselves you've given her very good reason in your delirium ravings."

" Jealous of Jessie ? Ha ! ha ! Ho ! ho ! The darling !— jealous of my brother's little ward ! This is lovely ; this is funny ! This is delightful," laughs the invalid.

" You wouldn't laugh if you'd seen her look at you when you were raving about the other girl," mutters Bovee who is an observer.

" I brought tears to her ? " murmurs Harry.

" Yes ! "

" Then as God's above me, those tears shall be her last ! "

" All right ! To keep your oath pull yourself together, get well, and we'll ship you off to Paris after her ! " answers his friend.

Which Mr. Larchmont does, and a week after Miss Minturn has sailed from Colon, Harry reaches that place, to follow her to Paris. He is much stronger now, and the sea-breeze adds to his strength, day by day, as he sails to cooler climes.

He carries with him something that keeps his mind occupied during the voyage.

As he is leaving Panama, right at the depot, Mrs. Winterburn catches him. She cries eagerly, for the locomotive has already whistled : " Here's something my husband says belongs to Louise ; " and gives him the beautiful string of pearls found in the powder canister. "And here's something Miss Minturn left in the hurry of bolting. It's a book of writing : she had only an hour to pack, and forgot it." With this Susie presses into Larchmont's hand a large manuscript volume.

" Great goodness ! It's her diary ! " he gasps, gazing at the outside of it, and would give it back to Mrs. Winterburn, but the train is already moving, for a curiosity has come upon him of which he is afraid.

But he locks the book up in his trunk, and fights with himself, saying : " No, no. I'll not—read this—if I die of wanting." But one day as he moves it, gazing at it with longing eyes, some things fall out of it.

With a cry of love and joy he picks them up and looking on them mutters : " These are mine—they were mine before they were hers." And goes about happy but expectant. They are his bunch of violets and card of the blizzard.

And so, coming into Paris, about six o'clock in the evening, of an early June day, Harry Larchmont is pretty much his old self again, though his face is still pale, and there is a very anxious expression in his eyes.

Driving up to the hotel of his brother in the *Boulevard Malesherbes*, near the Park Monceau, he is let in by Robert the old-time servitor, with exclamations of delight and welcome, and finds something that astounds him— that something that often comes to us—the great—the UNEXPECTED !

BOOK V.

THE HURLY-BURLY IN PARIS.

CHAPTER XXII.

THE MIND OF A LUNATIC.

The door is closed behind him. Harry says to the old man : "Robert, just get my baggage up-stairs ; and where is my brother ? "

" Trunks, yes, sir," replies Robert. Then he turns to Mr. Larchmont, and astonishes him. For he says : " Thank God, you have come, sir ! It was on my mind to speak to a lawyer to-morrow ! "

" What's the matter ? " asks Harry. " Anything wrong ? " for Robert's manner is alarming.

" Yes, sir ! Mr. Frank, your brother—he's sick. I think it's his head." The man waves his hand about his honest Breton brow, as if driving away phantoms. " But you had better go in and see him yourself, sir, at once."

" Very well," says Harry. " Is he at dinner ? "

" Oh ! he don't dine much, sir, and Miss Jessie and her governess generally eat up-stairs, sir."

" Where is he ? "

" In the library."

And Robert shows Harry Larchmont in to a dimly lighted room, where a man is seated before a writing table, his head in his hands.

Harry cries out : " Frank, I've come back from Panama safe ! The fever didn't kill me ! "

" Ah, thank God ! Harry ! You are come ! " answers the brother, rising, and the two wring each other's hands ; though François after the manner of the French would kiss.

"Let me have a little light to look at you," says the younger one, for the tones of François Leroy Larchmont's voice have given him a peculiar thrill, they are so nervous yet so muffled ; the timbre of the voice seems to be changed. It is as if his tongue were clumsy.

Lighting the room, Harry Larchmont looks at his brother, and can hardly restrain an exclamation, the shock of his appearance is so great.

The face that had been round and rather full, has grown thin and drawn. The eyes have a watchful furtive glance, as if looking for something, partly in terror, partly in surprise—a something that is always coming but never comes.

Before the younger man can speak, the elder breaks out : "Thank God ! You've come to save Jessie from marrying that infernal villain—that Montez of Panama and Paris !" Then, not waiting for an answer, he jumps on, the words coming from him in jerks : "I've had cables from him ! Threatening cables !—from New York ! cables that alarmed me so much ! cables !—that I had all the preparations made for the wedding—the *trousseau* ordered here—knick-knacks and folderols ! He is coming to-morrow ! But you—thank God !—in time ! Henri, my brother ! save me from him !" and he shudders as if frightened.

."Let me look at his cables," remarks Harry grimly.

The other exhibits to him rapidly, three—one from Panama, two from New York. The general tenor of these is for François to make all the preparations for the wedding, that must take place on Montez' arrival in Paris, though there is a peculiar ambiguous threatening in them.

"What does he mean by his hints?" asks Harry, and is astounded at the reply.

His brother suddenly giggles : "Ah, ha ! I bribed the deputies for him ! The deputies for the Canal Bill ! The Lottery Bill ! It went through the Bureau of Deputies, a few nights ago ! I bribed them ! He hints, he absolutely dares to hint, at threatening me with this, the wretch ! for doing his work—oh ho ! his orders !" Then he shudders : "Henri, protect me !"

"Certainly!" mutters the younger man, almost too overcome to speak, for there is something in his brother's manner that makes him fear for his intellect, though he meditates: "Why could I not threaten Montez also? If it is against the law for my brother, it is against the law for him!"

But as Harry looks on François Leroy Larchmont, who has suddenly begun to tell him of a new opera, he casts this from his mind, speculating: "What jury would believe his evidence?"

François is never quiet long. He breaks in suddenly: "But about this marriage. I have had a plan—a great plan. Within the last three days I have discovered how to postpone the wedding! What do you think I have done? I have made Jessie younger!"

"Made Jessie *younger?*"

"Yes! she is now only eleven!"

To this Harry returns, his voice very serious: "Where is she?"

"Oh, up-stairs, studying her lessons, I presume. You'll see her in a moment!" François rings the bell, and Robert making his appearance, he commands sternly: "Bring the child down!"

At which, stifling a grin, the servant goes away; but a minute after, reappears with a subdued but frightened giggle, saying: "The child says she won't come down!"

"Very well, I'll see her myself!" answers Harry. "Never mind about coming with me, Frank! You stay here quietly," for there is an indefinite fear in his mind—a fear of something, he does not know what, as he steps in the hall.

Noting his face, the servant whispers to him: "Miss Severn is all right! She's up-stairs with her governess, locked in. They're frightened to death of him!"

So Harry, going up, raps on the door, and the faint voice of the governess comes faltering through the panels: "Miss Jessie is at her lessons—she can't be disturbed, M-m-monsieur François."

"Never mind whether she's at her lessons, or not," cries Harry. "It is I, Harry Larchmont! Open the door!"

In a second the key is turned in the lock, the bolt slipped, and he finds himself with both the governess

and Miss Severn hugging him together, and sobbing :
"Thank God, you have come ! Thank God !"

But here he utters a cry of astonishment, and ejaculates : "What's this ? The ballet, or skirt dancers ?"

And Miss Jessie cries : "Good heavens ! don't you
know ? I'm a child again !"

"Yes, and a very pretty child !" laughs Harry, for
relief has come to him.

At which the young lady puts on a very blushing face,
and says : "Now don't be awful ! No joking ! I had to
do it ! Frank came up three days ago, and frightened
me and my governess to death. He said I was a child
once more ! He had my governess make short dresses
for me. He said that would prevent Montez from marrying me so soon ! I would be too young !"

"How dared you do this ?" asks Larchmont savagely
of the governess.

The woman bursts out sobbing, and gasps, her nerves
having given way : "Wouldn't you do anything, if he
had a pistol in his hands, and said it was the will of
God ?"

"But why didn't you escape from here ?" asks Harry,
turning to Miss Jessie.

"How could I go out in these clothes ? He took all
the rest away ! Look at me !" Then she suddenly cries,
"No ! For heaven's sake don't look !" for Harry is obey-
ing her, and turning his eyes upon a babyish but alluring
picture. Miss Severn is dressed as a Parisian child of
eleven, with very short skirts, with very pink silk stockings and *petite* slippers, and baby waist with blue knots of
ribbon upon her gleaming shoulders and round white
arms, and golden hair hanging in one long juvenile *pigtail*.

"Then why didn't your governess go ?" mutters
Larchmont, stifling a guffaw.

"She was too frightened to move, so we just locked
ourselves in. Please—please don't laugh at me ! I—
it's awful !"

"And Mrs. Dewitt ?"

"Mrs. Dewitt has been in Switzerland for a week.
She will return soon."

"We knew you were coming also," continues Jessie.
"We had seen your telegram. We thought it best to

await your arrival. It would make such an awful scandal about poor Frank ! But, oh," here her eyes grow frightened, "don't leave me with him !"

" How long has this thing been coming on the poor fellow down-stairs?"

" Well, when we came back, Frank was all right, and I had a very pleasant time in society here, but each day, for the last two months, he's been growing more nervous. I think it's the threats of that awful man, the Baron Montez, made to him before he left for Panama. Then he has been very busy doing something political, he says ; but only three days ago did this peculiar freak come upon him."

"You saw Baron Montez when he left for Panama?"

"Oh, yes, once. He left Paris just as we got here. To please Frank I went down to see him. I—I had to—Frank is frightened to death of him." Then she whispers "He is making preparations for my wedding. The *trousseau* is here. The time has been fixed by cable ;" next giggles : "Would you like to see the bride's dress?"

This is said so carelessly that Larchmont is astonished. He asks : "Did you not fear that Montez might really marry you?"

" No," replies the girl, looking with trustful blue eyes into his, with such faith that it gives him a shock. "No, because you had sworn that I should never marry him!"

Then Larchmont says quietly to the governess : "I will make proper arrangements for Miss Severn so that she can come down-stairs with—propriety."

At which the girl gives a little affrighted "Oh !" and stands a beautiful and blushing picture.

From this the young man turns with a sad but stern face, and goes down-stairs to see his brother, and coming into the library is greeted with : " Is the child still sulky?"

" No," returns Harry, "the child is quiescent."

" Ah !" remarks François, contemplatively. Then he suddenly giggles : " She was in a devil of a temper till I kodaked her !"

" You—did—what ?" ejaculates Harry, for the term is a new one.

" Yes, snapped her in—photographed her—I've her picture here. I'm going to send one to Montez." And François, who is an amateur at everything, produces a

carte de visite of Miss Jessie that makes Harry Larchmont,
serious as is the situation, guffaw.

"Would even Montez dare to marry such an awful
child as that?" remarks Frank.

"No. I'm blowed if he would!" returns Harry : for
he is looking at the most *enfant terrible* on record.

Miss Jessie's blue eyes are starting out of her head in
horror, but have tears in them ; her mouth is pouting, but
wildly savage ; her pigtail is flying out in the breeze ;
she seems about to fly at the camera and destroy it ; in
fact, this had been her idea, but Frank had snapped too
quickly and too deftly.

"Wouldn't that make an artist's fortune!" remarks
François. "I shall ask her to pose for me—you know I
daub a little—at least I did before that villain Montez
made me walk the floor all night!" Then he moans,
"Save me! He'll put me in prison!"

Meeting Harry's eyes, François Leroy Larchmont
droops his, as his brother says : "There is only one thing
to do, Frank! You, yourself, when you think of it,
must conclude that I am the only one to protect you
from Baron Montez!"

"Yes," answers the other, "I have prayed for your
coming!"

"Very well then, in order to save you from the man
you fear, I must have the full direction of everything.
You must assign your guardianship, under the French
law, of Miss Severn, to me. She will assent to it in
writing, and at her age, it will be legal."

"You—you—" gasps the weak man, "will give me a
receipt for Jessie's property, so that they cannot prose-
cute me for losing it—a *full* receipt?"

"Yes," says the other quietly, "a full receipt, to save
your name!" And he breaks out : "Good heavens!
You don't suppose that I could ever let a child, your
ward, lose her property through you! That would be a
disgrace upon our family forever. But you must turn me
over everything you have."

"All right! Only save me from Montez!"

"Very well!" remarks Harry, "give me your keys!"

He steps into the hall and says to Robert : "Do you
know a notary near here?"

"Yes, sir."

"Send for him!"

But Robert, about to go, suddenly whispers: "Look out for his pistol!"

"His pistol! Where is it?"

"He's got it on, sir," says the man. "That's the reason I obey him so quickly."

"Has he?" says Larchmont, and stepping back into the library, he remarks: "Frank, I've got to go out this evening, after I get through my business with you. I left my revolver in Panama. I have got so used to carrying one, I shall not feel safe without it."

"Oh, take mine!" cries his brother, cheerfully, and he hands him a very impressive looking weapon, remarking casually: "I brought it to coerce the governess, but have lately used it upon mice in the cellar. It will slay a mouse at four yards!" Then a sudden and awful tone coming into his voice, which makes Harry very happy he has the pistol in his own hands, he mutters: "Besides, on the wedding day—after the bride was married—I had thoughts——"

"Thoughts of what?" asks Harry uneasily.

"Thoughts! thoughts!" says the other. "Just thoughts!"

"Won't you come in to dinner?" suggests the younger Larchmont, anxious to cut short this musing of his brother.

"No, I never dine now. Perpetual Lent with me, *mon ami*. Perhaps, after all is over, and I have tried everything, I may turn monk! It is well to learn to fast." Then François' tone becomes suddenly anxious, and he murmurs: "If I do not do what he tells me, he has threatened to turn me out of here—to turn me into the streets to starve—I—a Larchmont, starve—I—who have never been hungry before! I am educating myself for this."

"You need have no fear of that now," remarks Harry confidently. "Here's the notary."

And that official being shown in shortly thereafter, François Leroy Larchmont assigns his guardianship of Miss Severn to Harry; and Harry acknowledges receiving the fortune of the young lady.

To the first of this it is best to get Jessie's assent, which she is delighted to give; the notary going up to her to take her signature.

So coming from this interview, telling Robert to send
one of the other servants out for a doctor, and to watch
at the door to see his brother does not leave the room,
Harry Larchmont goes to dinner, with but very little
appetite.   He has, however, made arrangements for the
restoration of Miss Severn's wardrobe, and that young
lady flits down to him, in a very pretty dignified evening
dress, though she sometimes pulls down her skirt as if
anxious to make it longer, and once or twice takes a look
at her train to be sure it is there.   As he eats she proceeds to give him further details of the last three days,
some of which would make him laugh, were they not
additional evidences that François Leroy Larchmont has
lost the weak mind he had, through his fears of Baron
Montez.

An hour after this, a distinguished French physician
comes, and after examination tells Harry that just at
present these peculiar disorders are so ambiguous, he
cannot tell whether the disease of his brother will be
permanent, or not.   He must study the case for a few
days.

"It may be only the nerves—it may be the brain.   If
the latter, it is probably hopeless !   At any event, he
must have attendants. · He must be watched.   He must
not be let go out of the house alone.   If Mr. Larchmont
wishes, he will send him two reliable men."

"Very well," says Harry ; "I am much obliged to
you, doctor.   Do as you suggest."

An hour afterwards, two quiet but determined-looking
men come.

"Who are these ?" asks François uneasily.

"Two secret police to guard you from Baron Montez,"
whispers his brother.

"Ho, ho !   Then we have Fernando !" chuckles
Frank as the men attend him up-stairs.

Satisfied that his brother will be taken care of, Harry
thinks he would like a cigar in the open air.

The night is a beautiful one.   He has been accustomed to open rooms on the Isthmus, and to sea-breezes
on the steamer.   He thinks he can better meditate upon
the awful situation in which he is placed, in the open air.
He must turn over several things in his mind.   Of
course his brother's signature to the document, making

him Jessie's guardian, will legally amount to nothing ; still, with her consent, he knows a French court will doubtless transfer the guardianship to him.

Then he suddenly thinks of the paper that he has signed, receipting for all of this girl's fortune—a million dollars—five million francs! He is no lunatic. He is liable for all of it!

He knows that his brother can turn over to him but very little of the orphan's estate, and he mutters : " I am afraid I have crippled myself ! Unless I can force Montez to disgorge, I am now comparatively poor ! If I marry, I shall not have wealth enough to retain my position in New York society ! "

Then he communes with himself : " There is but one I want to marry, and if she will have me, we can be happy in a flat ! I imagine she was living in one when I first met her ! "

The servants, tired with their duties of the day, have all gone to bed. Harry hesitates to trouble them. He opens the front door himself, to receive another sensation of this night in Paris.

Almost as his hand is on the door, there is a ring, and as he throws the portal open, he finds himself standing face to face with Louise Minturn—her bosom panting, her eyes bright. She mutters to him : " Thank God, you are here on time ! "

Then she thrusts something into his hand and whispers, a frightened tone in her voice : " That will save your brother's and his ward's fortune from Baron Montez ! Hold to it, as to your life ! It contains the secrets of the man you are to fight against ! I think I have saved your fortune, but fear I am pursued by the police ! "

THE SOMETHING IS THE BULKY, BIG POCKETBOOK OF BARON FERNANDO MONTEZ !

CHAPTER XXIII.

THE HONOR OF FRANCE.

MISS LOUISE MINTURN arrives in Paris on schedule time. The weather has been very pleasant—the sun

bright.   She has sailed over a summer sea ; so it comes
to pass, that early one morning, in the latter part of May,
arriving by the *Chemin de Fer de l'Ouest* she drives straight
from the *Rue Saint Lazare*, and presents her letter of
introduction from Aguilla, to Monsieur Jacques Pichoir,
a shopkeeper, who has a jewelry store on the *Boulevard
des Italiens*, and a comfortable home near by on the *Rue
Lafitte.*

By this gentleman she is most cordially received.   Besides being an old friend, he is under considerable trade
obligations to Aguilla, whose letter is a pressing one ;
therefore Louise shortly afterward finds herself very comfortably domiciled with the family of the jeweller.   At
noon that day, she stating that her business is pressing, he
kindly takes her through the crowds congregating about
that temple of Paris speculation, the *Bourse*, to the office
of Montez, Aguilla et Cie., on the *Rue Vivienne*, just off
the *Boulevard Montmartre.*

Here she presents her business letter from Aguilla
in Panama, to the manager, one Achille Gascoigne, and is
informed by him that Baron Montez sails this very day
from New York on the *Normandie.*   He has just received
a cable to that effect.

This news is received by Louise with a sigh of relief,
though she succeeds in making it inaudible.

Then Monsieur Gascoigne, begging her to be seated,
examines her despatches from Panama, and looks a little
troubled.   They are direct orders from the junior partner, for the bearer of the letter, Mademoiselle Minturn,
to make such copies of the ledgers as she has been
directed ;   and, furthermore, for Monsieur Gascoigne
himself to certify to their correctness.   Still that gentleman hesitates.

He would cable Baron Montez, if that were possible,
but his chief is on the ocean.

He comes in and suggests affably, for Achille Gascoigne is a man of compromises : " Mademoiselle Minturn, you had better wait until Baron Montez arrives."

" Impossible ! " falters the girl, and her heart nearly
stops beating at the suggestion.

" Why not ?   You can have a pleasant time in gay
Paris for a week.   Your salary will, of course, go on ! "

" In a week I must be on my way back to Panama ! "

says Louise, determinedly, almost desperately. "You have your written orders from the junior partner of the firm. I have mine also. If I do not obey them—" here feminine artifice comes to her, and she mutters : "I shall lose my position ! " tears in her lovely eyes—partly those of artifice, partly those of disappointment.

This remark about losing her position impresses itself upon Gascoigne, for he has also a very good one. He is now between two mill-stones. He does not know what Montez will say to this ; but he knows very well what Aguilla will say to disobedience of his orders.

"I would cable——" he murmurs hesitatingly.

"Cable ! " answers Louise. "That's right ! Cable Panama quickly, if you have any doubt of my authority and my directions."

"I will do so," murmurs Gascoigne. "You will excuse me—it is a matter of such importance ! "

He cables, and receives such an answer from Aguilla, that the next morning he throws open the old ledgers of the firm, in hurry and trepidation, to the young lady's prying eyes and ready pen.

These back ledgers are all kept in an office adjoining the private one of the firm ; a door opens into it, so that ready access can be had to the books in case it should be necessary to refer to them. These ledgers are locked up in a large safe. This is opened, and they are placed at Miss Minturn's disposal.

Then the girl finds an enormous work before her. She has four months of very heavy and diverse transactions to take down from that great ledger. It must be done before Montez' arrival.

She works at this from early morning until they close the office ; and, telling Gascoigne she must labor at night, this gentleman kindly unlocks the office and safe doors for her in the evening, as he goes to some place of amusement ; and coming back, on his return from *café chantant*, or operetta, or some other nocturnal enjoyment, puts away the ledgers, lets the young lady out, and locks up. For her evening visits Louise hires a carriage. Promenading the streets of Paris alone at night would be very unpleasant for a lady, and Aguilla has told her to spare no expense.

While looking over these accounts, the name of Fran-

çois Leroy Larchmont comes under her eyes, and in copying the ledger, the peculiarity of the entries astonishes
her. Wonderment comes into her face—then, sudden
hope.

So in making memoranda of the general ledger for
Aguilla, she takes a complete account, through all the
back years, as the ledgers are at her hand, of the transactions in stocks of the Panama Canal and other securities, made for François Leroy Larchmont, and thinks :
" Perhaps these are what Harry wants."

These accounts, she unites with the general accounts
of the firm, and gets Monsieur Gascoigne's signature to
their correctness before a notary, day by day, ostensibly
for the use of Aguilla in Panama.

But time has flown ! While she has been doing this
work in Paris, the two steamers, one bearing Baron Fernando Montez from New York, and the other bringing
Harry Sturgis Larchmont from Colon, are ploughing
their way towards the shores of France.

The days have passed rapidly. Louise has forgotten
that Montez will shortly be due, and one evening, having
been let in to do this work, she scribbles away until
eleven o'clock, and looking up, with tired hands and
pallid face, murmurs : " It is done, thank God, *in
time !* "

Is IT ?

Then she waits for Monsieur Gascoigne to come and
lock up the place, and let her out.

But in the silence of the night, voices come to her, and
she hears two steps instead of one. Her cheeks grow
suddenly ashen, she hurriedly turns out the light in her
room ; for one is the voice of Baron Fernando Montez
of Panama, and the other that of Herr Alsatius Wernig of
Paris. Both are angry and excited.

The girl's lips tremble ; she wonders : " What will
Montez do to me when he finds me here alone, at night,
and unprotected—a spy upon him ? "

As she thinks, she thrusts her memoranda made this
evening into her pocket. Suddenly there is a match
struck ; the gas blazes in the next room, the private
office of the firm. Then the voices of the man of all
nations, and the German, come to her ; for the door is
slightly open.

She peeps in. The Baron is in travelling costume, a little grip-sack in his hand; the German, in the full evening-dress of the *Boulevards*, with white vest, snowy shirt, diamond studs, and opera hat and coat.

Montez says: "My friend, if you will permit me, I will go and have a little dinner. I simply drove here direct from the *Gare Saint Lazare* to get my mail, and I find you waiting at the door of my office for me."

"Yes, I knew you would come here first," answers the German, "and I made up my mind to see you before you saw anyone else. The Lottery Bill has passed the Chamber of Deputies."

"Of course—two weeks ago! But not the Senate," remarks Montez. "That will come later."

"To be sure! And now I come to you for my dividend!"

"Your dividend on what?"

"My dividend on the money left from what you received to assist the passing of this bill. The money you did *not* give to press writers or deputies—the residue— the large residue!"

Then he goes on, laughingly: "Ah, you are a deep one, Montez! You made this François Leroy Larchmont your tool. While bribery and corruption have been going on, you who directed it were not even in Paris— you were in Panama! Ah, you are safe forever! But I wish a little statement of your accounts! You know I was to have my share!"

"Oh!" laughs Fernando, unlocking the safe in the private office and selecting his mail, which has been kept for him in an inner and stronger compartment. "Call to-morrow and get it. At present, I am going to my dinner!"

He looks over the documents waiting for him carefully —among them are two long envelopes, very carefully sealed.

"To dinner?" echoes Wernig, gazing curiously at the envelopes.

"Yes, to dinner, of course—or supper—I don't care what you call it. I'm hungry after my railroad journey from Havre. Will you join me in a *petit souper* at the *Café de Paris?* We cannot have the company of Mademoiselle Bébé. You have heard, I suppose, the sad news

that she died in Panama?" rejoins Montez, producing a
handkerchief and wiping his eyes as if affected. Then
he opens the two envelopes, draws out his black pocketbook and deftly places their contents within its morocco
binding ; next, as it is now very full, secures it with a
rubber guard.

" What do I care about your Mademoiselle Bébés, or
your suppers at the Paris?" says the German.

" No?" and Montez throws the residue of his mail
back into the safe and locks it ; and gazing at the pocketbook, a curious triumph in his eye, is returning it to his
pocket. He says affably, " If you are not going to
supper, I am."

" Not yet," growls the German.

" Why?"

" If you get away from me now, I know you will have
accounts to show me that will prove you have spent *all*
the money upon the journalists and the deputies," answers
Alsatius Wernig. Then he says slowly but doggedly :
" My share I have NOW ! "

"Permit me to go to supper," returns Fernando.
Then facing the German, he says : " I have no accounts
with me this evening ! "

" You have those accounts in that black pocketbook ! "
cries Wernig. Louise can see Montez' delicate fingers
tremble as they clutch the morocco thing he holds in his
hands. " That contains everything I want ! " snarls the
German, his eye with the cast growing bright. " Let me
look at them now ! Give me a statement before you get
away to prepare another ! "

" Impossible ! " and Montez' eyes flash fire. " You
are a fool, Herr Wernig, to refuse my offer to supper ! "

" Why? "

" Because "—here Fernando's hand goes slowly behind
him—"that is all you will get ! "

But, quick as a flash, Wernig has seized a ruler from
an office desk, and struck the hand Montez has behind
him, and his pistol drops to the floor.

Then the German, who is stronger, seizes the little man
by the throat, and clutches for the pocketbook ; but
Montez, struggling, holds it up, away from the German.
So the two, fighting, one like a bear, and the other like a
tiger cat, writhe and wrestle, each moment coming nearer

the door that is ajar—the one leading to the room where a trembling girl stands gazing through the crevice, with dilated eyes of curious resolution, one dainty arm upraised, as if for action.

And they struggle nearer, Montez holding his hand behind him—the right one that grips the pocketbook; and nearer still, until he is forced back, and his right hand is pushed through the opening door into the other room, and there is a quick rustle of feminine draperies, and a quick clutch upon his hand, and he shrieks: "Good God, Wernig! It's gone!"

"What's gone?" A ruse!"

"No! Let me go! Some one has taken it! The black pocketbook that holds the safety of us both!"

But the other cries out: "It is a ruse! You cannot fool Alsatius so!" and squeezes Montez all the closer.

But the Baron tears himself loose, and throws open the door, and cries: "Where is it? There was some one here!" And the two cautiously grope about the floor and corners of the dark room.

Then they start up with a cry, for there is a noise of closing doors of the office, and they rush to the door and shake it, and kick it, and throw their bodies against it; but it has been locked upon them from—the outside.

On this they turn and gaze upon each other—these two conspirators; and both grow pale, as Montez gasps: "My God! If the secrets of that book come out, we will be torn in pieces by the Paris mob!"

"We?"

"Yes! It is the record of the bribed Deputies!" sighs Montez. Then he laughs ironically: "With your name as well as mine attached to it!"

"*Mein Gott!*"

And the two men imprisoned glare at each other, and drops of perspiration gather on their brows—as they whisper with trembling lips: "What is to be done?"

But a moment later there is a step upon the stairs, and the door is unlocked and thrown open, and Monsieur Gascoigne enters the office, saying: "Mademoiselle Minturn, are you finished?"

To him Montez screams: "Mademoiselle Minturn! Explain—what do you mean?"

"Why, the girl from Panama!"

"She has stolen my pocketbook!"

"Yes, and taken record of your ledgers, also!" gasps Gascoigne.

"Fool! Dolt! Idiot! *Misérable!*" shrieks the Baron, the blood of Morgan's desperado coming into his eyes, and he and Wernig fall upon the astonished clerk, and beat him, and strike him insensible.

Then Wernig whispers: "I go to notify the police of the stolen pocketbook!" and would run out.

But Montez stays him, whispering: "No, no!" as if in fright.

"Why not? It is a theft!"

"But if France knows WHAT is stolen? Do you think the populace will spare us foreigners who have debauched their Deputies? If the tribunals of justice get that pocketbook in their hands, it is WE who shall suffer. No, no! No notice! I have another way," mutters Montez.

So leaving Wernig, pale and unnerved, he calls a cab and goes fast as horse can carry him, and waking up one of the great Ministers of France, tells him of the pocketbook, and to his affrighted exclamations whispers: "If it falls into wrong hands, your head also—HIGH AS IT IS!"

And so it might be; for Louise Minturn, as she drives, not to her dwelling at the *Rue Lafitte*, for she guesses that may be searched, but towards the hotel on the *Boulevard Malesherbes*, the place where Harry Larchmont will be, if he is in Paris, carries, clasped to her fair, panting breast, not only the secrets of Baron Montez, but THE HONOR OF FRANCE!

CHAPTER XXIV.

BARON MONTEZ' WEDDING DAY.

WITHIN two hours a few of the detective force of the *Rue de Jérusalem* are on this young lady's trail—only a few that the minister thinks he may trust.

They soon find out where Louise has been living, and at two A. M. the household of Monsieur Pichoir is

aroused with inquiries for the lady who has been stopping with him.

To their astonishment he says : " She has not yet
returned. She is still at the office of Baron Montez ! "

Then the town is searched, and railroad stations
guarded, and for two days the gentlemen of the *Rue de
Jérusalem* make every effort—but Louise Minturn has
disappeared !

Word of their failure being brought to Montez, he has
exclaimed : " These policemen are idiots ! "

But in this he has not treated the officers of *sureté*
fairly. For the minister and he have not *dared* to tell
the truth to the detectives. They have described Louise
Minturn as an adventuress, not a clerk ; they have stated
what she stole was a pocketbook containing securities,
stocks, bonds, etc.—not what it really did hold.

Here Montez stops the search, for an idea has come to
him. After reading the letters given Miss Minturn by
Aguilla, he has chuckled to himself : " It is only the
attempt of my partner to protect himself ! " and felt a
great relief.

Though he has had the passenger lists of all ships
bound for the Isthmus searched, and finds no record of
her, still he imagines Louise must have gone by some
steam line from England, if not by way of the United
States ; or perchance by some tramp ship carrying mer-
chandise to the port of Colon, for a great many vessels
laden with supplies and plant for the Panama Canal sail
to that point.

Then Fernando has communed with himself cheerily :
" Does my charming little stenographer think she will
get back to Panama and Aguilla with her plunder in
her hands ? My smart little Yankee girl will find an
Isthmus jail less comfortable than the Mazas."

Therefore he cables to Colon, to an agent of his ; and
if Miss Minturn arrives there, she will probably find it
necessary to apply to the American consul for protection, if she can get a chance to have word with him, for
they have a way of putting people in dungeons there,
and holding them, without notifying authorities or troub-
ling courts—when the power requesting it is potent.

But Fernando is relieved. From the reports of the
police, he is satisfied the pocketbook is not in Paris, the

place where he fears it may be used against him.   The other is a bagatelle.

All this makes him anxious to press his suit in regard to Miss Severn.   He has her guardian under his thumb. The marriage must take place immediately !   Then he will be free, if the worst comes to the worst, to leave France, a very rich man.

So Fernando writes to Mr. François Leroy Larchmont, asking him to call at his apartments on the *Rue Auber*, to arrange for the immediate marriage of his ward, and receives in reply the following most satisfactory note :

"238½ BOULEVARD MALESHERBES,
June 3, 1888.

" MY DEAR BARON :

" Your letter has come to me.   I am so glad you are here.   My brother Henri, who has returned from Panama, has treated me most unkindly.   He would, if he dared, prevent Mademoiselle Severn marrying you.   But of course that is impossible !   I am her guardian !   I have ordered the ceremony to take place at one P. M. to-morrow.   The notary will be here for signing the civil contract.

" The *trousseau* is here—all that is necessary is the bridegroom !

" I did not like you, *mio* Fernando, a few months ago.   You were dictatorial !   But my brother is more so ; and I love you—and hate him !   My brother is very foolish since he has come back.   He thinks he can destroy you by a black pocketbook.   He is a fool ! How can a black pocketbook destroy anybody ?   Just the same, I saw a girl bring it to him two nights ago—I went down and saw it from the hall—I heard him say to her, 'I think that will settle Montez !'   And the girl said, 'Destroy the bandit !'   Neither my brother nor the girl likes you.   I think they do not like each other.

" The girl stays here.   Henri has taken apartments on the *Boulevard Haussmann.*

" Don't forget—to-morrow at one, punctually, the bridegroom must be here.

" Yours till then,

" FRANÇOIS LEROY LARCHMONT,

"*Franco-American.*

" P. S.   I have taken a beautiful photograph of the bride when she was at the age of eleven.   I call it *l'enfant gâtée.*"

As he reads, Montez gives a shudder. The black pocketbook is here in Paris, in the hands of his enemy !

He thinks over the matter deeply. He knows he cannot obtain it from the strong hand of the young American, without recourse to the processes of civil law. The examination of the papers contained therein, which must take place, cannot be kept entirely secret—even a French court could hardly do that ; and if it once became known —one little bit of it—there would be such a hue and cry from the Parisian public, that everything within its morocco case must be given to the citizens of Paris.

Here he mutters with a shudder : "*Diablo!* the Parisian mob! They would tear me and Wernig in pieces ! Even the Government could not save us—if they could save themselves ! Besides, the Lottery Bill would then never go through the Senate, and that is necessary for my full success ! "

After an hour's thought he murmurs with a great sigh : "I must do it—there is nothing else ; " and finally brings his teeth together with a snap, and says : " It is he, or I! it shall be he ! "

So, putting on his oldest clothes, and making himself as seedy as possible, Fernando walks out of his rooms, and strolls to a far-off quarter of Paris, where the anarchists live—on a curious errand.

He goes by himself, taking no carriage ; and there comes to a Russian nihilist, one who had helped blow up the Czar of the Russias. This personage Montez had once done a favor. The man is a mechanical genius. He had made an invention of some little appliance to a dredger. This small piece of machinery Fernando had induced the Canal Company to buy.

He holds a short conversation with the mechanic, and comes away quite relieved. " It is arranged," he thinks, " quite easily." Then he mutters : " *Sapristi!* I don't like it ; but it is the best I can do ! "

However, he goes quite contentedly to a jeweller's that afternoon and orders sent to his coming bride a magnificent parure of diamonds.

Next morning he looks over the papers and is astonished. *It* is not there ! but he mutters : " They have not discovered yet. These reporters are lazy."

But there is no more triumphant creature in gay Paris

this day than Baron Montez of Panama, as he drives to his nuptials, his horses jingling with chains, and his lackeys laced with silver, as he comes along the *Boulevard Malesherbes* about one P.M., and gazes at the *Parc Monceau*, gay with the bright dresses of playing children and their attendant *bonnes* and *nounous*.

.   .   .   .

Now, all that François wrote to Baron Montez is as true as the letter of any irregular mind can be.

Louise Minturn has hardly said her words to Harry Larchmont, as he stands at the door of his brother's house on the night of his return to Paris, before she finds both herself and the pocketbook drawn into the library, and Harry looking at her with eyes of joy.

Her trembling lips, throbbing bosom, and agitated eyes make her beautiful as an excited Venus—and she has got a new gown—what woman in Paris would not? Gazing on this loveliness, the young man would speak to her now—to his tender nurse of Panama—but other things are imperative first.

Louise hastily tells him her story, concluding, "When I had the pocketbook, I knew it was so valuable that great efforts would be made to recover it."

"Undoubtedly!" answers Harry, looking hurriedly over its contents, and growing more and more excited as he examines.

Then he gets up, seizes both the girl's hands in his, and whispers : "God bless you ! By your aid, I think I will win ! "

"You think so ? " cries Louise, excitedly.

"Yes ; I think this pocketbook will settle Montez," returns Harry. "But these are things for anxious conference with some great lawyer ! Besides, the police ! I must make some arrangements to protect both you and this ! You cannot leave here ! "

"Why not ? "

"By this time your description is all over Paris. You must stay in this house very quietly ! "

"Here ! " exclaims the girl, astonished.

"Yes, with Miss Severn. She will make you perfectly at home—you will be treated *en princesse !* " Then he goes on eagerly, for he sees signs of refusal : " I beg— I entreat you——"

To this Louise rises, and says : " Impossible ! "

" But if you go into the streets, you wiil be subject to arrest. This is stolen property ! " He holds up the pocketbook of Montez.

" Yes, stolen ! " cries the girl ; " but stolen from a bandit ! Don't you think this must destroy the murderer of, my relatives ? " for she has now some inkling of what she has pilfered means.

Then he looks tenderly at her, and says : " So much the more reason for my keeping you from danger from this man. You must let me protect you ! I will introduce you to Miss Severn. Her governess is with her. I shall not be here ! "

" You are going away ? "

" Yes ! What you have brought me gives me business this very night. After that I shall not return here, but take apartments. You must let me guide you till this is over."

But the girl looks at him, a kind of despair in her eyes, and sighs : " You do not know ! "

" I know everything that is necessary ! I took care of you faithfully and truly in the blizzard ? "

" Y–e–s."

" Don't you think I will take care of you more carefully now that I have to thank you for this chance against the bandit who has robbed my brother—and you ? "

" Very well ! " falters Louise, his mention of the blizzard seeming to make her pliable.

But Harry, about to ring the bell, checks himself, and says : " The servants are not up. Besides, it is better that they do not see you this evening. Please remain here. I will see Miss Jessie ! "

Then he goes up-stairs, leaving Louise tremendously agitated. She will speak, for the first time, to this girl who has the heart she loves—this one whose fortune she is saving so that she may become his !

Then Harry, returning, announces: " Miss Severn had not gone to bed yet. In a minute she and her governess will be here."

Almost as he speaks, that young lady enters, and he introduces her : " Miss Minturn, this is my ward, Miss Severn.—Jessie, this young lady is to be our honored guest. She nursed me through the fever in Panama ; to her I owe my life—and much else ! "

And Jessie, who had been about to bow, for the attitude of Louise is haughty as that of Diana of the Greeks, suddenly runs forward, kisses her, and says : "Thank Heaven ! you saved him ! I don't know what we should have done without our Harry ! " and so puts anguish into the heart of the woman standing before her, whose face grows very pale. So pale that Miss Severn cries out : " You are sick—you are going to faint ! "

" No—but I—I have not had anything to eat—I— I—have been so agitated this evening ! "

" Quick, Jessie—the pantry ! " cries Larchmont. " Don't arouse the servants—run about yourself ! "

Then she and the governess go about in an fidgety kind of manner, and do not find much in the larder, for they don't know where to look for it. But finally they get wine, biscuits, and something cold. And the wine gives strength to Louise, who has gone through a great deal this evening—more than any of them think she has.

As she eats and drinks, Larchmont suddenly says : " The memoranda of my brother's accounts from Montez' ledger—I believe you told me you had them ! "

" Yes—in my pocket ! " And Louise producing them, he, after inspection, suddenly says : " I must go ! "

So, after a few more words, impressing secrecy on both the governess and Miss Jessie as to their sudden guest, Larchmont leaves them, and departs upon business that will take him all night.

Before morning Harry has the pocketbook where he considers it safe, though he has made a very careful examination of the matters therein.

He has not slept all night, making these arrangements. Early the next morning he engages apartments for himself in the *Boulevard Haussmann*, and thinks : " That's pretty well for a man only three weeks over the fever. But before I go to bed, something else ! "

He hies himself to a celebrated American lawyer, who is at present on his summer vacation in Paris, and, telling him the whole matter, gets from him certain opinions of American law, and certain advice, that please him so much that he acts upon them at once, cables to America, and then goes to bed satisfied that he has done a good night's work.

Being very anxious to get a glimpse once more of a face that he has become accustomed to seeing during his sickness in Panama, the next afternoon finds Harry at his brother's hotel again. There he learns that the invalid is well taken care of.

·ʻBut while there, one of the attendants says : " Mr. Larchmont, your brother has demanded writing materials."

" Very well," answers Harry, " let him have them. I don't think they will do him any harm. Perhaps they will do him good !" and thinks nothing more about the matter.

Then the physician comes and gives his advice ; which is, to humor the patient. " Let him do what he likes !" This Harry is very much pleased to do, thinking it will keep Frank's mind off subjects that agitate him.

Then he asks for Miss Minturn, but Jessie says she is not well enough to see him—" She is worn out !"

He sends a message to her, but the answer comes back : Will Mr. Larchmont please excuse her—unless it is imperative ! For the girl has read an article in one of the Parisian papers, which briefly states that last evening Baron Montez was robbed by an adventuress ! And this makes her ashamed.

She has thought : " For his sake I endure calumny— and what does he give me in return—misery ! "

Perchance, were it not for this unfortunate newspaper article, she would consent to see the man hungering for sight of her fair face, and these days might be happy ones to Louise Minturn instead of miserable ones.

As it is, were it not for absolute fear of arrest by the police, she would fly from him, and from his house, and from the girl she thinks his betrothed.

So Larchmont is compelled to content himself with messages from her, for he is tremendously busy, and under his lawyer's direction is cabling to and receiving messages from America. But he consoles himself with the sage thought : " *Wait !* "

This lasts for two days, when coming to his room in the *Boulevard Haussmann*, late at night, after a long interview with his New York lawyer, he remarks : " Now I'm ready for Señor Montez !"

Then, careless of everything but fatigue, he springs into bed to go to sleep and awake the next morning with a very peculiar headache. He looks astonished and rubs his eyes, half in amazement, half in agony, for the pain is excruciating.

Then he suddenly exclaims : " *The headache of Cule-bra !*—that came from—what can have given it to me in Paris ? There's no——"

His valet entering about this time—for Harry has fallen into his old style of luxurious living—he says to him : " Amadie—since I left yesterday morning, what have you done to my rooms ? "

" Nothing ! I'm going to leave them—I don't think they are healthy."

" Humph !—you remained in all last night ? "

" Yes, sir ; I was too unwell—I had a fearful head-ache ! "

" Ah !—when did it come on ? "

" About ten o'clock last evening. I was too sick to get up to assist you, though I wished to, as there is a package—a present, I think it is—that came for you about five yesterday."

" How was it sent ? "

" It was left with the *concierge*—I do not know who brought it."

" Ah, ha ! it came at *five* and your headache at *ten*. Describe your pain to me."

" Oh ! " exclaims Amadie—" how can I ? My head was in four pieces—each at the other side of the room."

" The same !—Let's look at my *present !* " remarks Larchmont, grimly. And removing its paper covers, a beautiful enamelled box of peculiar design is seen ; but no card is with it.

Harry looks at this curiously a moment, then thinks deeply, and makes an investigation.

And this being over, Harry Larchmont, looking very serious and much impressed, goes off to the hotel on the *Boulevard Malesherbes*, where excitement destroys his headache ; for he learns that his brother, Mr. François Leroy Larchmont, has just announced that it is the wedding-day of Miss Jessie Severn and Baron Montez of Panama.

The vagaries of this gentleman, his attendants and

servants have been instructed to obey, as far as is consistent with his and their safety. So they have followed his directions. And his orders have been that Jessie's *trousseau* and her wedding presents—those that he has made her, and a very handsome one that has just come in from Baron Montez—be arranged in the parlor; he has also announced that his ward is to be wedded this day by civil contract.

François is just about to send for the necessary notary, but his brother, who comes hurriedly in, says: "There is one in the house now, preparing other documents."

"Very well," remarks François, "he'll do! Baron Montez, the bridegroom, will come at one P.M. Let the bride be ready!"

"What makes you think that?" asks Harry, looking astounded.

"Why, I wrote to Montez that the ceremony would occur at that time."

"The dickens you did!" murmurs his brother, and goes to privately questioning the sick man's attendants.

They tell him that a letter was received, and answered, by the invalid. They did not suppose it would do any harm, as Monsieur Larchmont had told them to let Monsieur François do all the writing he might wish.

"Quite right!" remarks Larchmont, and he goes to his brother most cheerily, and says: "Very well! I shall be delighted to see your friend, Baron Montez. If he had not called to-day, I was about to see him myself!"

Then suddenly a peculiar look comes in his face, and he chuckles to himself, thinking: "Egad! I have what will fetch him, in more ways than one—this bridegroom! I'll weaken his nerves first. It takes spinal vibrations to make gentlemen of his kidney sign away what I'll make him disgorge!"

Calling Miss Severn to him, he says: "Jessie, I must ask you to remain up-stairs this afternoon. I expect a visitor—one I do not care for you to see."

"Who's that?"

"Baron Montez!"

"Oh, I'm delighted to keep out of his way. Ugly faces are not pleasant to me!"

"Thank you!" whispers Larchmont; next asks eagerly, "Where is Louise—Miss Minturn?"

16

"Oh, she's in her room, I think. I have not seen much
of her.   She seems so quiet—and reserved—I think she's
sad ! "

"Sad ? " ejaculates Harry.

" Yes, sad ! I don't think she likes me, either."

" What have you done to her ? "

" I ? " gasps Jessie.   " N–nothing ! " for Mr. Larchmont's tone is awe inspiring.

" Nothing ? "

" Nothing except to give her every dainty I could
think of to eat, and ask her to tell me all about your
doings in Panama."

" Oh ! Ah ! Very well ! Run up-stairs—that's a good
little girl," mutters Harry, remembering his friend's words
in that city, and a suspicion that is rather pleasing to him
than otherwise coming to his mind.

So, coming to Miss Minturn's door, he knocks and
says : " Can I see you for a minute?   It is important ! "

" Certainly ! " comes a voice from within—a voice that
astounds him, it is so unhappy.

She comes out ; he looks in her face and falters :
" Good heavens ! You have been miserable here ! You
have not mingled with the family to any extent ! "

" How could I ? " answers Louise, attempting a *moue*,
"without any clothes ?   I have only this dress ! "

" I—I beg your pardon ! Forgive me ! I am a man !
I forgot your trunks were at Pichoir's. You have not
dared to send for them ! "

" Of course not, without your directions ! " says the
young lady.

He stands meditating a second, then replies : " You'll
have to wait till this afternoon. "

" Why till then ? "

" Then I shall have annihilated your enemy and my
own—Baron Montez ! "

" This afternoon ! "

" Yes—in the parlor down-stairs. After that I think I
can promise you toilettes *ad libitum*—Worth, Pingat, and
Félix ! "

" Impossible ! Remember I am a poor girl ! You said
you wished to see me on a matter of importance ! " answers Louise, reproach in her eyes, for she likes not his
tones, which are nervous, perhaps bantering.

"Yes, of great importance!" he says, growing very earnest, for the girl's manner makes him think she is suffering. "This afternoon I hope to have two interviews—one with Baron Montez; it will probably deeply affect you. Will you put your interests into my hands?" As he says this he looks at her with all his eyes.

"Y-e-s."

"Understand me," he goes on, "this interview may affect you—financially."

"Oh, what have I to do with the matter? Regain your brother's and your ward's fortune from him. That is all. Don't think of me; let me go away as soon as I can!"

"Your interest first of all!" returns Harry, determinedly. "Then for the other interview!"

"What one is that?"

"The one with *you!*" And his heart is very tender as he clasps her pretty fingers and whispers: "*You*—my interview with you! It is the most important!" and perhaps would say more, but there is a ring at the doorbell. So he mutters: "Afterwards! I must go now," wrings her hand, and departs, leaving her a mixture of blushes and anxiety.

At one o'clock in the afternoon Harry has every preparation made—a notary with papers drawn up—an *attaché* of the American Consulate to make acknowledgments good for the United States.

So he, in perfect afternoon costume, a big white chrysanthemum in his buttonhole, strolls into the great parlor of the house, and looking around grins—for the room is *en fête*, the wedding presents are arranged upon a table, one great parure of diamonds from the bridegroom quite prominent; besides, a portion of the bride's *trousseau* is displayed, which is decidedly out of form, but is the idea of the erratic François.

Then François Leroy Larchmont comes in crying, "Flowers for the bride!" and tosses rare exotics all over the table in his old artistic style—and begins singing a little French wedding song and dancing a *pas seul.*

But Harry quietly gets him from the room, saying: "You must not make your appearance until you bring down the bride!"

"Oh, certainly!" and François returns to his room,

where his brother tells his two attendants to keep him.

Then, looking everything over, Harry adds to the presents his own.

He places upon the table, next to the magnificent parure of diamonds of Baron Montez, a box of enamel of curious design, a little key hanging from its ornamental lock, and chuckles, " Now let the bridegroom come ! "

But sitting down to wait, this big ex-athlete, who has stood unmoved facing a foot-ball wedge that is going to throw upon him two thousand pounds of undergraduate college veal, and smite him to the earth, and trample upon him with twenty-two murderous foot-ball shoes, grows nervous—the stake he will play for to-day is so large—the goal seems so dim and distant.

Next, he suddenly jumps up and rather curiously locks all the windows of the room, which seems a needless precaution against prying eyes, as the curtains have been already drawn and blinds closed by Mr. François' order, he having had the gas lighted to give effect to the bride's toilette.

A moment after there is the rattle of a carriage drawing up outside, and, peeping from the window, Harry Larchmont mutters : " Jingo ! What a carriage ! What liveries ! "

For Fernando's equipage is of South American and barbaric splendor this day.

A short half minute, and Robert announces : " Baron Montez ! " And the door being thrown open, in comes the bridegroom, a smile of expectancy upon his olive face, and his white teeth a little whiter than ever ; his hair done up very barbarously, and a white chrysanthemum in his buttonhole.

As he enters, he gives a little gasp of joy.   The room is prepared ;   the wedding is beyond peradventure. Then a look of expectancy comes into his subtle eyes as he rolls them about, thinking to see the blonde hair, blue eyes, and graceful figure of Miss Jessie, his bride.   But just here the Baron gives a start.   His eye catches Harry Larchmont.

" You—here ? " he falters.   " I—" he stops strangely agitated.

But Larchmont, springing up, breaks in rather easily :

"Baron—your hand! This affair has gone so far, that, though I opposed it, I presume it must continue now. My brother will be down shortly. The bride——"

"Ah, yes—of course, brides are always late. It is their little way!" interjects Fernando, who has glanced about, and is reassured.

The room is *en fête*, the wedding presents on exhibi-·tion, and through the open door leading to the library he can see a notary, and another official gentleman, with legal documents upon a table before them, that are doubtless wedding contracts ready for signature; though most of this comes to him in a kind of a daze, he is so astonished at seeing Harry Larchmont.

His view of the case is surely correct. In fact, Larchmont proves it to him, for he continues chattily: "The notary in the next room is preparing the nuptial documents." `Ringing the bell, he says to Robert: "Find out when Monsieur Lebeau will have the contracts ready."

During the servant's absence, Larchmont casually remarks: "What exquisite jewels you sent the bride, Monsieur le Baron! Jessie was overcome at the sight of them!"

But the Baron seems overcome also at the sight of them.

As he has followed Larchmont's careless wave of the hand, his eye has lighted on the beautiful enamelled casket with its curious ornaments, standing beside his sparkling gift. A little hectic flush flies into each cheek, making them look like chocolate ice-cream with spots of strawberry—that melt away, to leave deadly, ashy pallor such as only comes to those who have a little of the blood of Africa in their veins.

Then Robert, returning, announces, "The notary will be ready in five minutes."

"All right!" replies Harry, cheerily.

But Montez does not reply to this. He seems to be interested in the casket beside the jewel-case. His eyes never leave it. It appears to fascinate him, as a snake does its prey. He gets one awful, close look at it, and for a moment it seems to paralyze him. He appears amazed.

"Then before the notary—let's get to the bride's settlement," remarks Larchmont. "As my brother is not strong, I must act for him, and account for Miss Severn's *dot* to you, as her husband, under the contract. The securities, receipts, and deeds belonging to Miss Severn are, my brother has informed me, *in this box*." He lays his hand upon the ornamental casket that has brought coma upon Fernando.

At this, the Baron, looking at him, gives a little hoarse rattle with his tongue, as if it were parched. The perspiration of fear is on the palms of his hands, though his fingers move nervously. He contrives to mutter : " The bride—she is coming ! " and totters towards the door.

"Ho ! ho ! impatient bridegroom !" laughs Harry. " But your anxiety duped you. The bride is not here yet, but her fortune is."

But Montez cares no more for brides—HE ONLY CARES TO GET OUT OF THIS ROOM ALIVE.

Then Larchmont, placing the box on a little table beside him, continues quite calmly : " We will examine the securities together. Take a seat on the other side of the table."

But Fernando, who seems to have shrivelled up, his eyes never leaving the casket, sinks down on a sofa across the room from Larchmont. Looking at his agony Harry thinks he has won.

But at that moment there is a sound of light footsteps and rustle of feminine skirts on the staircase in the hall. Montez staggering up cries frantically, " The bride ! "

. For one second Harry grows pale himself, thinking : " Hang Jessie ! She may spoil my *coup*."

But he strides over to Fernando, laughing : " Not so fast, Romeo ! Business first ! We must examine these securities while we have time ! "

" No business for me ! " gasps Montez, " when I have —ah !—rapture in my heart ! " Then he gives a sudden affrighted shrieking, " A-a-ah ! " for Harry is holding the box right up to his face, and is putting the key in the lock.

" No, no ! Not now ! " he screams. Next moans, " I am not feeling well ! " His hand goes up in a spasm, for Harry is turning the key. Then there is a click of shooting bolt.

" It's unlocked ! Now for Jessie's securities ! " continues Harry, gazing at the Baron. The blue eyes are very calm, for there is Saxon blood behind them. The dark eyes, very drooping and timorous, for there is all nations' blood behind them, and the drop of the timid Cingalese is on top, and the drop of Morgan's buccaneer is at the bottom.

Harry Larchmont.is opening the case !

There is a howl of terror ! That makes the notary ·and the official in the next room spring up.

Then Montez, clutching both Larchmont's arms, cries hoarsely : " For your life, don't open it ! By the Virgin ! don't open it ! You will blow *me* to pieces ! It is an infernal machine *that will blow me up !* IT IS DYNAMITE ! IT IS DEATH ! "

" IT IS WHAT YOU SENT ME, YOU INFERNAL ASSASSIN ! " cries Harry Larchmont, with awful mien and awful voice.

And Montez would run away, but Harry has him in a grip of steel. And the notary and the official gentleman in the other room would run away also, for there is a sound of commotion from them, and cries of astonished terror ; and Larchmont knows he has all the witnesses he wants. So he goes on jeeringly : " Ah ! ha ! condemned by your own lips ! "

And the other gasps : " Be careful how you handle it ! " for Harry's hands are on the box again.

" Pshaw ! I don't fear it ! " And with a snap Larchmont throws open the lid, as Montez, with a shriek of terror, grovels upon the floor, and the clerk and the notary yell with fright.

" Pooh ! Baron ! " jeers Harry. " This does not contain nitro-glycerine NOW ! Your gift arrived last night. Fortunately I did not open it. I awoke this morning with an awful headache—one I recognized—such as no man can have once, and not remember—the peculiar headache from the fumes of nitro-glycerine. With due precautions I opened the box, and I replaced what you had sent me by THIS ! " He produces several papers. " These documents represent Miss Severn's estate."

Then he steps quietly to the door and says to the notary : " You will remember this gentleman's confession. In a few minutes I shall have some documents for you to acknowledge ! "

Coming back from this, he picks the Baron up, who

is still gasping, and palpitating, and trembling, and puts him into a chair, with his strong hands. Then laughingly fans Fernando Gomez Montez back to life, for fright has nearly killed him, and Harry does not want him to die until he has signed some papers.

So, after a little, the Baron recovers somewhat, and grows very angry, and swears and curses, though his hands still shake and quiver.

But here Larchmont astounds Montez, for he suddenly asks this curious question : " My dear Baron, have you ever played the game of foot-ball ? "

" No ! *Sacré ! Diablo !* What do I care for your beastly, idiotic game ? " snarls the Baron.

" Well, in the game of foot-ball there is one point—one great point," remarks Larchmont, easily, " that is to .get the ball. The side that has the ball generally kicks the goal. Now, Baron, I am ready to play with you, because I have got the ball—I have got your pocketbook ! I know what it contains, and though there are no bank-bills nor certificates of deposit in it, it is worth to you your whole fortune ! "

" My whole fortune ! Absurd ! Bah ! It is a bagatelle ! You frighten me, and you think that makes me a fool ! "

" The pocketbook will kill you as surely as dynamite," whispers Larchmont, " if I make this thing public in the present state of feeling in Paris ! I blow you up and the Panama Canal together ! You and your friend Herr Wernig will be torn to pieces by the mob ! Let it but be known that you bribed the Deputies, the Minister of——"

Here Montez cries : " My God ! no, no ! never ! "

" Then," remarks Larchmont, " supposing I let you go —supposing I give you your pocketbook—what will you give me of the plunder of which you have robbed my brother, and the girl you said you loved—the girl whom you expected to call your bride to-day, but robbed also ? "

" A million francs ! "

" Pooh ! when I have all your American securities ? "

" Impossible ! What do you mean ? What do you know about my American securities ? "

" I know that you did have three million dollars'

worth of the best in the world, in the hands of your New York bankers."

" Did have ? "

" Yes, DID have, for I have attached them all now in New York."

" It is a lie ! "

" If you had gone to your office this morning, Mr. Bridegroom, instead of coming here, you would have found a cable from your New York bankers to that effect. You are an alien—it was easy ! "

" It is a lie ! "

" Now, look here, Baron ! " says Larchmont. " I've taken dynamite from you and two lies. The next time you say that to me I'll put your little round head through the back of your chair ! " Then he goes on again : " I have proofs—written evidence from your books—that you never made the investments in the Panama Canal stocks you reported to my brother. You simply said you made them. You simply charged them to him on your ledger, but your stock book shows no such purchases, at that time, nor at any other time. You put my brother's and his ward's money into your own pocket, but *never* bought the shares. I know well enough, if I bring suit in America, where I will bring it, having nailed your securities there, for I have had advice on this point, that American courts will follow a precedent they have already established, and decide in favor of my brother."

" But this is even more than I have taken from him and your ward," falters Montez.

" There is a young lady up-stairs you have robbed."

" Who ? "

" Miss Minturn."

" What—my stenographer ? She shall have her salary," says Fernando, grimly.

" She wants *more!* She is the sole heir of George Merritt Ripley, and Alice his wife, whom you murdered on the Isthmus, and robbed of their gold—some sixty thousand dollars ! "

" You can't prove it ! "

" Whether I prove it or not, I'm going to collect it. I have notes and an assignment covering the value of all your New York securities, made out to me, in that room.

Will you sign them, or shall the contents of your pocket-book be given to the papers to-night?"

"There is no Parisian paper that would dare to publish them."

"There is one!"

"*Imbecile!* You rave! What one?"

"The Parisian edition of the New York *Herald!*"

"Yes," mutters Montez, "you're right! That terrible American paper would publish any news!"

"Now will you sign, or not?"

"No!" cries Montez, desperately, and rises to go.

"Ah, you hope to slip away from town before the *Herald* can give them the news—but you don't go!"

"What will stop me?"

"The contents of this box you sent me! I've got witnesses in there of your own confession! I'll have you under lock and key in half an hour! You can't get out on bail even, before I'll spread over town the knowledge of the contents of that pocketbook. Then you know you will never leave Paris alive!"

"No!" cries Fernando, desperately, for he knows he could not exist two hours before the Parisian mob, knowing its contents, would rise up against him. "I'll sign!"

Then he puts his hand to his brow, and mutters: "Three million piastres! Give me the pocketbook!"

"When you have signed! Not before! I also want an assignment of your contract with the young American lady, Miss Minturn."

"Oh—certainly! You ask a small thing after very great ones."

So Harry leads him into the room, where there is an affrighted notary and an astonished *attaché* of the American consulate. Here Baron Montez, the agony of restitution being on him, does the hardest five minutes' work of his life—he signs over, in proper legal form, all his American securities to Harry Sturgis Larchmont, in trust for various other parties. These acknowledgments are certified to by the notary, and made good in the United States by the seal of the American consulate in Paris.

Then Montez whispers: "The pocketbook? Quick!"

"You did not think I had it upon me with such gentle-men as you about!" laughs Larchmont, who has grown faint himself now that he has won. "I'll give you an order on the American Legation for it—good after three o'clock to-morrow. By that time the American stocks are in my hands, or there are no ocean cables."

This being done, Montez turns to go. Larchmont follows him to the hall, for he thinks it just as well to see this gentleman outside his portals, as he has heard female voices up-stairs, and fears descent from inquisitive young ladies.

At the door, Montez turns and hisses : "It was for this you brought me here—so that you might play with me and conquer me !"

"Oh," replies Harry, very modestly, though the triumph of victory is on his face, "I did not conquer you —it was a young lady—Miss Minturn !"

"Ah, that damned stenographer !" shrieks Montez. "She who plotted with you, and entered my employ to destroy me ! She—your accomplice—your tool—your——"

"I'll trouble you not to say anything about her !" mutters Harry, his face growing very stern. "Please go away !" He has opened the door.

But up-stairs there is a maniac chuckle : "Lo, the bridegroom goeth—Let me at him ! I'm going to throw an orange peel at Baron Montez of Panama !"

"What is that ?" says the Baron with a start.

"That is the voice of my brother whom you have made a lunatic !" whispers Harry. Then he says : "For God's sake go away. If I hear him again I shall kill you !"

Montez with a gasp runs down the stairs of the mansion, and springs into his carriage very nimbly, as Harry Larchmont, closing the door, mutters to himself : "Damn him ! I don't think he'll forget his wedding-day in a hurry !" Then tears come into his eyes and he murmurs, "Poor Frank !"

CHAPTER XXV.

THE PREFERRED CREDITOR.

THEN Mr. Larchmont looks at his watch. He has just time. He springs up-stairs to the door of Louise's

room, raps on it, and would shout : " Victory ! " but the
girl knows his step, and is before him.   His face tells its
own tale.

She cries : "You've won !   Thank Heaven !   I—I
am so happy for you."

" Yes, *we've* won ! " answers Harry—" won in full !
But to nail our flag over his—I must go at once —I have
just time to do it !   Good-by—*our* interview this evening ! "   His voice grows very tender, and wringing her
hand, he mutters : " God bless you !   It was all you ! "

By this time he is down the stairs, but at the foot of
them he turns and cries : " I'll attend to your dress ! "
then opens the front door, springs down the steps, and
gets into his brother's carriage, which has been waiting for him for the last hour.

In it he drives, with even more than Parisian reckless-
ness, to his American lawyer, Mr. Evarts Barlow, and
getting him into his carriage, the two post off to the
Paris agents of the New York bankers who hold the
American securities of Fernando Montez.   At their suggestion, the agency cables their home house, that all the
stocks, bonds, and investments of Baron Montez in their
hands have been transferred and made over to Harry
Sturgis Larchmont, by personal deed of their former
owner, properly acknowledged and registered, which they
(the agency) now hold ; that all further dividends upon
said securities, earned now or in future, are to be paid in
to Mr. Larchmont's account, at his bankers in New York.

This being done, Harry remembers he has another
errand, and telling it to his lawyer, the latter laughs :
" What ?—A Parisian *modiste, so soon !* "

" Certainly !   She's worn one dress three days running ! " replies Harry.   Then he says, in a voice that
makes Barlow glance very sharply at him : " She's like a
dream in muslin !   What will she be under the genius of a
Worth or a Félix ?   You've a treat before you to-night ! "

So it comes to pass that, about four o'clock this afternoon, a forewoman of a great Parisian dressmaker calls
upon Louise, and presents a note which reads :

My Dear Miss Minturn:

With this I send you some robes to choose from. You need
not fear the expense. If you take them all, they are easily within

your income. I'll explain the financial part of it this evening. I've nailed everything—by your aid.

"Yours most sincerely,

HARRY LARCHMONT.

P. S. Please, *for my sake*, put on the prettiest to-night. The great lawyer I told you of will call with me—upon your business."

This kind of a note dazes the girl. The dresses displayed to her delight but astound her. In her present state of mind, she would send the woman away and tell her : "To-morrow—any other time!" But Harry's note says : "For my sake !"

So Louise looks over the robes, and now the legacy left her by Mother Eve comes into play. The dresses fight their own battle ; for they are exquisite conglomerations of tulle and gauze—the tissues and webs of Lyons thrown together by a genius for such effects.

Just at this moment Jessie adds her efforts to this scene. She comes in and chirps : "My ! How lovely! " and looks over the gowns with exclamations of delight, but not of envy. For she cries : "How beautiful you will be this evening!"

"This evening ! Mr. Larchmont has written you ? "

"Yes—this unsatisfactory note, half an hour ago," pouts Jessie. It only says : 'Have a nice dinner for four this evening at eight sharp. I shall bring Mr. Evarts Barlow with me.' Evarts Barlow ?—he is one of the great lawyers of Manhattan. I saw him last season. He's not so old, either," goes on Jessie, contemplatively. " I think I'll put my best foot forward. I've got some dresses of the Montez *trousseau* that are rather *comme il faut*, I imagine. I'll go at that *trousseau* and wear it out quick, before I'm promised again. It shan't do *double* duty ! "

She goes away, and Louise, thinking of Miss Severn's remarks about putting her best foot forward, says to herself : "Why should not I do the same ? My foot is also a pretty one, I believe ! " Then she laughs, for there is something in all these remarks of Mr. Larchmont's and Jessie's, that brings a sudden spasm of doubt to an idea that had burned itself into her brain in those hot days on the Isthmus, when Harry had raved in the delirium of the fever.

Then Mother Eve flying up in this lovely creature, with the assistance of the forewoman, who is very expert in such matters, Louise finds herself in such a toilette by dinner-time, that, looking on herself, she is amazed, perchance a little awed, by her own image ; for she is a dream of fairy beauty.

So Miss Minturn coming down into the great parlor of François Larchmont, with its wealth of *bric-a-brac*, statues, and paintings, Jessie runs to her and says : "Don't we contrast just right !—only you overpower me—you have so much *esprit!*" for Jessie has a dear, generous heart, and there is a great soul in Louise's eyes this night.

As they stand together, two gentlemen in evening dress enter and gaze upon them amazed.

"Great heavens, Larchmont ! " whispers the lawyer to Harry. "Why didn't you tell me I had such pretty clients? I would have worked for them as if inspired."

"I—I didn't know *she* was *quite* so pretty, myself!" mutters Harry, who has eyes for only one of them.

A moment after, the introductions are made, and Barlow and Jessie, followed by Louise and Larchmont, go in to one of those pretty little dinners, that are all the more pleasing because they are not quite banquets.

As they sit down, Miss Minturn's thoughts give a jump to the time she first saw the gentleman beside her in evening costume—to the night of the dinner party at Larchmont Delafield's, when she was not guest, but stenographer. Then recollections bring blushes. It is her pretty shoulders Mr. Larchmont is *now* looking at, not Miss Severn's.

Into this reminiscence Jessie breaks : "Guardy Harry, have you got me into your clutches thoroughly? Are you legally my guardian now?"

"Yes ! " replies Larchmont. Then he looks curiously but anxiously at Louise, and says : "I am also the guardian of another young lady ! "

"Another ward? You wholesale guardian ; who is she?" laughs Jessie.

"Miss Minturn ! "

"I ! " gasps Louise, her eyes growing astonished and almost affrighted.

"Why, certainly ! " remarks Barlow. "I had the order of court made to-day. You're only nineteen?"

" Y-e-s ! "

"Then not of age in Paris, though you may be in
America. It was necessary for the proper protection of
your interests and property, that a guardian should be
appointed. Heiresses must be looked after."

" Heiress !—I— ? " stammers Louise.

"Of course," interjects Harry, "if you don't like it,
you can have some one else appointed to-morrow—Mr.
Barlow, for instance—but for to-night," he rises and bows
profoundly to her, " I believe I have the honor of being
your guardian and your trustee."

Here Jessie suddenly exclaims : " Both Harry's wards !
Delightful ! Louise, we can do our lessons together and
have the same governess. Half of the present one will
be enough for me ! "

" Jessie ! " cries Larchmont, sternly, for Louise's eyes
have looked rebellious at the mention of lessons and a
governess. " Miss Minturn is a little older than you.
This appointment is more form than otherwise."

" Oh !—Well, it don't matter being Harry's ward,"
giggles Miss Severn. " He is a good, indulgent guardian. He lets you do as you like. But if it was Frank !
—Whew !—Louise, he might decree that you were only
eleven or twelve years old to-morrow morning ! "

" And if you were sullen, kodak you," interjects Harry,
grimly.

But a scream from Jessie interrupts him. " Oh, goodness ! " she ejaculates. " He didn't get a picture of
me ! "

" Yes—a very charming one. It is labelled, '*L'enfant
gâtée*.' You look as if you were springing at the camera."

" And so I was ! " mutters poor Jessie. " I thought
he had not snapped it in time. Did he really get one ? "
The tears come into her eyes, and she begs : " Please
don't show it—Please——"

" Not if you're a good, obedient little girl ! " says
Harry, with great magnanimity.

As for Louise, she has been silent during this. The
word " heiress " has put her into a kind of coma; the
term " guardian " has given her a fearful start, and sometimes her eyes look at Harry Larchmont in a half-bash-
ful, half-frightened sort of way.

Then the conversation runs pleasantly on, Harry telling Barlow of his Isthmus adventures; some of his stories making Miss Minturn, who has gradually been regaining her intellect, blush, though they make her more tender to the man relating them, for they bring back the days she had struggled for his life by his bedside in the room of young George Bovee.

This talk of the Isthmus leads to talk of the Panama Canal, Barlow remarking: "The Senate will probably pass the Lottery Bill to-night."

"That will give the enterprise six months longer to exist, I imagine; but more empty pocketbooks and more bankrupt stockholders, when the inevitable crash comes," rejoins Larchmont. "By the by, I wonder if the Baron is looking after it this evening! Eh, Jessie? What would you have said to journeying to Italy about now, with his chocolate face beside you?"

At this Miss Severn shudders, grows pale, but says firmly: "He has kinks in his hair. I would have said, 'No!' right in his face, to both notary and priest."

With this, as the dinner is over, Miss Jessie rises, and going to the door, turns, and lifting her skirts a little, courtesies, after manner of dancing-school children, and says: "I bid you *adieu* till *après le cigar*, my guardian!"

And Louise, who has risen also, a kind of reckless mirth coming to her, follows Jessie's example, and, courtesying to the floor, murmurs: "Your obedient ward, Monsieur Larchmont!"

Then the two go off laughing towards the parlor, leaving the gentlemen to cigars and coffee. But they don't take very long over these, for Barlow says: "We owe a little explanation to Miss Minturn about her affairs."

To this Harry replies: "Very well! Let's get it over!" a curiously anxious look passing over his face.

Then the two coming into the parlor, Mr. Larchmont takes Jessie aside, and whispers: "Would you mind running up-stairs for a little? Mr. Barlow and I have some business with Louise—Miss Minturn."

"Shall I not come down again?" falters Jessie.

"No, perhaps you had better not. Perhaps it would be well to bid Mr. Barlow good-evening now! I imagine you have lessons to learn!"

At which Miss Jessie astonishes him. She says: "Yes, and you have something to say to Louise. But—

I'll be down to congratulate!" and so with a bow to Barlow moves out of the room.

Then Harry and Mr. Barlow go into a business conversation with Miss Minturn.

Mr. Larchmont says : " I have received a number of millions of francs in trust for three creditors of Baron Montez. You, Miss Minturn, are the preferred creditor. Your dividend first ! "

" My dividend on what ? "

Here the lawyer remarks : " You are the sole heir to your mother, and she was the sole heir of her parents. They were robbed, I understand from Mr. Larchmont, of sixty thousand dollars on the Isthmus, in 1856. This at interest at six per cent., for thirty-two years, compounded yearly, amounts to nearly four hundred thousand dollars—two millions of francs."

" Oh, goodness !—So much ? "

" Certainly ! " answers Harry, " I've computed it ! " and he bows before her, and says : " Behold another American heiress ! "

Here Louise astounds the lawyer and stabs Harry to the heart. She says in broken voice : " You, Mr. Barlow, take it for me — you be my guardian. You can be appointed to-morrow ! "

" Good heavens ! " cries Larchmont. " What have I done ? Can't you trust me ? "

" Trust you ? Of course I can ! " murmurs Louise ; " but two wards will be too much for you to guide." Then she says faintly : " Yes, let Mr. Barlow be my guardian—take care of my money—I'll leave it to his judgment ! "

" Of course, if you ask it I can hardly refuse," returns the lawyer ; " but you had better think over it till to-morrow."

And noting that the girl is strangely agitated, Evarts Barlow remarks : " I will go now, and see you in the morning. Your interests this evening are thoroughly safe in the hands of Mr. Larchmont ! "

So this diplomat makes his bow, and taking Larchmont with him to the hall door, he whispers : " This strain has been too much for your pretty ward. If you're not careful, she'll require the doctor, not the lawyer ! I'm afraid she has wounded your feelings."

17

"My heart!" replies Harry, with a sigh. And Barlow bidding him adieu, Larchmont marches in to his fate, and goes into the great parlor where Miss Minturn stands, more beautiful than ever before this evening. It is the beauty of resolution.

As he looks at her, the laces and tissues clinging about her exquisite figure are so still, she would seem a statue, were it not for the quick heaving of a maiden bosom that throbs up white and round and trembling beneath its laces, and a little nervous twitching of lips that should be red, but are now pale. There is a fear in her eye She uplifts a dainty hand almost in warning, for he has come up to her, pride upon his face, agony in his heart, and anguish in his eyes, and said sternly : "How *dare* you do it ? "

"Do what ? "

"Refuse to accept me as your guardian ! Imply I was not worthy of the trust—I, who think more of it than any man upon earth ! "

"Oh," says the girl, "I presume I can choose my mentor—I have arrived at years of discretion enough for that ! " Then she falters : " Let me go away ! I—I have saved your bride for you ! "

" Have you ? " mutters Harry, surlily. " That's some little blessing ! "

" Yes—let me go away——"

" Not out of this house to-night ! "

" Why not ? "

" Because I *forbid* you ! " answers Harry. " To-morrow you may have Barlow—or any one else you like— but to-day the courts of France made me your guardian — and to night *you obey me !* "

"You forget—to-morrow—you are not my guardian then ! Let me go ! May you be happy ! " And, fearing for herself, Louise glides towards the door. But his hand is upon her white arm, and his voice whispers : " Not without me ! "

On this the girl pulls herself away, faces him with eyes that blaze like stars, and stabs him with these cutting words : " Do you want to compel me to run away from you as I did from Montez that awful night ? "

" Why won't you have me for your guardian ? "

"*One* ward is enough ! "

"Ah! You are jealous of Jessie!"

"Pish! Of that child?"

"Yes—jealous of her!" answers Harry, who has discovered that the Roman way is the only true method of winning this Sabine virgin. Then he astounds and petrifies her, for he murmurs: "You love me!"

"I? My Heaven! How dare you?" And the girl is before him with flaming eyes.

But he smites her with: "Because I have your DIARY!"

"Impossible!"

"Yes, from Mrs. Winterburn in Panama!"

"Ah! the traitress!" Louise's hands fly to her affrighted face; she bows her drooping head, tell-tale blushes cover her face, her neck, and even her snowy shoulders, making what had been glistening white, gleaming pink. But she forces herself to again look at this man, and her eyes seem to be scornful, and disdain is on her lips, as she mutters: "And you dared to read it?"

"No!"

"Then how did you discover——?"

"Ah! I have you—ah!"

"O Heaven!"

"A bunch of violets and a card dropped out of it—my tokens of the blizzard. They were mine before—they are mine now!" cries Harry, and pulls them out of his breast and kisses them. Then he says tenderly: "I stole your confession—I give you mine! I love you with my soul! good angel of my life—whose scorn kept me from making a fool of myself in Panama—whose kind nursing saved me from the fever! I love you! Without you for my wife, life has but little for me—what does the kind nurse—who saved it in far-away Panama—say?"

And Louise stands fluttering before him—loveliness personified—loveliness astounded—loveliness in doubt —loveliness blushing—loveliness that is about to be happy; for a sturdy arm that has played in many a foot-ball game is round her waist, and is giving her such a grip as never Princeton man received in college *jouissance.*

The girl gives no answer save a little sigh; she has almost fainted in his arms. But a moment after, her happy eyes seek his, and she falters: "Was it only to save your brother? Was it only to save your fortune you went to Panama?"

"That at first," answers Harry, stoutly. "But afterwards I fought to be rich enough to put you in the place in society that you will adorn!" Then he queries: "Shall I continue to be your guardian? Shall I tell Barlow he need not oust me in court to-morrow?"

"Since you are going to be my permanent guide," returns the young lady with a piquant *moue*, "I suppose you might as well get into practice as my guardian."

"Then may God treat me as I treat you!"

There are tears in her beautiful eyes, there are kisses on her cherry lips, as Louise says playfully: "Dear Guardy! I shall give you even more trouble than Jessie!"

"Then I will cut my guardianship very short!" cries Larchmont, a gleam of joy flying into his face as he walks up to the girl, who can't now meet his eyes, as his arm goes around her waist again. For he says: "I, Harry Sturgis Larchmont of New York, demand of you, Harry Sturgis Larchmont, at present of Paris, the hand of your ward, Miss Louise Ripley Minturn, in marriage! And I, Harry Sturgis Larchmont, guardian of said young lady, accept your proposition, my worthy young man, for I have a deuced good opinion of you, and solemnly betroth her to you, and announce that the nuptials shall take place WITHIN THE MONTH."

"Within the month!" falters Louise. "But I have only known you four!"

"Yes, but guardians must be obeyed!"

Then there are more kisses, and Mr. Larchmont walks out, and mutters to himself: "By Jove! that was a harder battle than I had with the Baron this morning!"

About half an hour afterward, meeting his friend Barlow at the *Café de la Paix*, he says: "You need not make any motion about that guardianship business! The young lady has had the good taste to accept me, after all!"

"As a guardian?" asks Barlow, in tones of cross-examination.

"As a husband as well!" remarks Larchmont, "and the sooner you get to work at the wedding settlements, the better it will please both the guardian and ward."

The next morning Mr. Larchmont, coming from his

apartments on the *Boulevard Haussmann*, takes Louise, and says to Jessie quite solemnly: "This young lady is to be my wife. As the wife of your guardian you will obey her, eh, rebellious one?"

But Jessie gives a mocking bow, and laughs: "Oh, I know all about it! She told me last night! We have been talking about you most of the time since. I have promised to be obedient, if she asks me to do just what I want to!"

"Ah!" replies Harry, "then I shall exhibit the kodak."

And Jessie cries: "No! no!"

But he is in a merry mood, and shows the picture of *l'enfant gâtée* to Louise, and they all laugh over it.

But though Jessie giggles, she also begs; so piteously he gives it to her. Then she tears it into a hundred pieces, and tossing them over her head, dances on them, crying: "That's how I leave my childhood behind me!" next says: "No more governesses! Eh, Guardy?" with a pleading look.

"AFTER the wedding!" remarks Mr. Larchmont, for he has thought upon this subject, and he has concluded that a governess for Jessie will be very convenient during the honeymoon.

But the next morning he is relieved to find Mrs. Dewitt has returned from Switzerland. He introduces her to his coming bride, and this lady is most happy to take charge of Miss Jessie during his wedding tour.

In one of their numerous communings, within the next day or two, Louise says to Harry: "We are so happy! Can't we do a little to make others happy?"

"To whom do you refer?"

"To a dear little friend of mine in New York, who is going to be married also, Miss Sally Broughton," answers Louise. "Could I send her a thousand dollars?"

"Of course! ten thousand if you like. It's your money, dearest," answers Harry, cheerfully.

"Oh, thank you!" replies Louise. "A thousand is enough. It will mean a great deal to Mrs. Alfred Tompkins."

"So Sally is going to marry Tompkins!" remarks Larchmont, grimly. Then he suddenly continues: "Tompkins was the man who shook his fist at me when

he saw me sail away on the *Colon* with you ?   Eh ? " and
his eyes ask awful questions.

" Y–e–s ! "

" Ho–oh ! "   Then Larchmont smiles a little and says :
" Any other gentleman you want to do a good turn ? "

" Yes, to George Bovee, who nursed you on the
Isthmus so tenderly—who was such a good chum to you
out there.   He is growing pale also—some day he may
have the fever, and there will be no one to nurse him.
Could not you ?—you need some one to manage your
affairs—" For Harry had been complaining about the
amount of business that had suddenly come upon him,
from his brother's incapacity.

" Oh, I cabled George yesterday ; he is now on his way
to Paris ! "

" On his way already ? "

" Yes, so as to be my best man."

" Oh," cries Louise, " you are always talking of the
wedding ! "

" Of course ! I am always thinking of it ! "

Probably Louise is too, for she and Jessie are driving
about town, from milliner to dressmaker, and dressmaker
to jeweller ; and all the gorgeous paraphernalia of a
mighty *trousseau* is being manufactured in this the town of
trousseaux, as fast as nimble fingers of French working-
women can put together things worthy of the beauty of
the bride.

So one morning, at the American Legation, Louise
Minturn is married to Harry Larchmont, and Evarts
Barlow, who has stayed over for the ceremony, gives the
bride away.   George Bovee stands behind his old chum
of the Isthmus, with Miss Jessie, the only bridesmaid,
but with the concentrated beauty of six average ones in
her pretty self.

Then bride and bridegroom go to Italy—southern Italy
and the isles of the Mediterranean—where they see
palms and orange trees, and dream they are in Panama
—but there is no fever !   And coming back from this
trip, they linger out the happy autumn time in Paris.

But one evening François Leroy Larchmont, in a careless moment of his keepers, escapes from them, and is
out all night.   The next morning, he comes back with a
sleepy look upon his face.

But Harry Larchmont, reading the morning journals, gives an awful start ! Two days after, the whole party are *en route* for America, taking the brother, whose mind is now permanently gone, with them.

. . . .

Crushed, defeated, but not altogether subdued and dis- ,mayed, Baron Montez staggered down the steps of the Larchmont mansion.

The next day he calls at the American embassy, and delivering up his order, receives, after identification, a sealed envelope, which he tears open, and finds his pocket-book—not one memorandum gone, and his eyes glisten.

He thinks : " With this I have enough to feed upon the vitals of this republic. Some of their public men are in my power ! " Besides, his fortune, outside of his American investments, is large, and the Lottery Bill almost immediately passes the Senate of France and becomes a law. He receives large sums of money, delinquent payments due from the Canal Company, and though he is forced, by the record of the ledgers Louise has taken, to make some restitution to Aguilla, still, as he does not make restitution to any one else, his fortune is enormous.

Though the shares of the Canal go down and down, he has no interest in them, and lives the life of a gay bachelor in Paris.

In the course of time, the deluded investors will take no more lottery bonds, and in December an assignment is made to a receiver, and the work practically stops on the Canal Interoceanic.

As this happens, Fernando Montez becomes possessed of a shadow. Though he does not know it, as he walks along the boulevards, a shabby creature slinks along behind him. When he goes to the opera or theatre, the creature is waiting for him as he comes out. This unfortunate one evening stands outside the gay *Café de la Paix*, with its flashing lights, and sees Montez eating the meal of Lucullus. As Fernando comes out, well fed, contented, even happy, this shabby creature mutters to himself : "*Nom de Dieu !* for his dinner he paid more money than I saved in my whole first year of deprivation ! "

And Bastien Lefort, the miser, who has been sold out of his glove store on the *Rue Rivoli*, utterly ruined by his

grand investment in the Canal Interoceanic, follows, shiv-
ering with cold, and brushing the snow off his rags, the
steps of the well-dressed, *debonnair*, and happy Baron
Montez.

But there is another—a black man with snowy wool,
and two great red gashes upon his cheeks, and a form
bent by age, but strong with hate. He comes alongside
Lefort and whispers : " How now, miser ! Are you on
the track of your enemy ? I, Domingo of Porto Bello,
have come a long way to see him, also ! "

And the two become bloodhounds, and follow the
Baron Montez of Panama all that evening to the haunts
of gay bachelors in Paris : to the Eden Theatre, where
there is a ballet ; to the Palais Royal, where he laughs
at a suggestive farce. But whenever he comes to the
streets—these two dog his footsteps.

So it comes to pass, late that night, returning from
a *petit souper* with some fair sirens of the gay world of
Paris, who are very kind to rich men, Montez enters his
apartments, to find his valet is not in them, and mutters
to himself :

" The worthless beast ! I will discharge him to-morrow ! "

Then Fernando sits down to await the coming of Herr
Wernig ; for these two are hunting in couples again.

So Montez meditates and is happy ; but, chancing to
think of his lost American securities, he utters a snort of
savage remembrance, and taking the poker in his hands
breaks up the coals burning in his porcelain ornamental
stove—and as the blaze flickers up, thinks he sees a face.
He starts and gazes round, and sees *three* faces—the
faces of the wronged, the faces of the past—Domingo's
pirate head, the miser's wistful face, and the pallid cheeks
and big eyes of the lunatic, François Larchmont.

Fernando thinks it a dream. The lunatic says with
cunning chuckle : " I enticed your valet away, my dear
Baron—ha, ha !—and let myself in with my old pass-key
—you forgot the pass-key—ha, ha ! I was coming in
here to do your business myself—but these two gentlemen joined me—ho ! ho! ho ! "

THEN MONTEZ' DREAM BECOMES REAL !

He springs up to cry out and defend himself—but the
lunatic's hands close round his throat, and the voice of

a madman cries : " Oh, ho ! my friend ! Baron Montez of Panama and Paris ! "

And though Montez struggles he cannot say anything, and his eyes have despair in them, for three men have surrounded him. He sees, half in a dream, the form of Domingo, the ex-pirate, whom he has robbed, who whispers in hoarse voice : " Ah, ha !—the punishment of the buccaneer—who steals from his fellows ! "

And the miser cries : " For the gold of my ruined life ! "

Then a surging is in his ears ; there is the report of a pistol, and three forms glide out into the darkness ; and on the floor, his own revolver in his hand, lies the form that was once—Baron Montez of Panama and Paris !

A few minutes after, his old chum, Alsatius Wernig, comes in with laughing voice and merry mood, crying : " Oh, ho ! my dear Fernando ! you leave your door open. You should be careful ! You might be robbed ! " then utters a horrified " *Mein Gott!* " and staggers from the prostrate form before him. Next he says slowly, with pale lips : " Murder ! If they have stolen the pocketbook ! " With this his hand, trembling, goes deep into the bosom of the dead man, and he gives a gasp of joy as it draws forth the black pocketbook of Montez.

Then Wernig mutters : " In other hands, this would have been my ruin ! But NOW ! " and the German's form becomes larger, and his eyes grow luminous with coming potency, as he jeers : " I own the secrets of many Deputies and some Ministers ! I will bleed them till they die ! I will be rich forever. I hold the politics—perhaps the destinies—of France ! "

Then he cautiously leaves the room, and none see him come down the stairs.

The next morning it is reported that Montez of Panama must have committed suicide—though it is hinted to the police not to make too thorough an investigation of the affair—some of the powers that be seeming to fear Baron Montez, *dead* as he is, will rise up like Banquo's ghost.

But Herr Wernig lives on the fat of the land, and bleeds some of the potentates of France, right and left. He spares not Ministers nor Deputies who have been bribed, and would keep on so forever ; but one day,

years afterward, scandal comes, and investigation follows, and he flies from France, fearing that more than
any other country upon earth—the country he has debauched and plundered. For the foreign adventurers
who came to Paris, lured by the millions spent or squandered upon the Canal, were the greediest, the most
devouring—the Swiss, the German, the man of all nations.

One afternoon in 1892, in the autumn, there is a great
naval parade upon the Hudson River, and the flags of all
nations are thrown into the air from vessels belonging to
the great countries of the world.

And from a private retreat, situated on the Palisades
overlooking the river, kept by a doctor well known for
his skill in treating diseases of the mind, a gentleman
comes forth onto the lawn. He is very elaborately
dressed in the latest fashion, and seems happy, as he
should be, for a beautiful woman and handsome man
walk by his side, and he calls them sister and brother.
He looks over the great river, and jabbers, "Ha!" to
the guns.

Then, seeing the flag of France, he cries : "It is the
opening of the Panama Canal ! Montez was right !
My dividends ! My dividends !" And gazing over the
beautiful Hudson he chuckles: "*Mon Dieu!* What a
glorious canal this is at my feet ! What dividends we'll
make ! Hurrah for De Lesseps, François Leroy Larchmont, and Baron Montez of Panama and Paris !"

www.ingramcontent.com/pod-product-compliance
Lightning Source LLC
Chambersburg PA
CBHW020350030726
47496CB00007B/2082